Islands in the Mist

J.M. Hofer

ISBN-10: 149092633X
ISBN-13: 978-1490926339

Islands in the Mist

J.M. Hofer

Character Index

AELHAEARN (ile HAY arn) - iron brow

ARAWN (air-a-oon) - ruler of the Otherworld/Underworld, Annwn (AH-noon)

AVETA (ah-VET-a) - goddess of healing waters and childbirth

BELENUS - (BEL-an-nuss) - brilliant, to shine, god of the sun, god of reason

BRAN - raven

CADOC (KAH-dok) - battle

CAMULOS (KAH-mulos) - Gaulish god associated with the Roman god, Mars

CERRIDWEN (KER-id-wen)

CORDELIA - Celtic goddess of summer flowers, love, the "May Queen"

CREIRWY (CREE-wee) - a token or jewel

DYRNWYN (DUHRN-win) - white-hilt

ELAYN (ee-LAYN) - maiden aspect of the Goddess

EIRWEN (AYR-wen) - snow white

EINON (AY-nen) – anvil

EIRCHEARD (ER-chart) – master craftsman

ENYD (EE-nid) - soul, life

FFRAID (fryde) - Welsh form of Brigid meaning exalted one or high goddess

GARETH (GAH-reth) - spear-master

GETHEN (GETH-in) - dark, swarthy

GWION (GWEE-un) - fair boy, little innocent

LUCIA (loo-CHEE-ah) - from the light, born in the first hours

LLYGODEN (hluh-GO-den) - mouse

LLWYNOG (hluh-WIN-og) - fox

MEILYR (MY-lur) - man of iron, leader

MORVRAN (MORV-ran) - legendary son of Tegid

NEIRIN (NIGH-rin) - all gold, precious

ROWAN (ROW-an) - little red one

SEREN (SEH-ren) - star

TALHAIARN (TAL-hayrn) - iron forehead

TARANIS (TER-an-iss) - thunder

ULA (OO-la) - gem of the sea

PROLOGUE

He lit the pyre with blistered hands, and then watched in a trance as the flames danced quickly across the dried grass and twigs between the tree limbs, engulfing his mother's body. Soon the smell of burning flesh and hair met his nostrils, but he did not flinch or look away. The flames rose high and burned hot and long upon her burial mound, and he had stayed until the very last ember died and nothing but her bones and ashes remained.

What had killed his mother and her great protector, Cadoc, and why?

The clan thought it had been a wolf, but his mother had insisted on her deathbed that it was not.

Now, his sister would take his mother's place as priestess, their clan was without a chieftain, and he was left hungry for answers and revenge....

CHAPTER ONE
A Stranger

"Someone is coming!" Gwion called, running toward the house.

The sun shone off the boy's golden hair like a torch as he loped awkwardly up the hill toward where Lucia stood in the doorway, and she smiled. She often wondered how he had gotten such hair. His mother, Aveta, had very dark hair with deep brown eyes. Lucia often teased Gwion about it, saying the Roman sun-god Apollo must have fathered him by filling his mother's womb with sunbeams.

She stood in the doorway and watched cautiously as a man led a black horse up the path that ran along her fields, slowly making his way toward her. She quickly determined from his clothing that he was not a Roman soldier, and his horse was too fine to be from any of the surrounding villages. As he drew nearer, she noticed he was enormous, at least a head taller than any man she had ever seen, and that worried her. He seemed to be traveling alone and he did not look like he meant any harm, but just in case, she put a kitchen knife in the pocket of her apron.

"Are you the lady of this house?" he asked her gruffly when he finally reached her door. He had clearly been traveling hard, and for some time, for he had a month's growth of beard on his jaw and smelled strongly of sweat and woodsmoke.

"I am," she answered, a bit offended that it was not obvious.

"I must ask you if my horse and I can sleep in your stable for the night. He is exhausted and recovering from a few wounds, and I am not much better off."

Lucia fondled the knife handle in her pocket as she considered his request, knowing that every man, even the best of them, could become dangerous when desperate. She glanced over at Gwion, who was stroking the man's horse looking very concerned. The animal obviously needed some attention. She finally resolved to give the man and his horse food and shelter, so he would have no need to take them by force.

"You're welcome to stay in the barn, if you like."

"Thank you." The look of gratitude on the man's face helped ease her apprehensions somewhat. He began to walk off toward the stable, and after a few moments of consideration, she called after him.

"You must be hungry. Come to the kitchen and I'll find you something to eat."

He turned toward her. "I am," he replied. "I would be grateful for whatever you can spare. Let me tend to my horse and I will come."

Gwion had caught a few rabbits that morning, and she had made a rabbit stew which had been simmering for a few hours. She enjoyed being in the kitchen. Next to the lake and the library, it was her favorite place to be. Whenever her late husband's duties had taken him away, she had always asked him to bring back whatever spices he could find for her to experiment with. She had also pestered Aveta into teaching her about herbs and all of their uses, first for cooking, but later for medicine. In a short time she had gotten quite skilled at using all of the herbs and plants that grew in the surrounding woods and meadows.

Within the hour, the large visitor came striding across the garden toward the house with Gwion at his heels. He entered slowly, his head barely passing underneath the doorway. She thought back to the stories her husband had told her of savage giants hailing from across the sea that pillaged their shores, and wondered if perhaps that was where he was from. He leaned a long spear against the wall and then tossed a large satchel from his shoulder to the floor.

"Please sit down," she offered awkwardly, growing a bit nervous about making conversation. She quickly set a bowl of stew in front of him, along with a board of bread and cheese, and Gwion brought him a large mug of ale, causing his eyes to light up considerably.

"Thank you, again," he said to them. He drank the ale down first and then began wolfing down his meal. Gwion filled a bowl and sat down next to him, and then she joined them. She did not regard Gwion, or his mother, Aveta, for that matter, as her servants, though that was what they were. With only the three of them there to take care of the villa and each other, they had become like family over the past few years, and that was the way she liked it. Gwion had recently come back from a five-year apprenticeship and had been with them for a season. Though only twelve, he could do the work of a grown man and was just as mature, but unlike a husband, she didn't have to answer to him. Having him there was both a joy and a comfort.

"What brings you this way?" she finally asked her guest, not knowing what else to say.

"I have business north of here," he replied.

"I see," she said. His chest was broad and his arms large, with thick arteries running through his forearms feeding strong, calloused hands. She wondered what kind of work he did. Soldier? Blacksmith?

A cold breeze suddenly gusted in through the cracks in the windows. "Winter will soon be here," she said, getting up to add a log to the fire.

"Lady, is your husband away?" he asked her suddenly.

She knew it would be prudent to tell him her husband would soon be back, but decided to risk the truth instead.

"My husband died in battle a year ago."

He looked up at her, "I see. I am sorry for your loss." He waited until she began to eat again, perhaps out of respect, she thought, and then tore off a piece of bread and went back to his stew. After he finished he said, "This is quite a large villa. How many slaves do you have?"

"I have no slaves. Aveta and Gwion and I manage well enough," she answered without thinking. *Damn. You stupid girl. Now he knows there are only three of you. Two silly women and a boy!*

"And you have not been set upon?" he asked, surprised, as if he had read her mind. Her heart pounded in fear wondering what he might be implying. She gripped her knife again under the table, ready to stab him in the eye with it if necessary.

"We are all quite good with a knife," she said confidently, "and there are many strong men within earshot who work my land. I have but to call out and they will come to my aid." She kicked Gwion under the table as a signal to be alert.

The stranger nodded. "I see. Well, that is good. I hope they can run fast enough. I would caution you against telling strangers that you live here alone. Say your husband is out in the field, or somewhere close by. Though the Saxons stay mainly in the east, it will not be long before they force themselves into our lands."

"Yes, I know," she said, fear still sticking in her throat. "What about you? Do you have a wife?" she asked, hoping he had a family. It would ease her fear to know he was a father or a husband.

"No," he answered to her disappointment.

"You look to be a warrior," she ventured, glancing over at his spear. "For whom do you fight?"

"I fight for my own people, and the clans we consider friends."

"I see," she replied, growing more curious. "I've not seen anyone like you traveling this way before. Your village must be far from here."

"Not so far. A hard two days' ride. Some call us the 'Firefolk.' Perhaps you've heard of us? Many come to us to commission swords and buy horses."

She had heard this name used occasionally by those who farmed her land, but never knew if the people they spoke of were real or not, like the faerie they sang of.

"Then I have heard mention of your people, yes." she said, searching her memory for any bit of information it might hold. She noticed her guest kept running his bread around the bottom of his bowl, sopping up every last drop of his meal, so she quickly filled it again.

"Thank you," he said softly, and Lucia noted a bit of shame in his voice. His grateful look as he pulled the bowl back toward him plumbed a well of compassion in her heart, dissolving what remained of her fears.

Gods, but he looks weary, she thought. He had washed his face to reveal quite a handsome profile, she noticed, though it seemed older than it likely was.

"I am going to make you something that will make you feel even better than that ale," she told him.

"That I cannot imagine," he said, smiling for the first time. His grin shocked Lucia, for he suddenly looked ten years younger and capable of more than a fair measure of mischief.

She smiled back at him, pleased to see it, and got up to make him a tonic. She soon returned with a cup of steaming liquid and set it proudly in front of him.

"Drink this," she commanded. "You'll be glad for it."

He picked up the cup and smelled the brew. "Gods, woman!" he said, wincing. "You mean for me to *drink* this?"

"I know it smells dreadful, but I promise it will help to restore you."

She had learned how to make many tonics thanks to Aveta, and though she was not the expert Aveta was, she felt confident that she had succeeded in brewing something that would ease his muscles. That was not so difficult to do.

He looked at her skeptically, but put it to his lips. Lucia tried her best to keep the conversation going while he sipped it, but he was obviously a man of few words.

"I fear your brew is doing its job," he said suddenly, his eyes heavy. "I will leave you now."

She nodded. "You should sleep well tonight, I daresay."

"Half-way there already. Hope I make it to the barn," he said, collecting his spear and satchel. "I'll find a way to re-pay you for your kindness," he added. "Perhaps with some work when I pass through this way again."

"That would be welcome," Lucia replied sincerely. "I have need of strong hands like yours. There are certain things mine simply cannot do."

She glanced again at his hands and noted they could surely crush her skull. She shuddered and then added, "Gwion, will you please take our guest some blankets?"

"Of course," the boy answered, standing up from the table.

The stranger made his way toward the door, then stopped and turned toward her.

"Might I ask your name?"

Instinctively she almost said "Lady Camulos," but didn't.

9

"Lucia," she replied.

"*Loo-CHEE-ah*," he said, sounding it out. "What beautiful names the Romans give their daughters! I am Bran."

"Thank you, Lord Bran," she replied, flustered by his compliment, and nervously turned to busy herself with the dishes. "I wish you a good night, then."

He nodded toward her, surely noting her discomfort, she thought, and then left her alone with her thoughts.

***

The next morning Lucia woke just after sunrise and found Aveta in the kitchen cooking breakfast.

"Good morning," she said to her groggily. She went to the window and looked outside, and saw Bran pacing outside the barn.

"Good morning," Aveta replied, setting bread on the table. "I see we have a visitor. What do you know of him?"

"Not much. His village lies two days from here. He says he is of the Firefolk. Horsemen and blacksmiths, apparently. He was on his way north, but his horse was wounded and needed attention. Gwion is tending to the animal."

Aveta's expression changed, her brow wrinkling slightly. "Did he give his name?"

"Yes. Bran."

"Bran?" Aveta said, pausing for a moment. She joined Lucia at the window, tucking the wayward hairs out of her eyes up into the hastily-twisted chestnut bun on her head to get a better look. "He must be Agarah's son."

"Agarah? Who is that?"

"Agarah of the Firefolk. They are people of Sarmatian blood who live in a village to the south. They came here as Roman cavalry a few generations ago. After their service to Rome was fulfilled, they chose to remain here. I have traded with their people on occasion. The story of Agarah was well-known to me as a girl. She is something of a legend where I come from."

"Really?" Lucia prompted, intrigued. She looked out the window at Bran with renewed curiosity.

"Her village was attacked by giants from across the sea when she was a young woman. Though the men of her clan were skilled warriors, the invaders were massive and fought with a brutality they had not seen before. They say the Firefolk would have been wiped out that day had it not been for her bravery."

Lucia loved hearing stories of strong women, and turned from the window to give Aveta her full attention.

"When the invaders were spotted, Agarah led the women of her clan into the surrounding forest. The strongest archers among them took to the trees to provide cover for their clan sisters, and Agarah led the rest of them fiercely into battle alongside their men. They burst out of the forest bare-breasted and shrieking with rage, hair flying and spears held high. The men were quick to take advantage of the bewilderment of the enemy, and Agarah's clan gained the advantage in the battle; an advantage for which she paid a high price, for the enemy chieftain was overtaken by mad desire when he spied her running bare-chested across the field leading the charge. Fueled by the excitement of taking such a wild creature, he gave chase. Agarah ran back into the forest, seeking to lure him as far from her village as possible. She managed to evade him for some time, but he pursued her tirelessly and eventually overtook her. She was no match for him in combat, and he stole her away to his land. No one really knows how, but she managed to escape and return home to her village. She refused to ever speak of it. Nine moons later she gave birth to a son."

Aveta handed her a mug of tea.

"And you think our visitor is her son?"

"Yes."

Aveta went to the window to take another look, and Lucia went to the door and called out to him.

"Lord Bran—please come in and have some breakfast!"

He hesitated a moment, glancing back into the barn, but then made his way across the garden and ducked under the doorframe.

"Bran, this is Aveta, Gwion's mother," Lucia announced, motioning to her.

Bran nodded respectfully toward Aveta. "Your son has been a blessing to my horse, and to me. I am grateful."

"He is a wonder with animals," Aveta agreed. "Please, sit down. I trust eggs are welcome to you?"

"More than welcome, thank you."

Lucia found herself relieved that Bran did not ogle Aveta's large breasts as she leaned over to serve him, for most men did. At times even she was guilty of looking at them, but with envy rather than lust. Though over twenty, Lucia felt she still had the body of a girl in many ways, with breasts not much bigger than apples and narrow hips. Aveta truly had the body of a woman, like the statues the Romans so favored.

Suddenly Gwion came through the kitchen door. "Good morning," he said, setting a basket of blackberries on the table next to Lucia. "These are for you." His fingers were stained purple.

"Gwion!" Lucia cooed. "How did you know I was craving berries this morning?"

"A little bird told me," he whispered and then headed back outside. He hated being indoors, and always slept outside; sometimes under the apple trees, sometimes in the loft of the barn, sometimes down by the lake. She could not remember a single night he had ever slept in a bed.

"We also have a bit of salt pork and potatoes this morning," Aveta announced, setting more plates on the table. She took a good look at Bran as she did so, no doubt seeking to confirm her suspicions, and then left to attend to her other duties.

"Lord Bran, would you walk with me?" Lucia ventured. "I make it a habit to walk about my land each morning to see what needs tending. I would be glad of some company."

Bran drained his mug of goat's milk and set it down. "Please don't call me lord. Bran is enough. And yes, I will come. Perhaps I can be of service to you."

She imagined he could, and was glad to have him as a companion for the morning. They set out through the back door of the kitchen and passed through the garden. She motioned toward the heavy vines and healthy-looking rows as she spoke.

"We've managed well this season. Aveta merely touches something and it grows. There is no tree, herb or flower for miles around that she doesn't know the uses for. Gwion is gifted as well, but more so with animals. Your horse is in the best hands for miles around."

"That I believe," he answered. Though his hair was tied back, she could see it would hang to his shoulders if unbound. It flashed gold in the sunlight, and she noticed for the first time his beard had flecks of crimson in it.

"I would like to look in on him again, if you don't mind."

"Of course," she agreed.

She led the way down the path to a large and well-built stable next to the barn. She unlatched the large door and he followed her inside, welcomed by the smell of fresh hay and leather.

"There he is, already looking much better, I think."

Gwion rose up from behind the horse, brush in hand, and greeted them. Bran looked at his horse, stroking his muzzle and side of his neck, then walked around and patted him on his side.

"I can't believe it," he finally said.

Gwion smiled. "I've done my best for him. He will make a quick recovery given a few days' rest and good feed. I would say you could plan to leave two mornings hence."

Bran patted the horse again. "You indeed have a gift, my young friend."

Lucia had no children, but Gwion felt like a son to her. The pride he inspired in her was endless.

"It seems you live in a household of healers," Bran said as they left.

"I do. I have tried to learn as much from them as I can, though I am not as capable. What can be learned, I am learning. What has been gifted by the gods is another matter."

They walked down to the path that ran along the lake and followed it. Gradually with some coaxing on her part, Bran spoke more. She asked many questions about the places he had seen, and he told her of the many battles he and the men from his clan had fought in the lands to the east.

"Where are your men now?"

"Still there, fighting the bloody Saxons without me," he said and spat, shaking his head in disgust.

"Will you return to them?"

"Yes, as soon as my business is done."

"I know the Saxons come from the lands across the sea. Do you fight them on the shores?"

"Yes, we do our best to destroy their ships and kill them as soon as they crawl out of the water, before they can move inland."

"Tell me of the sea," she asked suddenly in wonder, for she had never been anywhere but her own small village and her husband's villa. "What is it like?"

"The sea?" His scowl suddenly faded away. "As powerful and mysterious as a woman you can never have," he said smiling faintly. "Something magnificent to behold."

"I would like to see it someday," she said wistfully. "I envy your journeys. I have only had one, and that was leaving my home to marry my husband." She stopped walking and looked across the lake. "That was the most exciting day of my life. Finally, to see something beyond the horizon of that tiny place."

"Don't envy my travels, Lucia," he replied curtly. "The places I've seen have all been bathed in blood."

She did not say anything for awhile, convinced that Aveta's suspicion of his identity was right.

"I am worried for you, Lucia," he said after a moment. "These are dangerous times. With the Romans gone, the Saxons flow in by the boatload and don't leave. It's just a matter of time before they come to your door, and you three would not stand a chance against them."

Times had indeed changed. Her husband had often talked of how Rome had forsaken its citizens in "Britannia", as he called it. His father had not returned to Rome when Macsen Wledig, or Maximus, as the Romans called him, had summoned his troops back from Britain, instead choosing to stay. Her husband had therefore been born and raised here, educated in the Roman tradition, but had never seen the country his father had come from.

"What of your family? Your parents? Do they still live?" he asked. "If so, you should consider returning and living with your people. Take the boy and his mother with you. The Romans no longer rule this land. You have no protection here, and plenty of things worth taking. Not to mention what might happen to you. I've seen what the Saxons do to the women they capture."

Lucia shook her head. "No. I'll never go back."

Bran looked at her in disappointment. "Never is a word for fools, Lucia," he said. "Think at least of the boy and his mother, if not for yourself."

"We're not alone!" she finally burst out in exasperation, offended by his condescending tone. "There are five families that share my land, all of them with several grown sons who know their way around a weapon, as do I!"

At this, Bran let out a laugh. "Is that so?" He shook his head as a parent would while listening to the foolishness of a child, and it made her blood boil.

"Yes," she said defiantly, and within seconds she had the hilt of his dagger in her fist and pointed toward his throat.

"Well, well," he said softly, taken by surprise. "It seems you do know a thing or two. Just enough to kill one, and get raped and beaten by the other ten. Well done."

She turned the dagger around, handed it back to him and stormed down to the water's edge. She went to work on a large berry bush near the bank. She had a temper she found hard to control at times. She had been shy as a girl, and often teased. Bran's dismissal of her had brought back all those painful memories, but he was right and she knew it. She cooled off, and after she had amassed a handful she went back to find him sitting by the water. She sat down next to him, offering the fruit in her hand as a truce. He took a few, absent-mindedly, and stared out across the water.

"Bran, the Saxons you speak of, how close are they?"

"They mainly attack the eastern shores, but I can promise you they won't stay there."

"I see," she said, desperate at the thought of losing her home. *Damn Camulos for dying, and damn Rome for abandoning its citizens,* she thought.

"I assume you came to us from the battlefield, from the state you arrived in."

"No. From my village, actually."

"What?" she asked, confused. "Was your village attacked?"

She was suddenly seized with fear, remembering he had said his village was a mere two days away. He was silent a moment before continuing.

18

"My mother and our chieftain were attacked in the night and both recently died from their wounds. Some say it was a wolf, but my mother insisted it was not. I buried her three nights ago."

"May the gods protect her," Lucia said sincerely after a moment, suddenly sickened at the idea of losing her own mother. She had been her only confidante growing up; the only one she could talk to about her terrible dreams. The day she died would be a dark one for her, indeed.

Bran's gaze darkened as he stared out across the lake, and Lucia left him to his thoughts. They sat there for some time, watching the sun glint off the water, Lucia occasionally stealing the opportunity to look more closely at his face. His scars and weather-worn skin sang a warrior's ballad, but the deep crow's feet in the corners of his eyes hinted of a man who had also known much joy over the years.

"I was too eager for answers," he continued, almost to himself. "It was foolishness that brought me to your door."

"Well, what's done is done," she said simply. In truth, she was thankful for his foolishness.

They returned after a few hours, boots muddy. Knowing he would be staying on a few more days Bran insisted on repairing the damage to the rock wall which surrounded the villa, and started on it that afternoon. Eventually, he came to a part of the wall directly outside of where Lucia sat at her loom. She watched him through the window from behind the long threads, the parts of him that she could see changing as she worked. She found her thoughts wandering back to the Beltane festivities in the spring, and images of hilltop bonfires flickered through her mind. She remembered venturing outside and hearing couples in the fields as they made love under the stars; sparks and smoke rising up into the sky.

Gwion brought in some fish in the afternoon, which Aveta cleaned and prepared for dinner. Bran was still outside working when supper was ready, so she went outside to fetch him. When she turned the corner she found him setting a stone in place, bare from the waist up.

"There is food on the table," she offered, wishing she had more to say.

"I'll be in," he replied, giving her a quick smile that made her heart race. She stole a few more glances when his back was turned, and then left him.

The following day unfolded much the same, with Bran spending the day finishing the wall and chopping logs. By dusk he had chopped enough wood for a month's worth of fires.

Aveta and Gwion retired early that night, leaving Lucia alone with Bran. Deliberately, she suspected.

Perhaps it was the comfort of the fire, or the keg of ale she had opened, but gradually he became quite relaxed and talkative for the first time since arriving on her doorstep. Encouraged, she was soon telling him animated stories and succeeding in getting a few full belly laughs out of him. He shared a few tales of his own from his travels and the battles he had fought, and Lucia asked many questions, surprising him with her knowledge of the places he mentioned. She had her late husband's library to thank for that.

Their conversation wound on, flowing more effortlessly through the night, and from time to time she looked up and found his eyes fixed fondly on her, that soft boyish smile upon his lips.

Eventually the fire burned down to its coals, and he stood up.

"Lucia, thank you. Tonight will be my last night here. I cannot delay my journey any longer. I must ride at first light."

She hid her disappointment the best she could and then dared to ask him why he was going north.

"To visit someone who may know something about what attacked my mother," he told her.

"I see," she said, glad of his trust in her. "I hope he can help you. Take what food and supplies you need. You've more than paid for them with the work you've done here."

"Thank you," he said. "Good night, Lucia."

***

The next morning Lucia woke to the cock's crow and laid in bed, knowing Bran was likely already gone. She stretched her limbs, pulled herself out of bed, and walked to the window. The birds had all joined the rooster now in a loud dawn-heralding cacophony.

Aveta was not up yet, so she stoked the still-hot coals in the hearth and poured some water in the kettle, absent-mindedly nibbling on an oatcake. She sat and stared blankly into the fire as she waited for the water to boil, noticing that each moment suddenly seemed heavier.

21

CHAPTER TWO

The Crossroads

He had grown soft.

Much too soft.

Over the past few days his brow had relaxed and a smile had sparked where nothing but the stern focus of a warrior had been for years. It vexed him, for he knew he could afford no such distractions.

He had not slept much the night before and rose eagerly at the first sign of dawn. He collected his things and visited Lucia's pantry to take the provisions she had offered, and then went down to the stable, pleased to find Gwion waiting for him and Gethen already saddled.

"Good morning," he said to the boy with a grateful smile.

"Good morning, Lord Bran," the boy replied. He seemed a bit melancholy, and Bran suspected it was because of how attached he had grown to Gethen over the past few days.

Gwion had worked miracles in the short time they had been at the villa. Gethen's black coat gleamed from brushing, the cracks in his hooves had all but disappeared, and the wounds he had suffered in battle were nearly healed. The night before in passing, he had overheard Gwion speaking to his horse in the stable and stopped to listen. He had not been able to make out the words as they were muffled from inside the stable, but the cadence and rhythm of the boy's voice had been full of gentleness. He wondered if he might ever have been that kind and innocent when he was a boy, but did not think so.

"I want to thank you for what you've done for Gethen," he said to Gwion sincerely.

The boy smiled and nodded, reluctantly handing over the reins, and then wrapped his arms around Gethen's neck and stroked his muzzle in farewell.

"He will never forget you," Bran reassured him, "and neither will I, lad."

The look in the boy's eyes was heartbreaking.

"I will be sure to stop and visit whenever my travels take me this way," he added, hoping to cheer him up.

"Until next time, then," Gwion finally said with acceptance.

"Yes," Bran nodded, tousling the boy's hair affectionately. "Until next time."

He wished he could promise a visit sometime soon, but he knew that was a promise he could not make, and he dared not disappoint him.

The sky was beginning to grow rosy above the hills and Gethen pawed the ground restlessly, ready for the ride. Bran put his foot in the stirrup, swung his leg over and settled into the saddle. He set off toward the treeline, and just before reaching it, made sure to turn round and wave a final farewell to Gwion before disappearing.

The sun finally peered over the horizon as he reached the lake and he took a deep long breath of the fresh earthy air, relieved to be on his way again.

It was time to find Talhaiarn.

***

Bran needed to reach the river by nightfall, so kept Gethen at a good pace. Summer was dying, but the day grew extremely warm in defiance as the sun climbed higher into the sky. They continued along the tree line for the remainder of the afternoon, finally reaching the river towards evening, as planned, where they meandered along its banks until Bran found a suitable place to bed down.

Bran soon had a fire going, and then pulled off his tunic and went to the river to wash and fill his goatskin. Gethen came over to drink beside him, and Bran enjoyed the moment with his companion, grateful that he was well again. As if sensing Bran's thoughts, Gethen pushed his nose against him affectionately. Bran splashed and played with him awhile, happy for a distraction from his dark thoughts, but it wasn't long before they returned.

"What the hell was it, boy?" he whispered to Gethen, peering into his black eyes as if the answer might be found there.

The horse looked at him blankly in response and shook his mane, as if to say, *how should I know?* and then nuzzled him in reassurance. Either that, or he smelled the apple in his pack.

Bran smiled and pulled out the fruit. "Here you go, you greedy vulture!"

Gethen nobly ignored the insult, took the apple gracefully between his teeth, and was soon chewing contentedly.

Good idea, Bran thought, sitting down by the fire and digging into his pack for his own supper. He found a loaf of bread and tore off a piece, eating it quickly. Gethen dined far more leisurely. He finished the apple and then went to work on his second course: a nice patch of long, green grass by the river.

Bran shoved his pack under his head and stretched out to sleep. He tried calming his mind by looking up at the stars and listening to the steady flow of the river, but sleep did not come. His thoughts wandered inevitably to his mother, bringing fresh pangs of guilt and sorrow, and then to Talhaiarn.

Talhaiarn had held the title of High Priest of the Crossroads and was the Druid counselor to the clan chieftains of the Great Circle since before Bran was born. He had always held Bran's mother in high regard, both as a queen and a priestess. No doubt as a favor to her, he agreed to teach young Bran to read and write when everyone else had given up on him.

To study under Talhaiarn was an honor envied by many, but Bran suspected it was nothing more than a plot by his stepfather to get rid of him. Cadoc had always resented the bond between Bran and his mother, envious of his wife's fierce love for her son.

From a very young age, Bran had tried to win Cadoc over by becoming the strongest and most promising warrior in the clan, but Cadoc never once offered him any praise or encouragement. One day, he had asked his mother why.

"You're not his, Bran," she told him without apology, "and that is the simple truth of it. Before you dare to pity yourself, though, remember that Cadoc treats you fairly, beats you only when you deserve it, and feeds and clothes you. That is more generous than most men would be to another man's bastard."

Cruel words, perhaps, but they were true, and from that day on Bran had no longer sought Cadoc's love or approval.

His mother had sent him away soon after, and insisted it was her will, not Cadoc's. Bran could not help but feel forsaken. He did as he was bid, however, for he would never shame his mother with disobedience.

Whether it was Talhaiarn's methods, the peacefulness of the Crossroads, or simply being away from the horses and swordplay that constantly called to him, Bran ended up flourishing more than his mother could have hoped for under the guidance of his wise teacher. When the year was over, reading and writing were the least of things he had mastered, and he returned proudly to her.

He and his mother had sat and talked for hours the day he had come home, and though she had said a great many things to him, there was one he had never forgotten:

"The Great Father wears many faces, my son."

It was then that he had realized the true reason she had sent him to Talhaiarn, and he had indeed regarded him as his father ever since.

***

The next morning Bran woke to the sound of Gethen nuzzling in his pack, searching for oats. He rose and stretched, pushed Gethen's nose out of the pack and scolded him.

"By the gods, you're impatient. I'll feed you, don't worry."

He rubbed his eyes and looked up at the sky. It was still dark overhead, but light was beginning to break in the East. He fumbled about tending to Gethen's breakfast while crunching down on an apple for his own, and then swung himself up into the saddle, eager to continue their journey.

As they made their way along the river, he thought back on the times he had come this way in the past. Happier times. Throughout his boyhood he had made this journey many times with his clan to celebrate the Greater Sabbats, meeting with their sister clans for a week of high council meetings, rituals and celebrations. Those were the source of his most cherished childhood memories; leaving home on horseback, sleeping beneath the stars, traveling through land where he did not already know every rock and tree and bend in the trail…These were the things that had given him an unquenchable thirst for what lay beyond. Once at the Crossroads, the adults would meet to discuss dry matters or make preparations for the rituals, and he and his tribal brothers would spar or explore the forest with their friends from the other clans. As they became young men, they traded running wildly through the camp at night for spending the evenings flirting with whatever beautiful girl they happened to fancy at the time. He wistfully thought back on their innocence, and how overwhelming the thrill of a simple kiss had been at that age.

Bran no longer knew that boy. He had long ago been eclipsed by a hardened countenance, forged by dark times and bathed in blood. His mother had hopes he would become a council leader, but his strong appetite for the thrill of battle had taken him far from their small village. At sixteen, he departed with his cousin Gareth to follow the older warriors in his clan into battle against the invaders, and had not returned more than a handful of times since then. His mother blamed his father's blood for this, but Bran had never known his father. As a boy he had often asked her about him, but she had revealed very little. The most he could recall her ever saying was, "He was a barbarian and a thief, but I, a better one; I captured his heart and stole the very best of him, and with it knit your bones together inside my womb. You have his strength and fearlessness in your blood. It's your destiny to become a great warrior."

Even at that age, before he knew anything about the ways of men and women and the treacherous sea of emotions that churned between them, he noted the change in his mother's tone whenever she spoke of his father – she became tense, like a bowstring. Not wanting to upset her, he eventually gave up his attempts to construct an accurate portrait of his father, and instead embraced the myth she offered. His mother's prediction had come true. He had indeed became a great warrior, but for what? He had been away when she needed him most.

His guilt moved in on him again, and he knew he had to kill it for the beast it was lest it lead him into another poor decision. He should have stayed with his clan a few days longer before setting out for the Crossroads, but the beast had not let him sleep nor eat, demanding he *do something*. Unfortunately, in his haste he had nearly lost Gethen. Thank the gods for Lucia and Gwion.

He thought about how Gwion had run out to greet him, cutting across the field and waving. He had been so trusting – *too trusting*, greeting him with an enthusiastic, "Good evening, my lord," as if he had been expecting him.

Then, there was Lucia. She was another blessing he had not expected. He pictured her in the doorway, looking at him suspiciously, the orange sunset casting a fiery glow on her copper hair. Her green eyes had searched his face boldly and without fear, flashing like the sun on a restless sea. The thought of her still made his blood rise, and he allowed himself to indulge in the pleasure of thinking about her as he rode along, for it was the only pleasure he had known in many long moons.

Suddenly, the cry of a raven overhead snapped his thoughts back to the present. It soared overhead, black wings stretched out in the sun, and Bran felt encouraged, having always regarded seeing his namesake as a good omen.

He and Gethen traveled steadily throughout the rest of the day, stopping only briefly for water. When the shadows grew long and began swallowing up the road, he fished himself some dinner out of the river and then leaned up against a tree to rest.

He watched the moon rise over the hills, covering everything in pale blue silk except for the river which she adorned with ribbons of silver. The river wore the moon's gifts as proudly as a young maiden, and they bounced and sparkled upon her curves as she danced.

Bran watched her dance all night, anxious thoughts again keeping sleep at bay.

Finally, the sky hinted at the sun's return and Bran rose, grateful the night was over.

CHAPTER THREE

The Sight

The morning broke crisply and Lucia went down to the lake for her swim, knowing she would not be able to enjoy them much longer. Summer was coming to a close, and the water would soon become too cold. She loosened her laces as she walked along, and then once upon the shore undressed quickly and dove in. The lake swallowed her up happily, welcoming her back with an icy embrace.

Her breathing instantly fell into a familiar rhythm, in perfect harmony with the strokes of her arms and legs as her feet gracefully moved her forward across the water's surface. She had always been a strong swimmer, and felt completely free in the water. In fact, she had been told she could swim before she could walk. She remembered her mother continuously warning her not to stay in the water so long when she was younger, saying the *Gwragedd Annwn* would surely notice her beauty and steal her away. "Then what would I do?" she would say, grabbing her and holding her tight.

Lucia felt especially strong that morning, and swam steadily for quite some time out toward the island. Eventually, she began to grow tired and stopped to rest, turning about to get her bearings. She looked back toward shore, and to her shock found she was much farther out than she had ever been before. So far, in fact, that the island seemed much closer than the shore she had left from.

She rested a moment, treading water, watching as the island mysteriously disappeared and then reappeared in the mist, beckoning to her.

Do I dare? she thought, heart pounding.

She had been warned many times by the field folk never to try and swim to the island, for though it may appear to be close, it was said to be nothing more than a faerie trick.

There was at least one story in every family of someone who had drowned or gone mad trying to reach it, and a few rare ones about those who had actually succeeded, but eventually met the same fate. Those who claimed they had been there returned with stories of the island's pristine beauty, and bewitching women who swam faster than river otters and moved through the trees without a sound. Forever compelled to return, the poor souls had all eventually died in the attempt.

Then there was the famous tale of the three Roman soldiers, disgusted by the superstitions of the peasants and intrigued by the descriptions of the island's female inhabitants, who set out for the island vowing to return with the "witches" and make slaves of them. Over the next moon all three of them were found washed up on the lakeshore, arrows lodged in their hearts.

Thus, the island and the women who dwelled upon it were said to be cursed, but Lucia did not believe it. She longed to see the women for herself. Besides, no one could swim as well as she could, and lately she had been getting close enough to see smoke rising from the island, or figures walking along its shores...but never had she been this close.

I can do it, she told herself, convinced she could reach it.

She surged toward the island powerfully, putting all of her effort into her strokes, but to her dismay, no matter how long or how vigorously she swam, she got no closer. Eventually, the island disappeared completely from view.

She waited for it to appear again, but the mist stubbornly refused to reveal it. Finally, she knew she had no choice. She would have to find the strength to return home.

Lucia was worried. She had never been out for so long before. She turned over on her back, trying to relax, breathing calmly, stroke after stroke steadily taking her back towards home. By sheer will, she finally made it back, dragging herself out of the lake, gasping and crawling out onto the bank, squeezing the land between her fingers gratefully. Exhausted, she lay there until her breath returned to normal, and then dressed and began walking back.

So close, she thought. *Next time, I will make it.*

Exhilaration returned to her body as she walked. It was a warm day, which was quite rare this late in the season, and she went to the field to practice. It was a good day for it. With Aveta's help, she had been working on controlling her visions - how to trigger them, explore them, and most importantly, understand their messages.

The first time she had received one was the night a man had come to her father's villa to speak with him and stayed for dinner. In her dreams that night, she saw the man stabbed to death, face down in a pool of his own blood, with his murderer standing over him. She had awakened instinctively knowing something was different about that dream, and it frightened her. Weeks later, what she had seen came to pass. Her fear turned to terror, believing that she somehow had a hand in what had happened to him.

She kept her secret for weeks, but finally could stand it no longer and told her mother about it, confessing her fear that she had caused it. Her mother comforted her, telling her she had done no such thing; that she had merely seen that which was yet to be. She told Lucia she had been blessed with a special gift from the Great Mother called 'the Sight', and that her great, great grandmother had also had it. She said it was something her father's people would be very frightened of, however, and made Lucia promise to share her visions with no one but her. Though they once worshipped many gods, the Romans now worshipped only one, called the Christ, and they would not understand.

Her mother never went to the Roman church if she could help it, but sometimes her father would insist upon it. Lucia had tried to speak to their priest once. He had mentioned a messenger called an angel, and she asked him if angels were the same as Fae. He said no, the Fae served the old gods and the old gods served Satan. They were not to be trusted. She had gone home that day and told her mother what he had said, and she had called him a stupid old goat. That was the last time Lucia asked the priest any questions.

Aveta worshipped the Great Mother, like her own mother did, and after Camulos died, Lucia had spent more and more time with her, eventually feeling safe enough to confide in her about her visions. Aveta offered to teach her what she knew, and help guide her as best she could. She taught her ways to call upon the

36

Sight, but encouraged her to find ways of her own. Lucia found that singing, weaving or gazing into a fire or pool of water most quickly took her into that place where the door would open, but sometimes, like now, it opened without her asking and beckoned to her.

She felt a desire to lie down and let the sun shine on her, so she went and collapsed in the barley field, crushing the long grain beneath her body. She felt hidden and safe and closed her eyes, surrendering to the sound of the wind shaking the barley all around her. Her heartbeat and breath slowed down, and soon she was drifting in and out of sleep.

She began to feel things shifting around her. Fear rose, as it always did, but she had been learning to ignore it. She knew it would happen soon; soon the door would open....

The colors of a sunset began flashing in front of her eyes, and then suddenly, she was running through the barley field. The grain came up to her waist, and she could feel it rushing against her legs and hands. She felt like the linen she had hung to dry yesterday afternoon, blowing in the wind...her strides effortless, taking her twice as far as they should....The ground springing beneath her feet, propelling her farther and farther forward. The field stretched on forever in front of her, its sheaves moving and swaying around her...She looked up into the sky as she ran, stretching her arms out like wings, feeling as if she could soar into it. Gradually she felt her arms changing, lengthening, thinning out gracefully, becoming light as air, and then suddenly her feet no longer fell upon the earth and the wind picked her up, flowing beneath them. Instinctively she thrust away from the ground, catching another current, and soon was soaring above the field, blue-black wings stretching out under the sun. She weighed nothing, flying high above her land, her vision becoming sharper with each moment...She saw the villa, the stable, the lake beyond, and the river which fed it. She was sailing smoothly upon the skirts of Danu's zephyrs, flying along the river, mesmerized by the sun dancing on it. She followed the river for miles, riding the wind. She flew low enough to skim the surface of the river, and then up above the trees, until suddenly she spied a horse and rider far below. She flew closer, and then recognized who she had managed to find.

When she finally awoke, the sun was high in the sky. She sat up, light-headed, her whole body humming. She sat for some time, until she was sure her legs would not give out under her when she stood. The dizziness eventually faded and she walked back to the house, searching out Aveta.

She finally spied her just beyond the gate in the orchard, relieving a heavy-limbed apple tree of its burden. Her hair had partially fallen out of its bun as it often did and was hanging about her shoulders. She had already filled three baskets and was working on a fourth. It was easy to spot Gwion.

"Aveta," she called as she made her way to the orchard. "I am sorry. I meant to come earlier." She climbed up the tree next to hers and began filling her own basket.

"I can see the light of the Otherworld in your eyes," Aveta said after a moment. "Something's happened."

Lucia nodded and picked a few more apples, seeking the right words. "This time it was different," she began. "This time I wasn't merely looking through the door, watching something."

"Go on," Aveta encouraged. Gwion abandoned his tree to come and listen to her tale as well.

"This time I was *in* the place I opened the door to. At first I was running through the barley field as myself, in my own body, but then, my body changed....my arms turned into wings, and I flew up out of the field. I *felt* them, carrying me upon the wind...I could see with different eyes, in a way I could never describe to you in words. I saw the lake, the villa from above -- the roof needs mending, by the way...we have work to do before the winter comes ---the orchard and garden, and then I came to the place where the river enters the lake, and I followed it for many miles north...how many, I don't know...and then, as I flew along the river, I spied a dark horse and rider far below."

"Ah, Lord Bran?" said Aveta, her brown eyes widening.

"Yes," Lucia confirmed. Aveta didn't seem surprised at all to hear this.

"Give thanks, Lucia," Aveta said. "You've been blessed by the raven. The spirits of animals do not invite many to see through their eyes."

"No, they don't," Gwion added.

"What do you think it means?" Lucia asked.

"What does it mean to you?" Aveta answered. "What it means to *me* will not help you, but I think we could agree your spirit is

39

drawn to Bran's for some reason, and took the form of his namesake. I would start there and see what comes to you."

The three of them picked apples for the rest of the afternoon, and Lucia thought much on it indeed - too much, for her liking. Finally the daylight began to fade, the hills pulling shadows up to their chins, and they went in to eat supper together. Aveta had prepared a stew with some venison that a neighboring farmer had brought by that morning for them. Such gifts came often, as it seemed most of the farmers fancied Aveta, although Lucia never saw that Aveta gave them any reason to expect anything at all in return. They sat down to it with some bread and apples. Gwion ate quickly and went to say good night to the horses, leaving the two women to sit together by the fire, exhausted from the day.

"Aveta," she said suddenly.

"Yes?"

"Thank you."

Smiling, Aveta reached over and gave her hand a squeeze.

Lucia was surprised to find herself holding back tears. "Such a secret is like a heavy stone you must carry on your back everywhere you go. You cannot imagine how comforting it is to know I can set it down when I'm with you. "

Then it was Aveta who looked as though she would weep. "Oh, but I can. Such stones I am most familiar with."

Lucia squeezed her hand in return and then let out a tired sigh. "I've spent my whole life hiding that part of me. There's so much I have to learn."

Aveta laughed. "We all do, Lucia." she said, consolingly. "Remember, all things have a season, and they turn according to the Great Mother's will. Think of your past as your winter. Perhaps now is your time to blossom."

Lucia smiled, comforted by her words, and then looked over at her. She seemed very tired.

"Please, Aveta. Go to bed. We've had a long day. We can talk tomorrow."

"Yes, we have," Aveta said, standing up. "Until the morning, then." She rose to leave, putting her hand on Lucia's shoulder in reassurance.

Lucia was tired as well, but her mind was racing, and she knew sleep would not come for some time. She went to the library to read.

Her late husband Camulos had won her over not with wealth or charm, though he had had a bit of both, but rather with books and the promise of an education. Fourteen years her senior, Camulos had been appointed as a procurator by the Romans. Loyal to the Empire but of strong Celtic descent, they believed him a perfect candidate to keep peace in the region. He was amply rewarded with good land and all the privileges the Empire could provide. Her father had him to dinner on regular occasion, and it soon became obvious to Lucia what was going on. Thankfully, she liked him, for it could have been far worse. Being a keen man, he noticed her eyes would light up whenever he spoke of anything beyond the horizon of her small world. She would forget propriety and ask many questions, enthusiastic over any detail he would provide. He soon brought books to her as gifts rather than jewelry when he would visit, and eventually offered to have her tutored in Latin. When he asked for her hand in marriage, her father was quick to agree. Though she was a great beauty, she knew her father constantly lived in fear that someone would find out about her "affliction" and he would be unable to find her a husband. That a man of such standing had offered to marry her must have been a great relief to him.

Lucia had Camulos to thank for everything she had, and unlike many women, very happy with the man she had been given to. Sadly, they had only spent a few short moons together before he had gone off to settle a skirmish with raiding tribes from the north and not come home.

Two years had passed since the day the messenger had brought the terrible news that he had been killed, and she had not wanted to remarry. She was luckily in a position where she did not have to, either. She had been perfectly content to spend the rest of her days as his widow, reading her way through his library, enjoying the land and the company of her adopted family.

Until Bran, that is. Now, longing had crept in, disturbing the peace in her heart. She found it extremely unsettling that in such a small amount of time, he had come and changed everything.

CHAPTER FOUR
A Reunion

The sun rose and the day began much as it had the morning
before, the first hints of autumn beginning to float upon the air.
Bran and Gethen continued up the river for the better part of the
morning, reaching the foothills of the mountains late in the
afternoon. From there, the countryside grew steadily less inviting.
The path became choked with growth, nearly disappearing
completely. For an hour after sundown they traveled through the
forest, their path obscured in darkness except for the rare sliver of
moonlight that managed to make its way through the thick
latticework of branches overhead. Eventually they emerged and
the trail began a steep ascent into a narrow mountain pass along a
series of switchbacks that carried them higher and higher across
the stone skirts of the mountainside. Bran looked out over the
valley past the dense forest to where the river flowed out, a mere
thread of silver glinting through the landscape far below. Gethen's
breath billowed white against his black coat as they continued to
climb, the night air growing ever colder, flooded with the light of
the nearly full moon and the crisp smell of the coming snow.

They finally arrived at the mouth of a cave that served as one of
the entrances to Talhaiarn's fortress. It was obscured by rocks and
brush, barely high enough for a horse but wide enough for two.
He dismounted and entered, leading Gethen in by the reins. They
followed a narrow passageway carved out of the rock that rose
steeply ever upward. Deeper and higher into the mountain they
traveled, the echo of Gethen's hooves reverberating against the
close rock walls in a steady hypnotic rhythm. Soon the

passageway opened up into a large cavern that served as a small stable. On the wall he spied saddles that he knew well.

Belenus and Taranis. Why are they here? Bran thought.

Belenus and Taranis were chieftains to the clans of the East and North. With his notorious reputation in battle, Bran was well-respected by both, and always welcomed to eat and drink in a place of honor at their feasts. He was anxious to greet them and hear what news they brought from their lands.

He fed and watered Gethen and then went up a staircase and down a corridor where the beams of the fortress began, solidly built into the side of the mountain. He could hear voices coming from the hall, and called out loudly to announce his arrival.

He heard a massive door open and walked briskly toward the sound. There, waiting for him in the doorway, was Talhaiarn.

"Bran?" he exclaimed, a pleased yet worried look upon his face.

"Lord Talhaiarn, I have come seeking your counsel on a disturbing matter," Bran said somberly, grateful to see his old master's face.

"Come in," Talhaiarn said, opening the door widely. "Belenus and Taranis are here as well with terrible news of their own. I suspect it all flows from the same poisonous well."

Bran entered and instantly felt more at ease. The fortress was the source of many treasured memories for him; a place of both refuge and learning. A fire burned in the center of the hall, smoke exiting through a hole in the rock ceiling overhead. Over it bubbled a pot of stew, and the smell of it filled the air.

"Greetings, my brother," said Taranis gladly from across the room, approaching to grab Bran strongly by the hand and forearm.

"Taranis, it's good to see you," Bran said, clapping him on the back several times.

Taranis had become more rugged-looking in the face since Bran had last seen him. His body looked especially strong and muscular, the result of much work during the harvest, no doubt. Taranis and his clan were the most hard-working folk he had ever met, but they celebrated just as much as they worked. Bran tried never to miss celebrating *Calan Awst* among them, but he had not made it this year. The harvest festival lasted a week, with more food and ale than anyone could eat or drink.

"It has been too long," Belenus said, greeting him as well. His beautiful white hawk, Gwyn, was perched upon his forearm. Those of the East often gave their sons a hawk or falcon to train when they were old enough to manage one. Gwyn and Belenus had been together since Belenus was a boy of five, but she had not been given to him. She chose him, which was considered one of the highest honors among his people.

Belenus does not age, Bran thought as he embraced him. His hair trailed down his back in a long, white-blonde braid, and his clear sky-blue eyes peered out from above a fine nose, missing nothing.

"Come, there is food," Talhaiarn offered.

More importantly, there is ale, thought Bran gratefully as he looked toward the table. He filled his drinking horn and sat down by the fire with the others.

"Bran, what news do you bring?" Talhaiarn asked, concerned.

"My mother and Lord Cadoc were attacked by something in the night," he answered heavily. "Both have died from their wounds."

"*Gods, no,*" exclaimed Taranis wearily, putting his head in his hands. Belenus closed his eyes and shook his head slowly.

Talhaiarn reached over and put a reassuring hand on Bran's knee, meeting his eyes. "Your mother walks among the gods, now, Bran. Of that you can be certain."

"I know she does," Bran answered and mustered a smile. "My cousin Gareth brought me the news. He told me Cadoc and my mother had been attacked by a wolf while they slept. By the time we made it to the village, Cadoc had died and my mother had but a few hours of life left to her. She insisted that sorcery was to blame. It was her dying request that I come to you for help."

The three men looked at each other expectantly after hearing the news, as if they knew something Bran did not, and then Taranis spoke, his baritone voice deep and heavy with the accent of the North.

"We were attacked in the night as well," he began. "The bastards hid inside our mines by day, and then under cover of darkness slipped into our village, unseen and unheard."

Bran looked down and saw Taranis' knuckles were white from clenching his fist around his mug.

"Cursed bastards!" he suddenly boomed out, nearly shaking the mountain. "Did they attack our warriors? *No*. No, they *slunk* in, the cowards, like snakes, and stole our children from their beds."

"Children?" Bran thought aloud, confused. "Why the children?"

"Why, indeed?" Taranis said with a disgusted expression. "Some of the poor bairns we found ripped apart in the woods, limbs torn from their bodies, drained of their blood. Some we found eaten down to nothing but their bones and some were simply gone, without a trace."

Gods, they must have fed them to their dogs, Bran thought in horror.

"I left the next morning for the Crossroads," Taranis continued. "I could hear the wailing of our women as they buried what remained of our sons and daughters for at least a mile as I rode away." He stopped and looked right into Bran's eyes with a fierce passion. "I swear to the gods, I will tear their throats out when I find them!" he vowed.

Bran took Taranis' mug and poured him more ale, setting it gently by his clenched fist.

"Strange things have been happening in the forests surrounding our lands, as well," Belenus began. "We lost a few of our shepherds who had been outside the walls after dark. It was clear they had been attacked and dragged into the forest. We followed the trail and found them in the same state Taranis described. Since then, we have insisted upon everyone being inside the walls by sundown, and keep our hawks on watch at all times. Though we have seen nothing since, we dare not let down our guard."

47

Suddenly a cold mountain wind rose up, blowing beneath the heavy oak doors which led out to the lookout. Talhaiarn placed another log on the fire and then spoke.

"Brothers, I believe Agarah was right. We are not dealing with Saxon or wolf. I suspect we are indeed dealing with sorcery, and that Cerridwen may be to blame."

"Cerridwen?" Bran exclaimed.

He was not familiar with everyone from every clan, least of all the mysterious women of the Sisterhood, but he definitely knew who Priestess Rowan was, as well as her infamous daughter, Cerridwen. Cerridwen had stolen the Sisterhood's sacred Cauldron and fled with her deformed son Morvran some years ago and had not been heard of since.

"Yes," Talhaiarn continued. "Recently tales have begun to spring up among the village folk of a grotesque giant who has been sighted on more than one occasion roaming the countryside at dusk. They call him Avagdu, but I am convinced that it is Morvran they have seen, which means Cerridwen has returned."

"And you think *she* is responsible for the attacks on our clans?" Bran asked.

"I find it very likely. She has always had an insatiable lust for power, and to that end I suspect she has raised an army and intends to steal the remaining clan relics. She vowed as much when she left the Sisterhood. If she manages to do so, she would be able to control the passage to the in-between."

"We cannot allow that to happen," Belenus said.

48

"No," Talhaiarn replied. "We most certainly cannot. We must act quickly, for it is obvious the enemy has been on the move. They attacked in the North, then some days later the East, and now Bran has brought us terrible news from the South. They are either growing stronger or far more ambitious, for they've gone from snatching babies from cradles to attacking and overwhelming warriors the likes of Cadoc, which we all know is no easy feat. We will need your best trackers, Belenus. Send them south to Bran's village. We must find out everything we can about the enemy we are dealing with."

"You'll have them in two days, led by my son, Neirin," Belenus promised. "He is the best tracker we have. If he cannot find them, no one can."

"We will be honored to host your son and his men," Bran said, "and as surely as they can find the bastards, I assure you mine can kill them."

"I will send all the men I can spare as well," Taranis pledged to Bran. "Believe me, they are ravenous for revenge, and want nothing more than to slaughter the vermin who murdered their sons and daughters."

***

Everyone slept except Bran, unable to free his mind from the day his mother had died.

He had been on the battlefield far to the East when Gareth had arrived with the terrible news. They had set out early the following morning, but even with good horses it was a long journey before the familiar roundhouses and stables of their village winked into view.

As they made their final approach across the meadow, a woman had come running toward them in the dying daylight, quite tall and slender. As she drew nearer, Bran had suddenly realized it was his sister, her long blonde hair giving her away. She had become a woman in the time he had been gone, and he had not recognized her at first. She told him how their mother and Cadoc had been attacked in their sleep. Their wounds had festered terribly, resistant to every poultice and salve. Cadoc had suffered the worst of it, his wounds so deep and infected he had not lasted two days. His mother had fared better, but slowly she had begun to lose the fight, and Seren knew she did not have long to live.

Bran had gone in to see her, and though he had been warned by his sister, had been completely shocked by what he had seen. Her face was gaunt and ashen, except for the yellow bruised flesh under her eyes, and her hair was wet against her cheeks. Her neck had a poultice of herbs pressed against it with bandages wrapped around to hold it in place. He could still see her in his mind, and was overcome with dread remembering the weakness and immense pain in her face.

How long had she suffered, waiting for him?

He had gone quickly to her side, lifted her up and held her against him, willing the strength of life that flowed through him to enter her body, but instantly he knew it was no use. Arawn was coming for her, and as he laid her back down he could feel the great god's presence descending around them like a massive, black cloud. Bran had felt the god's arrival many times before, beholding the faces of fellow fallen warriors upon the battlefield, but this time he could almost see him patiently looming over his mother's bed, flanked by his white hounds and their red, unblinking eyes.

"Mother, I'm sorry," was all he could think of to say.

"Don't be," she had told him faintly. "You're here, and now I can die," she said with simple acceptance. "I have fought with everything in me, but I have come to see it is my time."

He had not wanted to hear it, but he had seen death's shadow looming over enough faces in his life to know she spoke the truth. She would not last the night.

"You are our strongest warrior, Bran. The clan will need your strength in the days to come. Whatever attacked us was not a wolf. Go to Talhaiarn and ask his counsel on what has happened here."

He had sworn to do so, and then she had smiled and closed her eyes.

"I want you to build my pyre, Bran. Your hands alone. No one else."

"It shall be done as you wish," he promised. "Go, Mother," he had said softly. "The Summerlands are waiting."

She looked relieved, and then relaxed into death's waiting arms.

His sister had then lay down next to her and wept through the night, and he had sworn an oath of revenge on the one who had stolen her from them.

He spent the rest of that terrible day chopping wood and building his mother's pyre, as promised. He remembered how shocked he had been as he lifted her from her bed; she had been as light as a child, as if her body were filled with autumn leaves instead of bones.

That evening at dusk everyone gathered for her funeral, as they had no doubt done but a few nights before for Cadoc. Seren had come and stood near him, quiet and strong, and he remembered being proud of her courage. After everyone had arrived, Bran raised his hands over his mother toward the heavens, and said his clan's burial prayer.

He found himself whispering it again, now, to the flames in Talhaiarn's hearth.

"Guardians of the South, Keepers of the Flame, recognize your daughter Agarah, and burn the confusion from her soul with your fire, purifying her heart. Protect and guide her through the in-between, to the Summerland, beyond the realm of Arawn."

Suddenly, the flames began to play tricks on him. He began to see the image of his mother on her pyre, burning within the fire. The flames then began to change to resemble her features, flowing in the shape of her body and the contours of her face, undulating in waves forming her hair, until eventually a perfect replica of his mother's body appeared before him within the fire. She sat up and shifted, turning toward him, billowing in blue, orange and gold, her eyes watching him.

Mother? he whispered tentatively.

He leaned in closer, the smoke and heat making his eyes water, watching intently as the flames turned and flowed lengthwise forming a fiery river, out of which slinking demons emerged, crawling swiftly through the familiar landscape of his childhood.

The loud crack of a log splitting woke him suddenly to find he was drenched in sweat. The smell of smoke filled his nostrils, his damp hair, and his clothes. Disturbed and desperate for fresh air, Bran went outside to the look-out where he found Talhaiarn standing in the bright moonlight, looking down over the valley below.

"What did they show you?" Talhaiarn said without turning around.

"Who?" Bran asked weakly, dizziness slowly leaving him with the help of the cool night air.

"The Guardians of the South. They are here, with your mother's spirit," Talhaiarn said, turning to face him.

"What did they show you?"

Bran had hoped he had simply had a nightmare, but it seemed that was not so.

"My mother appeared to me in the fire, and then I saw what I can only describe as men bewitched, moving through the countryside around our village," he finally replied.

"Bran, where is *Dyrnwyn*?" Talhaiarn then asked. "Is it safe?"

"Only my sister knows," Bran answered.

"You must protect them both. With your mother and Cadoc gone, your clan is weak. Your sister will one day be a powerful priestess, but she is still very young with little experience in battle. I fear Cerridwen may attempt to force her to reveal where *Dyrnwyn* is. You must understand, with each relic Cerridwen gains, the others become easier to obtain. Look what she's managed to do with the Cauldron alone."

The thought of Seren being taken pushed Bran over the edge.

"I assure you, Talhaiarn, I will not let that happen," he vowed.

"See that you do not. The Guardians have helped your mother send you a warning," he said to Bran solemnly. "You must return home at once."

CHAPTER FIVE
The Island

Lucia had gone to bed early, shortly before sundown, scarcely able to keep her eyes open. She had slept only a few hours when she felt herself being pulled between the worlds. She had come to recognize the call well, as it had been happening more and more as of late.

Images began to come to her in flashes, and she relaxed, allowing them in. A hooded man with a torch…her villa…the orchard…The images were like the many threads on a loom that she had to weave together. She remembered the incantation Aveta had taught her to say…

"Sacred Guardians of Earth, power of bone, stone and soil, root this vision, plant it deep, so I may walk within it."

She repeated it over and over within her mind, and gradually, the threads materialized into one solid tapestry in time.

She found herself standing in her garden, the ground beneath her feet as solid as if she had gotten up from her bed and walked outside. She watched intently as the grotesque hooded figure with the torch emerged from the trees, surrounded by pale figures crawling on all fours. They moved in her direction and terror seized her. Although she knew they could not see her, she couldn't help but crouch behind the small stone wall that surrounded the garden. Some of them went into the fields, sniffing like dogs, and others slunk along the ground to enter the house. They were becoming more agitated, not finding what they were looking for.

Where are Gwion and Aveta? She ran to their little cottage, afraid she would find them set upon. Luckily the door was open. She looked inside but found no one there.

She checked the stable. No horses.

Where are they?

Suddenly she smelled smoke, and to her horror turned around to see the hooded man had set fire to her fields and thrown his torch upon her rooftop. Soon clouds of smoke were billowing up into the night sky, pouring from the roof of the villa, blacking out her vision…

No, she thought, terrified. *Please, no!*

Desperately she searched for clues as to when this would happen. It was still autumn. The apples they had picked earlier were still in baskets next to Aveta's cottage, and her garden hoe was in the same place she had left it earlier that evening.

I must see one more thing, she told herself. She breathed in deeply, focusing, and willed herself up, high into the sky, shooting her consciousness above the trees, out toward the lake, far from the smoke and flames…

Finally she could see the heavens, and there she found the object she had been looking for. The moon. It was full, its intense light shining down upon the lake.

She was about to force herself from the vision, but then spied something on the water far below…*What was it?* She willed herself closer, and then saw it was a small boat with three figures onboard, slowly rowing toward the island in the middle of the lake. She tried to get closer, but the boat began to disappear in the mist, as did the lake, then the house, then the orchard and the horizon.

Gradually she became aware of her body, her bed, and her surroundings. She tried fighting for more time, but it was no use; the fabric was unraveling. She finally let it go.

She opened her eyes. Her heart was pounding. Sweat had drenched the bed linens. She lay there for some time, motionless, willing herself to memorize every detail, burning it into her consciousness.

Moments later, Aveta pushed her door open and whispered urgently into Lucia's bedroom. "My lady? I heard you cry out in your sleep."

"We need to leave," Lucia said frantically, jumping from the bed. "Something is coming, Aveta. Coming here, and soon--the villa will burn, and nothing will be left!"

"Lucia, what did you see, exactly?" Aveta asked calmly.

"Aveta, please, trust me. We must leave--I am afraid they will come tonight!"

Aveta saw the terror in Lucia's eyes and did not ask any more questions. "Very well. I know a place where we will be safe. I will go and tell Gwion."

Lucia stuffed her warmest dress and cloak into a large leather bag, and her fear as far back in her mind as possible. As she ran past the library, her stomach seized up with the thought of it going up in flames. Tears in her eyes, she grabbed an armful of her favorites and frantically buried them in the orchard along with the coffer of gold her husband had kept hidden for her in case he had not returned. She had never used any of it, having always been able to manage the land well. She would not suffer it to be stolen now.

On her way back, she passed the stables and Gwion came out to meet her. "I've spoken to the horses," he said, looking at her. "They will go to pasture far from here until we come back."

"What do you mean you've spoken to the horses?" Lucia asked, panicked. "Where have they gone? We *need* the horses!"

"Don't worry, Lady Lucia. We are going home," he smiled.

"Going home?" she asked, confused.

"To the island," he proclaimed simply, pointing to the mist far off in the moonlit lake.

Aveta then emerged from the house with an authority emanating from her that took Lucia by surprise.

"Come," she said. "Now, you must trust me, Lucia."

The three of them made their way down to the tiny dock on the lake where the rowboat was tied. They dragged the fish nets aside and Aveta and Lucia climbed in, facing each other in the small boat. Gwion gave them a little push away from the dock and then jumped in himself, taking the oars. He was soon rowing in a steady, powerful rhythm out towards the island, far off in the center of the lake.

Were they really going to attempt to reach the island?

Lucia's heart pounded with the idea of finally landing upon the fabled island she had longed to see for so long.

As if reading Lucia's mind, Aveta began to speak.

"Lucia, I'm going to tell you something that will be hard for you to believe, but it is the truth. I've wanted to tell you for a long time, but I simply couldn't until now."

"What?" Lucia said, intrigued.

"Your mother is my older sister, and your grandmother is High Priestess of the Sisterhood on the island. Your mother and I were born and grew up there."

"What?"

Lucia sat silently in the boat, shocked.

"I am sorry, Lucia," Aveta apologized.

"You're my mother's *sister*?" Lucia cried in shock. "Aveta, how could you have kept this from me?

"I did not want to. Believe me. I promise you, when all is explained you will see why it had to be this way."

Lucia said nothing for a long while, in disbelief over Aveta's deception, but eventually decided if Aveta said it had to be that way, then perhaps it had. She had always felt especially close to Aveta and Gwion. Truly, they *had* become family to her, so finding out they actually were was not so very hard to believe.

Finally her anger gave way to curiosity, for although her temper flared up suddenly, it died down just as quickly, and she was eager for answers.

"You truly grew up on the island?"

"Yes."

"Why did you leave? Why did my mother leave?"

"Your mother left to be with your father. It happens, from time to time, that someone manages to reach the island; sometimes the spirits of the lake lead them there, and sometimes the mist is thin and they slip through. It so happened with your father. He washed up on the shore, and your mother was the one to find him. We in the Sisterhood are taught from a very young age that any men who land upon our shores are to be killed, but your mother claimed your father appeared to be dead already, lying face down on the shore where she found him. She was fifteen at the time, had never been off the island, and had never seen a man before. Of course, he was not dead. I am not sure what he said to her to gain her trust, but she led him secretly to the far side of the island and hid him there, quite well, for moons from what I understand. Nature took its course and they became lovers. "

"They were discovered, of course," Aveta sighed, "and then they were brought before the Sisterhood for judgment."

"What do you mean, judgment?"

"Unfortunately, there are only two choices for a woman of the Sisterhood in a situation such as your mother's. Either the man she loves is banished and she rejoins her sisters, or she chooses exile and leaves the island with him. Your mother chose the latter."

Oh, Mother, Lucia thought sadly. Her father was rarely home while she was growing up. In fact, she scarcely knew him. She and her mother were near inseparable because of it. When the time came, Lucia had suffered tremendous guilt leaving her mother behind to marry Camulos, but her father had insisted on it.

She gave up everything for a life of loneliness.

"Your grandmother was very unhappy about it, I can assure you. Daughters of the island have been known to leave for a man, but always for a man of one of the Guardian clans. Marry a Roman? No. Our mother was heart-broken, as was I. I was a small girl when Cordelia left, but I still remember her. I missed her terribly."

"Aveta, why did *you* leave? For Gwion's father?"

"No," Aveta said, her eyes tearing up. "Not for Gwion's father, though had fate been kinder, I would have." She looked down into the bottom of the boat, breathing a deep sigh.

Aveta changed the subject, and Lucia let her.

"Your mother and I have another sister. Her name is Cerridwen. As you know, we all have our faults, and hers are immense pride and a terrible temper. She felt Gwion had stolen something from her son."

"What?" Lucia looked over at Gwion.

Gwion looked over at his mother, but said nothing, and simply continued to row.

"I will tell you of that another time," Aveta said. "Let us just say that we needed to flee the island. You only have to witness my sister's anger once to know you never want to witness it again. Cerridwen is very dangerous and irrational when she is angry, and her son takes after her."

"So that is why you left? She can't have stayed angry with you for that long," Lucia said, thinking of her own inability to hold a grudge.

"You underestimate her wrath. There is much more to the story," Aveta assured her, and Gwion's face seemed to confirm her statement.

"So, where did you go, then?" Lucia asked.

"To find your mother. I had always wondered what path her life had taken. Luckily, Talhaiarn had kept himself apprised of where she was, as a daughter of the Order is always a daughter of the Order, whether she chooses to live as one or not. He knows of you as well. The journey to find her took me a nearly a week on horseback. I remember arriving at her door, my heart pounding at having found her. At first she didn't recognize me. So many years had passed. When she left, I had been a young girl. Once I told her who I was, she embraced me and we both sobbed for a long time. Over a meal she told me all that had happened since she left the island. Her Roman took her to his city and married her, as he had promised to do. She had given birth to a baby girl nine moons later, and named her Lucia – a name in her new tongue, meaning "light." She told me that she and your father had recently accepted a marriage proposal for you. She also confided in me that you had the Sight, and that she did not know what to do about it. I was shocked to hear this."

Aveta stopped and reached over to put her hand on Lucia's knee.

"Lucia, you need to know that you have been given one of the Great Mother's most precious gifts, though at times I know it can feel like a curse. This is only because you don't understand it yet, nor know how to use it. The priestesses on the island pray and pray for their daughters to be blessed with the Sight – it happens very rarely. I knew this. As your mother could no longer help you, I came up with a plan. I suggested that she offer me as a household servant to Lord Camulos, as a wedding present. This way, I could stay close to you while I waited for Gwion to finish his apprenticeship."

Lucia sat thinking about the sacrifices that had been made on her behalf.

"Aveta, you gave up your freedom! What if Camulos had been a brute? Or had treated you poorly?"

"Then we would have suffered by his hand together, I imagine. I would have been there for you, either way. In fact, if such a thing had been the case, I would have been even gladder that I were there for you."

Lucia thought again of her mother and what she had heard, and shook her head.

"I know this is a lot to bear. I wish I could have told you sooner. I'm sorry. I hate secrets, but they are necessary at times," Aveta said, consolingly.

After a moment Lucia spoke. "My mother left her home and her family behind for a man who was never there for her, Aveta. She was so lonely...I would sleep in her bed when my father wasn't home, and that was most every night I can remember. Now, I find out the way things should have been. None of us are where we should be."

Aveta smiled at her final comment. "That is where I think you are wrong, Lucia. Here is what I believe, for whatever it is worth; I believe the Great Mother puts us *exactly* where we need to be, *exactly* when we need to be there. I don't think that it was by accident that Gwion ended up with the blessings of Cerridwen's potion, nor do I think it was chance that your father found his way to our shores, or that you were born away from them. Life is ever unfolding, and the path the Great Mother sets us upon has a purpose. Have faith that you are where you are supposed to be. All will be revealed in time."

Lucia felt Aveta's words ring true, but she could not help but feel lost. She suddenly missed her mother deeply.

"Well, I suppose there is nothing to be done about it."

"Lucia, your mother has chosen her life. She loves your father, absent or not, and would never leave him. Even though she only sees him rarely, she truly loves him."

"You're right," Lucia said, "but I don't think he realizes how much she gave up for him."

"Perhaps. Perhaps not. Love cannot be measured by those watching from the outside. Only your mother and father know what they mean to each other. Have faith that your mother is a stronger woman than you are giving her credit for. No Daughter of the Isle is ever a victim. Remember that."

"Yes," Lucia said, realizing the truth of Aveta's words. Her mother would never leave her father's home, until she buried him. And even then, Lucia wasn't sure she would leave.

She changed the subject.

"Why is the island so difficult to reach?"

"The answer to that is not an easy one, but I will try to explain. For one, like water, it moves; drifting like a boat upon the sea of time, ever fading in and out. This is why we only leave as a clan four times a year, and when we do, we ask the Great Mother and the spirits of the lake to guide us safely to and from our home. Together, we are able to leave and return safely. Alone, it is much trickier. If you try to reach it using your senses, you will fail. To your eyes and ears it will always seem to be just a few strokes away, but you will never reach it. Many have drowned or gone mad in this way. I have received much training, but I must be honest with you, Lucia - I am not sure I would be able to do this alone. Luckily we have Gwion with us, who has been there as well, and has perhaps more talent than I. Between the two of us I am hoping we can manage." She smiled at Gwion, who smiled back.

"The Great Mother expects us," he said simply. "She will raise her veil."

The shoreline they had come from was no longer visible, and a thick mist surrounded their boat completely. Nothing but the sound of the water and the oars dipping in and out of the lake surrounded them. If she were by herself, she would not have the faintest idea which way to go.

"The island is the western-most point of the Great Circle, and home to the Sisterhood. We have lived there in peace for generations, keeping it safe from outsiders. We have three sister clans that also serve and worship the Great Mother, as we do. Up north are the people of Taranis, to the east live Belenus and his clan, and to the south are the Firefolk, Bran's people. Each clan has an ancient relic that its chieftain protects. For Lord Taranis it is a shield, Lord Belenus, a helm, and Lord Cadoc, the sword *Dyrnwyn*. Ours is the only clan that does not have a chieftain. Instead, we have a High Priestess - your grandmother, Rowan - and our sacred relic is a cauldron. Our clan villages were all built on the four points of a large cross, spanning many miles, at the center of which lies the Crossroads. There we meet four times a year to celebrate the Greater Sabbats, presided over by our High Priest, Talhaiarn, as well as trade goods and learn what is happening with our clan brothers and sisters."

"Why are there no men on the island?" Lucia asked, thinking back to the story of her parents.

"We learned long ago at great cost that it must be this way. One day I will explain."

Lucia wondered if she could be happy in such a place.

"Aveta, when a woman from the island takes a lover, does he wait for her?"

Aveta laughed. "Some do, but they are rare. Most do not. Nor do we expect them to. To make love to a woman only a few times a year is not enough for any man of a fathering age."

"Or woman, I suspect," Lucia said.

"And yet, you have gone without a man in your bed for two years, have you not?" Aveta pointed out.

"Well, yes," she answered. Truth be told, though she had missed her husband's touch, the freedom had been wonderful.

"If your life is fulfilling, you might be surprised how little this can matter. Perhaps it is the idea of not having a lover that disturbs you more than the truth of it," Aveta ventured.

"I don't know, Aveta," she answered, her thoughts leaping to Bran. "It seems like a lonely life."

"That depends on many things."

"Perhaps," Lucia conceded.

Aveta moved toward the bow of the little boat, her hands upturned upon her knees, quiet. Lucia sat motionless and silent herself, not wanting to disturb her.

Much time passed, and Lucia could not tell if they were getting any closer to the island or not. The mist continued to rise from the surface of the water, keeping everything beyond their little boat obscured. She could not tell what time of night or day it was. At times, it seemed to be late in the night, at others, dawn or early

67

evening. Then, the sky would cloud over, and the nearly full moon would appear from between the clouds. Glimpses of the island would appear close, only to disappear within the mist a moment later. Finally she gave up trying to spot the shoreline. She trusted Aveta knew whether or not they were headed in the right direction, and instead simply concentrated on Gwion's rowing, listening to the oars leave and enter the water, over and over. At least that was consistent.

Suddenly the little boat slid to a stop and the oars hit land. Lucia looked up in surprise, and saw that the bow had glided smoothly upon a sandy shore. From nowhere come women dressed in blue wool, squealing with delight, running toward them and grasping the sides of the boat, pulling it up on land.

"Sister Aveta, you have finally returned!" one said. Two women came to help her out of the bow, as she was a bit dizzy and weak.

"And you are Lucia," one of the brown-eyed women said, definitely more statement than question, and helped her ashore as well.

The youngest of them jumped into the water up to her thighs and grabbed Gwion from over the side of the boat. With only him left in it, it quickly tipped and he fell in. They both emerged from the water laughing. Once upright, they wrapped their arms around each other and embraced for a long time.

Aveta turned to Lucia and explained, "That is Gwion's cousin, Creirwy. She is Cerridwen's daughter. Cerridwen only had enough time for Morvran, as he required so much of her, so I took Creirwy and raised her as my own."

A barrage of emotions and realizations collapsed in on Lucia, sending her heart and mind in all directions, as she struggled again to find a foothold within her new world.

"Come, Lucia," Aveta said, her arms around both of her children, holding Creirwy especially close, tears pooling in the corners of her enigmatic eyes. She turned and led the way toward the trees.

CHAPTER SIX

Ruins

They soon had their horses saddled and left Talhaiarn's fortress with the moon still high in the crisp, clear coldness of the night's final hour. They made their way down the steep mountain trail in silence, moonlight reflecting off the frosted leaves and tree branches, and swirls of phantom breath coming from their horses' mouths and nostrils.

As they reached the bottom of the mountain, paths diverged. Talhaiarn reined his horse in and turned to speak. His wrinkled brow was damp with sweat, his silver hair escaping from its leather cord in pieces around his face. Talhaiarn had indeed aged since Bran had last seen him, and it shocked him a little to see it.

"This is where we must take our leave, brothers," Talhaiarn said. "Keep the relics safe."

"Rest assured, if you find the Shield out of my possession, it will have my severed arm within it," Taranis promised Talhaiarn.

"And my head inside the Helm," Belenus added. "We will await your message anxiously." He bid farewell to Bran and Taranis, and then turned and rode toward the breaking dawn, his white horse moving like a ghost through the forest.

"I will ride as fast I can, Bran, but it will be at least four days before my men will be able to reach you, even if there are no delays," said Taranis.

"Understood," Bran said. "We'll manage."

"I'm sure you will. Rest easy, I'll not let you down."

"You never have, my friend," Bran said. "I am disappointed I missed celebrating the harvest with you this year, now that this hell has crawled up out of the pits to our doors, but I promise, when this is over, we will raise the rooftops!"

"We will indeed, gods willing," Taranis smiled, and then turned his horse toward home as well.

Bran looked fondly after him as he rode away. He had been a good friend for many years.

"Ride on, Bran," Talhaiarn then encouraged. "Gethen is much faster than my horse and you a far better rider. I will send word after I've learned what I can from Lady Rowan. There is much that I suspect, but I will not know for certain until I speak with her."

"In my experience," Bran said somberly, "if you suspect something, it is very likely true."

"In mine as well, unfortunately," Talhaiarn replied, "but I am hopeful that this time I am wrong. Now, go! Your sister needs you."

Bran did not pry any further and took off, riding south along the wider roads, stopping very seldom. He was worried about his clan, but also for Lucia and her small family. It was not safe at the villa, not until whatever savages were roaming the countryside were found and killed. Two women and a twelve-year old boy would be no match for them. He would insist they come south with him to his village, where he could protect them.

The afternoon sun began to turn to dusk when Bran and Gethen emerged from the last of the forest. Now they could cut across the open spaces instead of following the river to make the most of the day's dying light. They stopped to rest only until the moon rose, and then continued through the night, the full moon's silver light illuminating their path. The next morning they rode hard again, and by early afternoon they had reached the lake road. Bran found himself increasingly eager to see Lucia again, but as they neared her villa, Gethen became anxious.

Bran smelled the burned villa before he saw it, the stench curdling his stomach. His heart sunk as the road wound around the last of the trees blocking his view to find smoke rising into the sky from a still-burning field.

He rode closer, and the charred remains of her stable and house came into view. Gethen tarried, not wanting to go any closer, but Bran held him steady. He dismounted and took him by the reins, his voice as reassuring as he could muster. He approached the villa slowly, sword at the ready, until he stood within the destroyed remains of Lucia's once beautiful garden, and then walked through what was left of the villa, filled with dread at the possibility of finding bones inside.

He stepped carefully in between the stone walls where the rooms of the villa used to stand, lifting charred objects up and looking for any clues that might explain what had happened. Sadly, the library she had so loved was completely burned, no more than a few books spared.

Finally tired of poring over the ashes, he raised his eyes to the horizon. His heart jumped into his throat as he spied a woman's body lying in the distance, face down in what was left of the barley field. He leapt the stone wall he had mended but days before and ran out to her, his worst fears choked in his throat. A pool of blood had formed around her head. He turned her over gently, and was shocked to see she had been fed upon in several places on her body, as if by wild dogs. A wave of nausea overwhelmed him at the smell of her and he looked away.

It was then that he saw more bodies in the field crushing the grain, three at first glance. *Gods.* He visited each of them in turn, and all had been fed on in the same way. They must have been the folk who farmed Lucia's land. No doubt they saw the field burning and came to help. They had been sadly rewarded for it.

Where is Lucia? And the boy and his mother? Bran thought, frantically searching for them, but they were nowhere to be found.

Again, he had been too late. Too late for his mother. Too late for Lucia.

Suddenly Bran was overcome with rage, and let out a gruesome cry as he ripped down the few charred rafters that remained of Lucia's villa.

Filled with vengeance, he leapt quickly back in the saddle and thundered south with fury.

He would not be late a third time.

CHAPTER SEVEN
Chieftain of the South

Bran reached the forest that surrounded his village by late afternoon. The trees had turned, ready to shed their leaves and sleep through winter, and the air smelled of coming snow.

Riding through the forest brought back childhood memories. He thought back on a summer, long ago, when his sister had found a twisted walnut tree with a perfect hollow in it, just her height, where she would hide things she loved.

"Bran, do you want to know something? A secret?" she had asked him.

"I don't know – is it someone else's secret? It's not good to reveal secrets. It means you can't be trusted."

"No, Bran, it's my secret, and I'm going to tell you! Just you. No one else. When I die, I want you to know about it."

"Great Mother, Seren, you're only ten! You're not going to die for a very long time."

"One day I will," she replied simply. "Do you want to know or not?" she asked, disappointed that he had not been more enthusiastic toward her offer.

"Yes, go ahead and tell me. I hope it isn't anything terrible."

"No, it's not. It's my secret place," she confided.

She had taken him to the gnarled tree. After looking around to make sure they had not been followed, she reached into its large hollow and pulled out a box.

75

"See? Isn't it the perfect hiding place?" she asked him. "Look at my treasures! The tree promised to protect them."

Inside the box he found a shell, a pressed flower, a small gold ring, and a tiny dagger with a bone handle.

"Don't tell anyone--only you know!"

He took the time to leave her a few gifts in the tree that summer for her to find. Soon after, however, he had gone off to war and the tree was forgotten.

Forgotten until now. Passing through the grove, he followed his intuition to the tree. Curious, he reached into the hollow and was shocked to feel Seren's wooden box still inside of it, still there after so many years. He took it out and opened it, and found her little childhood treasures; the shell, the ring, the flower and the dagger…all undisturbed.

After a few moments, he took his mother's amber pendant from around his neck. Seren had always loved it. He remembered her sitting on their mother's lap as a small girl, turning it over and over in her tiny hands, holding it up to the sunlight and pointing to the tiny cracks and bubbles, fascinated. He kissed it and laid it among Seren's things, and returned the box to its hiding place.

He continued along the grove path, grateful for a moment of happiness after all the pain of the past few weeks. He came to the river and found a place to cross, and soon the trail emerged from the trees and traversed the meadow. Miles of rolling hills spanned out in all directions, the late afternoon sun giving them a golden glow.

Once he had crossed the meadow the trail split, the right fork climbing steeply upward into the hills. He spied a woman coming down the path, beckoning to him. After a moment he recognized his sister. He waved in return and dismounted to meet her.

She ran until she reached him. "I'm so glad you've made it back! What news do you have?"

"Not good, I'm afraid," he answered bluntly. "Seren, where is *Dyrnwyn*? I trust it is safe?"

"Yes," she said with a concerned look.

"Has anything happened since I've left?"

"There have been more stories of vicious attacks on the road and in some of the farms in the area. The men have taken to keeping watch through the night, but so far nothing has come into our village while you've been gone," Seren replied.

"They also laid waste to the villa of a Roman woman who gave me food and shelter on my way north. She treated me as clan. On my way back I passed that way, intending to bring her and her servants back to our village. I found the house and fields burned to the ground, her livestock mutilated, and the folk who farmed her land ripped apart. I searched for her body, but did not find it."

"*Gods*, Bran," Seren exclaimed, horrified. "What the hell do they want? They attack only at night, refusing to show themselves, yet have made no demands! What did Talhaiarn say?"

"I'll tell you everything I know tonight, which unfortunately isn't much."

"Of course," Seren agreed, "but first, help me bring down a few more weapons from the caves above. We thought it best to arm ourselves more heavily. The others have already gone ahead. I saw you coming and told them I would wait for you."

Bran agreed and followed her up the path.

"We moved the armory up into these caves a few years ago," Seren told him as they climbed. "It was Uncle Einon's idea. He thought our weapons would be safer here, away from where the Saxons or raiders could find them. If ever the village were taken, the swords would be hidden from our enemies and could not be used against us."

"He's a wise man. How does he fare?"

"Well," Seren said hesitantly, "but troubled."

"As are we all."

Bran sighed heavily. Next to himself, he suspected Einon was taking his mother's death the hardest. Her elder brother by only a few years, the two of them had always been very close. He had nearly died fighting the leader of the Saxons that attacked their village and carried her off, but like her, he was very young and no match for a battle-seasoned barbarian twice his size. Driven by the guilt and weakness he had suffered on that fateful day, he had spent the rest of his life forging and mastering weapons. Regardless, he had again been unable to prevent the tragedy that had befallen her, and Bran knew it surely weighed as heavily on him as it did himself.

Bran followed his sister to a narrow opening in the mountainside. She turned sideways and entered, and he did his best to follow her. She had a torch lit by the time he managed to squeeze his way in. It was considerably larger on the inside, the ceiling at least eight feet tall. Iron nails bent upward had been hammered into the rock walls, and hung upon them rested the hilts of a good many swords forged by the famous blacksmiths of their village.

"Some of the boys were up here playing one afternoon and found this cave. We made the opening larger and turned it into what you see now. The cave extends back into the mountain for quite a distance, but we haven't explored it enough to know if there is another way out. Between this chamber and the passageway, there is enough room in here to hide all the women and children if the village is attacked. We have a few days' food and water stored here as well," she said, pointing to several clay pots.

"Good work," said Bran, hoping he would not need to be sending the women and children here anytime soon.

She smiled and quickly took a few swords down from their perches. Bran lingered a bit more on his choices. Once he was satisfied, they returned to where Gethen waited. Bran jumped in the saddle and pulled his sister up behind him, and soon they arrived in the village.

"Come to the motherhouse," said Seren, bidding one of the young boys who had come running to take Gethen's reins. "We have venison and good ale."

Bran followed his sister into the impressive motherhouse at the center of their village and ducked under its ornate arched doorway.

As he entered, cries of "Lord Bran, you've returned!" and "Thank the gods!" filled the air, and a few young women eagerly jumped up to serve him meat and ale.

He had always been well-loved by his people. Everyone looked upon him fondly; the men with respect, the women with desire or gratefulness, and the children with awe. If not for his ever-present conflict with Cadoc, he would have returned home far more often.

"You have been missed, brother," Seren smiled.

Just then, a man nearly as large as Bran entered the motherhouse, and at first Bran did not recognize him, for he had cut his hair and beard short, but the dark eyes beneath his heavy brow gave him away and Bran cringed. *Aelhaearn.*

"How go the preparations?" Seren asked him.

"Very well," he replied, sitting down. He looked like a dark mountain opposite Bran. A woman quickly brought him food and drink, and Bran noticed his arms had been burned badly, no doubt at the forge.

"The look-out posts have been reinforced. We can put as many as six archers up on all of them. They'll be able to see for miles." He then motioned toward Bran. "And this was the first invader we spotted!" he joked, clapping Bran on the shoulder. "I saw you crossing the meadow this afternoon. What news do you bring from the Crossroads?"

"Bad, I'm afraid," Bran replied.

"Well, let's have a drink then before we all have to hear it," Aelhaearn suggested, raising his drinking horn.

At least that was something Bran found agreeable. He raised his as well and they both took a long drink.

"Seren tells me there have been no sightings of anything out of the ordinary in the village since the attack," Bran said to him.

"None at all," Aelhaearn replied after swallowing. "The morning after, we searched around and found the tracks of what I can only surmise is the biggest wolf to ever walk the face of the earth. But what was strangest of all was that we also found *hand* and bare footprints leading away from the house into the trees behind it. The others are all convinced the handprints were made by one of us down on hands and knees searching for clues, but if that were true, why would they move off into the forest? Besides, no one in the clan goes barefoot now. The summer has left us."

Again, there it was. Wolf. *But his mother had insisted it had not been a wolf...*

"You're certain *nothing* out of the ordinary has happened since?" he inquired again.

"No. Not on our people. Reports have reached us of attacks on the roads, but they've left us alone. Perhaps they've moved on and won't return," Aelhaearn replied.

Bran ignored his comment, knowing it was overly optimistic.

"Where are the rest of the men?" he asked, eager to end the conversation.

"Setting snares," Aelhaearn replied. "They'll return when the sun has set."

"Good," Bran said. "I'll be back then."

***

The air had grown extremely cold outside. Enemy attack or not, one thing was sure to fall upon their village that night, and that was snow. Dark shadows were already beginning to ripen, reaching their long fingers in between the trees and thatched huts of his people.

He took a long, slow walk around the perimeter of the village, scouring the ground for the tracks Aelhaearn had described with what was left of the day's light. He searched intently for the better part of an hour until darkness finally swallowed everything.

He returned to the motherhouse where Seren was tending the fire in the large pit at its center. Tending the fire in the motherhouse was something that was done exclusively by their priestess and the women who served her, to honor the Guardians of the South. He had watched his mother do it for years. Now, his sister would carry on the tradition. When she finished, he walked over to her side and the two of them stood quietly watching the flames dance.

"Bran," his sister said quietly, "The Council and I have made a decision. We want you to be Chieftain."

Bran was taken aback by the news. He had not expected this.

"You are our strongest warrior," she continued, noticing his face. "The clan looks to you when there is danger from abroad. You have never once let any of us fall into the hands of the raiders. We need you now more than ever."

Suddenly Aelhaearn approached and Seren fell silent.

"The men will soon be here," he announced.

"Good," Seren said. "Aelhaearn, I want to speak to you before they arrive."

"Yes, what is it?" he asked.

She hesitated a moment, looking around. "Privately." She lit a torch and he followed her outside into the crisp darkness, but Bran could still overhear their conversation from inside the motherhouse.

"The Council and I have chosen Bran to take Cadoc's place as chieftain. I wanted tell you before we announced it to the clan."

A long silence followed, and Bran wondered if they had perhaps walked off where he could no longer hear them, but suddenly his sister said, "Aelhaearn, please understand."

"Understand what?" Aelhaearn yelled.

Bran went outside, fearful he might strike her. Aelhaearn looked over and glared at him, the air heavy with his anger. Strangely, Bran noticed steam starting to rise from the man's chest and arms into the chill night surrounding them.

"Aelhaearn, you've served the clan well," Seren said, attempting to placate him.

"Spare me your speech, woman! After everything we've been through, and all I've done for you? Gods, Seren--you come regularly to my bed! Have you no honor?"

Bran raised his arm to backhand the brute for his insolence, but Seren stopped him. "Let him speak," she said.

"When have I *ever* failed you? Or the clan?" Aelhaearn continued, unrelenting. "You know your father would have chosen me to follow him! And you!" he yelled, turning on Bran, "You've been gone for the better part of ten years! What do you know of this clan anymore? Believe me, when the Council calls out for challengers, you can be certain I will answer!"

"Why wait? Let it be done now!" Bran said, no longer able to control himself. He moved toward Aelhaearn and Seren tried again to intervene.

"Stay out of this!" Bran warned, giving her a look that stopped her in her tracks. "*Yes*," he growled in Aelhaearn's face, "I have been long absent, but do not forget it was to put blade and shield between our clan and those who would take what is ours. You know this. You rode by my side not so very long ago. Have you forgotten what the Saxons are like? I can assure you, they have not changed, and come in ever larger numbers!"

Aelhaearn was unmoved. "Don't play the spring lamb with me, Bran. You've ached for battle from the moment you were strong enough to hold a spear. You've been off fighting Saxons not as some great sacrifice for all of us, but because you couldn't stand to be here. From as far back as I can remember you've lusted after the horizon. I dare you to deny it. You are out of touch with your people, and you know it. *You don't belong here anymore.*"

Bran grew livid, wanting nothing more than to pound him into the earth.

"Believe me," he shot back instead, "what is coming our way is far worse than Saxons, and you have me to thank for knowledge of it! I have given up all the comforts of home for years, so that cowardly men like you may rest easy, in your warm beds, staying 'in touch' with your people!"

At this Seren yelled, "Enough!" and forced herself between them. "Save your fight for the enemy!"

Bran looked at Seren's panicked face, and somehow found the will to keep his hands from strangling the man across from him. He reminded himself that Aelhaearn knew nothing of the enemy they spoke of, and his sister was right. Though it tasted like caustic poison, he swallowed his pride and forced himself to walk away.

"I am sorry, Aelhaearn," he heard Seren say. She lowered her voice as to speak to him alone, but Bran's keen ears heard her.

"This is my brother's destiny. The Great Mother has shown it to me. She waits for you to surrender your will to her, and when you do, I know your path will surely wind to greatness far beyond that of this clan!"

Aelhaearn looked at her in disgust. "Far be it from you, woman, to advise me on where my destiny lies," he said, turning and walking off angrily into the night.

"Damn the gods, now I have to go after him!" Bran cursed. He didn't need to consult the Great Mother to know what destiny might be waiting for Aelhaearn in the woods, and though he was furious with him, he was nevertheless a clan-brother.

"Let him go," Seren said dismissively.

"No, Seren, we cannot let him go off alone into the night."

"He'll be fine," she insisted.

Bran ignored her and stomped off toward the trees, shaking his head.

"Bran!" she finally called out after him, "Aelhaearn is a Firebrand."

Bran stopped in his tracks and wheeled about. *"What?"*

A male Firebrand hadn't been born in their clan for five generations. It was a gift almost exclusively bestowed upon females. His sister had been blessed with it. He remembered when Seren had been born and it was discovered, how terribly jealous he had been, and asking his mother why the Guardians favored girls. She had answered that it was because boys were generally more aggressive, which could have dire consequences when you were granted the power to engulf things in flames. As soon as it became apparent a child carried the Firebrand, much care was taken to be sure she did not become inconsolable or upset. When the child was old enough, she was apprenticed by an older Firebrand who taught her how to wield the power she possessed. In Seren's case, it was her grandmother's sister, Lady Ffraid, who thankfully lived long enough to teach her.

He walked back to where his sister was. "Why did you not tell me this before?" he demanded, growing impatient with her. "It's clear why he feels entitled to be Protector. *He is a male Firebrand,* Seren. How is it that this was not discovered sooner?"

"The brand didn't manifest itself until a few years ago," Seren explained.

"Even rarer," Bran chided. "The last thing we need is a Firebrand as our enemy right now."

"I know," she cried out in frustration. She sat down upon a boulder and put her face in her hands, letting out a defeated sigh, and Bran regretted his harshness with her. He was not accustomed to dealing with women.

"I'm sorry this burden has come to you so young, sister," he said with a softer tone, "but it has."

She looked up at him. "However young I may be, I know that you are meant to be chieftain, and my protector. No one knows Aelhaearn the way I do. I blame myself for the way he is. It was me who mentored him, and I've obviously done a poor job. I wish Lady Ffraid had been alive to mentor him instead of me. "

"Don't blame yourself for the way he is," Bran consoled. "He's always had a temper. You know that!"

"Yes, I do," she said, "which is why the Council and I have chosen you." She stood up and pulled *Dyrnwyn* out from beneath her robe, the moonlight dancing upon its perfect blade.

"Take it, brother," she said, holding it out to him. "It's yours to protect, now."

Bran reached forward with hesitation, in awe of the sword's beauty, and finally took the hilt in his hand, marveling at its perfection. To wield such a weapon was every warrior's dream.

"I hope never to give you any cause to doubt your decision," he finally said.

"I know you won't," she replied. "Let's lose no more time. The sun has left us to our enemies." She ducked into the roundhouse and Bran followed her.

"Bran! Welcome home!"

He looked across the room and saw Gareth coming to embrace him, and it drained his heart of all the anger of the past hour. Gareth was his cousin and had been his closest friend in childhood. After a few good strong claps on the back, Gareth pulled away and smiled.

"How have you been, cousin?" he asked kindly. "We are so glad to have you home."

"Much has happened," Bran said. "We must talk soon over some ale."

"That we shall," Gareth agreed enthusiastically.

His uncle, who had been silently standing by the fire, walked over to greet him as well. "I am happy to see you have returned, nephew."

"Thank you, Uncle," Bran said. He then glanced quickly about and quietly added, "Later, I would like to speak with you both privately about Lord Aelhaearn."

"Of course," Einon said. Gareth simply nodded. Bran noted that neither of them looked very surprised by this request.

"Speaking of Aelhaearn, where is he?" Gareth asked, looking around the hall.

"That is what I wish to discuss," Bran said.

"I see. Until later, then," Einon replied, worry crossing his face. He and Gareth took a seat among the others, and Seren stepped forward to speak first.

"Clan brothers and sisters, I have sat in prayer for days listening to the voice of the Great Mother, asking her to guide me in naming my new Protector. The Council and I are now all in agreement," she said, "and Lord Bran is our choice."

Bran raised his spear at the mention of his name, and the clan responded by clapping, shouting approval and sending smiles and nods his direction. He had been anxious that perhaps Aelhaearn was right, and that he had been away too long to inspire any loyalty or devotion, but the scene in front of him spoke to the contrary.

"The rites shall be performed on *Nos Galan Gaeaf*," Seren continued, "when we will have proper ceremony and celebration, but for now we must instead turn our efforts toward our new enemy."

She sat down and Bran spoke to his people.

"I know you are all anxious to hear the news from the Crossroads. When I arrived, Lords Belenus and Taranis were there with news of similar attacks on their villages, but the North has suffered the worst of it. The enemy hid in their mines by day, and then attacked at night, taking all their small children."

Bran wondered how much detail to give, but thought it best that his people know what sort of evil they were up against.

"They found the bairns eaten or ripped to pieces and drained of blood, and many have not been found at all."

Looks of horror crossed the faces of his clansfolk, and soon the men were in an uproar and the mothers pulling their wee ones close.

"Talhaiarn believes Cerridwen may be to blame, and he's gone to the island to consult with Priestess Rowan."

"Cerridwen?" Seren interrupted in shock. "What makes Talhaiarn believe it's her?"

"He suspects she has gathered an army to obtain the remaining relics of the Great Circle, and with them, overtake the Crossroads. As she believes we are the weakest of the three clans right now, he's predicted that she will come for *Dyrnwyn* first..."

Bran unsheathed the sword from its scabbard and hoisted it high by its white-gold hilt. The firelight flashed along the blade, searing up and down its edges.

"...but I swear to you all upon my life, she'll not have it!"

"She will sooner die upon it!" Balin cried out. The other men passionately voiced their agreement and Bran returned the sword to his side.

"The North and East are sending what men they can spare to aid us. Once they arrive, we can make battle plans and seek this enemy out, but for now we will have to fend for ourselves. The women and children will sleep here in the motherhouse from dusk until dawn. This way we have but one house to defend rather than several."

"My men and I will take the first watch," Balin offered. "We've been working all day setting snares and other such things. May as well keep the same company and see things through 'til dawn." He looked around the hall and added, "Where the hell is Aelhaearn?"

"He is already in the forest," Bran said, not wanting to raise any suspicion. "We spoke earlier. Who are the best archers?" he asked, quickly changing the subject.

Einon stepped forward. "Allow me," he said, calling forth twenty or so men.

Once it was decided who would keep watch outside the hall, and who would be posted where, Balin stood up. "Well, let's move." He turned to his company. "Come on, men. She's beginning to cast snow, so take what you need for warmth and bring your dogs. You won't have your women tonight."

Seren watched as the men went to collect their weapons and move out, and Balin noticed her concerned face as he walked by.

"We'll not let them hurt any of you, my lady," he promised in reassurance. He then turned to Bran and extended his arm. "I'm proud you're with us, Bran. It'll be an honor to soon be addressing you as *Pennaeth*."

91

"Thank you, Balin. I am honored I have your trust. May the Great Mother keep you."

"You as well," Balin answered. "And you, my lady," he added, turning to Seren.

After Balin and his men had left, Gareth came over brandishing his sword.

"Shall I join the others, or stay behind and protect you, cousin?" he joked, doing his best to lighten the mood.

He and Gareth had argued since they were old enough to hold a blade over who was a better swordsman, and Bran chuckled. It felt good to laugh, even a little.

"Stay. I'd like you in my company, brother."

"Done," Gareth answered.

Bran then turned to Seren. "Get some sleep if you can."

"Now that you're here I'll finally be able to," she said. "Being responsible for *Dyrnwyn* has been a burden I'm glad to be rid of."

"Go," Bran encouraged.

She went to join the rest of the women and children. Everyone was on the floor near the fire, heads on balled up cloaks or blankets. The dogs lay nearby, ever vigilant.

Einon came over to where Gareth and Bran were standing. "I would join the two of you, if you'll have me. My eyesight is not what it once was, but I can still swing a sword. It will also give us the opportunity to discuss the matter you mentioned earlier," he added.

"You know my mind, Uncle," Bran said, leading the way outside.

Once away from the eyes and ears of the clan, Einon turned to Bran. "What of Aelhaearn?"

"Seren told me he has the Firebrand. I recall him being a fierce warrior, but don't know much else of him. When did it happen?"

"Five years ago, seemed it was triggered by his wife's death. For two days she suffered in childbirth and finally bled to death. He allowed the midwife to cut into her belly to try and save the child, but the poor thing did not live for more than an hour. He was like a wild animal after that. Would not let anyone help him with the funeral pyre. He worked through the night preparing it himself."

"The next day he sat next to the bodies of his wife and son on that pyre from dawn until dusk, when suddenly it went up in flames. Soon after, the trees surrounding it were burning, and then his own house. At first, he told us later, he thought the Guardians had set the pyre alight, but after everything surrounding him went up in flames as well, he realized it was his own fury that had caused it. He called out for help, and your sister came and prayed to the Guardians, who thankfully listened to her. The village and all the surrounding forest would surely have burned to the ground. From that day forward, she's mentored him."

Aelhaearn's rage made more sense to Bran now.

"He and I fought tonight over her choice to name me as chieftain," he said. "That is the truth of why he was not with us in the motherhouse tonight."

"I knew it," Einon said. "Where is he?"

"He went into the forest on foot," Bran replied. "He took the wood-gathering path."

His uncle glanced off toward the tree line, concern furrowing his brow. "I can bring him back."

Einon paused and then put his hand on Bran's shoulder.

"Bran, although she is quite young, your sister is wise for her years. No one knows him better than she does. I am sure she has given great thought to her choice, and for what it's worth, I believe she has made the right one. However, I am certain he feels deeply betrayed, and this is a problem. We cannot afford to have such a man as our enemy. Besides, in a way, he is like a son to me."

"Well then, let's stop standing about talking like a bunch of women, and go find him!" Gareth exclaimed.

"I agree," Einon said.

"I don't think it's wise for me to go with you," Bran said.

"Neither do I," Einon agreed. "Stay here and guard the motherhouse. Gareth and I will take the dogs and find him."

CHAPTER EIGHT

The Sisterhood

The Sisters of the Isle lived in small huts that surrounded a larger roundhouse, used for meetings. A bit away from their village were the ruins of an old castle, and there in the middle of its courtyard was the largest oak tree Lucia had ever seen, its branches spreading out in all directions. It was ripe for harvesting, and though it was clear the Sisters had collected a good many acorns from the ground, there were many more to be had. It was simply magnificent, and filled Lucia with a feeling of awe. More than that perhaps, she felt protected as she stood underneath it, looking up at the stars which were just beginning to wink into view.

She, Aveta and Gwion were shown to a hut that had been made available to them by some of the Sisters. Lucia did not intend to fall asleep, but she lay down to rest herself just a little. She didn't wake until the smell of roasted venison reached her nostrils. Her eyes shot open, and outside she no longer saw grey sky through tree branches, but rather the dark of night, the blanket of stars complete. She walked outside to find a full moon had risen overhead, and a knot of worry formed in her stomach, remembering her vision the previous night. She quickly rubbed her eyes and followed the smell of meat into the roundhouse where a dozen or so women were gathered, as well as Aveta and Gwion. They all turned toward her as she entered. Aveta came to her. "My lady, come and eat. There is much to discuss tonight."

"I am so sorry…I should have been here to help…I didn't intend to fall asleep," she whispered to Aveta, rubbing her hands over her eyes to clear her blurred vision.

"No matter. There will be many other opportunities for you to help. You needed to rest," Aveta smiled kindly. "There is someone waiting to meet you. Follow me."

Lucia followed her out to the old castle ruins and into the courtyard where a woman stood under the oak.

"Lucia, this is your grandmother, the Lady Rowan."

The woman turned to look at her. She had wolf-like grey eyes, and long raven hair shot through with silver that hung down her back in one thick, long braid. Like the other women, she wore a simple wool tunic dyed indigo blue, but she alone wore a large crescent-shaped neck torc. Upon seeing Lucia, she came over to where they stood.

"I have kept my daughter in my prayers all these years, but never dared hope that I would see her again. Now, I see her in you, Lucia."

She put her hand upon Lucia's face, as if to convince herself that she was real.

"Is your mother well?" she asked.

"I believe so. I have not seen her in some time, but we write letters to each other," Lucia replied, feeling guilty. *I should have visited my mother more. What if I never see her again?* she thought, a lump forming in her throat at the thought.

"Visit her soon. A mother needs her daughters," Rowan said, compounding Lucia's guilt. "Aveta has told me of your vision. I have seen similar things in my scrying pool. Follow me, we have much to talk about." She led them back to the large roundhouse where other women were waiting, seated in a large circle around the fire. She, Aveta and Gwion sat down among them and Gwion laid his hand over hers tenderly.

"All will be well," he said to her, so like a grown man, and so sweet because he wasn't quite yet.

"I know it will, Gwion. Everything we need we have right here, don't we?" she whispered.

All the women stood until Rowan took her place in the circle. She raised her hands and asked for blessings on their food, and then everyone sat down to eat and talk. Lucia was passed a plate of meat and then a cup of wine, which she drank gratefully. The last few days had worn on her in all ways. Her disturbing vision, her feelings toward Bran, the rushed and panicked departure from her home...*Is this all really happening? Perhaps what I saw was just a nightmare*, she mused half-heartedly. Ah, if only she could believe that.

After eating everyone moved closer to the fire which had died down a bit. Lucia relaxed as the heat eased her tired limbs. As she watched the flames dance, she couldn't help but wonder if her beloved home was also dancing in flames, burning to the ground at the hands of the strange men she had seen in her nightmare. With the panicked journey over and her hunger gone, fear and worry now flooded the empty spaces in her mind. What of the farmers and their families? What of her fields, the animals and her stable? And the library? So much knowledge and beauty lay to waste.

Her thoughts were interrupted by Rowan standing up to speak, and everyone grew quiet.

"I am full of gratitude that the Great Mother has brought my daughter and grandchildren home, reuniting our family. However, the circumstances that have reunited us are anything but fortunate. Granddaughter, would you please share with us of what you have seen?"

Lucia was surprised that she has been asked to say anything, but stood to speak as she had been bidden. "I had a vision of strange savages, for I have no other word, attacking my villa and setting fire to the barn and the fields." She paused a moment, gauging the reaction in the room, then continued. "They were men, but they crawled on all fours as animals and wore no clothes. They had pale skin and empty eyes, as if they had been born underground and had never seen the light of day."

The faces in the room bore varied expressions of fear, concern, and confusion, and the room erupted into speculations as to what the creatures might be. It shocked Lucia that not one of the women questioned her vision; they simply accepted it without hesitation. How odd that she doubted her own vision more than these complete strangers did.

Rowan raised her hand to speak again. She paused a moment, as if pondering carefully how to say what she needed to say.

"Daughters, dark times are coming. I regret to tell you that the troubles of the past five years will seem like a warm and gentle spring compared to what lies ahead of us. We must prepare ourselves for war."

Sounds of alarm and concern went around the room, and worried faces all gazed forward, awaiting Rowan's next words.

"For the past five years we've searched for Cerridwen and Morvran, but have heard nothing. We suspected they went to lands across the sea or deep into hiding in the Northlands. Our efforts to find them and bring the Cauldron back to the island have failed. However, Talhaiarn has brought news that there have been sightings of a man in the countryside so grotesque he strikes terror into the hearts of all who see him. We are both convinced it is Morvran the field folk have seen, and that Cerridwen has returned. Talhaiarn will speak to you of this."

She opened her hand toward the arched low doorway of the roundhouse, and a tall, silver-haired man entered. He wore dark traveling robes, and though he was an older man, his frame still seemed muscular and capable beneath it.

He walked forward, his quiet power filling the hall. Lucia noticed the expressions of the other women becoming much more anxious, and Aveta leaned over to whisper in her ear. "He only visits in times of great trouble."

"Greetings, daughters," he began. "Though she was once a dear sister to us, Priestess Rowan and I believe Cerridwen has been abusing the power of the Cauldron."

He glanced at Rowan as if to say, *I'm sorry*, and then continued.

"It has long been sung that the power of the Cauldron can be used to resurrect a corpse. From what Lady Rowan and I have seen in our visions, and the stories that have been brought to me by the chieftains of our sister clans, we believe Cerridwen has discovered the truth of this."

Lucia felt Aveta stiffen next to her.

"However, what the Cauldron gives birth to can never be a true and complete being, for what is *not* possible, is to bestow the gift of Spirit, for Spirit is not of this world."

Lucia wondered if she was the only one in the room who struggled to believe what was being said. She looked about furtively, but no one in the room had anything less than a look of complete concern on her face. *Stealing bodies from the peace of their graves and bringing them back to life?* Could such things actually be done? Even the thought of attempting them was appalling.

Talhaiarn continued.

"As there is no place for Cerridwen on the island, and no place for her son among the men of this world, it is our belief that during her absence she has been plotting to take over the Crossroads and name her son as Protector and High Chieftain. We believe she's reaping the corpses of soldiers from the many fertile battlegrounds that litter the countryside, and desecrating their bodies with a wretched half-life borne of the Cauldron."

"With no true blood of their own, these men are re-born with a ravenous hunger for the blood and flesh of the living. When brought back into this world, they are as animals, simply seeking to satisfy their hunger. They feed upon anything they can manage to subdue, which in the beginning is sadly a woman or a child. As they feed, they become stronger, smarter, and more dangerous. It is through this hunger that Lady Cerridwen controls them. They

100

have already attacked all three of the clans of the Great Circle, and though none of them have fallen, we have nevertheless suffered terrible losses at their hands."

He paused a moment and then said, "Lady Agarah, Priestess of the South, and her Protector, Lord Cadoc, have both died from wounds they suffered in an attack."

Many gasped, hands flying to mouths, and whispers of astonished anguish rippled through the hall.

Then Rowan stood to speak. Her face was ashen, and Lucia could only imagine how troubled she was, knowing the evil they were facing had come from her own womb.

"For generations, the four clans of the Great Circle have lived simply, managing to keep the Old Rites and our relics a secret from those that would desecrate or exploit them. It grieves me deeply that this time, the threat comes from within, and more grievous still, from my own daughter."

"Talhaiarn and I believe Cerridwen's heart has become poisoned by her desire for power and revenge, and that she plans to capture the remaining three clan relics to gain control of the passage to the in-between. With the power to bring back the dead and unlock the passage, none could oppose her. This cannot be allowed to happen. As you know, the Great Mother demands balance in all things, and the very existence of the cauldron-born in this world offends this balance. They are incomplete beings, neither living nor dead. Their souls are trapped in the in-between, a spiritual thread tethering their soul to their body, preventing it from being able to enter the Summerlands. They are tormented and to be pitied, these ghostly men. The only way to bring them peace is to return their bodies to the earth, where they were meant to be, and thus free their souls upon the other side, so that they may continue on their journey. Life is a sacred gift that only the Great Mother may bestow. When we attempt to do so, a terrible price must always be paid."

One of the women that Lucia did not know raised a hand to speak, which Rowan acknowledged.

"What of the South, now?" she asked. "How do they fare? Who will take the place of Lady Agarah and Lord Cadoc?"

Rowan turned to Talhaiarn and he answered.

"Lady Seren, Agarah's daughter, has been named Priestess, and has chosen her brother, Lord Bran, to be her Protector. They prepare for battle, and the East and North are sending them what warriors they can spare. Although the cauldron-born have been kept at bay, they grow ever stronger as they feed, and time is an advantage we must not fail to exploit."

"Daughters, I will now take my leave," he said. "Lady Rowan will tell you what must be done. I am sure that together, with the Guardians watching over us and the help of the other clans, we will overcome." He bowed his head in respect and disappeared through the archway as quietly as he had entered.

Rowan rose and took his place in the middle of the roundhouse.

"Prepare yourselves, sisters. We will need to make enough arrows to fill every quiver and then some. We have no time to waste.

From this moment until Cerridwen is defeated and the Cauldron once more rests in the grotto, we must be ever ready for war."

She walked over to Creirwy and whispered something to her, after which Creirwy nodded and left the hall.

The women went directly to work, grabbing armfuls of arrows from the far wall and filling their quivers, and strapping blades around their thighs. Once armed, they took turns braiding each other's hair tight against their heads, and then set to work making arrows. Their fingers flew, and arrows soon began to fill one large basket after another at the end of the table. Every one of them had a magnificent bow, all carved differently, and Lucia had no doubt they all knew how to use them well.

Lucia looked around at them. They didn't look frightened, but Lucia was. She had never wielded a knife for anything but paring vegetables or skinning a rabbit. She took some comfort in knowing she was a good shot with a bow, but she had only hunted animals, not men--and certainly not demonic soldiers. How could they possibly all look so calm?

Rowan came to where she stood with Aveta and Gwion and said, "I have matters that I would discuss in private with the three of you, if I may."

"Of course, Mother," said Aveta. They followed her out of the roundhouse again to the privacy of the old castle ruins under the massive oak.

They entered the old throne room, now decked with a ceiling of stars. There was an old fireplace made of massive stone where

Creirwy had built a fire, and a half dozen large stones about the hearth in a half-circle. Rowan motioned for them to sit.

"Children, this misfortune touches us most deeply of all. Cerridwen is daughter to me, mother to Creirwy, sister to Aveta, and aunt to Lucia and Gwion. She is family. We share the same blood."

"From the day Cerridwen left our shores, I have asked for her to be blessed with understanding, and for the waters of compassion to wash away the anger and resentment in her heart; I have prayed for mercy and goodness to pierce her blindness, but she has grown ever blinder, taking Morvran into the darkness with her. Talhaiarn's news means my worst fears have come to pass." She took a deep breath. "I gave her life, and my new prayer is that I not be called upon to take it from her."

She turned to Lucia. "Lucia, your presence here but proves that whatever the Great Mother takes away, she gives back in some way. We are never left bereft of her blessings. Though a daughter has been taken from me, I have been given one back, in you. Know that as it was your mother's destiny to leave the island, it was your destiny to come to it. This place is like a beating heart to our blood; it may leave the island in the veins of one of us, but it never fails to return in the veins of another. I am certain that you will have an important role in the days to come." Lucia sat silently, not knowing what to say. Luckily everyone's attention turned toward the sound of someone approaching. It was Talhaiarn, who came and sat upon one of the stones.

"Before I take my leave," he said, "I have come make you all an oath. You, most of all, Lady Rowan, for I know there is nothing

104

stronger than a mother's love for her child. I promise, if there is any way to bring Cerridwen and Morvran back from the darkness, I will."

"Thank you, my lord," Rowan said. "I fear to hope anymore, but thank you."

He then turned to Gwion. "Gwion, your gifts surpass even mine. Your destiny may be to become the most powerful High Priest the Crossroads have ever known. Cerridwen knows this, and if she means to follow through with her plan, you are in grave danger."

Gwion nodded.

"However, I believe that you will all be safe here for awhile. Cerridwen already possesses the Cauldron, and she is intent upon obtaining the other three relics. I feel it is the South that is in the most danger now. I am sure news of Agarah's and Cadoc's death was encouraging to Cerridwen, and that her next move will be to make another attempt at capturing *Dyrnwyn*."

Rowan suddenly looked concerned. "My lord, the journey from the North to the South is much farther than the journey from the East. It will be four days before the North can aid your cause. The women of the isle are skilled as both warriors and healers. Let some of us journey south."

Talhaiarn didn't seem to like the idea of sending the young women into battle, and it showed upon his face.

"Lady Rowan, it causes me pain to imagine even one of you perishing."

"Lord Talhaiarn, please," Rowan continued. "We are closest, and the enemy you face is one of our own. We may not be the best of warriors, but none are better healers. We have many skills that will give you a much better chance at victory. You know this to be true."

Lucia noticed Talhaiarn looked very tired all of a sudden, the power he had exuded in the roundhouse now seemed drained from him.

"Very well, my lady," he said after a moment. "I am sure the South would be honored if the Sisters would join the cause."

"It shall be done," Rowan stated and turned to Creirwy. "Creirwy, you are the best archer we have, but it is your mother we fight. You do not have to go if you do not wish it."

"She is not my mother," replied Creirwy quickly. She put an arm around Aveta, who was sitting next to her. "*This* is my mother. I will go."

"As you wish," replied Rowan. "Let us return to the motherhouse. We must make preparations for as many women as we can spare."

She turned to Talhaiarn. "Please, my lord. You are weary. You must sleep. It has clearly been days."

"I wish again that you were not correct, but you are. I must rest. My body is not what it used to be," he replied. "I will leave to return to the Crossroads as soon as the cock crows, which feels to be just a few hours away." With that he stood, and the women all rose in respect as he left.

"Let us return to the others," Rowan said.

They walked back to the roundhouse where the women were still working, and all fell silent when Rowan entered.

"Lord Talhaiarn believes strongly that Cerridwen's next move will be to attack the South in an attempt to capture *Dyrnwyn*," she began. "With the recent attack and the deaths of Lord Cadoc and Priestess Agarah, they are weak. Although the North and East are sending warriors to their aid, it will take two days for the East to make the journey, and four days at least for the North. We are much closer. I would send all who are willing to go to help defend the South at first light tomorrow."

Creirwy stepped forward first, and quickly thereafter most every young woman stood and stepped forward. It was obvious Creirwy had the respect of all of them. There were only a dozen or so older women who remain seated, she and Aveta included. Suddenly Lucia felt her heart pounding.

Without thinking, she stood and stepped forward as well, and Aveta reached up and grabbed her arm. "My lady," she whispered, with a tone of alarm that caused Lucia to doubt her decision, but it was too late. She had committed herself, and her pride would not allow her to back down now.

Rowan acknowledged her and nodded.

"Very well. Prepare the boats."

After Rowan finished speaking, Aveta took Lucia aside. "Lucia, are you sure? I had assumed that you would stay. You are not seasoned in battle. Do you know what that is like?"

"I'm no stranger to what it does to men. I've seen plenty of battle wounds in my life."

"Lucia, I must ask again, are you sure? The Sisters of the Isle have been trained from a very young age to handle knife and bow, and know a thousand ways to disappear…They also know how to call on the water spirits for help."

"Then I shall be in good company," Lucia said. "Aveta, this enemy has destroyed my home, and very likely all of the good people who live on my land. We will need to face these things sooner or later, and it may as well be now. I cannot lie, the idea of facing them frightens me, but I have faith I will be able to do what is necessary when the time comes. Perhaps my visions can give us an advantage. I would be burdened by heavy guilt if I were to stay here, knowing I could make a difference."

After some moments, the look upon Aveta's face changed from worry to acceptance. "You are right, Lucia. I'm sorry I doubted you. I am being selfish. I can't bear the thought of losing you or Creirwy. She is my only daughter, and you my dearest friend."

Aveta's face contorted and a few tears escaped her eyes. Lucia embraced her, and the two women held each other.

"I will return, Aveta, and so will Creirwy," Lucia promised. "We will see the end of this darkness, and celebrate on the other side. I'm sure of it."

Aveta pulled herself together and smiled. "You're right. We will indeed. The Great Mother will set things right." She wiped her eyes. "Now, let's go make some more bloody arrows."

They joined the others around the fire, for there was still much to be done. Lucia had learned quickly, and arrows piled up next to her.

"Aveta, tell me what happened to Gwion," Lucia said after a few arrows.

"Ah," Aveta sighed. "Very well. We have all night, and it is a long story." She tied another arrow and tossed it aside.

"Cerridwen was a very powerful priestess of the Sisterhood. One of the most powerful we've ever had, and was destined to take my mother's place as High Priestess when the time came. She had an insatiable passion for herb lore from the time she was very little, one that surpassed even mine, and she reached an unrivaled knowledge of all earthly substances. She currently possesses a mastery that I suspect no priestess of the isle has ever come close to, not even my mother."

"When she was sixteen, she gave birth to twins – Creirwy, whom you know, and Morvran, whom we spoke of earlier, who sadly was born extremely deformed. Only Cerridwen could bear to look upon him, and so Morvran spent his childhood almost entirely by her side."

Morvran was Creirwy's twin? thought Lucia. It seemed impossibly unfair for one child to be so beautiful, and the other a monster.

"As Morvran approached his thirteenth year, Cerridwen began to worry for him, for the father of her children was not a living man, but rather the lonely spirit of Tegid Voel, who is said to dwell within the waters of the very lake which surrounds us. As such, she had no father to send her son to when the time came."

109

"Cerridwen knew she could not keep him on the island, and she also knew that with his appearance he would struggle in the outside world. He would very likely never know the love of a woman, nor would any man would ever pledge allegiance to him in politics or battle. She appealed to our mother who went to Talhaiarn for help, and Talhaiarn agreed to take him as an apprentice the following year. In the meantime, Cerridwen employed all of her herblore knowledge on Morvran's behalf to transform his features. She worked incessantly, but time and time again, failed to produce a potion or magic that would correct his deformities. Finally, she decided that if she could not heal or transform his appearance, she would labor to grant him wisdom to compensate for it. And so, she began her most ambitious undertaking yet. For a year and a day she patiently brewed a potion for him, adding each herb and substance at precisely the right time of the year. She brewed it beneath the open sky, allowing the energy of the sun to infuse it during the day, and the calm of the moon to reflect upon it at night. She brewed hundreds of herbs and flowers, acorn from the mighty Oak for patience, yarrow for courage, mistletoe for fertility, sycamore for strength, clover for balance…All the gifts the earth could impart, she brewed into it, watching over it carefully. When finished, she hoped her potion would make up for the physical beauty her son lacked by giving him the power to inspire and do great things upon the earth."

Lucia was mesmerized by Aveta's tale. It was one of the things she loved most about her. A true master of stories, there was no voice she enjoyed listening to more.

"On the day the potion was nearly finished, she asked Gwion to stir it for her. Gwion helped her often, as it needed to be stirred constantly, day and night, until it was finished."

"On this particular day, she was gone longer than usual, and the fire under the cauldron began to die down, and Gwion knew that he would suffer her wrath terribly if he let it go out. In his eagerness, he put too much wood in the hearth, and the fire caused the potion to rapidly boil away. Panicked, he tried to pull it away from the heat to cool it a little, but the pot was so hot he dropped it, and the little bit of liquid that was left in the bottom splattered out onto his hand. He put his burned fingers into his mouth and accidentally sucked the few drops of potion that were left off of them."

"Cerridwen's potion gave Gwion extremely powerful abilities. He can indeed communicate with animals, as well as see and hear things none of us can. As a small boy, knowing nothing of what was happening to him, you can imagine how overwhelming this was. I went to my mother immediately, explaining what had happened. She insisted we go to Talhaiarn to put Gwion under his apprenticeship, and said she would deal with Cerridwen. We set out immediately. Unfortunately, this only made things worse, because the plan was for Talhaiarn to take Morvran as his apprentice that spring. Instead, in addition to receiving all the gifts of Cerridwen's potion, Gwion would have that privilege as well. But nothing could be done about it – he simply could not be left unguided with such powers, and not even my mother was qualified to help him. It was decided that he would stay with Talhaiarn for five years, and that Talhaiarn would take Morvran on as an apprentice after that time. I knew my sister would be furious, and I dreaded the day I would see her again. I promised Gwion I would stay close, but had to leave him with Talhaiarn until his studies were complete. You know the rest of the story."

Lucia looked about but noticed Gwion had not returned with them. She suddenly had an overwhelming desire to hold him close, and wished he were there.

They worked in silence for awhile, Lucia thinking of everything that Aveta had told her.

After awhile her thoughts wandered to Bran and his sister, and the trouble they were in.

"Aveta," she asked from across the table, "What does it mean now that Bran is Chieftain of the South?"

Aveta spoke without taking her fingers from her work. "It means he has pledged his life to protect the Priestess, his sister, the people of his clan, and the relic of the South - the sword *Dyrnwyn*."

"What will his life be like?" she asked.

"Well, for now, it means that until Cerridwen and Morvran are stopped, he and his people will be in constant danger, that is certain." she replied. "If Cerridwen indeed wants the sword he carries, she will likely stop at nothing to get it. I know my sister. She is relentless."

"Can he take a wife?"

Aveta looked up at her, eyes compassionate, as she finally comprehended the reason for Lucia's questions.

"He could, but it is doubtful he will as long as his sister remains the priestess. Were he to marry, his duties to his wife would interfere with his duties as her Protector. This is why traditionally a clan priestess chooses a lover to be her Protector."

Lucia realized in that moment how much she truly wanted Bran for herself. The hope of having him by her side someday had been feeding her courage. With that hope suddenly taken from her, the world suddenly began to look darker.

"Aveta, why do you think his sister made such a choice? Does she not have a man whom she loves?"

"I don't know, Lucia. I suppose it is possible that she has chosen to devote herself to study or worship. However, I know of very few women from the Southern clan like that. They are a passionate people. The last time I saw Lady Seren she was but fifteen. Even at that age, she was stunningly beautiful. She possessed many charms that did not go unnoticed by men. I am sure she is still beautiful and could have her pick of many lovers. "

"Then why would she choose her brother as her Protector?" Lucia wondered aloud.

Aveta was silent a moment, and made two arrows before she answered.

"I believe I know why Lady Seren chose him. Would you like me to share my thoughts with you?" Aveta asked.

"Yes, of course. Please," answered Lucia.

"In dark times such as these, I believe that Lady Seren has set aside what she wants as a woman, and rather chose what her clan needs, and by doing so, has proven that she was wisely appointed as priestess of her clan. She had a very important choice to make, and not much time to make it in. She needed to choose a man she could trust, the man in her clan best suited to defend her and protect the relic with his life. She must have felt that Lord Bran, although her brother, was that man, and chose him over a lover."

Lucia suddenly felt very small and selfish. She sat in silence for a few moments, and then answered.

"Aveta, I am ashamed. I am thinking only of myself."

Aveta stopped her work and looked up at her. "Lucia, I understand. I saw your eyes light up as they haven't for two years when Lord Bran was with us. Perhaps for longer than that, for I don't think you ever looked at Camulos that way." She smiled understandingly at her and reached across the table. "I long to see you happy again. You deserve a good man at your side. Please know I don't fault you for your disappointment."

Lucia finished winding the thin strip of leather around the arrowhead in her hands and tossed it into the basket. She nodded and left it at that.

The night wore on, until finally, every quiver was filled to bursting, and all baskets were full. Everyone retired for a few hours rest.

Lucia lay on the furs that served as her bed, grateful that she had slept earlier that evening, because she knew those few hours would be all the rest she would get that night.

CHAPTER NINE

Firebrand

Aelhaearn stormed furiously through the trees, passionately searching for something to torch to death. He left the path and surged through the forest, scanning everything around him with the skill of a hawk, flames barely contained within his hands and fingers, ready to leap and consume whatever pathetic creature dared to cross his path.

The forest grew denser, branches reaching out and snagging at his clothes as he charged through the trees. They scratched his skin and jabbed him in the thighs and ribs, but he welcomed the pain. He ran quite some time, until finally he burst out of the trees into a glade with a deep pool that he had never seen before.

He looked for any sign of the enemy, but nothing but falling snow came toward him, winking around the placid silver face of the moon, and covering the autumn leaves.

He went to the edge of the pool and unleashed the full fury of his fire into the water. Soon it was steaming in front of him, and he collapsed to his knees from exhaustion.

After a bit, he looked up. The surface of the water had turned smooth and glassy, steam rising toward the stars above. He found it peaceful to watch, and allowed himself to be soothed by it.

Suddenly, something began rising out of the water. He arched his hands to burn it, but then realized it was a woman's head. She emerged slowly into the moonlight, water flowing from her silky dark hair down over her breasts and shoulders, and steam rising off her skin into the cold air around them. She stayed where she was, coming out no further and staring at him, the water lapping at her breasts. He dared not move nor speak for fear he would wake from his dream, and she would disappear.

"Thank you for warming the water," she said. "It feels like Summer making love to the Winter."

She looked up into the sky, letting the snowflakes fall and melt on her face, and then met his eyes. After staring at him for some time, she asked him, "Are you a king?"

Spellbound, he did not answer.

"Why will you not speak to me? Are you mute?"

"No," he finally responded.

"Ah, good--you are not mute."

"No, I am not a king," he said, watching the moonlight dance on the water around her.

"Not a king? A priest, then?"

He didn't answer.

"Not a king, nor a priest? Well, what are you, then? The Guardians do not bestow the Firebrand on ordinary men."

She bathed languidly in front of him, never taking her eyes off him, her breasts or knees occasionally coming to the surface of the water like lilies. He didn't answer her, because he was ashamed of the truth. He could not bring himself to tell her he was a man of no rank whatsoever, with few possessions, no wife, no children, and a simple trade. He had been waiting for a future that had suddenly been snatched away from him that night.

"I am a seeker," he finally answered.

"A seeker?" she responded softly. "Then what is it that you seek, Firebrand?"

"Justice," he replied, feeling himself growing angry again.

"Is that all?" she asked, swimming closer. Though her dark beauty drew him to her, he was wary. He thought back to the many childhood stories of men being lured into the water by the mischievous faerie, and then pulled to the bottom and drowned.

"Who are you?" he asked again.

She ignored his question a second time.

"Come now, Firebrand. Surely you want more than that. What of power? Fortune? Glory? These are the things a *great* man seeks and longs for…Imagine, having your name sung around the campfires of future generations, echoing through the ages. What of these things? Do they not call to you?"

They indeed called to him. They had for as long as he could remember, and until Bran returned, he had been sure they would all be his. The clan trusted him, they respected him, and Seren loved him.

This is not how it was to be. He was to rule as chieftain of his people, and protector of the woman he loved.

"Ahhhhh. They do call to you, don't they?" she said, interrupting his thoughts and swimming closer.

"You say you seek justice. Justice for what?"

Her beauty tempted him to reach in and pull her warm body out of the water, but he resisted, staying where he was.

"I have long served my people, but they have betrayed me tonight," Aelhaearn told her. "Our chieftain passed not long ago, a great man who I know favored me to follow in his place, but our priestess has convinced the clan to choose another."

"I see," she said. "Why do you suffer this man to come and take what is yours? Learn from your brother, the .tag…When another challenges him, he does not slink like a coward into the forest. He fights until he is either defeated or victorious. Great men seize what they desire."

Her words stung.

"What if I told you I could help you?" she ventured.

"What do you mean?" he asked, growing irritated.

"I can help you, Firebrand. I can see you are meant for great things. I can help you become Chieftain, if that is what you desire."

"I don't need your help," Aelhaearn replied angrily. He had suffered enough assaults on his pride for one night.

"As you wish," she said, a smirk crossing her face. "Farewell, Firebrand."

With that she dove down beneath the steaming water and disappeared.

Aelhaearn sat by the pool for some time after his mysterious visit. She had been right, whoever, or whatever, she was.

He could not run away and give up everything he had worked for, yet he could not go back as she suggested and slay Bran to take it, either. *I am no murderer,* he thought.

There was only one way. He would make the clan see that he was the better choice, and on *Nos Galan Gaeaf,* he would challenge Bran for the title.

He got up off the ground and began walking back to the village. He cast a small ball of fire out in front of him to illuminate his way, and it was not long before he heard dogs barking and Einon's voice calling to him from a distance.

"Einon!" he yelled back, angry that the old man was out in the forest alone. *Old fool.* He would never forgive himself if anything happened to him. He ran in the direction of Einon's voice, worried, knowing that any enemy who might be hiding in the forest could surely hear him as well.

Finally he found him, Gareth by his side with spears at the ready.

"Thank the gods you haven't left us," Einon said.

The relief he saw in the old man's eyes melted the last of his anger.

"No, I have not left." he answered, feeling guilty that he had most definitely considered it not an hour earlier. "I needed to think."

"Then think when the sun rises. We need you, Aelhaearn," Einon chided. "More than ever. We have no idea what type of enemy we're up against, so what gifts the gods have given you, please don't take them from your people now. "

"Indeed," Gareth agreed. "The men are asking for you. Things are graver than we thought. The Northmen arrive in two days, and we mean to hunt this enemy out. We need you."

"Let us get back, then," Aelhaearn said, feeling encouraged.

The men are asking for you. The words gave him hope. In time, they would see.

They would see, and he would have his opportunity.

CHAPTER TEN
What Lurks

The Sisters made their way south on foot in small groups, traveling as inconspicuously as possible. They wore fur-lined hooded cloaks the color of brush and traveled along rivers or lakes whenever they could, for a mist would willingly roll off the surface of the water to conceal them.

Lucia's company consisted of five women in addition to herself – Lady Elayn, one of the higher initiates, Llygoden, so called because of her small size and quickness, the twins, Ina and Ivy, and the beautiful Creirwy. She and Creirwy were a pair, then Lady Elayn and Llygoden, and the twins, obviously. They never left each other's side anyway.

They trudged along in silence, their soft boots crushing the long rushes beneath their footsteps. Lucia kept her eyes on Lady Elayn's dark braid as it swung back and forth down her back, its pendular dance and the steady rhythm the march lulling her into a quiet state of reflection.

Her mind wandered to many places, the happiest being the time she had recently spent with Bran. At times she thought of seeing him again and her stomach leapt, but those little sparks of joy were quickly snuffed out by her ever-growing worries. *What if she and her companions never made it to his village? What if his village had already been attacked? What if he were dead?*

They moved quietly yet quickly, rarely stopping to rest. She was glad of her morning runs to the lake, for she was sure she would not have been able to keep up otherwise. As the day progressed, occasionally Elayn stopped and motioned to the rest of them in sign language which she didn't completely understand. She just did whatever Creirwy did, and that seemed to work. They virtually disappeared into the landscape, crouching deep down in the long grass, until Elayn gave the signal indicating whatever possible danger she had perceived was no longer there.

"Tell me about your mother," she asked Creirwy later that afternoon. "About Cerridwen, I mean," she corrected herself quickly, feeling clumsy. "Forgive me."

Creirwy was silent for awhile, to the point that Lucia regretted asking. Finally, to her relief, she answered.

"I have not seen her for years, but I remember her being stubborn. I was always very careful not to make her angry. Sometimes I would feel relieved that she did not pay much attention to me, because that meant if I forgot something or did it wrong, she would not notice. I don't ever remember being alone with her, or even being held by her. She was always with my brother. My fondest childhood memories are of Gwion and Aveta. To me they are my true mother and brother, and I was devastated when they left. I wanted so badly to go with them, but I had just reached the age of initiation, and Aveta pleaded with me to stay with my grandmother to begin my training. I did as she wished. I missed them so much…so much that I grew to hate her, for I knew it was because of her that they had to leave."

"I thought I had overcome my anger towards her, but hearing of what she has done now, I realize I have overcome nothing. My anger still burns whenever I think of her. Right in here," she said, putting her hand over her chest. "Again, she seeks to destroy everything I love and respect."

"I hate that she gave birth to me, and I hate that I despise the woman I should hold most dear in life. I often pray to the Great Mother, asking why this is so, and why I was not truly born to Aveta instead."

"Does she answer?" Lucia asked, after a moment.

"Yes. She tells me to be patient. That one day I will know why."

"That's not much of an answer, is it?" Lucia commented.

Creirwy smiled. "No, I suppose not, but I have at least learned that the Great Mother reveals things in her own time, and it's foolish to expect her to reveal them on yours."

Lucia suddenly felt like the more childish of the two of them, though Creirwy was younger than she was. She suddenly found herself missing her own mother again. How wonderful it would be to return to the island with her, after all of this fearful trouble is over. She wondered if she could convince her to come.

"Creirwy, did you know my mother left the island to marry my father?"

"Yes. I've heard her story. My grandmother does not like to speak of it. She becomes very upset."

"I've been told," Lucia said. "Do you think, when my father passes away, that my mother would be allowed to return to the island?"

"I don't know," Creirwy answered. "You should ask Lady Elayn, or Aveta. They are wiser about such things."

The thought of her father's death, though dark, started her thinking. It was likely her mother would outlive her father, and Lucia longed to reunite her with her family, and for all of them to be together. She resolved to speak to her grandmother about it. Surely something could be done.

The other women kept mostly silent that day. The twins followed quietly behind them. They were thin and blonde, with very pale skin. *Like two stars*, Lucia thought.

Soon it was dusk, and after some searching, Elayn decided they would set up camp at the base of a large oak.

"We will sleep here tonight," she announced. "Sisters, help me cast a circle." The women pulled handfuls of salt from pouches on their belts, and moving clockwise, cast a wide circle of protection around the tree.

Elayn turned to her. "Lucia, watch and learn. We are asking the Spirit of the Oak, the Great Mother and the Guardians to watch over us tonight. The salt we are casting marks the edges of a sacred space for us to sleep within. Do not step outside the circle until the sun rises tomorrow, and even then, not without Creirwy by your side."

Lucia nodded, fear rising again, and she chided herself for it. She had grown so sick of fear. She watched as Creirwy and Llygoden moved intently and carefully, sprinkling salt and chanting an incantation as they circled the tree. Lady Elayn prayed to the tree directly, asking for protection for all of them by name, one by one.

Though their ways were strange to her, Lucia felt safe with these women. Lady Elayn, especially - she reminded her so much of Aveta. She stood very close to her, listening to her supplications, and then to her singing in a language she did not understand. She dared not speak or move for fear of disturbing her.

After some time, the circle was cast and the women gathered at the base of the tree.

"She will cast snow tonight, which is a blessing, but we cannot build a fire. It will call too much attention," Elayn advised. "We will have to sleep close together and share all the blankets and cloaks we have for warmth."

Lucia was confused. "Why would snow be a blessing? We will freeze tonight."

Elayn smiled, "Lucia, what is snow, but frozen water? The Mother is sending us the best protection she can."

Each woman pulled a blanket from her pack. Some they laid upon the ground, and with the others they covered themselves, overlapping each other as much as possible. The roots at the base of the tree provided a nice natural crescent for them all to lean into, and in addition to being lined with fur, the cloaks they wore were made of thick wool. Even without a fire, they would be warm.

After settling in, Lucia felt compelled to speak. "I fear I should not have come. Though I've hunted, I've never been attacked by man or animal, and I'm afraid that when the time comes I will be too frightened to act."

She felt better after getting it out, and then a small warm hand patted her thigh in reassurance.

"I'm scared too, Lucia." Llygoden admitted. "I've never been off the island before. I was to go to Beltane for the first time in about a moon."

"And you still shall," said Creirwy, trying to lighten the mood.

"We are all anxious," said Elayn. "Myself, included. We are dealing with powerful magic, and as women of the Sisterhood, we know better than any the power Cerridwen commands as a sorceress. I, perhaps more than the rest of you. She and I are the same age, and were trained at the same time. She surpassed everyone in our group from the very beginning, and soon the initiates had no more to teach her. I can offer you this comfort only - if she has not changed, she lacks patience, prudence, and humility. I am hoping she is still as arrogant and stubborn as ever, and that we can work these faults to our advantage. However, for now, we must sleep. We will accomplish far less if we are not rested tomorrow."

Lucia still had a million questions she wanted to ask, but willed herself to save them for the next day. Her world was a different place now, and her voracious mind was fighting for a foothold within it.

***

Lucia was drifting in and out of consciousness, being brought back regularly by her stiff muscles and recurrent anxious thoughts.

126

She woke to see large snowflakes falling outside the umbrella of branches their oaken host provided. She gave up on sleep, and instead watched as the ground surrounding the tree became whiter and whiter, the flakes falling rapidly, covering the ground in an ever-thickening blanket that she found comforting.

Suddenly, out of the corner of her eye, she noticed a small greenish glow appear and then disappear from between tree trunks in the distance. She focused on it and watched intently until it stopped at the base of a large birch tree not far from where they slept. Then, it disappeared again. She kept her eyes on the place where it had been, not daring to blink. Then, again she saw it--not one, but two round spheres of pale greenish light, like fairy baubles. *Could they be fae?* she wondered, delighted with the thought, her mother's stories jumping to life in her mind.

As the lights drew nearer, her delight turned to dread. They were not of the fae. Not at all. Eyes. The eyes of an animal, surely. *Wolf?* she thought, fear swelling up in her stomach. There had been no howl to his brothers, however. It moved closer, its eyes growing larger as it neared. She did not move, except to turn her head ever so slowly and look toward the other women.

They were all asleep, except for Elayn, who met her gaze and brought her finger to her lips, motioning for her to remain silent.

She looked back out into the darkness, and then watched as the animal slunk slowly out from behind a tree toward an open clearing. The moonlight on the snow provided a large pool of light, and her heart jumped into her throat as the creature moved fully into view.

It was a man.

He smelled the air tentatively, following a scent, moving ever nearer to their tree. His stained teeth were visible from a slightly open and deformed mouth, and all of his hair was gone, save a few stringy pieces that hung down in front of his limpid nocturnal eyes.

Suddenly, he found their scent. He moved quickly on contorted hands and feet toward the tree, circling the perimeter where the women had poured the salt and growing ever more agitated as he searched for a way to the blood he knew was there.

Lucia kept her eyes locked on him, and Elayn reached over and wrapped the hilt of a dagger in her palm.

The grotesque thing continued to pace futilely around the tree. She didn't know if it was the spell or the snow that kept it from coming in, but either way, she was grateful.

Then, to her horror, the ghostly corpse began climbing the tree next to theirs.

"It seeks a way around the spell. It's going to try and come down upon us from above," Elayn whispered urgently.

Lucia nodded, but inwardly swam in terror. She gripped the dagger and leather pouch of salt Aveta had blessed and given to her, and realized she valued them more than any of the books or jewels she had ever owned.

The half-man slunk smoothly from limb to limb, attempting to cross over from the branches of its tree into the branches of theirs, but still, to no avail. The protective spell extended over them as well as around them, and the falling snowflakes seemed to confuse it. It became more frustrated, strange sounds gurgling from its throat.

Elayn nudged the others, who were all awake now, looking upwards to indicate where the half-man was, and motioning for a silent kill. Creirwy took action, carefully bringing out her bow and creeping around the side of the large tree trunk where the creature could not see her. The rest of them sat in silence.

Seconds later, Lucia heard the sound of an arrow being shot, and then down from the treetop fell the hideous thing, an arrow lodged in its neck. The body lay but feet from them, twisted and partially decomposed. She didn't dare take her eyes off it, for fear it would rise again, but it did not.

They all breathed a sigh of relief, but Elayn quickly motioned for silence. "There could be more," she said. "They may hunt as a pack."

Creirwy moved back to her spot and they sat in heavy silence, all looking out into the woods, watching for any sign of others until the glow of morning began to grow.

After the sun rose, Elayn got up and closed the circle. She then took out her hunting knife and severed the half-man's head.

"Creirwy, go and bury this, far from here. The rest of you, help me with the body."

The stench of the freshly opened corpse rose up and overwhelmed Lucia, and she knew she was going to vomit. She ran a few steps away and retched behind a tree, leaning against it for support.

Once she was sure there was nothing left, she took a deep breath, wiped her mouth and strengthened her resolve. The others had already dragged the body several feet away and were covering it with tree boughs and leaves.

"Why did you sever the head?" she asked Elayn.

"So that this body may never rise again. A body without a head is of no use to anyone, alive or dead." Elayn answered.

Creirwy soon returned, dirt beneath her fingernails, and helped them cover what was left of her kill. Even with blood and dirt covering her, the girl was a shocking beauty. Her hair was the whitest blonde, almost like moonlight, and her eyes clearer than the crispest winter sky. She had no blemish or mark upon her skin, as if she were carved from marble, like the statues the Romans worshipped in their temples. She found it impossible to believe that Cerridwen had not cherished Creirwy and kept her close. She was so like her name, "a jewel"; she imagined her as a babe, and thought she must have been exactly that - a tiny precious pearl that you could hold in your arms and marvel at.

After the corpse was dealt with, Elayn opened her goatskin and poured water into the palms of all the women, and then her own, washing away the blood and soil.

"We must quicken our pace. We cannot risk being found. If Cerridwen learns we have left the isle and are moving south, she will know the Southerners suspect an attack. I only hope the others have been able to cover their tracks. However, we haven't eaten in some time, and we need something more substantial than berries before we move on. Ina, Ivy – seek out some meat. The rest of you gather some wood and get a fire started."

The others seemed much less affected by what had just happened, so Lucia did her best to shake it off by focusing on the task at hand. She and Llygoden collected as much wood as they could carry. Most of the kindling they found was covered in snow, and she didn't understand why Llygoden even bothered picking it up. It would never catch fire. The trees were heavy and thick, so luckily there were many lower branches that were sheltered and dry, which she collected instead. With enough dry kindling, the wet logs would eventually light. Once they had collected a large pile, they took it back to their camp. Lucia soon saw that her painstaking care was completely unnecessary. Elayn took all the wood and performed a spell which drew all the water out of it, and soon had a fire roaring. She smiled to herself. It was a beautiful thing to be repeatedly astonished. Wondrous women these were, and the knowledge that her blood bound her to them filled her with pride.

The twins were back within a half hour with three rabbits, and began skinning them.

"You caught three that quickly?" she exclaimed.

"Yes, we hunt well together," said Ina, proudly. Ivy just looked at her and smiled. She realized she had never heard Ivy utter a word. She wondered if she was mute or had taken a vow of silence, like the Christian nuns did.

"Ina, can Ivy not speak?" she asked.

"She could, I suppose. She can make birdsong and animal sounds just fine," Ina responded. "But words she doesn't care for. We have always known each other's thoughts. I learned to speak, but she never did. Or as you say, maybe she chose not to. I speak for her when she wishes to."

Ina put the skinned rabbits on a spit that Ivy had fashioned, and soon the smell of roasting meat had Lucia's stomach growling and mouth watering. It seemed the nausea of this morning had passed. They were all famished, and soon had all three of the rabbits eaten down to the barest of bones. When they were finished, Elayn moved close to the fire to brew some tea. "This will keep you alert today," she said. "Licorice root."

The food, fire, and hot liquid put the women in better spirits, and they paired up and set off, moving with swift focus. They emerged from the forest early in the afternoon, and then traveled across wide, open hills. Lucia was relieved to be out of the darkness of the trees and out in the open. She felt much safer out there where she could see for miles around, with the sunlight on her face. The wind blew strongly as they crested the hills, whipping her hair and clothes about. She breathed the air in deeply, exhilarated by it.

They came to the ridge of yet another hill, and the landscape opened up into a vast beautiful meadow of long grass. She could see far off into the distance to where the meadow eventually met a serpentine tree line, which she knew marked the river's edge.

Elayn turned to them and said, "We won't reach the village by nightfall, but we can at least reach the safety of the river."

Lucia suddenly felt sick. *Another night out here, alone?* She looked at Creirwy, and must have looked worried, because Creirwy put her graceful arm around her shoulders and said, "It will be fine, Lucia. Our Guardians rule the rivers. We will be safe there."

Lucia forced a smile and nodded in understanding, but what if there were more of them this time? And wasn't Cerridwen of the isle as well? Would not she have just as much of an advantage along the river?

As they traversed the meadow, Lucia resolved herself to another encounter with the creatures. In the process, she became angry, which she found a welcome replacement for fear. She had grown fiercely attached to these women, and her blood boiled at the thought of anything hurting any of them.

Suddenly Ina called out. "Stop! Ivy sees something."

Everyone turned to look toward the small girl, pointing a finger toward the horizon, pieces of her hair that had come loose from her braids blowing across her face.

"Help is coming." Ina reported. "We must wait here, where they can see us."

Lucia didn't see anything, but kept watching in the direction Ivy was pointing.

Minutes passed, and still nothing. Then, small specks appeared on the horizon, moving quickly and slowly taking form.

"Southern riders!" Elayn exclaimed with a smile. "Thank the gods." She took out a long red scarf and held it high above her head, flying her crimson banner high and strong in the fierce wind.

The riders could soon be seen galloping across the meadow to meet them. There were four of them, men dressed like Bran, in heavy wool tunics, leather gauntlets and boots lined with fox fur. They wore thick bronze torcs around their necks beneath full beards and long hair.

They dismounted and bowed their heads toward Elayn, then turned and respectfully acknowledged the rest of them. Lucia's companions all bowed their heads in return, and Lucia did the same.

A man with reddish hair spoke first. Hair much like her own, Lucia thought. "Sisters, we're honored you have made the journey south. We've come to escort you the rest of the way."

"Thank you," Elayn replied. "We are glad you reached us before nightfall. We encountered one of enemy last night."

The man looked surprised. "Is that so? The clan will want to hear of this. Let's lose no time. Please," he said, motioning to two horses without riders.

Elayn quickly mounted one and pulled Llygoden up behind her, and the twins climbed upon the second. One of the riders was quick to offer an arm to Creirwy, no doubt stunned by her beauty, and so it was that the man who had spoken to Elayn rode up beside Lucia and offered her his arm. She took it, swiftly swinging her leg over the horse and settling in behind him.

Soon they were riding across the meadow toward the river, and a wave of relief washed over Lucia. She noticed her rider was almost hot to the touch, as if he were suffering from a fever. Perhaps he was? She hoped not. However, with the air growing colder as the sun went down, she found herself grateful for his heat.

"What is your name, Sister?" he asked.

"Lucia, my lord."

"Lucia?" he asked in surprise. "Isn't that a Roman name?"

"It is," she answered hesitantly, disturbed by his sudden change of tone.

"How is it that a Roman woman travels with the Sisters?" he asked.

Lucia thought of Aveta and Gwion, and everything that had happened over the past few weeks, and was not sure how much she should share with this man.

"It's a long story," she said, hoping to stall any further questions until she spoke with Elayn.

"Yes, I'm sure it is," he said. "One I'd like to hear."

Lucia couldn't tell what his motives were, and it made her uncomfortable. She changed the subject.

"Has Lord Bran returned home?" she asked, tentatively.

She felt her host stiffen at her question, and worried she had committed yet another folly.

"How is it that you know Lord Bran?" he asked her.

"He was a guest of mine not long ago," she ventured carefully.

"A guest?"

"Yes, he needed a place to rest for a few days," she replied. *Surely there could be no trouble in telling him that much, could there?*

"I see," he said dryly. "He is well. He has ridden out with another scout party looking for the rest of you."

"I am glad to hear he's well." Knowing this, she wished desperately it had been Bran and his party that had found hers instead of this man's, but so be it. She was safe and warm for the moment, and for this she was very grateful.

Some time later they arrived at the Southerners village and stopped within a circle of low huts, one very large and round, like the Sisters had, with an elaborate arched doorway leading into it. Lucia's host dismounted and helped her off his horse, and many people came out to greet them. Some of them Elayn or her other companions recognized, and many embraces and greetings were exchanged.

Then, out of the large roundhouse, a tall young woman strode out toward them. She wore a sword girded about her waist over a long blood-red tunic, and her blonde wavy hair flowed unbound to her waist. She seemed rather serious for her years, Lucia thought. She spoke to the man whom Lucia had ridden behind.

"Well done, Aelhaearn," she smiled, and then turned to address Elayn. "The South welcomes the Sisterhood most gratefully," she said, bowing her head gracefully. "For those who do not know me, I am Seren, priestess here. We are honored you've come to help. Please follow me." She walked to the roundhouse and led them through the doors beneath the archway Lucia had noticed earlier. They were built of heavy oak, fashioned with iron handles, and intricately carved with a woven pattern of fierce dragonheads breathing fire. Inside the hall, large beams carved in the same fashion held up the roof and a great fire burned hot in the center of the great structure, smoke rising up through a hole above it.

"There is food. Please eat," Seren said.

Elayn spoke up, looking worried. "Thank you, Priestess Seren, but I am concerned that I do not see any more of us here. Have none of the others arrived?"

Seren turned to her, the firelight dancing on her high cheekbones.

"A dozen or so of you arrived earlier today. They have gone out to help deliver blankets, food and weapons to the posts for the watch tonight. They will return in the morning."

"Only a dozen?" Elayn exclaimed. "We set out numbering almost thirty. With us, that means almost half have still not arrived."

"We have not found all of you yet, true, but I am confident we will," she said. "The fastest riders from the East arrived this morning, and they are the shrewdest trackers in the Great Circle. We will find your sisters and bring them in before nightfall."

Her voice inspired confidence, Lucia thought; resonant and calm, but it was obvious Elayn was not as reassured as she was.

"Please, eat something," Seren offered in a softer voice, seeing Elayn's dismay.

137

Lucia, Llygoden and the twins set down their packs by the fire and bowls of food were brought to them, but Elayn approached Seren to speak with her privately. Lucia could not hear their conversation, and she found it unsettling. *What does Elayn not want them to hear?* Eventually the women finished their conversation and both came to sit beside the rest of them.

A few hours passed, and Elayn grew ever more restless. Lucia and her companions met many women of the Southern clan, learning their names and helping however they could with the tasks at hand. Lucia liked them; they were strong and capable, and quick to laugh and smile.

Suddenly, the sound of horses bursting into the village reached their ears.

"It seems more of you have arrived," Seren announced. Elayn jumped up and followed Seren outside, and Lucia and the other girls were close behind.

Outside many horsemen were dismounting, lifting women wearing the same brown traveling robes off the backs of their horses. Suddenly, Elayn looked as if she might cry, which surprised Lucia. She had been so stern since they had left the island.

A girl came running toward Elayn and when they embraced, Lucia finally understood.

"Great Mother!" Elayn cried. "I was so worried." She clutched the girl close to her chest, relief washing over her face.

"Mother, please," the girl said, smiling consolingly. "I'm fine."

No wonder Elayn's been so preoccupied all day, Lucia thought. She wondered why Elayn's daughter hadn't traveled with them in the first place. She began walking over to meet her, but just at that moment, another group of horsemen arrived. Out in front, on a black horse that Lucia knew all too well, rode Bran.

She was instantly seized by a desire to run to him, but something held her back. He was a different man than the one who had come so humbly to her door and sat with her by her hearth. No longer a travel-weary stranger in torn clothing, his mane of thick blonde hair was oiled and pulled back, revealing his broad forehead and the same high cheekbones as his sister. He wore a thick gold torc about his neck with dragon's heads on its ends that faced each other fiercely beneath his chin. A large bronze brooch held a fur cloak about his broad shoulders, and both of his great wrists bore gold cuffs. It seemed he had grown another foot since she last saw him.

He dismounted and helped a woman off his horse, and then began giving orders to the men in his company. Seren went to him and they were soon in serious conversation. By the time they had finished, there was a large crowd of people gathered, impatient for news, and Bran raised his hand for silence.

"Sisters of the West, Brothers of the East, we are grateful you have come to aid us in our time of need. In the past, a visit to our village has meant the joyful beating of drums, dancing round our bonfires, and chariot races, but unfortunately we've joined together for a much graver purpose. Seren has taken my mother's place as priestess of our clan, and our council has chosen me as chieftain. Sadly, we have come to be called by these names far too

139

soon. We hope to earn your respect and trust, as the Lady Agarah and Lord Cadoc earned it before us."

The crowd shouted their approval.

"I've been to see Talhaiarn, and there found the other lords of the Great Circle. All of our villages have been attacked by this new enemy. Talhaiarn went to the Sisters to discuss the matter, and Lady Elayn has brought us news from the isle. Lady Elayn, please..."

Elayn stood and went to the front of the crowd.

"Clan-brothers and sisters, as many of you know, our sister Cerridwen stole the cauldron from the isle some years ago, and she and her son Morvran have not been seen since. There have been rumors for years about what might have happened to them. Some believed they had sought out a life across the sea, and others were convinced they had perished, but sadly, neither of these rumors is true. Cerridwen has returned, and she is using the cauldron to create an army from the corpses that litter our war-torn countryside. These were the creatures that attacked Lady Agarah and your great chieftain, Cadoc, as well as the other clans, feeding upon their livestock, women and children."

"Wait a moment," Bran said. "Are you telling us she can *bring back the dead*?"

"I am. We've seen one of them with our own eyes," Elayn replied emphatically. "They hunt by night, and feast upon man and beast alike. " She looked toward her sisters who nodded in agreement. "I swear to you all, I speak the truth."

140

Murmurs of outrage rippled through the crowd, and the warriors began calling out for Cerridwen's blood. Bran finally raised his hand for silence and stepped forward, towering over Elayn. He thanked her and she returned to where her daughter stood.

"We will speak more of this tomorrow, but for tonight the time for talk is over!" he bellowed over everyone, and they quieted down. "This is the news the Sisters have brought us, as disturbing or unbelievable as it may be. We must assume her army of--" he stopped for a moment, obviously wondering what he should call them, "--her army of *cauldron-born* is coming this way. They will expect to find our clan weak after her cowardly worms murdered our chieftain and priestess, but she does not know the people of the South, nor what fierce warriors have come to aid them in their hour of need."

He hoisted *Dyrnwyn* high, inciting the crowd into furious battle cries, and then turned to acknowledge a slender man on his left with a beautiful falcon perched upon his arm.

"The great and noble Belenus has graciously sent us his son, Neirin, and a company of scouts from the East to track these creatures to their lair," he added, "and let us not forget, we are all blessed to have the healing skills of the Sisters of the Isle among us."

He looked toward where the women were standing. "Sisters, we are honored you have come. We know what it means for you to be here, and it shall not be forgotten."

The Sisters were respectfully acknowledged by the crowd as well, and then a plan for the evening's watch was decided upon.

Everyone seemed to know exactly what to do except for Lucia. Bran was surrounded by several men awaiting his counsel, but he allowed Elayn to approach him first. After speaking with her a few moments, the two of them turned and started walking toward where Lucia and the other women stood.

What am I doing here? Lucia thought suddenly, feeling foolish and slightly panicked, trying to think of what she would say if Bran noticed her. How could she possibly explain how she had come to be in his village? She took a few steps back behind the others and hid her face beneath her hood.

"Sisters, we will post you along the riverbanks tonight, where you may call upon your Guardians should you need to," Bran began. He suddenly glanced her way and hesitated a moment, and Lucia's heart leapt into her throat. *Had he recognized her?* Thankfully Aelhaearn approached a moment later, distracting him.

"Thank you again for coming," Bran said to them. "Aelhaearn will tell you what to do." With that, he turned and left and was quickly swallowed up by others seeking his counsel.

Aelhaearn was accompanied by some twenty men, a few of them obviously not from the Southern clan. The Southerners were muscular and strong, most of them dark-haired, with the exception of Bran and a few others, like his sister, who were blonde. The men from the East reminded Lucia of birch saplings, like the man who stood next to Bran - thin and tall, with fine features and lighter complexions. They wore simple clothing and very little ornament, unlike the Southerners who favored bright colors and thick bronze neck torcs, rings and cuffs…and the more of them the better.

"I have been charged to oversee you and your party, my lady," Aelhaearn said to Elayn. "We will make for the river. You and your kinswomen will be posted along the banks. The men and I will be seeking out the enemy in the forest on the other side of the river."

"A wise place for us to be," Elayn answered for all of them. Her daughter, whom Lucia had not yet met, was still with them and walked alongside her mother. She looked to be about fifteen years of age. No doubt Lady Elayn didn't want to let her out of her sight after the scare she had had earlier. The girl was most certainly her mother's daughter, Lucia noticed, both of them with big, deep brown eyes.

"Let us move, then," Aelhaearn concluded, looking suspiciously at Lucia and making her feel ever more out of place. She fought the impulse to say something to him. It was not the time, but she would see it done before long. She had never tolerated being treated disrespectfully by anyone, and he would be no exception.

They were soon rushing against the setting of the sun on horseback, Aelhaearn and some of the thin men in the lead, the others behind her and the rest of the women. Lucia rode closely behind the twins, who were obviously having a private conversation within their heads, giving each other repeated looks of *"Yes, I agree,"* or, *"I'm not certain."*

They eventually reached a place along the river with a grove of very high trees on its banks.

"I will leave you to decide among yourselves how best to defend the riverbanks," Aelhaearn said to Elayn. "Archers will be watching from the trees. Should the enemy approach tonight, they will shoot as many as they can spot from their perch overhead and signal the rest of us. Hopefully none will reach the river, however, should any of them succeed, they will have to deal with me and my men who will be on the other side. If any somehow make it past us, you will of course have the protection of the river in addition to your weapons. Your sisters have similar orders. There is no land around the village that will go unwatched tonight."

"Understood, my lord," Elayn said. The men went to assume their posts and the women were left alone.

Elayn turned to Ina and Ivy. "Take opposite ends up and downstream," she said to them. Lucia assumed this was due to their ability to communicate silently to each other. The advantages to having them on opposite flanks were obvious.

"The rest of you, choose a place in between, and have your bow ready at all times. Do not make the mistake of underestimating Cerridwen. You all know as well as I do that the magic of the isle can beguile the fiercest of warriors, and if men are all who stand between us and her, we are still in danger. Thankfully we are immune to her magic."

Creirwy smiled. "We can be quite wily bitches, can't we?"

They all laughed, grateful for some humor. Even Elayn could not resist the temptation to crack a smile and shook her head. "We can," she agreed.

144

They embraced each other and then chose which way to go. Lucia began to follow Creirwy, but Elayn reached out and took her aside.

"Lucia, I want to talk to you. I'm not sure it's obvious to you why the daughters have been given the task of defending the riverbanks. I want you to fully understand the deep relationship the Daughters of the Isle have with water. One that you have as well. One that can be called upon in times of need."

Lucia was intrigued. "Go on," she said.

"Have you ever noticed how easily swimming comes to you? That drowning seems impossible?"

How did Elayn know this? Lucia had never been fearful of water. She had been swimming for as long as she could remember. In fact, she couldn't remember ever learning to swim. She had always just known how. She thought about her mother, and how she had called her "my little seal".

"Yes." she answered. "Swimming is like breathing for me."

Elayn nodded. "This is because it is virtually impossible for a Daughter of the Isle to drown. Knowledge of water runs deep in your blood. It is your birthright."

"I see," Lucia said. "What exactly do you mean when you say *call upon the water?* Are you referring to an invocation of some sort?"

"No, not an invocation," Elayn said. "Names and words are weak webs we weave, trying to capture things. In truth, we, like all things, are like the sky. The world is ever-changing, beyond words--like trying to capture running water in a bucket, when you

145

name something, or tie it up in words, you limit its glory and power. This is not what I want you to do. What I speak of is something you clearly already *know* how to do, but I'm not sure you know you can *choose* to do it. You can call upon the water any time you're near it, not just when you are swimming. If you concentrate on becoming one with the water, and allow it to become one with you, you can fill it with your intent or desire and it can become a powerful ally. This may come instinctively to you, most especially in times of peril. Remember you have this ability, and use it when the time comes."

Surprisingly, Lucia felt she understood. "I will."

Elayn gave her a reassuring look and then walked off following the river's edge.

Elayn is wise, like Aveta, Lucia thought.

She then wondered how much wisdom her mother had, but could not, or chose not, to share with her. Her mother had never spoken to her of the things the women of the isle had shared with her. Living in a Roman Christian household, she could never teach her daughter to call upon the water, or embrace her visions, or unlock the power of herbs and flowers for healing. These things were considered witchcraft, and her mother, though she did not condemn them, had wisely taught her to keep them a secret.

Lucia remembered the swimming races she and the other children in the village used to have in the lake by her house. Her mother had told her to pretend to tire when the other children did, and not stay underwater too long. Whenever Lucia would have a vision of things to come, she made her promise to share them only with her. *Tell no one else.* She explained to her at a very young age that people feared things they did not understand, and would seek to destroy those things so that they could feel safe again. Instead of inciting fear in others, Lucia grew up a fearful child herself, burdened with many secrets. In fact, she had hidden her gifts for so long, she had forgotten they were there until Aveta had won her trust and began to teach her.

Lucia knew her mother wanted to protect her, or perhaps she had not lived on the island long enough to have learned its ways herself, but how wonderful it would have been to have known them at Llygoden or Creirwy's age.

Now, things were different. She was being asked not only to let her secrets out, but to harness and use them. In fact, lives depended on her ability to use them.

As the others went two and two both up and downstream, it seemed best for her to simply stay and watch the stretch of riverbank where she stood. The sun had set completely. She considered climbing one of the trees and watching the opposite riverbank from there, but decided the best place to "call upon the water" would be as near to it as possible. With this in mind, she scouted out a clump of thick brush which hung over the edge of the river, and used her dagger to cut away enough branches for her to stand within it. From there she had a clear view of quite a bit of the riverbank on the other side, and a completely hidden place to shoot her bow from. Her heart was racing, but slowly her fear faded away. She knew she was a good shot with a bow, there was no doubt in her mind about that. She remembered she had seen the eyes of the enemy glowing from a good distance the other night; if she were to see a pair of those eyes again, she would put an arrow right between them.

At first she peered intently, not missing one movement of a bird, rodent, or splash in the river, but the hours passed slowly, making it very difficult for her to stay alert in spite of the rushes of adrenalin she experienced every time a creature so much as twitched its tail within her line of sight. Fatigue slowly settled into every muscle and bone, her eyes grew sore, and lids heavy. The day had been long, and she did not sleep at all the night before, due to their unexpected visitor. The thought of it still chilled her blood, but she kept the memory of it within her mind's eye, in the hope that it would keep her awake.

Time dragged on. She wanted desperately to sit down, but knew if she did she will surely fall asleep, and so forced herself to stay standing.

A few times she felt her head drop, and then gratefully remembered something Aveta had given her in addition to the salt pouch before they had set off for the South. She opened her pouch and was relieved to see they were still there: mugwort leaves to help stave off sleep. She put them in her mouth and chewed them, expecting the worst, but found they were only slightly unpleasant. A bit bitter, but not bad. There had been many other things Aveta had given her over the years that were far worse. She smiled thinking back on some of the potions Aveta had made her gag down. One thing was for certain, though…it was always worth it, because they always worked. She expected no less from the wad of bitter leaves in her mouth.

Another few hours passed without incident, and Lucia found herself becoming colder and colder. Perhaps it was exhaustion, or perhaps that she was too accustomed to comfort, but she could no longer feel her fingers or toes. The leaves had indeed helped her to stay awake, but now her worry was that she would not be able to pull her bowstring when the time came.

Eventually, her need to move overpowered her misgivings and she left her hiding place to stretch her limbs and splash river water on her face. After all, she was there to fight, wasn't she? Why not move about, rather than hide in a bush all night long? She would welcome some action at this point. Waiting had always been the worst thing in the world for her. Patience was definitely not one of her gifts. After putting her hands in the river, they grew completely numb. In desperation, she relieved herself on them, and the heat far outweighed any squeamishness about uncleanliness. She could wash them in the morning. She dried them on the edge of her cloak and rubbed them together vigorously until she could feel them again.

It wasn't long before the cold encroached into her again, deeper than before. Suddenly, she thought she saw a hand reaching up out of the ground beneath her feet. She grabbed her knife and almost screamed, but then realized nothing was there. *What is happening to me?*

"Lucia," a voice suddenly whispered to her from the river.

She looked toward the river where the voice came from, but saw no one. Her heart beat like a rabbit as she waited, wondering if she had imagined it. She listened more carefully, but heard nothing but the sound of the river flowing.

Suddenly her late husband appeared a few feet from her, scaring her nearly to death. He was standing in the river up to his thighs, reaching his hand out to her. She stifled a scream and clamored away.

"Lucia, I'm coming for you," he said within her mind, moving toward her.

Terrified that this was one of Cerridwen's tricks, Lucia panicked and willed the water to pull him away from her. Up out of the river at her command floated misty tendrils which swirled around him, pulling him back down into the water. He fought against them, still trying to move toward her, desperately trying to tell her something.

"Lucia, I am coming, but you must refuse me…"

She poured all of her effort now into sending him away, ignoring his words, and finally he turned into mist and disappeared.

She dared not move for what seemed like forever, watching the water, scared he would re-appear.

She could feel a fever coming on, and the last of her strength draining out of her. Thankfully, the sky was beginning to turn from black to purple, and she sank down in relief. Dawn was only minutes away. Finally she could rest, couldn't she?

Somewhere, faintly she heard Elayn call, but she found she could not answer. She could hear footsteps splashing across the river, and voices speaking to one another, and then, nothing at all.

CHAPTER ELEVEN
A Warning

Aelhaearn wondered about the woman he was carrying. *How had she come to be among the Sisterhood?*

"She seemed quite well when we set out," Elayn said to him, interrupting his thoughts.

"Well, she is quite *un*well now," he replied irritably as they came upon his hut.

After the misfortune of burning his previous hut down many years ago, Aelhaearn had chosen wisely to re-build his new one out of slate. He had also built it a good distance away from the others. He liked his privacy. Unfortunately, it also meant that right now it was the closest place to take the woman.

He carried her through his door and dumped her on a pile of animal skins, and then threw wood in the firepit. He hovered his hands above it and within seconds had the logs blazing. He then took three large stones and laid them in the flames while Elayn took the woman's boots off and covered her with her cloak.

Elayn took his cooking pot from its hook and handed it to one of the girls.

"Ina, Ivy – please go to Seren and ask for a cup of mead for Lucia and something to fill this pot that we may eat. If there is no meat, get us a bird or a rabbit."

The girls obeyed, leaving quickly to take care of the things Elayn had requested.

Elayn then began vigorously rubbing the woman's hands and feet.

"Lucia? Can you hear me?" she asked her softly, but got nothing but mumbling in response.

The youngest one looked worried. "I don't think Lucia is accustomed to being out of doors as much as we are," she suggested.

"Surely not," Aelhaearn agreed. *Observant little thing*, he thought. "The Romans have weak women. Too many luxuries." He then turned to Elayn. "So tell me, how is it that she has come to be in your company?"

Elayn seemed offended by his tone or his question. Perhaps both.

"It doesn't matter. She is to be treated with the respect due a daughter of the isle, and that is all you need to know," Elayn said to him curtly.

Aelhaearn had half a mind to kick all of them all out into the cold, but after a moment thought better of it.

"As you wish, my lady," he said sarcastically. "Forget I asked."

He went to get water, staying away as long as possible, and returned to find that things had gotten far worse.

"She is still shivering," Elayn said anxiously.

That, at least he could fix, thank the gods. The sooner this woman could be moved, the sooner he could get rid of his unwanted visitors and get his bed back. He was tired from the watch.

He reached into the fire and retrieved the hot stones, wrapped them in skins and put them near Lucia's feet.

"That should help."

"Thank you," Elayn said, showing him some genuine gratitude for the first time.

Ina and Ivy soon returned with blankets, a cup of mead, some of the stew broth from the night before and a few vegetables.

"Please," he said to the girls, taking the tin cup in his hands. The liquid was steaming within moments. He handed it to Elayn, who looked at him again in astonishment. She had been doing it since they had arrived here. Aelhaearn knew she surely ached to ask him questions, but dared not, knowing that then he would have a right to some answers of his own. *Ah, the webs we weave,* he thought.

She raised Lucia's head gently. "Lucia, here…try and drink this." Lucia was awake enough to take small sips.

"Can we stay here until she is well again?" Elayn asked him. "I don't think it would be wise to move her."

"Yes, but when she recovers she should return to her people. She is no help to us, and we certainly don't need trouble with the Romans added to our problems."

"She has no one to return to, my lord," Elayn replied rather abruptly. "She is one of us now. Treat her as such."

Aelhaearn was surprised by Elayn's loyalty to the woman.

"You're upset," he said. "Perhaps there is more to her story than you are sharing?" He looked directly at her to let her know he was no fool.

"I will make us something to eat," she said, ignoring his question.

Aelhaearn watched as she pulled a knife from a sheath she wore under her robe, pared the vegetables and put them in the stew broth. Watching her stirring the pot in front of the hearth reminded him of his wife cooking for him long ago. His thoughts turned melancholy, and Seren's recent betrayal gained fresh sting in his gut. How could he have misunderstood so much? Had she not turned to him for everything? Trusted him? *Did she not love him?* Obviously not.

Soon the food was ready, and they all ate quickly without speaking. The night had been long and cold, and they were all tired and hungry, grateful for food.

Suddenly the woman on his bed became extremely agitated.

"They are coming," she started repeating, at first softly, then loudly, alarming everyone.

Fever talking, he thought. The women seemed to be taking her mumblings very seriously, however. The little one went to sit next to her and hold her hand.

"Who? Who is coming, Lucia?" she asked.

"She has a fever...pay her no mind," he told the girl. "Besides, we are well-prepared for an attack."

"She has the Sight, my lord," she said to him, in frustration. "Do not dismiss her warnings, fever or not."

Aha! Now we are getting somewhere. She had finally broken, as he had hoped. He was proud of his tactics.

"Creirwy, take Llygoden and go fetch Lady Seren and Lord Bran," Elayn ordered.

The last two people I want here, he thought.

The two girls ran out and some time later returned with the pair. Seren entered first, and then her giant brute of a brother.

Aelhaearn nodded in greeting toward each of them. "Seems we have a feverish seer on our hands with a warning."

Bran walked over to look at the woman on the bed and his expression changed drastically.

"Thank the gods," he said, going to her and taking her hand. "Lucia? Can you hear me?"

"You know this woman?" Seren asked in surprise.

"Yes, this is the Roman woman I told you of," Bran answered.

"Whose villa was burned and attacked by cauldron-born?" Seren asked. "Praise the Great Mother she lives, then."

Bran took her face in his hands. "Lucia?" Lucia's eyes were glazed and they seemed to look right through him.

Lovers, thought Aelhaearn, noting the tender way Bran touched her.

155

"She is too sick to recognize you, brother," Seren said consolingly.

Finally Aelhaearn's patience ran out.

"Will someone tell me who this woman is?" he demanded. "How is it she has come to be among the Sisterhood?"

"She came with you?" Bran said, turning expectantly toward Elayn, and Aelhaearn realized he wasn't the only one who wanted answers. Elayn was silent for a moment, apparently weighing what to say.

"Yes," she finally admitted. "Lucia is granddaughter to High Priestess Rowan."

Bran looked up in shock. *"What?"* he exclaimed, wondering how it could be.

Ever more interesting! thought Aelhaearn, pleased with the drama.

"There is a long story here," Elayn said.

"To be certain," Aelhaearn said, finally satisfied. "Let us hear it!"

Bran and Seren encouraged her to tell it as well, and Elayn began.

"Some of you may be too young to remember, but the Priestess Rowan had a third daughter, the Lady Cordelia. It was told that she died of sickness when she was fifteen, but that is not what happened. A Roman soldier somehow slipped through the mist and found his way to the shores of our island. Cordelia was the first to encounter him, and, the Sisters say, fell deeply in love with him. She harbored him to keep him safe from the fate she knew he would suffer, but eventually, of course, she and her lover were found out. Cordelia chose to leave with him and of course was never allowed to return. Lucia is the daughter of Cordelia and her Roman husband," Elayn explained, "and lest there be any doubt about her bloodline, she has the Sight. That we can all see for ourselves."

"Yes, but how is it she has come to be in your company?" Bran prompted.

"Aveta, Rowan's youngest daughter, brought her to us some days ago. Lucia had a vision of Cerridwen's cauldron-born before we knew of them. Aveta saw this as an omen and brought her to the island. I believe Lucia can see the creatures again now, in her fever. She speaks of them coming."

"No, she says they are *digging* toward us," Llygoden interjected.

"Digging?" Bran said, thinking. "If they hunt by night, is it possible they sleep underground, or in caves, by day?"

"Gods," Seren said, repulsed. "Could they be digging burrows? Or...*tunnels*?"

"What are you suggesting, exactly?" Aelhaearn asked. "That they are tunneling toward us, like worms, or badgers, beneath our feet?"

The thought clearly disturbed everyone in the room, for no one said anything for a moment.

Suddenly Lucia sat bolt upright in bed, startling everyone from their thoughts. Her head hung limply back, her eyes focused on nothing, and her voice was not her own.

"They are coming, those born of the black womb. They will rise up from the earth beneath your feet and swallow your children from their beds. Find them. Find them and kill them."

With that, she collapsed, and Bran scooped up her limp body.

"I am taking her," he announced, wrapping his cloak around her. "The Northmen should arrive today. Advise everyone to come to the motherhouse and we will plan our next move." He looked over at Aelhaearn and his sister. "See to it."

"Right away," Aelhaearn said. He would definitely see to it. The more leadership opportunities he could take from Bran the better. Let him go fawn over his weak Roman bitch.

Seren approached him, but he didn't give her an opportunity to speak.

"I think you should go with your Protector and the woman he is obviously in love with, my lady," he said dismissively. "Pity he can never make her his wife now, thanks to you."

Aelhaearn could tell by Seren's face that his words had hit the mark. She left quickly with the others, leaving him to enjoy the satisfaction of knowing he had hurt her.

Finally, his house was his again. Before enjoying his solitude, however, he needed to replenish his wood stores. He set out into the forest, axe in hand.

He found himself wondering about the strange glade he had found himself in a few nights ago, and the mysterious woman he had encountered. He went in the direction he remembered it to be, but found only the ever-familiar woods and trails he had known since boyhood. *Did I dream the encounter?* he wondered, finding the doubt in his mind a slippery slope, both emasculating and disorienting.

He put off his frustration by setting to work on a huge brittle dead tree, most of it sheltered from the recent snow by the trees around it. It would provide good wood. Blow after well-placed blow he worked on it, watching the blade cut into the trunk and small bits of wood fly from his axe. Soon he forgot about the glade, simply enjoying the rhythm and exertion of his work. After some time, the tree finally succumbed with a huge crack and made a noisy journey to the ground, taking many branches and leaves from its brothers as it fell.

Aelhaearn wiped his brow and leaned on his axe to rest a moment, smiling. He loved hard work. He always had. Growing up and working in the forge as Einon's apprentice he had never complained; the hotter the better, for him. It had been his favorite place to be as a boy and still was. The heat, the hypnotic, repeated hammer blows, the need for focus, strength and accuracy when forging a blade– these things came easily to him and the rewards were always great.

"Firebrand," A woman's voice suddenly said behind him, tearing him from his thoughts.

He whirled around to find the woman he had met before but a few feet from him, and the scene behind him completely changed. What lay in front of him stayed the same – the tree was felled, his feet were still planted firmly on the same grass….but behind him everything was new.

159

Her face was framed by the large cowl of a beautiful dark robe, her green eyes and pale skin nearly glowing from within it. She held out a flask to him. "You have been working very hard. I have been watching you for some time."

The warrior within him felt uncomfortable learning this. He had not felt her eyes on him. He could usually sense when he was being watched.

He took the flask she offered and looked at it suspiciously. "What is this?"

"A honey mead. I brew it myself," she answered.

It was warm within his hands. He uncorked it and the delicious aroma of honey and summer flowers rose up to meet his nose.

"I don't trust you," he said, looking up at her.

She gently took the flask back, put it to her lips and drank deeply, and then offered it back to him. Finally satisfied, he drank.

"An elixir fit for the gods!" he exclaimed after tasting it.

"I am flattered, Firebrand. Go ahead--drink it all."

He tipped the flask a few more times, and the liquid quickly had him in immensely good spirits. "Who are you?" he said to her, "and this time, do not pretend you do not hear me. I will have an answer."

She took her hood off and came a bit closer, and the smell of amber and roses met his nose. "I live alone, Firebrand. I have no village and no people. I grow my own food, and brew my own drink. I keep myself hidden from the brutal men who roam our

160

countryside and would take what is mine and enslave me. That is who I am."

He didn't know what to say to that, so said nothing, and gladly finished off the flask.

"Come with me," she said, leading him away from his work. "I want to show you something."

I want to show you something as well, he thought, remembering what her breasts looked like in the water when he had first seen her.

"I am pleased you have come back," she told him. "How do you fare among your people?

He smiled. "I will have my way in due time, lady." he boasts.

"This is good to hear, but don't wait too long," she cautioned. "If you remain agreeable to this new chieftain, he and your priestess may believe you are content with things."

"Content or no, it matters not."

He began to notice that as they walked, the sun seemed to grow stronger, and there was no longer any snow on the trail. The air felt warmer as well, his fur cloak seeming more and more of a burden. *Strange.*

Suddenly the trail left the woods and they entered the glade where he had first met her, the sun shining fully upon its green field which was filled with wildflowers. The pool he had seen her swimming in before was there, and he could hear birdsong coming from the trees around them.

"Impossible," he whispered. She turned around and looked up at him.

"If your chieftain were to die or abandon your clan, do you believe they would make you chieftain in his place?"

"Yes," he replied without hesitation. "I have no doubt."

She smiled. "It would thrill my heart to know a Firebrand sits upon the Southern throne, and that I had his favor. What if I could lure your chieftain away? In his absence, you would have your opportunity, and would use it to good end, I have no doubt. Once you became the chieftain of your clan, if you wished it, I would fill your hall with my mead, and devote myself as a healer to you. There is no wound I cannot heal. You would be safe from any who would try to take your throne by force."

"No harm would come to him?" Aelhaearn asked, considering her offer.

"No," she said. "He will live, but I will see to it that he does not return for a very long time."

"And what would you want in return for such a favor, woman?"

"I would do it for but one of your belongings, so that I can prove I have your favor, should I ever encounter any trouble."

"I care nothing for material possessions. What do you covet? Gold? A house? Jewelry? You shall have it."

"When you are named Chieftain of the South, I shall let you know," she said, moving near. Her closeness made his manhood

162

rise. "I seek nothing from you until I deliver what I have promised."

Emboldened by drink and the idea of becoming chieftain, he pulled her body to his and tasted her lips. She succumbed completely to his kiss, and he no longer cared what manner of woman or creature she was. He would have her. He picked her up and took her to a place in the full sun, took off her cloak and threw it on the grass, and then ripped off the rest of her clothes, revealing her beautiful breasts and everything beneath them.

"Yes, Firebrand, take what you want!" she told him.

CHAPTER TWELVE

Into the Caves

The night air blew cold through Bran's clothes as he made his way to his sister's hut where he had taken Lucia that morning. He found Elayn ever at her bedside, but she still looked pale and unwell.

"How is she?" he asked, dreading the answer.

"Her fever has broken, thankfully," she told him. "I expect she will be over the worst of it by morning."

"Good," he said with relief. "I must ask you, did she know I would be here? I never told her exactly where my village was."

"Yes, Lord Bran. She knew."

"I see," Bran said. "When she wakes, please tell her I will return soon and wish to speak with her."

"I will, my lord," Elayn said with a smile.

The Northmen had arrived that morning as expected, a robust party of men, stocky in build and eager to fight. Their arrival had enlivened everyone's spirits, and for that Bran was grateful. The Northerners always brought laughter in their wake, even in the worst of times, and that was something that had been sorely missed over the past month.

He left his sister's hut and walked toward the motherhouse. He could hear the boisterous voices of the Northmen long before he arrived, and couldn't help but smile. He ducked through the dragon arch and entered to the loud cheers of their newly arrived guests.

"Bran!" a familiar voice called out, "My old bones jump for joy at the sight of you."

He looked up to see Maur coming at him like a bear from across the hall. Bran was thrilled to see him and clapped his arms around him. Well, around most of him. Maur had always been a man of wide girth, even by Northern standards, but he was solid as a rock and could beat many a man to a pulp. Bran had witnessed the truth of this more than a few times. As boys, he, Gareth and Maur had been inseparable when their clans met at sabbat.

Bran loved visiting the Northerners. Their tables were always heavy with roasted meat, the ale never stopped flowing, and they loved music. They were simple, hard-working people who said exactly what they meant and knew how to hold a banquet.

"How have you been, my friend?" Bran asked, smiling.

"Well, we've had some misfortune, as you have, but it seems to have passed, at least for the moment," he said and then lowered his voice. "Seren gave us the news that the sisterhood brought, but I must ask you, friend, do you really believe it?"

"I must admit, I find it both difficult and disturbing, but I've never known Talhaiarn to be wrong about anything."

"But *cauldron-born*, Bran?" Maur replied skeptically. "Come on. I'll bet my bones we're just dealing with savages from the deep North or across the sea!"

166

"Perhaps you're right," Bran replied, "but those who have seen them insist we are not dealing with men."

Maur still looked unconvinced. "Well, whoever or whatever they are, I'm ready to carve my way through their bowels," he said in disgust. "I was so grieved to hear about your mother, Bran. And Cadoc, of course."

"Thank you," Bran said, appreciative of his friend's genuine compassion. "Now, back to what you were saying…are you telling me the enemy has disappeared completely from your lands? You've not seen any trace of them at all?"

"Not for weeks. Our dogs are vigilant through the night, and our men take turns keeping a small watch, but other than that, we have returned to our normal lives, thank the gods."

Bran looked down at Madoc who was ever at Maur's heels. The Northerners bred their dogs with wolves, and hand-fed them from the time they were pups. When Northern children reached the age of seven they were given a pup to train, both the boys and the girls, and from that day forward they were inseparable. A Northerner's dog was a faithful companion until death, often giving its own life protecting its master.

"I see," Bran said, wondering if the cauldron-born were indeed still in the North but hiding underground, as Lucia had warned, but he did not mention it. "and your wife and children?"

"All good. The boys favorite game these days is 'kill the forest-beasts' - they have all manner of knives and weapons strapped to their arms and legs that they never take off. I daresay they like the excitement. The little one insists on sleeping in our bed, though."

167

"I'm glad to hear they're safe," Bran said with relief.

Gareth walked over and then crouched down to pet Madoc.

"Bran, what's our next move, now that our Northern brothers have joined us?"

"And your Eastern," Neirin announced, approaching the party, his falcon upon his arm. "I am ready to track down these worms and put an end to them," he stated boldly.

"Yes," Gareth added. "I'd wager we've got enough brains and muscle in this hall now to destroy any enemy ten times over."

"Agreed," Neirin said. "There's nothing I've ever failed to track and find, dead or alive. I don't intend to start now."

Bran hoped the young man's skill matched his ego. It would make it easier to tolerate his arrogance. Bran's first instinct was to caution the youth against taunting the gods with his pride, but decided against it. He had enough to deal with.

"We look forward to seeing your skills tomorrow, Neirin," he said instead. "It's good to have you among us."

Neirin nodded at him respectfully. "I am honored to be here."

Then Bran turned toward the group. "I would speak to you all as one clan," he began. Everyone ceased their conversations and looked toward him expectantly.

"First, a warm welcome to our Northern brothers. We're grateful you have come. Doubly so now, as we have reason to believe the enemy may be planning to attack us by way of tunnels or the nearby caves, and we all know your clan possesses the greatest skill at navigating underground places."

This puzzled and alarmed most everyone present, with the exception of Aelhaearn, who stood silently by the fire, and Lucia's companions, who knew of this disturbing development already.

"We suspect they are planning to attack from the caves in the foothills just beyond the forest, so tomorrow at dawn I will set out with a company of men to track our enemies and take the fight to them. We will not wait here in fear any longer. These vermin will die so our women and children can sleep in peace again!"

At this the men cried out, raising their cups and howling for blood, the women cheered and the dogs howled, filling the motherhouse with the formidable mingled sounds of man and beast. The sound stirred the warrior within Bran and he felt the urge to leave right then, his blade thirsty for revenge.

When questions had been asked and answered, Aelhaearn promptly approached Bran.

"What would you have me do?" he asked.

Bran could not tell if he had asked the question in earnest or if he were baiting him, but either way, he felt it best if he and Aelhaearn saw as little of each other as possible. He did not want any conflicts from within.

"I want you here in the village to protect the women and children," he said. "It is possible the enemy is close, and they may attack while we are away."

"As you wish," Aelhaearn replied without argument.

Bran was wary of how agreeable he had suddenly become, but could not fault him for his obedience. He would be sure to caution Seren to keep a good eye on him.

***

Bran slept very little, anxious for the morning, and at the first sight of dawn gladly roused his men starting with Gareth.

"Let's go," he said to Gareth's groggy face. "I want to reach the foothills by mid-morning."

Gareth stretched and rubbed his eyes, widening them in the darkness. "Everything is ready. We just need to saddle the horses." he replied groggily.

"Good. Wake the others," Bran said.

In addition to Gareth and Neirin, he had asked Maur to come and bring two of his men. Maur had chosen Heilyn and Eurig, both young and strong with keen eyesight. Neirin was of course coming with two of his clansmen as well, the brothers Owain and Urien.

Bran left the motherhouse and was greeted by a cloudy grey sky. They would have rain, to be sure. He made his way over to the long stable and swung open the gate, and Gethen whinnied a greeting as he entered. He soon had him fed and saddled him for the ride and led him out of the stable.

He spied Neirin out in the meadow waiting for his falcon to return with her breakfast, and walked out to where the slender youth stood.

"Good morning, Lord Bran," Neirin said. "Did you sleep at all?"

"Not much," Bran answered truthfully.

"That's a fine horse," Neirin said, nodding in Gethen's direction.

Bran stroked Gethen's muzzle affectionately. "He's been a good friend to me for many years."

Neirin smiled. "I think often of how closely tied we are to our animal companions. Sometimes I feel as though I could more ably suffer the loss of a limb than the loss of my beloved Eirlys."

Bran knew well the bond the youth spoke of. Noticing the boy's softness toward the bird made him feel a bit remorseful at having judged him so harshly the night before.

"I know that feeling well," he said, thinking of how grieved he would be to lose Gethen.

As if she knew they were speaking of her, Eirlys flew their direction, sailing gracefully on the cold morning air, a fat mouse in her beak.

"Successful hunt," Bran said.

"She never misses a meal," Neirin replied. She landed on the perch Neirin had standing beside him and ate the mouse she had caught.

"We will leave as soon as the others have saddled their horses," Bran announced, growing anxious to depart.

Neirin nodded in understanding and Bran walked over to the other men in their party who were leading their horses from the stable.

"Morning, Bran," Maur said. A cold rain had begun to fall, and Bran envied the man's ample layer of muscle and fat, as well as the thick mink-lined cape he wore about him.

"We're ready when you are. How long before we reach the foothills, do you think?"

"We should be there by mid-day," Bran answered, swinging himself up astride Gethen. "Sooner if we ride hard and have no troubles with the trail. I want to give the trackers as much daylight as possible to search the area, so let's be off."

"Agreed," Maur said.

Soon the party was heading south. After riding along in silence for some time, each man lost in his own thoughts, Gareth rode up next to Bran.

"May I speak plainly?" he asked Bran.

Bran just looked at him expectantly.

"Good," Gareth said, continuing. "There's been no sign of this Cerridwen or her son, or these so-called cauldron-born. Are you certain these are what attacked Cadoc and your mother? I'm sorry, but it's difficult to believe in corpses brought back from the dead, and harder still to believe that they are somehow capable of uniting in purpose against us under the command of some bitch sorceress."

"Go on," Bran said.

"Well, perhaps we're just dealing with a strange tribe that's made its way down from the far North of the wall. There are wild tribes up there, you know -- tribes with strong magic."

"I admit I have not seen the enemy with my own eyes," Bran said, knowing such doubts would continue to arise among his men, "but I have seen those who have clearly been fed upon, and the bite marks were made by the mouths of men. Were that evidence not enough, I trust the word of Talhaiarn without question."

"As do I," Gareth said, "but if what he suggests is true, and these walking dead must feed upon the living, I don't understand their disappearance. Why haven't we seen them? Why haven't they attacked any of our villages again?"

They rode in silence awhile, Bran contemplating. Suddenly he had a thought.

"What?" Gareth asked, noticing his change in countenance. "What are you thinking?"

"Belanus said the ones they encountered in the East were easily overcome, which means they were likely newly-born. Talhaiarn said they are weak when they are reborn, which is why they seek easy prey, like children and small animals. As they feed, they grow stronger and more cunning, and become much better hunters."

"Yes, so what are you suggesting, exactly?" Gareth said, growing impatient.

"I am suggesting that Cerridwen has taken her cauldron-born elsewhere to feed, waiting for them to become stronger before she attacks. Gareth, you know as well as I do what a strong warrior Cadoc was. Whatever attacked him was certainly not easily overcome. What if *that* is what these cauldron-born are destined to become?"

Gareth grew visibly more anxious. "Then we need to slaughter them before that happens," he said in a low voice.

Maur rode not far from them.

"You've seen the enemy, right, Maur?" Gareth said, calling back to him. "These 'cauldron-born'?

"Aye," he grunted. "Not well, but I have."

"What do they look like?" Gareth asked.

Maur grimaced in disgust. "Pale, stinkin' men that wear nothin' but their own skin, move close to the ground and can climb like spiders in the trees. You can nearly smell 'em before you see 'em."

Gareth and Maur continued to discuss the particulars of the enemy and many of the others jumped in with their own speculations. Bran removed himself from the conversation, preferring to listen to the conversations between his men as they argued about who or what their enemy might be, and how or where they might find it.

They came upon the foothills earlier than expected, which was fortunate. The days were becoming shorter, and would continue to do so until *Lá an Dreoilín*, the winter solstice. Hopefully, by then, they would be celebrating the way they were accustomed to.

Neirin suddenly dismounted. "Wait!" he called.

Everyone stopped as Neirin disappeared into the woods that flanked the trail. His men soon followed.

"They must have found something," Maur said to Bran after fifteen minutes. "Should we follow?"

"No. Let's stay here. I don't want to risk disturbing anything."

"Right. I'll be resting myself a bit, then," Maur said, dismounting. Madoc was right there next to him, as always, and Maur reached in his pack to give him something to eat.

An hour or so passed, and then suddenly Neirin and his men reappeared.

"We found several trails made by bare hand and footprints. They are all over this area," Neirin announced. "They lead to the base of a steep mountain with a deep cleft in the side of its face, about a hundred feet up. We'll have to climb to reach it."

"Good thing I brought plenty of rope." Gareth announced.

"Bah!" exclaimed Maur. "I prefer my feet on the ground, or in it. Hauling this belly up the side of a mountain is no easy task."

Bran laughed, patting him on the back. "Fate has saved you this time, brother. Lucky for you we'll need a man to stay back with the horses."

"Gladly," he said with relief.

Bran smiled and looked to Neirin. "Lead the way."

They set off, riding behind Neirin and his companions, Owain and Urien. Eirlys flew high overhead, making an appearance every once in awhile, sailing gracefully over their heads. After a bit they came to the foot of the mountain Neirin spoke of.

"There," he said, dismounting and pointing up. "Do you see the bushes around the opening? The ones at the top have all their leaves, but the others, near the bottom, have very few. The branches have been grabbed or stepped upon many times."

Far overhead in the side of the mountain Bran saw the long dark crevice in the side of the rock face that Neirin spoke of.

"I see it," he said, squinting.

Gareth looked a little anxious, but nodded in agreement. "I have to say, I wish Aelhaearn were with us. His skills are invaluable when it comes to dark cold places, which this is sure to be."

Bran thought back to what happened two nights ago and felt a twinge of guilt. There was no doubt that Aelhaearn would indeed be an asset on an expedition such as this.

The men dismounted and Maur took the reins of their horses.

"I'll see they are fed and watered, as well as the dogs. You all come back, do you understand? I'll have a stew made."

"Gods, but you would make me a fine wife," Eurig teased. "Too bad you're not prettier!"

Maur gave him a look. "Pity you'd make such a poor husband. I have it on good authority from the women you bed."

Heilyn laughed heartily and gave Eurig a smack. "Ha! Good one, Maur."

Eurig smiled, taking Maur's comment in good sport. "I'll be lookin' forward to that stew when we get back, big man."

The men began climbing up the side of the mountain toward the opening equipped with ropes, axes, hammers and torches. Bran was anxious to get inside and look around. Neirin and his men silently led the way, Eirlys ever-circling high overhead. If Bran had not seen them with his own eyes, he would have sworn there was no one there. They moved as quietly as ghosts, and apparently weighed about as much, as nothing cracked or moved beneath their hands and feet as they scaled the slippery terrain up the side of the mountain. The men concentrated on their steps and handholds for awhile as the way became steeper and more treacherous. The Easterners reached the cave opening long before the rest and waited patiently for them to catch up.

Once inside, they found many passageways leading in different directions, obviously carved out by the hands of men.

"They are more than animals, if they've managed to do this," Eurig announced, holding his torch up and examining the walls. "I can see why we've not encountered them. They have obviously been busy."

"We will need to map out these passageways," Bran said, lighting torches and moving in.

"That we can do," Heilyn said, looking confidently at Eurig, who nodded in agreement.

"Hopefully without waking them," Eurig added.

"I propose we follow this one," Neirin said. "It is used the most."

As they followed Neirin and his men down the passageway, Bran noticed blood and drag marks, and a foul odor increased with each step; an odor Bran knew all too well from his many days on the battlefield. The passage finally opened into a small chamber where they were hit full force with the rank smell of rot.

"Gods," Gareth said somberly. "I believe we can safely say they've been feeding."

Heilyn moved in, covering his face with his cloak.

"Great Mother!" he exclaimed. "There are dozens of bodies in here."

Both animal and human corpses lay piled together in the chamber. Of the human, most are women and children, and most disturbing, quite a few babies. Some were Roman, others simple farm folk. It was clear the cauldron-born did not discriminate by race or rank. Bran moved into the chamber and examined them each in turn, looking to see if there were any he recognized.

"Babes!" exclaimed Heilyn in horror. "They feed upon babes!"

Heilyn became increasingly upset, to the point that Bran took Eurig aside. "Will he be alright to continue? Or shall we send him back to Maur?"

Eurig leaned in, no trace of his earlier joking manner, and spoke quietly in Bran's ear. "His wife gave birth to their first son but a moon ago."

"Ah, I see," Bran said, full of pity for all the new fathers and mothers whose children lay here in this terrible place.

Owain had been silently examining the corpses and finally spoke, holding up several pieces of jewelry between his fine long fingers.

"Some of these people are from tribes that lie east of our village. Why would they be traveling so far south? And so far from any road? There's no reason for them to be anywhere near here."

"Owain and Urien's father trades regularly with several tribes along the roads which lead from our village to the eastern sea," Neirin explained to Bran.

"Perhaps the bodies have been here longer?" Gareth proposed, covering his nose and mouth with his tunic as he bent down to examine them. "Preserved by the cold?"

"No," said Urien, "these are but a few weeks old, if that."

After Neirin and his men finished examining the corpses and the chamber, they decided to go back, as there appeared to be no way out.

"*Wait!*" Neirin suddenly whispered to Bran, grabbing his arm and motioning upwards. Bran squinted, and, being the tallest, held his torch up as high as he could. The firelight revealed holes in the rock overhead. "I saw something," Neirin said with complete conviction.

All the men followed Neirin's gaze overhead, waiting for whatever it was to make itself known to them.

"Take aim above my head," Bran finally said in a low voice. "If anything appears, kill it." He silently positioned himself underneath the largest hole and pulled himself quietly up upon the ledge. Once up, he listened, but sensed nothing up there but cold darkness.

"Torch," he whispered. Fire came his way and he caught it, extending it into the passageway he now found himself in. It was narrow, only wide enough for a man to crawl through, so for Bran, it was uncomfortably small.

"I'm going to see where this leads," he turned and said down to the others.

"Are you out of your mind?" Gareth exclaimed. "You can't go in there alone."

"Come, then," he said, tossing a rope down. "Someone must stay here and guard the opening so none may enter behind us. I'll kill whatever comes toward us. There is certainly no room for any other kind of attack."

He put a dagger between his teeth and crouched down, slowly making his way through. The others followed. He wondered who they chose to stand guard. Finally the passage opened up into another chamber with an underground stream. He could not see it, but he could hear it. He felt around over his head, and realized with relief that he was able to stand. There was a faint light coming from somewhere. Overhead, perhaps? He waited until he heard the others make their way out and then felt a hand on his arm.

"I can lead us from here if you like," Eurig offered. "I can see quite well."

The Northerners were blessed with a great ability to see in the dark, and Bran let him take the lead, moving to the back of the party in case they should be attacked. He felt his way along the shoulders of the men. One, two, three, four, five, six, himself, and whoever was left behind – eight.

Bran followed behind the man in front of him, whom he knew to be either Owain or Urien, for his shoulder had been thin and fine-boned when he touched it. He was handed a length of rope, which he tied around his waist, knowing it bound him to his brothers. They continued along the stream until the passageway opened up into a large cavern with what sounded to be a deep pool of water in it. They had found the source of the stream.

The men untied themselves and Eurig whispered for them to come closer. "My guess is this is their water source, and all creatures must drink, be they man or beast. It is high enough for us to fight freely inside, and we could shoot arrows down from above, through the clefts in the rock."

Neirin agreed. "There are hundreds of hand and footprints at the edge of the water. They come here daily."

"Let us find these clefts from outside, then," Bran said. "We will return with more men. I fear we don't have much daylight left, and we should be far from here when these things awake. We are clearly outnumbered."

"I agree," Neirin said. They didn't bother tying up as there had been no steep or dangerous places, and the way back was clear.

Eurig led and Bran took the rear, same as before, following the stream out of the cavern.

How many men should he bring upon their return? Bran thought. He didn't know. He would have to ask Neirin about how many cauldron-born he suspected were here. Or perhaps Eurig would have an opinion, based on the amount of work in the corridors. If they could somehow drive them out of the caves into the daylight, when they would be weaker and unsuspecting, and then they would have the advantage.

His thoughts wandered to Lucia, and he wondered if she had recovered, and then of her warning, which now rung with eerie truth. Where did all these corridors lead? How far do they go? How long had Cerridwen and her cauldron-born been living here, working on them? He could not remember exactly, but he was fairly sure Talhaiarn had said she fled the island with her son seven years ago. The idea of her being here creating seven years worth of cauldron-born was disturbing enough, but to think of them scraping out seven years worth of tunnels in all directions was even more disturbing.

Then, suddenly, he realized with alarm something was very wrong. Almost in an instant, the footsteps and voices ahead of him vanished, leaving only the sound of the stream flowing beside him. What had happened? He whispered urgently to the others, but no one answered. He quickened his pace, reaching blindly in front of him, but there was clearly no one ahead of him. He dared not call out to them for fear of awakening trouble and putting his companions in danger, so instead moved as quickly as he could, holding his hand out in front of him to feel for low-hanging ledges or rock, but still he encountered no one.

182

He traveled along the stream, keeping it on his left side at all times, as he remembered they had traveled with it on the right side when they entered and eventually found the cavern with the waterfall. Eventually the water would have to lead him out. He followed it for at least an hour, but it simply continued flowing, on and on, leading him nowhere. The men must surely be looking for him by now, and he hated the thought of them endangering themselves on his account. How could he have let himself get so far behind?

He kept following the stream, but for another hour nothing changed. *This makes no sense,* he thought, becoming more and more anxious. He knew that soon the sun would be down, and the creatures would wake to hunt. He hoped the men had had the sense to leave the area. Someone needed to make it back to the village so the clan would know where they were. They could return in the morning. He felt confident that Gareth knew him well enough to predict his wishes and keep the men and horses out of danger.

Finally he gave up and stopped walking, listening very closely to his surroundings, trying to figure out what it was that he had been missing. At first he heard only the water, but then began to hear other noises, like the whistle of air through the tunnel. He felt around on the wall of the cave next to him, moving along it, seeking other passageways. If only he had a torch! He felt around, expecting to find some clue that would tell him where he was, but everything seemed the same. Feeling the stream he realized he was quite thirsty. It was shallow, but in time he finally managed to fill his goatskin.

He found other passages that led off to the left or right, but he didn't dare leave the water, and so walked on along it for what seemed like hours. He could tell the passage was gradually descending, hopefully toward another opening in the mountain, but though it turned and twisted, it did not lead him out.

Finally, he could go no further. He found himself a place in the wall to lean into, and slept.

CHAPTER THIRTEEN
Neirin

The South had sent men to the caves every day for a week searching for Bran, but most did not come back. Finally, Seren insisted they send no more. Only Gareth would not give up hope, saying he would not return unless with Bran at his side. Sadly, he had never come home, either.

There had still not been another attack on the Southern village, nor any evidence of attacks anywhere near it, strangely. Though many were convinced the threat required strong attention, there were others who still believed Lord Cadoc and Priestess Agarah had been attacked by a wolf and that the cauldron-born did not exist, and some that believed the enemy had simply moved on. These divisions caused many problems within the clan, as those who felt there was no true threat argued fiercely that they were squandering precious time and resources chasing after ghosts when they should instead be preparing for the long winter ahead.

With Bran gone, the Council looked to Aelhaearn for guidance, who led well, even in the midst of all the discord. They urged Seren to name him Chieftain, but she refused, insisting her brother would return, and this too caused tension.

Frankly, Neirin was glad to have a break from it.

Today he journeyed home, sent by Aelhaearn with a request to his father to send more trackers. Having now found an entrance to the enemies' lair, what the South needed now were enough trackers to thoroughly search the entire area for other entrances to the caves, and enough warriors to watch each entrance through the night and behead anything that emerged from them. If his father agreed, Aelhaearn would be able to satisfy his clan's believers and non-believers alike – there would be enough men to deal with the enemy threat without sacrificing any of the winter preparations. In return, Aelhaearn had promised new swords for all their warriors, and his father's choice of ten newborn foals come springtime. The East had enjoyed a bountiful harvest and had already finished their preparations for the winter, so Neirin supposed his father would be more than pleased with his offer.

He was but a half day's ride from the South when suddenly he came upon a young woman running toward him and waving frantically.

"Have you seen a chestnut mare?" she called out to him from across the meadow.

"I haven't, my lady," he yelled back to her.

She looked distraught and anxious. "I have been searching for hours, but on foot I cannot cover enough ground! Without that horse I cannot survive out here."

Neirin was shocked. "Do you have no husband? No children?" he asked, concerned. "Where do you live?"

"There," she said, pointing across the field. He looked in the direction she indicated and spied a small house, not so very far away, but well-hidden. Most travelers would not see it from the road.

"Can you help me?" she asked. "There is a hot meal and a bed for the night if you wish."

Neirin thought of the meager bit of food he had in his pack, and a bed would indeed be preferable to sleeping out in the open tonight; not to mention safer.

"You are in luck," he told her. "I happen to be quite a good tracker. Return home, and I'll find your horse and bring him to you."

Relieved and thankful, she made her way back toward the small house and he set himself to the task. It wasn't long before he had found the mare, grazing contentedly a few miles away. He returned to the house proudly, her horse tied to his.

"Thank you!" she cried, relieved. "I'm in your debt!" She led the horse into the small stable at the back of the house and then quickly returned. "Please, come and eat something!"

"Gladly," he said. He had not eaten since the morning.

She fed him very well indeed, to the point where he could eat no more, and the bed she showed him to was clean and sweet-smelling. He rested well upon it with his full belly.

Early the next morning he went out into the field, as usual, and waited for Eirlys to catch her breakfast. The sky was growing dark and cloudy, and snow flurries were beginning to fall.

As soon as Eirlys returned he went to the house to collect his belongings, and to his dismay, the door nearly fell off its hinges when he entered. "Gods!" he exclaimed, surprised.

She turned suddenly from the breakfast she was cooking over the fire. "Oh, no!"

187

"I fear I've broken your door off its hinges," he said, feebly attempting to right it.

"Can it still be bolted?" she asked anxiously.

"I'm afraid not," he answered after examining it. "It doesn't sit well in its frame."

Knowing what roamed the countryside at night, Neirin's conscience would not allow him to leave his hostess alone without a secure door. Luckily, he was quite a skilled carpenter. He knew with the proper tools he could fix it without too much trouble.

"Let me mend it," he said, not asking. "Do you have tools?"

"I do," she answered, obviously relieved by his response. "In the barn."

He made his way to the barn. The holly hedges were in bloom all round the house, their red berries and deep green leaves standing out brightly against the brown scrub and leafless trees of the surrounding forest. They were tall and wild, and served as a good wall around her house. He found a decent set of tools in the barn, and thankfully some pieces of strong lumber that would do the job. He returned and set to work, removing the door completely and ripping out the rotted wood. She watched him intently, and they talked while he measured and cut the wood for the new frame.

"Where did you learn such skills?" she asked. "Did you apprentice?"

"In a way," he replied. "My father is an excellent carpenter. A great man. He started teaching me when I was a boy. Even now we often build things together."

"What is your father's name?"

"The Lord Belenus," Neirin answered proudly. "He is Chieftain of our clan."

"I know his name well!" she said, obviously impressed. "You are the son not only of a great carpenter, but also of a great leader and warrior, then!"

"I am," Neirin said, smiling, "and very proud of it."

"As you should be, my lord," she replied. "I am sorry I was unable to offer you better accommodations."

"Don't be ridiculous!" he countered. "I've not slept so well in weeks!"

She looked at him suspiciously.

"No, I am quite serious," he insisted, reassuring her.

Suddenly Eirlys flew down from the sky and perched next to him.

"What a beautiful creature!" she remarked, admiring the falcon. "Does she hunt with you?"

"Yes," he said. "She helps me track things."

The woman looked at him sideways. "I see. So you can track more than lost horses, I take it?"

At this he smiled. "There is nothing I cannot track, my lady," he said confidently, hammering the new wood into place.

"Is that so?"

"Yes. Quite so."

She looked at him coyly. "Very well, Tracker. I will make you a wager."

"What kind of wager?" he asked, curious.

"If you can manage to track and capture me, I will give you anything you desire that is mine, and if you cannot, you must promise me anything that is yours."

He smiled and thought a moment, and then said playfully, "I will take your wager."

He was eager to show off and then collect the kiss he would demand after he found her. He had wanted one since he had laid eyes on her.

"Ha! This shall be a lovely way to spend the day. How much time shall you give me to flee?" she asked.

"I could give you three days to run, and still find you, but sadly, I do not have that kind of time. I will give you an hour, if you feel that is time enough."

"Agreed!" she smiled.

"Very well, then. I need that much time to finish your door, anyway," he winked. "You had best start running."

***

It had been just over an hour by the time Neirin finished the new door frame to his satisfaction. The door itself was luckily quite hardy and well-made, and now that it had a strong frame to rest within, it would take quite an effort to break it down.

He set off in good spirits to find his beautiful hostess, quickly finding her trail and following it easily for some time. He had gone perhaps a mile or so when, suddenly, it disappeared completely. Certain that he had simply become careless, he gave the search his full attention and examined the area in earnest, but to his utter amazement he found nothing; no tracks, no broken branches, no earth disturbed – *nothing*.

She must have back-tracked, he thought, going back and searching with his keen eyes for the tracks or fork in the trail he knew must be there. For another hour he searched, taking in every detail, but it was if she had turned into a ghost and disappeared.

The day wore on, long past the time he had intended to be on the road. He considered calling out for her, but his pride would not allow it.

He continued searching, astonished that yet another hour later he still hadn't found her. Soon he had to admit to himself that he had lost the day and would need to spend another night under her roof. No matter, there were worse things than that, he supposed. He hadn't had a woman in some time, and she had looked at him in a way he recognized well enough. After the inconvenience she had caused him he had be sure to make it worth his while.

As the sun began to set, he discovered fresh wolf tracks, and more than a few of them. He became anxious. This was no longer a game.

"My lady! Please! Come out! You have won! There are wolves about!" *And other evil things which hunt at night that I do not dare tell you of, my darling.*

He walked briskly back along the tree line toward her house, calling into it until darkness had fallen completely. Perhaps she had returned home? His keen eyes looked in the direction of her house, and spied smoke rising from the chimney.

He grew angry and felt terribly foolish at having been outsmarted, but the relief from the guilt he would have felt had she been attacked by a wolf tempered his bruised ego.

He pushed on her door, noting how smoothly it opened, which was satisfying, and the woman turned from the hearth and greeted him with a smile.

"I win," she said smugly. "You could not find me, Tracker."

Her smugness angered him even more.

"I was worried for you, my lady! I found wolf tracks!" he said, irritated. "And you cheated, I'm sure of it! The wager is forfeit."

"I did no such thing!" she retorted. "How do you think I survive out here, Tracker? A woman out on her own? Certainly not with my brute strength!" she laughed sarcastically.

He knew she had somehow tricked him, but unfortunately he could not prove it.

"Very well," he conceded, "claim your prize. What would you have?" He hoped to the gods she didn't ask for his horse. It would be a long walk home.

"You have nothing I want at the moment," she said, surprising him.

"Is that so?" he asked, looking at her. "You let me know when I do, then." Neirin said with a frustrated sigh. "I've lost a day of travel and must sleep."

He left her, feeling both irritated and aroused by her taunting, but too tired to act on either. How she had managed to elude him he could not fathom, but he was determined to find a way to win back his honor.

***

At dawn he rose to find her sitting by the fire. "I thought you would be up early," she said. "I am sorry about yesterday. That was not a wise use of your time. I acted like a child."

Neirin appreciated her apology. "Somehow you managed to outwit me. Perhaps you have taught me a lesson, which happens rarely, so count yourself clever. However, now I must leave you and make up the time I have tarried here. There is trouble in the South."

Her eyes widened at his comment. "Is it Saxons?" she cried in alarm. "Please, do not leave me here! You cannot leave me!"

He noted panic in her eyes, and did not want to alarm her by telling her the truth.

"Yes…Saxons." he lied.

"Take me with you!" she blurted. "Let me stay with you until the threat is gone."

He considered it. Truthfully, he knew she was in danger far worse than she realized, and wondered how she had survived out there alone as long as she had, with wolves and cauldron-born about. He had already grappled with his conscience over whether or not to bring her with him. Besides, once home he was certain he could seduce her, and having a woman through the winter would bring him much pleasure. All the servant girls at home bored him with their prattle, and as he was not of the mind to take a wife yet, so the more interesting women were off limits. As long as she would not slow him down, he could think of no reason not to bring her.

"How well can you ride?" he asked.

"For days. I can also hunt, fish, skin, cook, weave and sew. I will do whatever you require." Her voice was full of desperation and submissiveness, devoid of the maddening smugness of the night before, and he found her irresistible.

"Come, then," he said magnanimously, pleased to have the upper hand. "I will saddle your horse for you."

Relieved and grateful, she grabbed his hand and kissed it, and they were soon on their way.

She was indeed a good rider. Even along the narrow trails and thundering across the open fields, she kept pace. They arrived at the great gates of his village not long before sundown, and they opened to receive them. Riding in, they were greeted by his father and two male servants.

"Welcome home, son." he said. His father then looked over at the woman he had brought with him.

"This woman seeks refuge," Neirin explained, dismounting and handing the reins to the stable boy waiting to attend their horses. He then turned to the other servant, happy to see it was Caerwyn, who did everything well and always with a pleasant smile.

"Caerwyn, please show the lady to Old Derwyn's hut. See to it there is fresh water and firewood for her."

Derwyn had passed on over the summer, and the hut had stood empty for moons. It was not lavish and a bit small, but it was safe within the high stone walls of the hillfort village that they lived in that kept food, water and livestock in, and cauldron-born out.

"Gladly, my lord," he answered.

"Caerwyn will see to your needs," Neirin said to his guest, helping her dismount.

She thanked him profusely and followed the young man.

His father watched them go, a puzzled look upon his face. "Who is she?"

"She was living alone a half day's ride from here. She approached me on the road."

His father was surprised. "She was living alone?"

"I assume her husband was killed by Saxons. She seems to have much fear of them. Somehow she avoided being captured or killed, but I did not think she would be so lucky against what currently roams the countryside at night."

"She would not," his father agreed. "Our walls are open to those who are willing to work. I'm sure a woman who has managed to live on her own and survive has skills that will serve the clan. Come and tell me what news you bring from the South."

People greeted Neirin and his father respectfully as they made their way across the village toward the stone towers of his father's house.

"We found an entrance to a vast network of caves within about half a day's ride from Bran's village. We explored some of them, but unfortunately we lost many men. Bran was the first."

"Bran?" His father stopped in his tracks. "This I cannot believe. Are you certain?"

"The South sent men to search for him day after day for a week, but every time they sent a party in, only a few men returned to tell of it. Finally, Lady Seren insisted we abandon the search."

Belenus thought on this, and after a moment replied, "If you did not find his body, I will not accept that he is dead. He has surprised me too many times over the years."

"I hope you're right," Neirin said.

"What of Owain and Urien?" his father asked. "Please don't tell me we've lost them as well!"

196

"No. They stayed in the South, as every man is needed. That is why I've come home. Aelhaearn leads in Bran's place for now, and has asked us to send whatever men we can spare. They are falling behind in their winter preparations. To show his gratitude he promised our warriors new swords, and that you will have your choice of ten foals in the spring."

Belenus considered his son's words. "I will send him forty. Perhaps more, but first I must meet with the Council. Meet us in the hall in an hour. You will tell them what you have told me."

"Yes, Father," Neirin replied dutifully.

That night the men of the East met to discuss the plight of the South, and all agreed that the threat must be addressed. It was quite possible that they, too, might come under attack and would then need help in return. The swords and horses made the vote unanimous.

***

It had been two weeks since Neirin returned home. The night before he and his father were to travel south with the additional trackers that Aelhaearn had requested, all of their cattle mysteriously escaped their pen, a near deadly blow to their clan with winter now upon them. Because of this, his father had instead sent Ioworth, his most trusted advisor, with the men promised to Aelhaearn, and he and Neirin remained behind to track down and retrieve the cattle.

The morning they were to set out, Neirin was approached by his mother.

"May I speak with you privately?" she asked him.

"Of course, Mother," he replied.

He followed her across the courtyard and up to the top of the tower his father had built for her. Every morning, at dawn, for as far back as he could remember, his mother had climbed the stone stairs of the tower to welcome her owl back from the night. After receiving her, she would stay to greet the first rays of the rising sun, and pray to the Guardians of the East. His father said the only sunrise she had ever missed was the morning she had given birth to him.

They stood together, looking toward the rising sun, waiting. Presently, he spotted Bloudewedd's white wings leaving the trees below, sailing up toward the tower, and then she landed on his mother's outstretched arm. As always, his mother was serene; as cool and graceful as the winter snow which had fallen the night before. She gave Bloudewedd over to the perch by her side and turned to speak to her son.

Her breath appeared as mist in the cold air as she spoke. "Neirin, I have misgivings about the woman you have brought here."

He looked at her expectantly, and she continued.

"You said you found her living alone?"

"Yes, except for her horse and a few goats and chickens," he replied casually.

"What else do you know of her? Who are her people? Where did her husband come from?"

Neirin was ashamed to admit he knew nothing about her, not even her given name. He had simply nicknamed her *Llwynog*, fox, since the day she had managed to trick him.

"I've been watching her the past three nights. She comes and goes from her hut at the same times I am here atop the tower. At sundown she leaves, and does not return until very early the next morning. I have asked Blodeuwedd to follow her."

"Are you certain?" Neirin asked, surprised.

"Yes," his mother said.

Not even a week had passed since Llwynog had invited him into her bed, Neirin realized. Where could she have spent the past three nights, except in another man's bed? There was no other explanation. He thought of how modest and shy she had acted with him, and how, like a fool, he had fallen for it. She had tricked him yet again, it seemed.

"Yes," he said, growing angrier by the moment. "I would like to know where she is going as well."

"I will find out," his mother said. "For now, set aside your jealousy and find the cattle. We need the milk and meat this winter."

"I'm not jealous!" he said in disgust. "Merely offended! You'd think she had bear me more gratitude!"

"Well, when you come back you can send her out on her own again," his mother stated calmly. "I imagine you made it clear to her that spreading her legs for you through the winter was the price for her safety?"

Neirin felt the harsh sting of his mother's criticism.

"Let me make something clear," she added, "her behavior has indeed raised my suspicions, but for now, that is all they are-- *suspicions*. We have no proof of any wrong-doing on her part, just some strange behavior. Your bruised ego and petty jealousy are not grounds enough for you to cast her out."

"You are right, Mother," he said feeling shamed.

They finished their conversation and Neirin descended the tower, looking toward the small hut he had arranged for Llwynog to live in. Out of curiosity he opened the door and looked inside, but found it empty. He wondered where she was, but had no time to look for her now. He would have to deal with her later. He made his way to the stable where his father was waiting impatiently with Ambisagrus, who already had their horses ready.

Ambisagrus was not one of their clan by blood. He hailed from the South, one of Cadoc's nephews. He married Neirin's only sister when she came of age, and had come to live in the East at Belenus' request, who asked him to train and breed their clan's horses. In return, Belenus gave Ambisagrus a large amount of land and cattle. Ambisagrus had made the most of everything he had been given and was highly respected within the clan, but his hot southern blood often clashed with the cooler nature of his wife's people. Still, of all the men in the clan, he was unanimously the one you would want by your side in a fight.

"Let's be off," his father said, irritated by his son's tardiness and anxious to leave.

Neirin and Ambisagrus quickly mounted their horses and followed him to where the cattle had escaped their pen. They followed the trail easily, Gwyn and Eirlys soaring overhead, until Neirin noticed the tracks suddenly changed; the impressions were deeper and there was quite a bit of turf thrown up.

"Look here," he said, stopping. "They were spooked by something."

The tracks indicated that the cattle had run quite a distance, and the three men rode for some time in search of them. His father then stopped and motioned toward a nearby hilltop rising up from where they were.

"I'm going up there to get a better view," he announced, turning his horse and charging up the hill.

About a quarter of an hour later he rode back down. "I can see cattle grazing directly on the other side of the forest," he said. "They look to be ours. If we cut through the forest rather than taking the drover's road we'll save ourselves a few hours time."

"Done," Ambisagrus agreed. He glanced up toward the overcast sky. "Besides, I don't like the look of that." Heavy grey clouds were moving in rapidly, surely pregnant with rain. It would be a long, cold night if they had to spend it out there.

They galloped to the edge of the woods, as the terrain was flat open grass, but once within the woods the forest trail narrowed and became uneven, slowing their pace considerably as his father had predicted.

"I find it strange this trail is so well-worn," Neirin remarked.

201

"I was thinking the same thing," his father agreed. "We've hosted no travelers as of late, and there are no villages in the area."

The trail sloped downward into a nearly dry riverbed where the mangled remains of one of their cows awaited them.

"Gods!" Ambisgrus exclaimed.

Neirin noticed huge paw prints next to the animal, and dismounted to take a closer look.

"Wolf tracks. The biggest I've ever seen! And there are human tracks as well through here."

His father also dismounted and crouched down by the mangled remains of the animal.

"Strange. No blood. Nothing but bones and hide. I don't understand…this is a recent kill. There should be blood!"

Neirin surveyed the area looking for anything out of the ordinary. The river had been strong in the summer, as the banks on both sides were quite high. He came to a place where the river had washed away all the earth from beneath the trunks of several large trees growing along the bank. Their huge roots were exposed, but they still stood without the earth around them, as every tree's roots were deeply intertwined with its brothers. As he explored beneath them he found what he was looking for: numerous hand and foot prints all over the soft mud in the riverbed.

He investigated further and noticed something deep behind the roots. He hacked them aside to reveal the tell-tale black entrance to a tunnel large enough for a man.

"*Cauldron-born,*" he announced with dread.

Even though Neirin didn't believe their enemies had truly been born of the missing Cauldron of the West, that was what everyone called them, for they were as savage and vicious as men without souls and attacked only by cover of night.

"And we've just sent our best men south with Iorworth," his father sighed in desperation.

"How do you explain the wolf tracks?" Ambisagrus asked.

"I don't know," Neirin admitted, quickly getting back on his horse. "Perhaps a lone wolf made the kill and the cauldron-born took it from him. It doesn't matter. We need to be as far from here by dusk as possible."

They moved quickly from the riverbed, Neirin wondering how many cauldron-born might be sleeping in that dirty hole as they rode toward the other side of the forest. The tunnel entrance they had found surely wasn't the only one. There was never only one.

"Father, we need to bring whatever men we have left to explore the forest and locate as many of these entrances as possible. We must hunt them before they begin hunting us," Neirin insisted.

"I agree," his father replied, looking up. "It must be mid-day by now. If we find the cattle quickly, we can make it home by sundown and return with more men tomorrow."

"And if we cannot?" Neirin asked anxiously. "Perhaps we should turn back now."

"What?" Ambisagrus exclaimed. "And risk those worms taking more of our cattle? I'll lead them back myself. Let the bastards come! My sword hasn't tasted blood in awhile."

"Easy, my friend. I'm not ready to abandon our search quite yet," his father said to Ambisagrus.

Much to Neirin's relief, the trees thinned out considerably in the next hour, allowing them to travel faster. Soon they were riding once more across open land where the rain fell steadily from a grey and cloudy sky. Blinking the raindrops from his eyelashes, Neirin kept his eyes firmly fixed on the horizon. It thankfully wasn't long before he was rewarded.

"There," he said, pointing with satisfaction.

His father squinted in the direction he indicated and smiled. "Eyes of a hawk, my son," he said proudly.

The three of them galloped swiftly through the tall grass toward the herd, approaching from different angles. Neirin was dismayed to count only fifteen head, about half their original number. They maneuvered around the small herd and were soon leading them back along the drover's road as planned, but the cattle stopped frequently which slowed their progress considerably.

"We'll not make it back at this rate," his father said, frustrated.

"They're spooked," Neirin remarked, worried. "There isn't much daylight left."

"We'll get them to the old hilltop fortress," his father announced. "It's big enough for all of us."

The old hilltop fortress was where the clan had lived in his grandfather's time, until the clan had outgrown it. Its walls were still tall and solid, and the clan still used it from time to time, keeping a small amount of supplies and caches of weapons hidden within it for times of trouble. They would be safe there. It was a good plan.

His father then wrote and fastened a note to Gwyn's foot and sent her off. "A message for your mother to send whatever warriors remain to meet us at the fort before nightfall, just in case," he explained.

They found water, let the animals drink and refilled their goatskins, and then drove them as hard as they could around the forest and up toward the old fortress. They somehow managed to be well-settled by sundown.

Ambisagrus stood at the wall, looking out anxiously in the direction of their village.

"Where are the men?" he asked finally. "They should have made it here by now."

"They should have indeed," his father replied heavily. "Perhaps they received the message too late. We'll have to do without them."

They rested in the early evening after a quick meal, not knowing what the night might require of them, taking turns watching at the wall. As Neirin and his father had better night vision, Ambisagrus took the first watch.

Neirin sat against the wall of the old fort, occasionally looking over at his father who was sitting with his back against some of the old stones that had fallen out of place. Neirin knew he only appeared to be sleeping. He had found that out the hard way plenty of times as a young boy, trying to sneak something past him. The great Belenus saw all, heard all, and, it seemed, knew all. No one could outwit him, with the exception of his mother, and Neirin suspected that was why his father had chosen her for his wife. He had longed to earn his father's respect for as far back as he could remember, and when given, his praise was received like bread to a starving man. Today had been no different. Neirin nibbled at it now in his mind, deeply satisfied that he had managed to impress his father earlier. He finally managed to sleep a short while, and then relieved Ambisagrus, taking his turn at the wall with Eirlys beside him as a second sentry. The hours passed agonizingly slowly, the moon making her silent journey across the sky like a crippled old woman, and Neirin grew ever more anxious for the dawn.

During his father's watch, Gwyn suddenly let out a shriek, and the cattle grew restless. Neirin and Ambisagrus grabbed their weapons and jumped to their feet, moving to the edge of the wall where Belenus stood, bow and arrow poised.

Neirin scanned the entire countryside with his keen eyes, sweeping the tree line and the faint path far below, waiting for something to move. Finally, his patience paid off. He spied a black form slinking out of the trees.

"There," he said, pointing it out, his stomach churning.

There was no need to point out what approached next. Limpid eyes began emerging from the dark forest below, shocking the three men who watched from above.

"What in Arawn's name?!" Ambisagrus exclaimed in disbelief.

Smooth and agile the eyes moved rapidly toward the hilltop, eerily winking in and out of view, and Neirin and his father responded quickly, raining arrows down upon them.

Ambisgrus spat and pulled out his sword. "Let it be known to the gods that I am ready to die a hero's death upon this mound of shit, and take a hundred of those....*whatever they are*....with me to shine my boots in the afterlife!"

Neirin and his father had been shooting arrows with faultless precision through Ambisagrus' tirade. "I've shot myself ten in the time you've blustered!" Neirin called out.

"I'll take care of any that make it up here!" he shouted back.

The eyes slowly disappeared as Neirin and his father shot them down, and Neirin looked hopefully across the hillside. For the moment, it seemed as though they had managed to hold them off, but soon, many more pairs of eyes appeared and Neirin's heart raced with terror.

Belenus looked down at the odds. "We will surely die if we stay here. There is no way we can take them all. We must leave the cattle and flee. They have no horses."

Ambisagrus didn't have time to argue, and soon they were galloping down the hill homeward. The cauldron-born were waiting for them at the bottom.

For the first time, Neirin peered into the lifeless eyes of the enemy and smelled their rotting bodies, and he knew without a doubt that the words of the Sisterhood were true. These were not men. Not anymore.

The horses were spooked but Ambisagrus had trained them well, and the three of them galloped at full speed through the enemy, slashing at their limbs as they rode by.

They surged across the land toward the safety of their walls, and Neirin was comforted, knowing the things could not outrun their horses. They had surely lost the cattle, but at least they would live.

Then, out of the corner of his eye, Neirin spied a black form running alongside them. *Gods, now what?* he wondered in fear. He looked over until finally he glimpsed it again. The creature was enormous.

"Father!" he bellowed as it came into view. *"Wolf!"*

Neirin knew his father heard him, but he did not turn around to look. They thundered on, Ambisagrus choosing the best path for their horses.

To Neirin's shock, the wolf kept pace with their horses. It seemed deformed, yet moved with amazing speed in spite of its strangely-formed limbs. It stayed ever within view, and soon the horses were lathered from fear and exertion.

In terror Neirin noticed his father beginning to lag behind. He had loaned his horse to Iorworth for the journey south, and though the steed he rode upon now was strong, it was struggling to keep up and the great wolf was gaining on him.

Neirin slowed to put himself between his father and the deadly pursuer.

"What are you doing!" his father yelled. "Ride for the gates!"

"Not without you!" Neirin cried.

The wolf slowly gained the advantage as Belenus argued with his son, insisting he ride ahead. Still Neirin refused, keeping his mount next to his father's. Finally, when it was clear the wolf could not be outrun, his father looked over at him and deliberately slowed his horse.

"*No!*" Neirin cried out.

The wolf quickly saw its opportunity and sprang, sinking its teeth into the thigh of Belanus and tearing him from his saddle.

Neirin nearly choked his mount turning back to help his father. Ambisagrus was faster and thundered by him, spearing the beast in passing and forcing it to release its bite. The wolf ran back toward the forest, Ambisagrus' spear still lodged in its side, and Neirin leapt off his horse and ran to where his father lay.

Blood was gushing from the deep puncture wounds left by the wolf's bite and had already formed an ominous black pool in the moonlight. Neirin ripped off his tunic and tied off his father's leg in a desperate attempt to stop the bleeding, but the wound was massive. He knew he needed to get his father's leg elevated above his heart, but they could not stay there. Tiny pinpricks of milky white eyes were already beginning to appear in the surrounding darkness, surely drawn to the blood he could not stop from flowing. Thankfully, Ambisagrus came galloping back with the other two horses.

"*Pennaeth*, you must ride! We must get safely behind the walls!" he yelled, jumping from his saddle.

His father could barely stand, so Ambisagrus and Neirin hoisted him quickly into his saddle as the cauldron-born started closing in. They rode as fast as they dared, Belenus in between them, the two of them galloping side-by-side to ensure he didn't fall from his mount. They yelled as loud as they could as soon as the walls of their village came within view. Thankfully they were heard and the fortress gates were open to receive them as they came thundering up the hill.

"Close the gates after us!" Neirin bellowed. "We're being pursued!"

The gates were quickly shut and barred behind them, and Neirin leapt off his horse to help his father off his mount.

"Ring the bell!" Neirin barked at Ambisagrus, who ran to the huge bell by the gates and pounded out ear-splitting clangs to wake the clan.

"Archers!" Neirin cried as the men emerged from their houses. "We need archers on the wall, everywhere! The bastards can climb!"

Neirin then spied his mother running toward them, her eyes filled with panic at seeing the pool of blood beneath his father; a look Neirin had never seen on her face before.

"What has happened!" she cried. "Healer! I need the Healer!"

"Don't worry, my light," Belenus whispered. "I'll recover."

Neirin could tell his mother didn't believe his father's lie.

"Of course you will," she said, returning the favor.

The Healer heard her queen's call and came quickly followed by men with a large board to lay the king upon. His mother reluctantly stepped aside, her hands covered in his father's blood, as they carried her husband off.

She somehow she willed herself back into her calm and composed nature and began organizing the women and gathering the children to take them to safety, and Neirin ran to help lead the defense of the wall.

The cauldron-born scaled the wall quickly. The Easterners didn't have enough men to keep them all off and eventually some of the cauldron-born managed to breach it. They moved powerfully, like crazed animals, lunging at the throats and thighs of his clansmen, seeking tirelessly to sink a fatal bite into a main artery.

They will not be easily overcome, Neirin thought with dread, but thankfully the dawn was near...if they could only hold out a few hours longer!

Thanks to their well-made defenses and archers, the clan managed to keep their casualties to a minimum, and their enemies confined to the wall and the courtyard, away from the women and children, until the dawn mercifully began to break. At the first sign of light, thankfully the grotesque creatures slunk back toward the cover of the forest, granting the East a reprieve.

"Open the gates!" Neirin cried as the cauldron-born fled.

The men followed him courageously out into the disgusting aftermath of the night's fighting, shooting as many down as they could before the beasts disappeared into the cover of the forest.

When no more could be seen, besides those that lay dead all around their feet, Neirin turned to his clansmen.

"Cut off their heads and burn the bodies," he ordered in disgust, "or I fear we'll see them again."

***

Neirin washed the dirt and blood from his face and hands and went to sit with his mother by his father's bedside. The Healer had worked tirelessly through the night to stop the bleeding and ease his father's pain.

"I have done everything I know to do," she told Neirin and his mother. "He has lost far too much blood. I fear he will not survive the day."

His mother didn't cry. She simply nodded her head, somberly accepting what would be, but then, as if in defiance, Belenus suddenly stirred and grasped his wife's hand, and Neirin saw hope leap into her eyes.

"Dawn of my heart, can you speak?" she asked him.

He opened his eyes and looked at them, managing a faint smile. "I have no illusions. This body will soon serve me no longer."

"No, my light…we will send for the Sisters!" his mother said encouragingly.

"There is no time for that," he replied kindly, reaching out to stroke her face. "Send for Ambisagrus and the Council."

"I'll do it," Neirin said, knowing his mother would rather die than leave his father's side. It didn't take him long to find them, as they were all close by, anxiously waiting to hear of their king. When they were all gathered round his bedside, Belenus spoke.

"Let it be known that I, Belenus, Chieftain of the Warriors of the Light, and humble servant of the Guardians of the Dawn, am entrusting the Helm of the East to my only son, Neirin. It is my hope that he will always deserve your respect, and that you will honor him with your loyalty as you have honored me."

The Council nodded in understanding, and then the Healer dismissed them. When they were alone again, his father motioned for Neirin to come closer.

"Keep Ambisagrus and Iorworth near, but trust no one else," he whispered. "We have a traitor within our walls."

"A traitor? Who?" Neirin asked.

"I am certain someone let the cattle loose the night before Iorworth and our warriors left, knowing we would stay behind to retrieve them and that we would be few in number. Gwyn never made it here with my message, which means she was killed. We were betrayed. You must find out by whom, and put them to death. Protect your mother and your sister, and send for our warriors. They must return to defend their own now."

"It shall be so, Father." Neirin promised.

With that, the great Belenus fell silent.

213

As the Healer had predicted, the great king did not live to see the sun rise again with his human eyes, but his people buried him standing up facing east, high upon Kings Tor, where they had buried all their chieftains for generations, and from there, his spirit would greet every future sunrise until the end of time.

Neirin ruled well in his father's place in the weeks to come, listening to the advice of Iorworth or his mother when in doubt of action, and in so doing, his clan began to trust and accept him as Chieftain.

One day, as suddenly as she had disappeared, Llwynog returned to Neirin's village. She had left without a word soon after his father had been buried. Neirin had ridden to her house to see if she had perhaps returned there, but he had found it as empty as the hut he had given her to live in. Weeks had passed and he had given her up for dead.

"The *llwynog* returns, I see," he said, a bit cross with her, yet very happy to see her alive. "Why did you leave without a farewell?"

"I am a solitary creature, my lord," she offered meekly in explanation. "I found that I could not live among others, as I once did. I must beg your forgiveness."

"It is forgotten," he said. "Why have you returned, then?"

"A debt," she answered.

"A debt?" he asked. "You were here but a few weeks! You owe us nothing."

"No, my lord. A debt you owe *me*," she explained.

"What do you mean?" he asked, laughing. "I owe you nothing!"

"Oh, but you do, my dear king. Do you remember the day we met?"

"Yes. I remember it well, lady. I retrieved your horse, mended your door, and agreed to shelter you for the winter," he said, growing irritated. "Perhaps it is you who suffers from a clouded memory, for otherwise I am quite certain you would not speak of debts."

"You accepted a wager from me, and lost," she reminded him.

"A wager?" he asked, truthfully not remembering.

"Oh, yes," she answered. "I offered anything I owned if you could track and capture me, for you said there was nothing you could not track. Do you remember accepting this wager?"

"Yes," he answered simply.

"And you could not track me, could you?" she added menacingly.

Everyone in the hall was now looking at him and the strange woman, surely wondering what she wanted of him, but most worried and anxious of all, was his mother.

"No, I could not," he replied, "but I am sure it was because you used sorcery!"

"Oh, please, my king," she said, shaking her head, "Do not appear ignoble before your people. You lost our wager, and I would claim what you promised."

Neirin grew sick inside, as he saw for the first time the woman in front of him for what she truly was. He suddenly knew what she would ask of him, and when the dreaded words came forth from her treacherous lips, he leapt at her, grabbing her tiny arms in his hands. Suddenly a huge, black wolf charged into the hall and Neirin backed away in horror, recognizing the beast that had killed his father. It had him on his back within seconds, nearly crushing him beneath its weight.

"Stop!" Neirin's mother screamed. "Stop! Please!"

The woman called to the beast and the great hound obediently walked up next to his mistress, his massive skull in line with her shoulders.

"Neirin! Does this woman speak the truth?" his mother asked him.

The disappointment and sorrow in his mother's voice was nearly as hard for Neirin to take as his father's death. He couldn't bring himself to answer, for shame strangled the words in his throat, refusing to let them out, but he finally managed to stand up and gather his words.

"Yes, she speaks the truth, but from a deceitful heart; she played the part of the innocent with me, and I sheltered her, not knowing that I'd let a black adder slither in behind our walls."

The woman smiled in a compassionate way, which confused Neirin.

"Let yourself be comforted by this, my young king," she said, stroking the beast at her side. "I do not wish to claim the Helm for myself. I wish to claim it for the unborn son I carry. You may pledge it to him with a clear conscience, for the blood of the East runs in his veins, thanks to you."

CHAPTER FOURTEEN
Taranis

Everyone was in good spirits, laughing and talking when Taranis entered the motherhouse. The boar he had speared that morning was roasting over a large fire in the sunken stone pit in its center, and the rich smell of roasted meat made his mouth water. He proudly hung the shield of his people in its place and then made himself comfortable upon the large pile of furs directly opposite the entrance to the massive circular hall. He whistled to the dogs waiting patiently at the door, and they eagerly came and sat at his feet. They had earned the privilege tonight, having bravely brought down the boar after he had speared it. Once he was settled his servant girl approached.

"Milord," she began softly, "The woman with the ale waits outside. Would it please you to speak to her?"

Ah, yes. Earlier that afternoon he had been told a woman had arrived in the village driving a horse-drawn wagon bearing several barrels of ale and had requested an audience with him. The men said she was a beauty, and there were two things he loved almost as much as a good hunt -- beautiful women and good ale. He had already had a good hunt today, so if luck were on his side, he would have the pleasure of all three before the sun rose again.

"Bring her in!" he barked, eager to see her.

The girl ran quickly to do his bidding, and a few moments later she returned, leading the woman to his feet. He was not disappointed.

219

The woman's eyes radiated above rouged cheeks and her hair spilled down in braids over a long shawl of many colors that she wore about her shoulders and brought attention to her ample bosom; a quality in women he had a special weakness for.

"Noble Taranis," she said, bowing her head. "I have come to humbly ask if I may trade my services as a brewer for lodging through the winter. A fire has taken my home. I can promise you, it will be the finest ale you have ever tasted."

His people were master brewers, and because of her beauty Taranis tolerated her boast like a parent indulging a small child.

"I sincerely doubt that, woman!" he said, chuckling along with his clansmen. "You obviously have no idea how much ale this king has tasted, or the talents our brewers possess!" To that several men in the hall gave a cheer and raised their horns in a toast to themselves, and the woman smiled.

"Then, gentle king, let me leave you a barrel as a gift for your feast tonight. I will return in the morning, and if it was truly not the finest ale to ever pass your lips, I will take my wares elsewhere and bother you no more."

Taranis enjoyed being generous, and had already decided that he had let her stay through the winter. However, there was no harm in letting her believe she needed to earn the privilege. He knew well that people didn't value things that came too easily, and he definitely wanted her to value being under his roof.

"Agreed." he said. "We'll see if your ale is worthy to be poured into the horns of the Northmen, and if it is, we'll provide you with what you need to keep them full of it."

"Thank you, kind Taranis." she said, bowing deeply in respect. "I'll leave you to your feast, then, and return tomorrow."

He turned to the two warriors closest to him. "See the lady out and fetch a barrel off her wagon. All this talk about ale is making me thirsty!"

The men did as he asked and soon returned with the promised barrel which they opened and set at his feet. Taranis then gestured to his servant girl, who quickly filled his gold-rimmed drinking horn and brought it to him.

He instantly liked what he saw. The head was thick and creamy, and the aroma greeted him like a lover in the morning. He took his first sip, and it was as if the summer sun had returned to shine solely upon him. He smelled vast fields of grain swaying along with wildflowers in a warm breeze as he swallowed, and then the golden aftertaste of honey filled his mouth.

He was overcome.

"Not a bad effort," he said, pretending not to be impressed, "but I will not serve it to my warriors on a feast day. Bring out our best!" he cried, and the men cheered again.

The clan's best ale was brought out and served all night, but it tasted like pig slop to Taranis. He could think of nothing but retiring with the barrel at his feet and drinking it alone. *Where had the wench come from, and where had she learned to brew ale so fine? He had to know.*

The feast carried on late into the night, and eventually all fell asleep on the great piles of furs beside the coals of the fire pit in the hall. Taranis then enjoyed another cup of the ale he had kept for himself, smiling at its perfection and eagerly looked forward to welcoming the woman into the clan.

The next morning, Taranis waited anxiously for the woman to return, but the morning came and went without her. As the day wore on, Taranis regretted that he had not granted her request the day before. What if she had found another clan to winter with, and had decided not to come back? He berated himself for his foolishness, but much to his relief, just before sunset, she returned.

"Ah, woman. You've returned! Let us speak in private." He dismissed everyone from the motherhouse and then beckoned for her to come closer.

"You do not boast of things idly. Your ale was indeed some of the finest I have ever tasted. Who taught you the craft? I would meet him, and bring him here to live with us in the North!"

She laughed. "I was taught long ago by one who now brews for no one but the Lord of the Underworld, I'm afraid."

"Just my luck!" Taranis said, sorry to hear such a master had died. "Then, you shall stay through the winter, and teach my brewers!"

She shook her head. "No, I will not teach my craft to others, but I will gladly brew for you, my king," she countered. "You must understand how teaching others would lower the value of my wares."

"Shrewd," Taranis remarked. He was irritated that he had been denied, but had to admit he respected the woman more.

"How much more of that ambrosia do you have right now, woman?" he asked her.

She motioned outside. "There are ten large barrels in my cart. These are what I have brought for your clan. For you, and you alone, I have the ale you tasted yesterday. Only the finest for a king. There are but three more barrels of that. If you require more, you will need to give me a place to brew alone, as well as a place to sleep."

Taranis knew exactly where he would have her sleep, but did not reveal his intentions. "Done. As agreed, lodging and food for the winter, in exchange for you keeping me in my cups. I warn you, I drink heartily."

"That is not a problem, my king. I will keep you far from thirst," she promised with a smile.

***

Within a few days, the woman had her workplace arranged. Taranis gave her everything she requested and visited her often in the evenings, when the demands of the day were over. She was no common woman, and he wanted to know of her family, but she refused to ever give him her name or speak of where she came from.

"I wish to forget my past," she explained one night. "I would have you give me a new name, my king."

Taranis was pleased. "Very well," he agreed. After giving it some good thought, he announced, "You shall be known as Enyd among my people."

"So be it," she said, smiling.

Night after night, Taranis drank the elixir Enyd brewed for him, hoarding it like liquid gold, but even that which she brewed for the clan far surpassed any they brewed for themselves, and Enyd was heartily welcomed at every feast and table.

Soon King Taranis could scarcely think of anything but the ale and the bewitching woman who brewed it. He summoned her frequently to sit with him at meals, finding she had knowledge he had only known men to possess. How had she come by it? She could also make him laugh, full and loud, with clever talk about what struck her as absurd or entertaining. These things alone would have been enough to captivate him for some time, but then one night he asked her to do something that would unwittingly serve to enslave him to her completely. Taranis loved music almost as much as he loved ale and women, and he asked her to dance for him.

"If it pleases you, my king," she agreed, re-filling his drinking horn.

"Music!" he yelled joyously. "Enyd will dance!"

The clan cheered and clapped, and several men picked up their drums and instruments, and Enyd rose to dance. She removed her shawl and unpinned her hair, letting it tumble down her back.

She began to move, and the king felt time suspend. He was transfixed, unable to take his eyes off her. Her arms rose and fell with the grace of birds in flight, and her hips moved like a river flowing over smooth white stones….as she turned faster and faster, her hair and many-colored skirts lifted to reveal her white neck and long legs, and as she slowed they all flowed delicately back down. Small tendrils of hair fell softly against her rosy cheeks, which grew damp and flushed. She danced and danced, possessed by the rhythm of the music, until finally the musicians released her from their grasp and she emerged from her trance.

From that night on he asked her to dance for him, which she did happily. He began lavishing her with gifts of clothing and jewelry, which she accepted graciously. Over the next few weeks, she grew to look more and more like a queen, which heightened the king's desire for her.

"Come to my bed," he finally said to her one night after everyone had either left or fallen asleep.

"No, my king," she answered to his surprise. He had never been refused by a woman, not before he became king, and certainly not after.

"You dare refuse me?" he asked.

"I do," she replied.

"Enyd!" He reached for her and she backed away. "Don't play with me!" he growled.

"I will not be your possession," she said defiantly, turning her back on him and leaving.

Taranis was unaccustomed to such behavior. Had he not provided her with everything? Shelter, food, clothing, jewelry? Where would she be without him now? Out peddling her ale in the clothes of a peasant! He fantasized about forcing himself on her, but his pride would not allow him to chase after her.

Overwhelmed with desire, he stood and threw his drinking horn on the stones of the fire pit, shattering it into pieces and storming out of the hall. He visited the hut where his servant girls slept and had them all in turn, but none could quench his desire for Enyd.

Bitter over her refusal, Taranis spoke very little to Enyd and took a different woman to his bed each night. He no longer asked her to dance for him. He hoped she would fear losing his favor, but night after night she seemed unaffected by the withdrawal of his attention. She simply brought him his ale, smiled graciously and took her leave. His pride let her go every night without a word, but behind his kingly stature her departure burned into him like hot iron.

One night, Taranis took his seat among his people in the hall, presiding over the evening meal as was his custom, watching the flames in the fire pit and the smoke rising up through the ceiling toward the sky. After the meal, the songs began. Enyd came in with his ale and turned to go, and he found he could feign disinterest no longer.

"Wait," he said to her.

"How may I serve my king?" she asked, kneeling.

He looked at her in exasperation and sighed.

"Enyd, have I not given you everything a woman could want?"

"You have been most generous, my king," she answered, looking at the ground.

"Do you not find me to your taste?" he ventured.

"I find you the most desirous man I have ever laid my eyes upon," she answered. Taranis was filled with passionate joy at her remark, but it confused him more than ever. *Could she be a virgin?* he thought. No, that was out of the question. No virgin could dance the way she did! *Perhaps she had been raped.*

He reached down and lifted her chin, looking into her eyes. "Do you fear lying with a man?" he asked.

She did not look away from him. "I do not. On the contrary, I enjoy it very much," she admitted boldly.

He leaned down to kiss her, but she turned her head and he was incensed.

"Damn the gods, woman! Why do you refuse me! What is it that you want!"

"I do not refuse you, my king," she said. "What I refuse, is to be one of many. If you truly want me, you must make me your queen, and have only me in your bed. There can be no others. *That is what I desire.*"

She rose and turned to go, but he grabbed her by the arm and pulled her back, and this time she let him kiss her. Finally tasting her brought his blood to a boil, and as his tongue and lips dominated her mouth he felt her slowly melt, sweetly yielding to him. *She is mine!* he thought, growing more excited by the second, but it was not to be. She pulled away and ran from him, and King Taranis was left with a hunger so great no number of women could satisfy him.

***

227

A week passed with no sign of Enyd, and Taranis felt as if all the light in the world has been taken from him. He tried to forget her in every way possible; drinking, hunting, fucking, dancing, music--but nothing helped. Thoughts of her vexed him ceaselessly, day and night.

Finally he went out searching for her, asking in all of the villages and farms within a day's ride in every direction, but no one knew whom he spoke of.

Heavy-hearted, Taranis returned to his clan, and resolved that if he ever saw her again, he would make her his queen. There was no woman on earth he had ever wanted more.

***

The air was cold and snow was falling outside, yet Taranis lay alone without a woman to warm his bed. In fact, he had not taken any women to his bed for some time. He could no longer muster any desire for them, and refused to be known as a man who could not satisfy a woman.

Suddenly, Taranis heard someone approaching and jumped up naked, blade in hand. He could see the form of someone creeping softly outside, and in one swift move reached out through the furs covering the opening of his hut and grabbed the intruder, throwing him down on the ground inside his hut and putting a blade to his throat.

"My king!" a woman cried, holding her hands out in fear.

Recognizing the voice, Taranis dropped the blade and pulled Enyd up off the floor, relief rushing through him.

"My queen!" he cried and clutched her to him, overjoyed.

"I am not your queen," she answered.

"You will be! Say you will be mine!" he said, squeezing her like a madman.

"Not yet."

"Why do you insist on torturing me!" he whispered angrily. What more do you want from me!"

"Your seed, and a promise."

There was nothing he desired to give her more than that, and he laughed. "Woman, you shall have it! More than you can carry!" he said, throwing her down into his furs.

She crawled quickly away from him. "*and* a promise!" she insisted.

"Anything you wish, you shall have it," he swore.

"Should I bear a son, you shall promise him the Shield of the North."

Taranis was overjoyed to hear this.

"Oh, indeed he shall have it! I shall lay the boy upon it and hold him up to the Guardians of the North, who will gasp in wonder at him!"

Before she had a chance to say anything more, he found her mouth and stripped off her clothes. Then, like a thunderstorm,

Taranis overcame every inch of her, finally tasting her, possessing her, taking her......

Finally. *Finally, she was his.*

CHAPTER FIFTEEN

The Bonfires of Samhain

Soon after the fateful expedition to the caves that had resulted in Bran's disappearance, Aelhaearn led a mixed company of two hundred warriors from the three clans of the Great Circle to the foot of the ominous mountain that sheltered the enemy, all of them restless from waiting in the village for an attack that had never come and eager for a fight.

The warriors used every hour of daylight to search for entrances to the enemy caves and tunnels, and then guarded all that they managed to find by night. Eventually their efforts paid off. A lone cauldron-born emerged from one of the entrances disturbingly near the camp, and the warriors on guard slayed it and brought it back. It was a grisly and ominous sight, eyes milky white and its flesh rotting off its bones. From that night on, no one doubted the story of the Sisters anymore.

Unfortunately, once the enemy knew they were being hunted, they proved to be stronger and more elusive than any had anticipated and did not make the same mistake again. They managed to come and go every night, but never through any of the guarded entrances, and the warriors that returned each morning always numbered less than the night before. They were indifferent to being set on fire, so being a Firebrand gave Aelhaearn no advantage, and arrows only stopped them until their brethren dragged them back into the mountain to be resurrected. The only way to truly stop them was to remove their heads from their bodies, which required close combat, and close combat meant casualties.

After a few nights of heavy losses it was decided that Neirin would return home to bring back as many more men as his clan could spare, for his village was closest. In fact, it was almost as close to the enemy mountain as the Southern village was. That itself warranted at least a message of warning, for their people could easily be in as much danger as the South.

Neirin had left over a week ago and had not returned nor sent word, however, and it could only be assumed that he had been ambushed or killed.

Aelhaearn then sent an urgent message asking Talhaiarn to come and lend his counsel, but Talhaiarn sent word he dared not leave the Crossroads at such a crucial time, and instead advised Aelhaearn to rely upon the Sisters for guidance in his place. Aelhaearn reluctantly sent a messenger to the village to ask the Sisters who were still there to please consider extending their stay through the winter and lending their services at the camp.

Lucia was among those who answered his call for help, and was glad she did, for the camp was in a desperate state when they arrived. She and the other women worked night and day nursing wounds, mending weapons and preparing meals and medicine. No one slept.

The warriors who managed to survive night after night learned quickly about the cauldron-born, and became more skilled at tracking and killing them. Occasionally, however, a cauldron-born would emerge that was nearly impossible to overcome. The warriors called them the *Gythreuliaid:* demons, for they could not be outrun, were nearly impervious to blade or spear, and could climb trees with inhuman agility. The Sisters advised they were the older cauldron-born; those who had fed regularly for some time and had grown in strength and cunning. Luckily, coming across an older cauldron-born was rare, but it was equally rare that a warrior ever returned to tell of it. Due to their elusiveness, it was suspected that the younger ones hunted and brought back food for them, or that there were simply very few. All hoped for the latter.

The first night Lucia spent in the camp, she discovered she had a very valuable skill to offer that would turn the tide of the battle they fought. She had been sitting by the fire when a feeling of panic came over her, as if a thousand bells had tolled inside of her. Soon after, the camp was attacked. She knew it had not been an accident. The next time the panic seized her, she ran to warn the warriors and directed them to where she knew the cauldron-born would be. Inevitably, the tell-tale eyes of the enemy gave their position away, and the warriors had the advantage. Since that night, Lucia had never once led the warriors astray and they had lost far less men. She had quickly gained the respect of the warriors. Even Aelhaearn treated her differently, and no longer referred to her as "the Roman woman".

She and the other women were dealt with honorably for the most part, but they numbered few, and it did worry Lucia a bit. Being the daughter of a soldier and the wife of a centurion, she knew all too well what war did to men. It favored the merciless and conjured the beast within every man, no matter how gentle he might seem, stoking his appetite for blood, violence and sex; all the more so when there was ale in his belly.

Some of the Sisters were quite young and very pretty, like Llygoden and Elayn's daughter, and had never seen a grown man before. Lucia worried about them, as did Elayn. The two of them kept a close eye on the girls at night, reminding them to stay away from the fires when the men would drink, and never to go anywhere alone. There was no reason to ask for trouble. Then, of course, there was Creirwy. Every man that laid eyes on her did so with awe, lust or longing. She seemed wholly unaffected by the attention she commanded, staying focused on her work, but Lucia worried about her most of all.

However, at times, she wondered if it were the Sisters that she should be worried about instead - not all of them had the focus Creirwy did. Despite Lucia and Elayn's best efforts, more than a few encounters had sprung up between a sister and a warrior. As far as Lucia knew, they had all been consensual, but she knew they were playing a dangerous game being so outnumbered – one that would continue to become more dangerous the longer they stayed.

The tents for the Sisters and the wounded were in the center of the camp, with the tents of the men set up in a tight perimeter around them. Each night at dusk, the Sisters cast a protective spell around the camp. As of yet, no cauldron-born had managed to get in, but the unearthly cries that filled the countryside at night made sleep hard to come by.

Lately, the stories around the campfire had become more and more alarming. The cauldron-born were growing ever more cunning, strengthened by the blood of the clansmen they happened to subdue as the battle waged on night after night. Most disturbing of all were the stories of familiar faces emerging from the caves, eyes turned the tell-tale milky white of the cauldron-born, requiring brother to slay brother.

234

Just when things seemed they could get no bleaker, a messenger arrived from the village with the tragic news of King Belenus' death. The Easterners left the camp to attend his burial, and would not be returning. They were needed at home now, to defend their own people against the cauldron-born that now roamed their own forests.

It had been two moons since Bran's disappearance. There had been no sign of him in the caves or anywhere around them. Einon and the Council had been urging Seren to name Aelhaearn their new chieftain for weeks. With the news of Belenus having fallen and the Easterners returning home, they became more insistent than ever. Finally she relented, saying that if Bran had not returned by *Nos Galan Gaeaf*, the New Year, she would concede to the Council's wishes. That long night was now upon them, and sadly Bran had not returned. True to her word, Seren kept her promise.

They all gathered in the motherhouse that evening to witness the performing of the rites and then celebrate. The preparations for the feast had taken them three days.

Seren stood in the center of the roundhouse and raised her hands, and the crowd fell silent.

"Brothers and sisters," she began, "Tonight we accept that our king and chieftain, Bran, son of Agarah, has died protecting his clan, not to return to us in this lifetime."

Pained expressions went around the room followed by shouts to Bran's bravery and honor, and blessings on his name.

She does not believe her own words, Lucia thought.

"Step forward, noble Aelhaearn." Seren continued. The crowd cheered, and warriors from all three clans raised their spears in tribute.

"Should there be any man here tonight that would challenge Lord Aelhaearn for the title of King and Chieftain of the South, let him step forward!"

No one did, and Lucia wanted to cry. She realized that somewhere within her she had suddenly expected Bran to appear at that moment, and the silence that had come in his stead drained all the joy from her heart.

"Then tonight we will celebrate the feast of the dead and drink to his name!" Seren announced, feigning her exuberance.

Cheering erupted in the camp and the drinking began. Einon was there to receive Seren with an understanding embrace, and Lucia and the Sisters left to help prepare the feast while the warriors drank to their new king.

To Aelhaearn's credit, however, they had accomplished more than Lucia thought possible over the past month. Somehow the fighting at the caves had been managed in addition to all of the other preparations for winter. The last of the apples were picked, the wheat from the fields cut and threshed, the prime livestock selected to be lodged in the barns through winter, and the rest of the pigs and cattle slaughtered. Meat had been set aside for the feast tonight, and the rest salted and cured.

Lucia sat deep in thought, baking bread over an open fire. It was her favorite chore now that the weather had become so much colder, and she thought back on prior celebrations of *Nos Galan*

Gaeaf that she had shared with Aveta and Gwion. Aveta would leave her door and windows open all night, and set out apples, wine and a bowl of stew that she made from potatoes, carrots, turnips, peas, parsnips, leeks, pepper, salt and new milk. Lucia would sit with her and Gwion in her tiny house by the fire which she would keep burning all night, and they would eat, talk and tell stories. Aveta shared with her that she left her door open for Gwion's father, explaining that on this night of the year, the veil between the worlds was at its thinnest point and the dead were free to roam the earth.

Tonight, it would be Bran's spirit that many in the camp would hope to see, but Lucia knew that would not happen. She knew he was still alive although she could not prove it, but dared not say anything to Seren for fear Aelhaearn would cast her out on her own. It was clear that however much she had helped the clan, he still did not trust her, and, alive or not, until Bran actually returned, the clan would continue to press for a new king.

The bonfire in the center of the camp would be huge, judging from the size of the woodpile that had been constructed. All of the bones from the slaughtered animals that weren't stewing in the many pots about the camp were beside it, to be thrown into the coals when the fire was raging.

Seren began the ceremony by lighting the bonfire and calling the Guardians, and the Sisters cast their circle of protection around the camp. There would be no hunting of the enemy tonight. Tonight they would celebrate, and the Great Mother would protect them.

Soon the fire was a pyramid of heat and light, its flames like the forked tongues of a thousand dragons tasting the stars. Everyone feasted together and threw the bones from their meat into the smoldering coals at the heart of it. Some time later, everyone lay down close to the fire upon furs with one another, their bellies full of meat and drink, and Aelhaearn made his first request as Chieftain.

"Grace us with a song," he asked Teirtu.

Lucia smiled. Teirtu the bard had come to the camp at Seren's request, and since his arrival, the spirits of everyone in the camp had been lifted. He sang ballads of their most-beloved heroes nightly that bolstered the men's courage, giving them the strength to return night after night to fight against the horrors which lurked all around them.

"Gladly, my king," Teirtu said, pulling his harp out. Everyone fell silent in anticipation until his fingers began moving along the strings, long and graceful, yet commanding and calloused from endless hours of playing. His harp wept and sang, telling a story without words, and when you thought the music could not possibly become any sweeter, his voice rose and filled the air like an ancient perfume, as rich and deep as dark honey.

Suddenly, Aelhaearn stood up and swiftly unsheathed his sword, breaking Teirtu's beautiful spell, and every warrior among them quickly jumped to his feet and did the same.

Cauldron-born?! Lucia thought in horror. How could she not have known?

No, not cauldron-born. Not this time. Everyone looked in the direction of their king's gaze to see a dark figure on horseback slowly approaching the camp from the forest.

"Name yourself friend or foe, man or spirit!" Aelhaearn called to him.

"I am man, and friend," The stranger replied.

"We feast in honor of the dead tonight, and all are welcome all who mean no harm," Aelhaearn said in a warning tone.

"I come peacefully," the man answered.

"Then come and eat, and share our fire this night," Aelhaearn offered generously.

The man came into view, an impressive figure astride a white horse, and Lucia gasped. *It cannot be!* she thought, her heart pounding. Many thoughts flooded her mind at once. A part of her wanted to run to him; another told her what she saw was surely an apparition. *The dead walk among the living this night!*

"I am Lord Camulos," he announced. "I come seeking my wife, the Lady Lucia."

Lucia felt uneasy. *Something was not right.* She quietly moved to leave…but it was too late.

"There she is!" the man cried, pointing in her direction.

Lucia shook her head in disbelief, looking at the man on the horse.

"This cannot be," she said. "My husband is dead!"

Aelhaearn looked the stranger up and down. "It appears not," he said. "Unless it is his spirit that has come for you instead."

Lucia considered the latter, but the man in front of them was as solid as the ground beneath her feet.

The stranger dismounted and approached Lucia, but was stopped by half a dozen warriors with spears.

"I am no ghost, you pagan fools! I am Camulos, a Centurion of the Roman Legion!" He pulled out his dagger and cut himself, and blood dripped down his arm onto the ground to prove his point.

Lucia saw the anger in Aelhaearn's eyes at Camulos' gross disrespect and ran to his side, knowing the king would not suffer his insult, especially on the night of his feast.

"My king, please, pardon my husband! He does not know his place!" She embraced Camulos to protect him and then distracted him with her affections.

"You are indeed flesh and blood! My prayers have been answered!" she cried.

Aelhaearn sheathed his sword and glared at Camulos.

"My hospitality expires with the morning sun, Roman dog. Be grateful your woman is well-loved among my clan, for otherwise you would not live to see it rise again."

He walked off and left them, and Lucia demanded her husband be quiet or else plan on returning to the grave he had somehow overcome.

"Superstitious fools," he said under his breath, looking with disgust at the people Lucia now considered closer than family, and then turned to face her.

"You look at me as if I am a stranger, wife. Have I changed so much?" he asked.

Truthfully, he had not changed at all, which was disturbing to her. He looked exactly the same as when she had last seen him. In fact, if anything, he looked *younger*.

"Lucia, are you not pleased to see me?" he asked.

"I am pleased, of course!" she said, forcing a smile and embracing him so he could not see that she was lying.

"How did you find me?" she asked.

"It is a long story that does not matter right now. There will be much time for stories tomorrow," he replied, smiling.

His answer did not satisfy her, but she asked no more questions. Soon everyone was carrying on just as they had before, drinking and dancing, as if nothing had happened. Everyone but Seren, who looked over as if to say, *"Do you need my help?"* But she could not help. No one could. Bran had not returned and her husband had come for her. Lucia felt as though she had fallen through a crack in the earth and was sliding down rocks and loose soil, unable to find anything to grasp onto and crawl back out.

"I will to bed," she said suddenly in desperation to Camulos.

"I will come with you," he replied eagerly.

"No. I sleep in a tent you cannot come to," she said, grateful her bed lay within the tent of the Sisters.

"What do you mean?" he barked. "Have you taken another husband?"

All the kindness disappeared from his face in an instant and he looked as if he might strike her. She backed away from him.

"No! I sleep with a company of women," she replied indignantly, angered by both his threatening manner and that he expected her to still be in mourning after two years.

"And what if I *did* have a husband? I was told by men in your command that you died upon the battlefield! Did you honestly expect me to never take another lover? To never marry again? I am not yet a crone, Lord Camulos!"

She turned to leave, but he reached out and pulled her back.

"Of course not, Lucia. Forgive me. It has been a long and wearisome journey to find you, and I am afraid I am not myself." he said. "Go and sleep."

She didn't know what to say, confused by his rapidly changing temperament, so simply turned and left.

She entered the tent she shared with her sisters, relieved to be away from him. Llygoden, Creirwy, the twins and Elayn's daughter Anwen were already asleep, but Elayn was waiting for her.

"Lucia," she said simply. "Are you happy your husband has returned?"

Lucia paused a moment before answering. "I am glad he lives," she began, "but he's--*different.*"

"What do you mean?" Elayn asked.

Lucia tried feebly to express how she felt. "I don't know. I can't explain it."

"More than likely it is you who has changed," Elayn offered kindly. "You are no longer the child he married."

"I have indeed, but that's not it," Lucia replied.

"Are you afraid of him?" she asked.

"I don't think he would strike me…It's just that I don't…*recognize* him. He makes me uneasy."

Elayn nodded and put her hand over Lucia's.

"Well, you do not have to decide whether or not to go with him now. Sleep on it and decide in the morning," Elayn advised. "Perhaps with some food and rest tonight he may yet become the husband you remember by morning. Who knows what he's been through these past few years."

It had been a long and arduous day with all of the feast preparations on top of their regular duties, and Lucia was indeed exhausted. She followed Elayn's advice, willing herself to think on it no more, and fell asleep to the sound of the men celebrating. She was happy for them. There had not been enough laughter lately.

***

The sun had not yet risen when she was awakened.

"Lucia, your husband is insisting you leave with him now," Elayn said gently. "He is outside."

Lucia grew sick at the realization that she had not dreamed everything that had happened the night before.

"If you do not wish to go with him, I will speak with Seren. I'm sure she would agree to have the warriors send him on his way, but you must know it could end in his death if he refuses to leave. He made the mistake of insulting Aelhaearn last night, and there will be no patience granted to him if he causes any further trouble."

"I do not know what has happened to him." Lucia said. "He was a stern man, but always diplomatic. Not like this."

"War hardens the heart of every man," Elayn said, "but a woman's love will often soften it again."

Lucia thought on this. Camulos had been generous and allowed her freedom where most men would not have, and a part of her still loved him.

"Tell him I will go with him," she finally said.

At that, Llygoden sat up. "Lucia, no! You can't go!" she said, rubbing the sleep from her eyes. "You're one of us now, and the Sisters don't have husbands!" She crawled over and put her arms around Lucia, refusing to let go. Llygoden had become something of a daughter to her, and Lucia had to hold back tears. "Tell him to go away!" she insisted.

Creirwy and the others were all awake as well, their faces somber in the pale light of the small lantern Elayn held.

244

"You'll be back," Creirwy said simply.

"I believe so, too," Ina agreed. Ivy said nothing, but went to give Lucia a parting embrace.

"I will return as soon as I can," Lucia promised, "but for now, I must go." She collected her few belongings and embraced each one of the others in turn, and then left the tent.

Elayn accompanied her to the edge of the camp where Camulos and Seren were waiting. She was surprised to see Gethen saddled next to Camulos' horse.

"I have decided to give him to you, Lucia. He is a strong horse, and he trusts you. Besides, he'll let no one else ride him," she said, smiling.

Lucia was overjoyed at the gesture. "Oh, thank you!"

She had cared for Gethen and rode him much over the past month, and the idea of having him with her on this journey made all the difference in the world.

"Lucia!" Camulos barked in disgust. "You are the wife of a Centurion, not a slave! Act like one!"

Anger boiled up in her heart, but she said nothing, knowing it would be best if they simply departed. She placated her temper by promising herself she would make him pay later.

She said her farewells to Elayn and then to Seren, who whispered in her ear as they embraced, "Gethen knows the way home, Lucia. If you desire it, he will bring you back."

She pulled away and nodded, letting Seren know she heard her.

They reached the moorlands by mid-day. She loved being able to see for such far distances in all directions, and with the wind whipping her hair back she felt as if she were flying. The air was biting cold but she didn't care, relishing the feeling of power and freedom. Camulos must have found her smile inviting, for he spoke to her for the first time since they had left that morning.

"I found the villa burned to the ground, and was sure I had lost you," he said. "I've since ordered it re-built. I've men working on it right now. It'll be bigger and more beautiful than before. I'm sure you'll be pleased."

She was surprised he said nothing about his maps or the books in the library. His maps were his most prized possessions, and the books were hers.

"How was it that you were not there?" he asked her, putting her on guard.

"We were warned there were invaders about, and fled before they found us," she lied. "The clan you found me with is well-known to Aveta, and they took us in. News reached us that the villa had burned, and knowing we had no home to return to, they allowed us to stay on through the winter."

"All of you? Aveta and Gwion as well?" he asked.

She nervously thought of a response. "We were together a short while, but then they left to rejoin family."

"I see," he said. "Where?"

She needed to change the subject before he pried any further, for she was decidedly not a good liar.

"Husband, you went to war two years ago and then some. How is it you have not returned to me until now, and yet look younger than when you left?"

"That's a long story, love," he said.

"We have a long journey," she replied. The question she really wanted an answer to was how he had managed to find her. No one but the Sisters and Talhaiarn knew she was with Bran's people.

"That is true," he agreed, taking a deep breath. "We were but a garrison of sixty men just north of Hadrian's Wall," he began. "The wall has always been fairly simple to defend - the might of the Empire against a few barbarians with spears - but lately our lady Rome has been shortening her skirts, calling many of her sons back home. When the hordes attacked in the night, we were completely outnumbered, ten to one. We managed to hold them off for a day or so, but we were given no rest. After three days, nearly all my men lay dead, as I would have been, if not for an old woman who found me bleeding to death upon the battlefield. She looked like one of them, and I expected her to carve my heart out and put me out of my damned misery, but to my surprise she spoke my language. She asked me if I were the Roman they called Camulos. I told her yes, and she asked me if I wanted to live. Again, I said yes. She said she could heal me, and that I would be stronger than I was before, if I agreed to help her in return someday. I agreed, of course."

Camulos looked off toward the horizon and said nothing for a moment.

"And?" she finally prodded.

He continued with his story, though she found his tone reluctant.

"The next thing I remember, I was being pulled from a huge vat of what seemed to be warm milk by a beast of a man who tossed me upon the ground, naked and wet as a newborn. We were in some kind of grotto. The woman said she would find me when she needed me, and I would be able to repay her kindness as promised. She gave me my clothes and weapons, and told me to follow the sound of the ocean and it would lead me out. I did, and came to the edge of a cliff. The sea battered against a small rocky beach several hundred feet below, clipped off at both ends by more cliffs. The only way for me to go was up. It took quite an effort; the rocks were wet with spray and moss, but the fates smiled upon me and finally I succeeded in making it to the top. I wandered for days, looking for a road or some kind of clue as to where I might be, but no feature of the landscape or horizon looked familiar. Eventually I was set upon by a tribe of Pictii, which I now look upon as a blessing, because it was then that I realized I must have been far north of the wall, deep within Caledonia. It was also then that I realized just how strong I had become. My sword felt light in my hands, and I never grew tired – I fought the Picts continually, one by one, until finally, they all lay dead at my feet. She indeed delivered what she promised, and more."

Lucia's anxiousness increased as she listened, slowly suspecting the identity of her husband's healer. It had to be her. Hadn't it? Or were there others who commanded such power? He didn't look or act like the cauldron-born, but he was certainly changed, and not for the better.

"Husband, I fear for you," she said after much consideration. "I am afraid you may have wagered with a very powerful sorceress. One who has the power to bring corpses back from the dead."

She was alarmed to find a strange pride had come over her as she said those words, for the blood of that powerful witch ran through her veins too. *Cerridwen, the woman who could bring men back from the dead.* The thrill shocked her and she recoiled from it.

Camulos smirked at her. "Lucia, please…Those are but stories the peasants you have been living with tell their children around the fire to frighten them into obedience! Do you honestly expect me, a literate Roman citizen, to believe anyone has the power to bring back the dead? No. I will hear no more of this nonsense."

The combination of his arrogance and ignorance overwhelmed Lucia.

"You just told me she brought *you* back from the dead!" she said with disdain, feeling insulted and disregarded.

"Don't be a stupid cow, Lucia! She merely healed my wounds, for which I am grateful! I would think you would be as well! She's the one who told me where I could find you, so you have her to thank for being spared a cold winter with a clan of pagans!"

Lucia reined Gethen to a stop. "Where to find me?" she asked warily. "A moment ago you said you returned to the villa and found it burned, and thought me dead! Now, you say this woman told you where to find me?"

Camulos did not reply, and Lucia grew ever more suspicious of him. "You've changed, husband, and not for the better!" she burst out angrily, unable to control her temper any longer. "I'd rather brave the winter with the pagans than follow a fool like you any further!"

She turned Gethen around abruptly and started back toward Bran's village, but Camulos was next to her in seconds. The back of his hand flew against her face so hard she would have been knocked out of her saddle if her feet had not been secured in the stirrups.

"Oh, I think not, wife," he seethed menacingly. "You will follow me home."

She was shocked by his violence, but her pride refused to give him the satisfaction of knowing it or seeing her tears. She glared back at him in defiance, resolving to create another opportunity for her escape. She would not fail the next time.

They traveled in silence for the rest of the day. Tears did come later in the night, but not from his blow. They came because she had to suffer the death of her husband a second time; he was not the man she married, and it grieved her deeply to see all the familiar contours of his face but feel nothing of his kind soul.

The next morning they traveled under the same heavy yoke of suffocating silence until she felt she would go mad from it. *Is this to be my life now?* she wondered. The prospect was intolerable to her.

She couldn't go back to the clan now, for that was exactly what he would expect. After what had happened, she didn't dare risk any more trouble, lest Aelhaearn banish her from ever returning. *No, she thought, I must seek refuge elsewhere, in a place he will never find me.*

She knew she had to return to the island. It was her only hope. She could sneak away while he slept, but this meant she would need to get him to drop his guard. Traveling alone at night would be risky, but well worth it to escape the life she saw herself fated for if she remained with him.

"Husband, forgive me," she pleaded, managing to eke out some tears in an effort to appear as remorseful as possible. "I don't know what came over me. I think seeing you after so much time has been trying on me."

Camulos seemed appeased by her words, which she found encouraging. After making camp and eating a small meal, she rolled out some blankets and furs for them to sleep upon. He was quick to stretch out upon them and pull her down next to him, immediately pulling her robe up and groping her roughly underneath it. Though she dreaded his hands on her body and having him inside her, she pretended to enjoy it. Thankfully it was over quickly, and soon he was sleeping deeply.

She waited patiently for the night to almost come to an end, knowing her chances of surviving the surrounding countryside increased the closer to dawn it was. When she felt the time was right, she mounted Gethen as silently as she could, but Camulos was no fool.

"Where do you think you're going, woman?" he said.

Lucia kicked Gethen and took off with her heart pounding like a war-drum in her chest, riding as fast as she dared through the forest. She tucked her head down into his mane to avoid low-hanging limbs and branches, peeking up as often as she could to seek out open space. There she knew Gethen had a good chance of outpacing the horse Camulos rode. She looked intently through the trees, every moment a terror, until finally they began to thin out and she saw her opportunity. She jabbed her heels into Gethen's flanks with a yell and he leapt forward into the open field.

"LUCIA!" she heard Camulos bellow. He was not far behind, and soon she was startled by a rope whizzing by her head, dangerously close to falling round her shoulders. She crushed her body even flatter against Gethen, whispering desperate prayers into his black mane. *Great Mother! Open your arms! Protect us!*

Slowly the sounds of her pursuer faded away, until all she heard was the sound of her own labored breathing and Gethen's strides. Still, she rode hard, wanting to put as much ground as possible between herself and the frightening man her husband had become. They eventually found their way back to the road leading north toward the lake and she slowed their pace, breathing deeply to calm herself. Only after they had traveled for the better part of an hour without incident did she let herself relax.

The night will soon be over, she thought, comforting herself. Old Colwyn would be up at first light, and she could ask to borrow his boat and get food and water for Gethen.

Suddenly she was shocked from her thoughts as if a lightning bolt had struck her from the inside, and Gethen reacted as well, spooked into a full gallop. *No! Not now!* she thought fearfully. *We're so close!* She knew there are cauldron-born about, for that feeling was now very familiar to her, but she sensed there was something far more menacing that now hunted them…Something she had never felt before.

"Don't stop, my love!" she pleaded to her dark companion, fear once again filling her chest. *"Don't stop!"*

It wasn't long before she began to see something out of the corner of her eye in the moonlight, running alongside them in the long grass flanking the road. She looked over in dread to see the black form of a huge wolf moving at terrifying speed, its eyes glowing yellow in the night, and its muscular body bleeding where tree branches and bracken had ripped at its flesh as it raced through the forest.

Gethen must have felt the creature gaining on them, for he suddenly found new strength and blasted through the countryside. She flattened herself against him, gripping his body as tightly as she could with her thighs. Then, like a blessing, the shimmer of the lake appeared, albeit far in the distance, and suddenly she heard Elayn's voice: *You can call upon the water in times of need.*

The lake! We must get to the lake! she realized, but poor Gethen was beginning to tire. She screamed in terror as the wolf gained on them, kicking him madly. "Don't give up!" she cried. "We cannot stop!"

The wolf's strides brought him ever closer and closer. She knew Gethen was too tired to increase his pace. She pulled out her dagger, readying herself for the inevitable.

The creature soon saw its opportunity and sprung, sinking its claws and teeth into Gethen's flank. Hearing him cry out in pain brought out the fury of a mother bear in Lucia, and she viciously stabbed her dagger deep into the creature's eye and yanked it back out again with a war cry. It snarled in rage and fell off Gethen's flank in a tumble of blackness, but to her amazement it quickly recovered and was soon in close pursuit again.

The wolf sprang again, this time managing to sink its fangs into her leg. Searing pain sent a fresh wave of adrenalin surging through her veins, and with it she managed to stab the animal in the throat, forcing it to release its bite. She looked in desperation toward the lake, which was now quite close, but Gethen's strides had lost their power.

No doubt drawn to the smell of fresh blood, cauldron-born soon emerged, closing in from all sides, moving swiftly toward horse and rider like snakes through the tall grass. The pain in her leg was unbearable, but Lucia willed herself to stay conscious.

"We're almost there! Almost there, just a bit further!" she pleaded in Gethen's ear.

Gethen seemed to understand, putting everything he could into reaching the lake until finally they galloped into the water. She slid off his back, pulling the foot of her injured leg out of the stirrup with a cry of agony, and then pulled him by the reins into the water.

The cauldron-born stopped abruptly at the waterline, seething and pacing, but the wolf dove in undeterred. Gethen was so tired he could barely keep his head above the surface, and in desperation Lucia used every ounce of her mental strength to focus her mind and call upon the water, asking for the Great Mother's protection.

Suddenly she felt a current come up from beneath them and wrap around her and Gethen forcefully. It carried them out toward the middle of the lake as if they were upon a raft in a rushing river, far away from their dark pursuer and the terrifying danger on the shore. Lucia turned her efforts toward picturing the island, holding it in her mind's eye with intense focus. She put her arms around Gethen's neck and rested her head against him, enduring wave after wave of pain and looking up toward the moon, remembering the fateful vision she had had two full moons ago that had started this journey.

After some time, Lucia felt the cauldron-born departing, retreating to wherever they had come from. Soon she could no longer feel her limbs, the icy water taking all feeling from them, and her teeth chattered uncontrollably. She must get them to the island soon, or they would both die from the cold.

With renewed focus Lucia willed the shore to appear, supplicating the Great Mother, the guardians, her ancestors – anyone that would listen. Then, finally, like a benediction, she felt land beneath her feet and looked up to see the shore. Sobbing in gratitude she refused to blink for fear it would disappear, hanging onto Gethen's neck for support as they stumbled out of the water, only daring to close her eyes when she could feel the solid ground against her cheek.

CHAPTER SIXTEEN

Prophecy of the Three Kings

Her grandmother's face appeared above her in a moonlit dream, the sound of her voice floating toward her faintly, as if from some faraway place.

"Lucia? Lucia! Can you hear me? Help me lift her...Tell the others to come and care for the horse. Quickly!"

"I hear you," she finally managed to say through the fog in her head. "Help Gethen..."

She felt herself being lifted onto a blanket and then up into the air, her body lying heavy in its center. She looked up at the sky and saw the moon still there, ever-present, faithfully gazing down on her. She kept her eyes upon it as she was carried through the trees and finally indoors where they laid her down close to the fire. Her sisters removed her wet clothes and wrapped furs around her and she relaxed gratefully into waves of warmth. Yet again she had been bested by the cold.

"Lucia!" said a familiar voice. Lucia smiled and her eyes filled with tears as she recognized the sound of her dear friend, and felt Aveta take her hand.

"Here, drink this," she said, lifting her head. She drank as much as she could manage from the cup held to her lips. Again, she thought of Gethen.

"Gethen...please, we cannot let him die. He saved my life," she said.

"Don't worry. Gwion is with him," Aveta answered, and relief washed over Lucia.

"Lucia, where are the others? What happened?" she demanded.

"They are fine," Lucia managed to say. "I left alone."

Aveta asked more questions, and Lucia did her best to answer, but with the increasing warmth she began to feel her leg, and soon the pain became unbearable. "My leg..." she cried out.

Aveta lifted the furs to examine it. "Gods!" she exclaimed in shock. "This bite is enormous! Lucia, damn the gods - *what happened!*"

"Wolf," Lucia answered weakly. "Huge. A wolf who ran with the cauldron-born."

"A wolf?" Lucia suddenly heard her grandmother say from across the room. Soon her face appeared by her side. "They say a giant black wolf pulled King Belenus from his mount, and with cauldron-born in pursuit as well. It is either the same creature that attacked you, or there are several."

Lucia's face must have spoken of her weakness, for Aveta stroked her hair and Rowan refrained from asking any further questions. "Sleep, granddaughter. We will speak in the morning." With that she was left in Aveta's care, who finished dressing her wound and then lay down next to her.

Early the next morning Lucia awoke to immense aching and throbbing in her leg. She threw the furs aside to look at it, and noticed with alarm she was bleeding profusely through the bandages.

258

Aveta was by the hearth in the center of the roundhouse stoking the fire. The other women must have already left to attend their duties.

"Ah. You're awake," she turned and said. "We must change the dressing."

She was stooped over a hanging pot that straddled the fire and prepared a new poultice, and came over to remove the old bandages. She gasped when Aveta revealed the wound. It was red and swollen, oozing blood and yellow pus, and hot to the touch.

"I am surprised it is not worse," Aveta offered consolingly. "This would have been a fatal bite, I'm sure. Though the icy water of the lake nearly claimed your life, I'm sure it also slowed the bleeding and prevented much swelling and bruising."

"I am glad for it then," she said through gritted teeth as Aveta dressed her wound.

"I long to see Gwion - I've missed you both so much. Can you ask him to come and visit me?" she asked.

"Yes, of course," Aveta replied, smiling and tying off her fresh bandages. "I will go and fetch him."

Within the hour Gwion came to visit her. She remarked he had gotten taller than when she last saw him. He knelt down into her outstretched arms and they embraced for some time, neither of them speaking.

"You and your mother are constant blessings to me," Lucia finally said as he pulled away. "I don't ever wish to be apart from you again."

Gwion smiled at her, looking quite mature for his age, she thought. "We're glad you've come back."

"How is Gethen?" she asked eagerly. "I put both our lives in danger. I should never have tried to travel by night. It was selfish of me."

"He will recover," Gwion answered. "As you will."

"Thank the gods," Lucia said, relieved.

Aveta came over with a wooden bowl. "Here, sit up and drink this."

Lucia sat up gingerly, and suddenly pain reached up from her leg and grabbed her, as if it had long pointed fingers and a hand of its own. She winced until it subsided and then carefully took the bowl.

"Damn this leg!" she said in frustration. "I won't be able to put any weight on it for days!"

"No, you won't," Aveta said, "and don't even think of getting up without help," she added in warning.

"I won't," Lucia lied, knowing the one thing she was incapable of was laying still for long stretches of time. The smell of the broth in her hands suddenly brought on a wave of ravenous hunger. She raised it carefully to her lips and sipped on it.

"Where is Lord Bran?" Gwion asked. Of course he must be wondering why Gethen was with her, and not with his master, Lucia realized.

"There is much to tell," she said, and a moment later, almost as if she had heard, her grandmother entered the motherhouse.

"You look better," she says as she knelt down to look at Lucia. "How do you feel?"

"Tired," Lucia answered truthfully, "but grateful."

"As you should be," Rowan remarked, matter-of-factly.

Lucia thankfully began to feel a bit of strength returning to her, and wondered what Aveta had put in her broth.

"About a month ago, trackers arrived from a tribe in the East. They helped Bran and his men track the cauldron-born to a remote area in the mountains, southwest of their village. It's a cold and lonely place, growing ever more so with the coming winter. The cauldron-born live there within a network of caves, and travel between them by way of underground tunnels that they have dug. Aelhaearn set up a camp in the foothills, and from there, warriors go up nightly into the mountains to ambush the cauldron-born."

"Why do they not go into the caves and kill them in their nest?" Rowan asked.

"None dare venture in any more. Of all that have, only a few have ever returned. They could not afford to lose any more men." Lucia sighed sadly before she continued with her next bit of news. "Bran was the first to disappear."

"What?" Aveta cried in shock. "No!"

"Many believe he is dead, but I don't, and neither does Seren."
Lucia said.

"Poor woman." Aveta added. "Both her parents, and now her
brother? It is no wonder she clings to hope."

"Who now leads the clan, then?" Rowan asked.

"Aelhaearn," Lucia answered, finding herself a bit irritated at her
grandmother's seeming lack of compassion. "It's been a month
since Bran disappeared. After weeks with no sign of him, the
council insisted that Seren choose a new Protector and King. She
finally agreed, and two nights ago on *Nos Galan Gaeaf* she gave her
blessing to Aelhaearn, and the clan does now call him Chieftain."

"Well, he does bear the Firebrand," Rowan said, thoughtfully.

Lucia grew indignant at this comment and Aveta seemed to
notice, because she quickly asked, "How do our sisters fare?"

"They are well," Lucia said, trying her best to shake off her
temper. "Tired, as all are, but well. They are in the mountain camp
tending to the warriors."

"What happened, then?" Rowan asked. "Why did you leave?
Alone, no less?"

Lucia looked to Aveta and said, "You will perhaps not believe me
when I say this, but Lord Camulos came for me."

"What?" Aveta said, her eyes widening. "He lives?"

"Yes," Lucia answered, taking a brief moment to finish the last of
her broth. "He came for me the same night Aelhaearn was named
Chieftain, very late in the night. I'd had my share of mead, and

262

when I first saw his specter emerging from the shadows, I did not dare believe my eyes until I heard it speak and ask for me by name. I then thought his ghost had come to comfort me; to let me know all was well and he had found the Summerlands...to free me at last from wondering what had happened to him."

"But it was not his ghost?" Aveta prodded.

"No," Lucia replied, and then hesitated, trying to think of how best to explain to them the man he had become. "He lives, but only what meets your eyes speaks of Camulos; in his heart is naught of his former spirit."

"What do you mean?" Aveta asked, gently taking her empty bowl from her.

"In truth, I had misgivings from the start. He was violent and demanding when he asked for me, and managed quickly to anger Aelhaearn and all his warriors. I did not want to go with him. Later that night, however, I changed my mind, thinking perhaps his aggression sprang from an empty belly and the hardships he had endured. Elayn also reminded me that war hardens the heart of every man, and said perhaps he would soften into the man I knew before. I decided to go with him foremost to spare his life; I feared he would be killed if I chose to stay and he protested. Aelhaearn had already extended him more patience than he deserved..."

"I see," Aveta nodded in understanding. "What story did he give? Where has he been these two years past?"

Lucia continued, "As he told it, he lay dying on the battlefield after a raid on the garrison he was leading. Nearly all of his men were killed or died shortly after from their wounds. He said a woman came to him and offered to save his life in exchange for his help in the future, and he agreed. He woke to find himself being pulled from what he described as a vat of hot milk and tossed naked on the floor of a grotto. She told him she would find him when she needed him, and bid him leave. I asked him where he had been for the past two years, and he told me he had eventually figured out he was far north of the wall, deep in Caledonia, but I think he lied to me."

"As do I," Rowan agreed. All were silent a moment, each inwardly assessing what such a thing could mean. "This is a turn of events I didn't see coming. I suspect Cerridwen has known for some time that you have the Sight, and that is precisely why she saved Camulos' life. I believe she sent him to get you away from the clan so that she would have an opportunity to win you over. The Sight is the one gift from the Goddess she does not possess, Lucia. If you were to accept an offer to be apprenticed by a sorceress as powerful as she, and aid her with your gift in her ambitions, I fear to think what would be possible."

"That will never happen," Lucia said. "I promise you that. Besides, she is surely no more powerful than you!"

Surprisingly, Rowan shook her head at her comment. "No, Lucia. She is far more powerful than I. Not as wise, unfortunately, but far more powerful."

Lucia was shocked by her comment. "What do you mean? How is that possible? Didn't you teach her?"

"I did, but there are some who are *born* knowing, Lucia," her grandmother explained. "So it was with Cerridwen. Even when she was very small, she seemed to have a natural grasp of anything I taught her, no matter how advanced. It was as if she were simply *remembering* them, rather than learning them for the first time. She never had to be shown anything more than once, no matter how complicated."

Lucia thought for a moment, fear setting her heart to pound. "She must have visited my mother."

"It's likely," Rowan said.

Aveta agreed. "It was through your mother that I found you, Lucia, and came to be in your husband's household," she said, "but she made no mention of Cerridwen ever having visited her, and that she surely would have told me."

Lucia suddenly became sick, the broth she had just had turning sour in her stomach.

"Lucia, I am sure your mother is fine," Aveta said consolingly, guessing her thoughts. "Cerridwen was devastated when your mother left," she added. "I'm sure she would not harm her."

Lucia heard Aveta's words, but was not comforted, unnerved by her grandmother's silence on the subject.

Suddenly they were interrupted by some of the other sisters coming into the roundhouse with armloads of firewood. Rowan turned round. "Leave the wood and go, please," she said, at once both kind and commanding.

"I never should have gone with him," Lucia rued. "I knew I'd made a mistake, but I couldn't go back. He would have come for me again and Aelhaearn would have killed him."

"And so you came to us," Rowan concluded.

"Yes," Lucia answered, unable to tell if her grandmother approved or not. "The only chance I had to escape was after he fell asleep, which is how I came to be traveling by night." Lucia took a deep breath and coughed. She was beginning to tire, and could feel a fever coming on.

"I fear the coming days," Rowan said. "King Belenus is dead, and, I'm sorry, Lucia, but it's likely Lord Bran is as well. Hopefully Aelhaearn will lead well, but I fear for the East. Neirin now sits in his father's place, and far too soon, in my opinion. Let us hope he has a good portion of his father's wisdom and will live a long life. I would hate to see Queen Eirwen both widowed and childless."

Gwion, who had said nothing throughout the entire conversation, suddenly spoke. "Lady Lucia, you say Aelhaearn was named Chieftain two nights past, on *Nos Galan Gaeaf*?"

"Yes," Lucia said.

"There is a ballad Talhaiarn used to sing about four kings," Gwion said. "Grandmother, do you know it?"

"Yes," Rowan said. "Three kings who will rise and fall…"

"…and a fourth, who will fall and rise," Aveta added thoughtfully.

"Yes," Gwion said, reciting the ballad softly:

266

Three kings will rise, and then will fall,
The first betrayed within's own walls,

The second will pledge his all away,
to the unborn son of's enemy,

The third a false crown is bequeathed
when flames rise high, with bones beneath

The fourth will rise up from below,
to him the Mother will bestow
all things lost when he didst fall,
to rise again, and rule them all

"*When flames rise high, with bones beneath,*" repeated Gwion.

"The bonfires of *Nos Galan Gaeaf,*" Rowan said softly, obviously comprehending Gwion's meaning, which Lucia did not.

Aveta noticed Lucia's confusion and explained. "The ballad is believed to be an old prophecy, one so old I'd forgotten it. Gwion suggests Aelhaearn may be the third king the ballad sings of, falsely crowned."

Because Bran still lives, Lucia realized. "If Aelhaearn is the third king, then who are the other three?"

"Time will reveal who they are," Rowan said. "It also means when all is said and done, we will have a High King who will unite all the clans, one chosen by the Great Mother, and that would be a good thing," she said. "A very good thing, indeed."

CHAPTER SEVENTEEN
Lucia

As soon as Gethen had fully healed, Gwion left the island. Convinced as well that Bran still lived, he promised Lucia he would find him. Aveta tried to be strong without him, but she struggled. Without her son she seemed ever far away, lost in her thoughts.

"You must stop worrying, daughter," Rowan said one night at the evening meal. "Gwion is wiser than men three times his age, and more gifted than all of us. He is no warrior, but with his abilities he has no need of strength."

"It is not that," Aveta said. "I don't doubt his abilities."

"Then what is it?"

"I cannot shake this horrible feeling that I shall never see him again," she finally admitted, nearly unable to voice the words.

"You cannot think such things!" Lucia cried abruptly. She sat down beside her and put her arms around Aveta's shoulders, as Aveta had done for her so many times in the past. "Of course you will see him again!" she encouraged. "He is the cleverest young man I have ever known! If he says he is going to find Bran, you can believe it! I am sure we will see both of them again!"

Aveta stared into the fire. "I hope you're right, Lucia," she said quietly.

"He will soon be a man, Aveta." Rowan said. "Better he leaves us to seek his place in the world. The Great Mother means Gwion for greater things than being your son, or my grandson."

"I know, Mother!" Aveta said defensively, but then checked herself and softened her tone. "I know, all too well."

The others looked at her with understanding, as surely many of them had also sent their own sons away and grieved as she was grieving.

***

Lucia's leg had healed enough for her to walk on it, save for a limp that she regarded as a gentle but constant reminder to be grateful to the Guardians for saving her life. She could now at least sit at the loom, prepare food and keep the fire burning, all things she was more than happy to do. Lying on her back with nothing but her worries to keep her occupied had been torture.

She was beginning to fall in step with the rhythm of life on the island, and found it was one she very much enjoyed. During the day the Sisters fished, hunted, collected water and firewood, worked at spinning and weaving, brewed mead, made candles, embroidered, swam, or practiced throwing a spear or shooting a bow. The older women taught the younger many things, and Lucia put strong effort into learning as much as she could, for it seemed even the youngest girls were beyond her in many of their skills.

Every night as the sun dipped close to the horizon they gathered around the fire in the motherhouse and prayed, each woman communing with the spirits in her own way. After a certain amount of time, never quite the same, Rowan would speak. Sometimes about mundane things important to their survival, like a shortage of wood or water that needed attending to, and sometimes about the messages or revelations she received in prayer. After she spoke, she would ask if there were others who wanted to share. Sometimes there were, and sometimes not. After everyone who wished to had spoken, they shared the evening meal together, which was either some kind of stew or fish roasted over the fire, bread, and apples--apples such as Lucia had never tasted before in her life. Apple trees grew all over the island, and the fruit they bore was better than any she had ever eaten. The Sisters made wine from it, and given her choice of mead or apple wine, Lucia always chose the latter.

All of the Sisters could play the harp and sing, but some had been gifted with voices that set the heart to soaring and eyes to weeping; voices so exquisite, that when they sang, the soul would leap in joyful recognition of the divine.

Lucia's mother was such a woman, and hearing the women of the isle took her back to the childhood hours she had spent sitting at her mother's feet listening to her, soothed, enraptured and mesmerized. She recalled how her mother had sung to her whenever she had suffered from the terrible visions which haunted her as a girl. All children have nightmares from time to time, and parents comfort them by saying they are naught but dreams, but not Lucia's. No, hers, unfortunately, *did* come true, and it was her mother's voice that had kept her from falling into the abyss; her beautiful voice, which flew into the dark storm cloud of her fear like a dove on silver vespers, white wings cutting through the blackness and revealing the light behind it, guiding her back out.

For hours each night before retiring, the Sisters took turns singing songs of great kings and queens, the gods and guardians, heroes who vanquished great enemies to save their people, women so radiant and glorious that no man nor god could refuse them anything, and common men with courageous hearts who were challenged by the gods and emerged victorious…

Night after night, as the sound of their music rose up through the thatched roof of their motherhouse, Lucia began to notice that she could feel the Guardians draw near to listen, a feeling so sublime she would weep for joy because she no longer only sensed when evil approached; she could feel when the divine leaned in closely as well.

As she learned more about the many faces of the Great Mother the Sisters worshipped, she found she already knew one of them very well. In the Christian faith, the Great Mother wore the mantle of Mary, the mother of Christ Jesus, and Lucia realized the altar dedicated to Mary that her mother had worshipped at was likely in truth an altar to the Great Mother whom she had grown up worshipping on the island. Yes, the Great Goddess was known by this name, but also by many others. She was Maiden, Mother, and Crone, constantly changing yet ever-willingly surrendering herself in love to her lord and consort, who also had many names—Cernunnos the Horned One, Warrior, Protector. Her power was not subordinate to his, but equal, and they stood forever loyal to one another, side by side. Together the Lord and Lady danced together, eternally, in a never-ending spiral, as many different partners throughout time and in all aspects of life; his strength shining forth as the sun to her moon, his passion overwhelming her as a lover to her maiden, his wrath as a champion for her protection, his obedience as a loyal son to a mother, his guidance as a father to her daughter, his knowledge as light penetrating the darkness of her mystery, and his action from her inspiration. The Lord to the Great Mother was all these things, but a suppressor, controller, or silencer of his beloved, he was not.

As the days passed, Lucia began caring less and less about the world that lay outside the mists of the island, and other than to see Bran and Gwion again, found she had no desire to return to it.

CHAPTER EIGHTEEN
The Crystal Cave

Bran awoke in misery, for he could not feel his fingers or toes, nor could he stop his teeth from chattering. His clothes were damp, and he wondered if somehow he might have rolled too near the stream as he slept. He had no idea what time of day or night it might be. After a moment of groping, he rose and felt his way along the walls of the black tunnel, seeking to know his surroundings better. He felt grooves along its sides, obviously scratched out by the fingernails of the cauldron-born as they scraped away the earth to form the tunnel. His only comfort was the sound of the stream flowing along the passage with him, like a friendly companion. He continued downstream, convinced the water must eventually lead him to freedom. *It must!* He tried not to think of how long he had been walking, reaching nothing, forcing down any impulse of panic or despondency, but soon even the stream sounded mocking and ominous to him.

Suddenly he heard something other than the sound of the water and his own breath. Whatever it was, it was coming toward him. He pressed his body against the side of the passage, waiting to strike. It was certainly the shuffling sound of bare feet or hands upon the earth, not the sound any of his companions would make, and so when it came near enough, he reached out, found its neck, and snapped it with one swift move.

He listened in the dark intently, wondering if more were soon to follow, but none came. He severed his victim's head and carried it by the hair with him, continuing along the stream.

Increasingly, he began to hear many sounds echoing through the corridor, carried on the foul air blowing through the tunnels. *They are waking*, he realized. *It must be night.* He was surprisingly grateful for the eerie cries, for they gave him something to focus on, as well as cued him which way to go, sometimes revealing a passage to his left or right. If he could find the creatures and secretly follow them, they would unwittingly lead him out of this terrible place. He moved along in the darkness until eventually the sounds led him to a place where cold air and a fine mist hit his face. He listened carefully and heard the stream he had been following flowing over what he felt to be a mossy ledge, cascading into a pool which seemed to be some distance below. He listened carefully for the sounds of the cauldron-born, but heard nothing but the water. He wondered how deep the pool was, and tossed a large rock over the ledge. The sound of the water when it splashed told Bran the pool was deep enough to swim in. *It could be a way out!*

He took a chance and dove into the pool from up above and the icy water swallowed him up. He cautiously swam to the surface, head and sword still in hand. He had no idea which way he should swim, as everything was as black as soot, and so he simply let the water's current carry him until he encountered a disheartening sight: several limpid eyes, all trained on him. *So much for finding them without being seen.* The current carried him directly toward them. Soon he felt rock beneath his feet, and in true warrior spirit, he burst forth from the water, a terrible force of vengeance, the head of his latest victim held high in his left hand, and *Dyrnwyn* vice-gripped in his right. They swarmed him like insects, their fingernails and teeth sinking into his flesh, but Bran was full of might and wrath, and though he had suffered many wounds, in the end he had ten more heads to add to the first.

He tossed them all into the water, letting the current carry them far from the bodies he had struck them from, and then waited, hoping eventually more would come into the chamber that he could secretly follow. He felt his way along in the darkness, trying to get an idea of how big the chamber was, and while he felt his way around his hand came upon a piece of rope; rope made of uniquely-braided horse-hair. The rope of his tribe. He wondered if somehow this was the same cavern that earlier in the day had been lit by small slivers of sunlight, where he and his men had discussed posting archers. Either that, or his companions did not make it out, and this rope was what is left of them. He felt around for bodies or other clues, but found nothing. He then realized this could not possibly be the same cavern. He had followed the stream, and water flowed downward. There was no way he could have traveled as far as he had, and ended up standing *above* the place he had started from!

He searched the cavern walls for passageways, and found many. He used his blade to carve a mark into the rock above the one he chose to explore first, so that he would know the place should he encounter it again. It took hours to come to the end of the first tunnel, his progress slow as he had to walk hunched over, his broad shoulders barely clearing the sides. Eventually he emerged, thrilled to stand up, but to his dismay he found himself not outside, but rather on yet another ledge within an echoing cavern. One that sounded too familiar. He looked above him, wondering if he would be able to see light from above. It had to be morning by now! He peered upward, but saw nothing but blackness. He was too tired to dive down and try another tunnel, and so laid down and slept there upon the ledge, desperately hoping he would see daylight when he awoke.

***

Bran did not wake to sunlight as he had wished. Again, only blackness greeted him when he opened his eyes, and again, he tested the depth of the water beneath him and jumped down into the pool. He listened carefully for the cauldron-born, looking for the sick light of their eyes, but this time there were none lurking about. It must indeed be daytime, he thought. He felt along the perimeter of the cavern above each of the tunnels, and eventually he found the mark he had made. He proceeded to the next tunnel to his right, carved a new symbol above it, and moved in to see where it led. He noticed right away that it was different. There were numerous tunnels leading off to the left and right as he made his way through, foul odors coming from some. He followed four of them in turn, making a mental map in his head, hoping they would lead him to the room where he and his companions had first encountered the corpses. The tunnels he followed invariably did lead to corpses, but unfortunately none led to a way out. They were simply dead ends, in the truest sense; deep holes filled with the bones and carcasses of the victims the cauldron-born had fed upon.

As he finished exploring yet another of their disgusting pits and was making his way back toward the main tunnel, he was alarmed by the sound of several cauldron-born making their way toward him. Had night fallen again so quickly? His sense of time was so impaired! He could scarcely move his body through the small tunnel, so he knew there was no way he would be able to swing a sword in such a small space. They decidedly had the advantage. Instead he returned to the pit, where the only option left to him was to jump down into it. The stench of rotting bodies overwhelmed him and he suppressed the urge to vomit, covering his mouth and nose tightly with his tunic and breathing through his mouth. The cauldron-born were dragging something behind them, and he heard the hideous sounds of what seemed to be at least three or four of them feeding upon whatever they've brought in, tearing it to pieces. He hoped it was an animal, but judging from the number of human bodies in the pit surrounding him, it probably wasn't.

They eventually tossed the remains of their victim down into the pit, and Bran waited until he could no longer hear them before he began searching the bodies in the pit for supplies. As he was there, he may as well make the best of it. He managed to find flint, old rope, a few small weapons and some clothing that would prove to be of use. He had the means now to light a torch, he realized. He took a long bone, wrapped it with rags and worked the flint until he was able to ignite it.

The moment he achieved his goal he regretted it, for the light of the torch fell upon a mangled body that he knew well.

"*Gareth!*" he whispered. "*Not you, brother! Not you! Not you!*"

A fire of rage then consumed him that could not be contained, and he let forth a thunderous, wrathful cry of agony, which echoed eerily through the chambers of hell. It wasn't long before he spied several cauldron-born peering down into the pit from above. To Bran's delight they began jumping in to attack him, trying to pull him down, and though he was outnumbered, they could not. Bran's feet were steady, as if rooted in the earth like an oak.

More poured in from above, and to Bran's shock *Dyrnwyn* suddenly alighted in blue fire, flames flowing up its blade, as if it had ignited from within. He remembered hearing the legend of the blade of *Dyrnwyn* acting so when righteously engaged, and was mightily encouraged. He mowed the creatures down with renewed vengeance, yelling in their faces like a mad man as he ruthlessly severed heads.

He soon stood soaked in their blood, their bodies piled knee-deep around him, yet the beast of his wrath was not yet satisfied. He yelled and yelled, calling out to his enemies, daring them to come, his chest rising and falling, his heart pounding, an iron grip around the hilt of the flaming sword of his people, until finally, no more came.

He looked over to where Gareth's body lay. He could not suffer this to be his final resting place. He would take his body with him and give him a proper Southern burial. He had to escape the pit, but it was clear the walls were far too high and too smooth to climb, especially carrying Gareth's body. After thinking a moment, he realized what must be done. He hacked the heads off every corpse in the pit so that none would ever rise again, and then proceeded to build a stairway with the only material available to him.

Two hours later, the gruesome structure stood towering over him. He picked up Gareth's body and climbed out of the pit upon the backs of the dead.

Weeks passed, and Bran learned to navigate quite well in the darkness, for his senses had grown much sharper. He could easily hear and even smell when the cauldron-born approached, and was getting much better at following them undetected.

He had a simple routine that kept him from going mad; sleep while the cauldron-born hunted, and work while the cauldron-born slept. He returned every night to the pit he had found Gareth in, hoping not to find any familiar faces among the new corpses. He stripped the new bodies of everything left on them, severed their heads, and then crawled back out upon his human staircase. So far he had managed to amass quite a bit of rope and a great many weapons which he placed strategically throughout the tunnels. From the jewelry he found, he made lures and fishhooks.

He had tried each tunnel leading from the main cavern in turn, traveling along some of them for hours, but to his disappointment they all eventually led him back to the main cavern. Neither had his efforts succeeded in following the cauldron-born out…somehow he was always detected or he lost them.

He saw only one other possible way to escape his prison, and that was to swim out. He bided his time until the cauldron-born left to feed, and then dove into the icy water to search for underwater passages. After several attempts he finally found what he was looking for. He attempted to swim through, but to his dismay it was far longer than he expected. He could not make it, and had to swim back. By the time he pulled out of the underwater tunnel his lungs were nearly bursting, and he broke the surface of the pool gasping desperately for air. He would have to swim faster. He tried again, getting a bit further, but still couldn't find any place to come up for air.

For the next few nights he continued to work at it, getting a bit further each time, but the span was simply too far to swim. He needed to find a place to breathe along the way. He tried swimming along the top of the corridor, face and hands up, feeling for any pocket in the rock where he could take a breath and rest. He counted as he moved along under the water, knowing exactly how much time he had before he had to turn back. At ten, fifteen, twenty, and twenty-five he had found nothing, but like a miracle, at thirty his hand felt air! He pushed his face up, holding on to crevices in the rock. There was not enough space to bring his head completely out of the water, but there was enough for his mouth and nose, and he breathed in gratefully. Now, he would be able to explore twice as far. He submerged again and pulled himself along the rock as rapidly as he could, feeling for more pockets. He found another at the count of thirteen, then another at seventeen, and another at twenty-seven, and then, finally, he felt the passage open up. Suddenly there was no longer rock over him, just water. He floated silently toward the surface and emerged. He breathed as slowly and quietly as he could, even though every fiber of his being wanted to greedily swallow huge lungfuls of air. He found he could stand, and so he did, silent as death, listening intently to his surroundings. He heard nothing but the sound of water dripping into the pool, and by the sound of it, from a place far above his head. He noticed he could no longer feel where his body ended and the water began.

Suddenly, he heard something moving far on the other side of the cavern. Then, he heard it slip into the water, barely disturbing the pool. He knew he had no time to lose. He swam furiously away from the sound and came to a wall. There was not much of a lip to stand on, but he could climb upwards from it. He pulled himself out of the pool swiftly and climbed furiously up the side of the cave, frantically feeling for foot and handholds. One thing was certain, he was not back in the main cavern. He had successfully found another chamber, but he wondered if he would soon regret it.

Upon the wall he felt hundreds of tiny clusters of pointed rock, some big, some small, jutting out in all directions with many facets and angles. He moved along slowly, struggling to find hand and footholds, but he managed. He was able to get some twenty feet from the surface of the pool before something obviously quite large lurched out of the water, its jaws snapping just below where he clung, and splashed back down into the water.

He knew he would not be safe for long. Whatever it was, it could navigate on both land and water, and it was not yet clear which one it preferred. He had to find some solid footing! He moved along the wall for what seemed like forever, knowing he was being silently followed by the creature below.

Eventually, he felt the wall he was climbing start to angle and turn. He wondered if there were still water beneath him, or if he might be able to stand on the floor of the cavern. He managed to find a good handhold on the other side, and then swung around. He was still facing the wall, unable to turn, but to his great joy he noticed he could faintly see his hands grasping clear stones that looked like ice. *Great Mother be praised, there is light in here!* he thought gratefully. He climbed toward it, ever higher, and finally leaning backward then saw the source of the pale light illuminating the cavern from overhead: a narrow crevice in the rock, just wide enough to let the light of the moon and stars through. He nearly cried for joy. *A way out!*

He moved along the wall slowly and carefully toward the crevice as silently as he could, looking for a secure place to put his feet. He finally found one that felt wide enough to stand upon and he was able to turn around and take a good look at his surroundings.

He was awestruck. Every bit of faint light that managed to make its way in from overhead was reflected off thousands of crystal facets in the walls, as if the entire cave were made of ice.

Then, he surveyed what lay below. The pool went on as far as he could see. There was nothing but water beneath him except for a small peninsula formed from crystals and stalagmites that stretched out into the center of the pool. Then, Bran's heart leapt, *for on that peninsula, sat the Cauldron.*

He wondered if the Cauldron had somehow transformed the cavern into the glittering citadel it now was, or if it had always been so. Either way, it was clear why Cerridwen had chosen it. Smoke from the many fires that had been burned beneath the cauldron could rise and escape, and there were only two ways in or out that Bran could see – either through the crevice overhead, which he doubted any man could fit through, save a small child, or through the watery passage, which had taken him four nights to manage. *How does she come and go?* he wondered.

Bran heard a splash and looked down. He could now see the creature that had been stalking him in the clear water below. It was an eel-like fish the length of a man, with silvery skin. It had a lower jaw longer than its upper, featuring needle-like protruding teeth, and Bran smiled. Those teeth meant the creature ate meat, which meant its own flesh would very likely offer much more sustenance than the tiny meager fare he had been surviving on. He was ravenous for something other than the small fish, insects and bats he had been eating over the past month, and the idea of a large fish dinner set his mouth to watering.

He had to make it to the peninsula. He continued to move along the wall toward his destination, surveying all of the angles in the crevice overhead with his sharp cave-conditioned eyesight, and patiently made his way there. When he finally reached it, he noticed that the gap in the rock above him was far larger than he had originally thought, and his heart pounded with the thrilling prospect of escape.

The Cauldron sat but feet from him, looming ominously within the crystal chamber, filled with a pearlescent liquid that seemed to churn on its own. Though he wanted nothing more than to return it to its rightful place, he knew it was impossible. Even if he were strong enough to turn it over and pour out the liquid, it would be too heavy for him to lift, and even if he were strong enough to lift it, it would be impossible to fit it through the gap overhead. It would need to remain where it was.

Bran surveyed the gap overhead, thinking about how he was going to climb out, when suddenly his senses screamed at him. He looked around him and saw dozens of eel-fish swimming toward the peninsula, but he knew that was not the only cause for his alarm. He turned around to see an enormous dark wolf emerging from the darkness on the opposite end of the peninsula.

Bran unsheathed *Dyrnwyn*. It ignited as it had before, flames flowing toward the top of the blade, and the eel-fish swarmed toward the light in a frenzy. The sound of splashing water echoed ominously through the cavern as the thing bared its jaws, slowly closing in on him.

It finally leapt and attacked, its jaws snapping inches from Bran's neck. In that instant, Bran's memory flashed back to the wounds he remembered seeing on his mother's neck, and on Cadoc's corpse. *Wolf attack,* many had said. *Wolf attack.* A flood of purpose flowed into his veins as he surmised the truth of what had happened, strengthening his focus. He waited, calmly, for the beast to come to him.

He lunged with renewed fury against the black abomination, hungry to avenge his mother, but it easily overpowered him, this time picking him up and hurling him toward the mouth of the Cauldron. Bran managed to avoid its milky maw, but came dangerously close to falling into the lake in doing so. *Was it was **trying** to throw him into the Cauldron?* he wondered in horror.

He thought out his next move carefully. He was weary of darkness and his hunger for revenge, and knew this would be perhaps his only chance to rid himself of both. He ran toward where he had seen the beast emerge from the darkness, trading positions with the beast and putting it in the compromised position out on the peninsula, and waited for his enemy's next move.

The beast surprised him by leaping over the water and onto the cavern wall, high above where Bran stood, gaining the advantage back. Its long claw-like fingers held it securely, and Bran realized quickly he would not win this battle with brute force. He looked desperately around him for anything or any place he could use to secure his victory.

The beast attacked again, jumping from above to try and knock him back toward the Cauldron once more. Bran maneuvered out of the way and quickly delivered a blow which sent the wolf-man into a rage. It attacked yet again, within seconds. Bran tried repeatedly to get his sword into the beast's vulnerable neck or underbelly, but to no avail. *Dyrnwyn* was too big and too long to thrust up into its belly. He would have to use a dagger, and that meant he would have to let himself be pinned.

He sheathed *Dyrnwyn* and pulled out Gareth's dagger, staring into the creature's face as they circled one another. He knew the passage behind him might possibly lead to a way out, but he refused to trade the possibility of escape for the guarantee of it. He had seen the stars through that gap in the cavern, and he would get himself through it. Tonight. *He would not return to darkness without stars.*

Bran waited patiently for it to attack again, but this time allowed it to pin him, and then thrust the dagger of his fallen brother deep into the heart of the black beast. The creature let forth an eerily human sounding cry of pain, but still managed to sink its teeth into Bran's flesh before it died, and Bran heard his own howl reverberate through the cavern.

Then, something strange happened. Still pinned beneath the beast, Bran felt his adversary change; twisting and shrinking…he pushed away from it in shock and disgust, leapt to his feet and unsheathed *Dyrnwyn*, its blade again rimmed in blue flames. The light of his sword now revealed nothing more than a severely deformed man, Gareth's dagger plunged deep within his breast.

Bran stood over the horrific scene, covered in blood, its tell-tale rusty, metallic smell filling his nostrils and assailing his mind with memories of the battlefield. After catching his breath, he reclaimed his dagger and dragged the hideous thing to the edge of the pool where he hewed off its deformed head and then heaved both head and body into the water. The eel-fish were soon swarming around the body. By morning, there would be nothing left of it but bones.

Blood poured from the wound on his shoulder. He knew he would bleed to death if he didn't find a way to stop it. He rinsed it in the pool the best he could and then cauterized the three deep gashes left behind by the wolf's claws with the flames of *Dyrnwyn*.

Bran then weakly made his way out to the end of the peninsula. He tied his rope to the hilt of his sword and sent it sailing up into the pale light above through the crevice until the blade wedged itself securely into the rock overhead. He wrapped himself about the rope and climbed up toward the surface, using his good arm and legs. His injured shoulder burned as if it were being branded by a hot iron, but it was nothing compared to his frantic desperation for freedom. He soon reached the top, but to his dismay the opening was not quite wide enough. With some difficulty he managed to fashion himself a sling with his rope and chipped away at the rock and soil, focusing on the sight of the moon and stars until the hole he had carved was big enough for him to crawl through. Tears came to his eyes as the sight of the sky and smell of fresh air greeted him. He climbed victoriously out of his prison, pulling his body out of the crevice with the last bit of strength he had left.

More exhausted than he had ever been in his life, he rolled over on his back and lay under the open sky gazing up at the moon, filled with boundless gratitude.

CHAPTER NINETEEN
Ula

Bran woke to the blush of the dawn on his sensitive eyes, and a soothing sound in the distance. He sat up and found himself in a completely foreign terrain. The mountains he was used to seeing no longer sat on the eastern horizon. He stood up and looked all around, finding himself upon a wide bluff, but recognized nothing in any direction. He looked down at the ground where he had dug himself out of the cavern only a few hours before, but found there was nothing there but earth and grass.

He explored the land and eventually came to the edge of a tremendous cliff covered in yellow gorse bushes, where the vast blue expanse of the sea greeted him from far below. *Impossible,* he thought, trying to grasp how this could be. The sea lay miles from where his clan lived, nearly four days travel on horseback, yet he could not deny what he saw. Regardless of the seeming impossibility of it, Bran felt immense joy at the majestic sight. From the time he had first seen the sea, he had longed to return to it, like a lover from his past he could never forget. One day, when he could no longer lift his sword in battle, he would go and live quietly by her side with a few horses and a small forge, and a woman to keep his bed warm. He suddenly thought of Lucia, and imagined living with her there in peace.

He winced as his shoulder suddenly throbbed with pain, pulling him from his thoughts and reminding him that it badly needed attention. He would need to make a paste from ashes or mud for the wound, as there were few herbs that could be found growing or blooming this time of year. Winter had taken most all of them beneath her blanket. He luckily happened across some witch hazel shrubs, and though they were of little use for wood, the bark and leaves mashed into a poultice would curb the bleeding and keep the wound from becoming infected. He went to a small stream running nearby and removed his tunic. He rinsed the wound clean and then examined it well for the first time. He had not been able to clearly see it until now. To his disappointment it was far worse than he had imagined. He found some flat rocks and worked the bark and leaves into a mud paste which he then smeared on the wound. He tore the bottom of his tunic off and soaked it in the stream, and then tied it around his shoulder, bandaging the poultice in place. It would have to do for now.

He suddenly felt the urge to run; he had been trapped in small tunnels for so long, unable to stretch his limbs or stand up fully. He took off toward the cliffs overlooking the sea, striding along the edge, exhilarated by the space around him, his blood running freely through his veins, watching the birds sailing on the winds gusting up from the sea far below. Such stunning landscape he had never seen before. *Finally, free!* To see the sky, breathe fresh air, and feel the cold wind upon his face...*Great Mother, thank you!*

He didn't stop except to drink. For the entire length of the day he ran along the cliffs, tasting the salty air upon his lips and watching the sunlight glint upon the water until the sun began to dip down once again toward the horizon.

He stopped near a place where he could climb down to a small beach below. There, he collected driftwood and lit a fire, feeding it slowly until it blazed, warming his hands and face. He thought of Seren, for if she still lived she would now be lighting the nightly bonfire for his clan. *Please, protect my sister,* he prayed to the Guardians. He would never forgive himself if anything happened to her before he made it home. She was the only family left to him, and guilt seized him thinking of how he had sworn before the clan to protect her. He had accepted the title of Protector and then disappeared, leaving her and the rest of the clan to fend for themselves. Who knew what sort of misfortune had befallen his people while he had been away? *Gareth certainly paid for it with his life*, he thought, sickened.

Perhaps Aelhaearn had been right about him that day they had nearly come to blows. Could he resist a battle call when duty demanded he stay behind? Was it possible for him to tolerate the thought of another warrior bringing home a victory that could have been his? He had to admit it was his selfish pride that had prodded him to lead the search party to the caves. He had convinced himself he needed to go, but truly, he went because he could not stand the thought of staying behind with the women and children.

Again, his thoughts were interrupted by his shoulder which ached terribly. He had been so busy he had paid it no mind, but now sitting quietly it had begun to rebel, insisting he pay it some attention.

He removed his bandage to examine it. *Ugh, ghastly!* The salt water would do it good, and he needed to catch himself some dinner, anyway. After a few moments of searching he found a long slim piece of driftwood. He whittled it to a sharp point and undressed and walked into the surf, bracing himself for the icy water. Once in, he rubbed the old mud and poultice off and waded deep enough to soak the wound. It burned fiercely, reassuring Bran the salt was doing its job. He then set himself to the task of spearing some fish, which he accomplished quickly. He had become quite skilled at spear-fishing in the caves, and he was soon drying off and roasting them over his fire. Great Mother, how good they would taste! His mouth watered at the thought of finally having a proper meal.

He watched the sun set for the first time in over a month while he ate his catch, and then slept more soundly than an infant in his mother's arms.

***

Bran woke to the dawn and sound of the gulls crying overhead, hunting for their breakfast. He would do the same before setting out. He put more wood on the coals which were still hot from the night before, and ventured out on the rocks. He was patient and clever, and eventually fortune granted him a few crabs. After cooking and breaking them open, he had the gulls to fight off, eager to take his breakfast rather than hunt for their own. He would normally be irritated, but it delighted him to interact with any living creature after what he had been through.

While enjoying the sunrise and sucking the last bit of meat out of his first crab, he noticed something bobbing out in the surf. He watched it intently, and after some time determined it must be a head, but too small to belong to a person. It came closer, disappeared, and then reappeared close enough for him to realize he had been watching a seal playing in the waves.

He broke open the second crab with his dagger and went to sit on the outcropping of rocks where he had caught it. The seal stayed bobbing in the water, watching, obviously curious about him. He smiled.

"Come closer!" he called, holding out a meat-filled claw. When the little seal was close enough that the gulls couldn't intercept it, he tossed it to her.

She munched eagerly on the claw and came closer, hoping to receive another gift.

"I worked hard for that. I hope you enjoyed it!" he said, tossing her another piece and taking one for himself. He shared the rest of it with her until there was not a morsel left, and then rose to leave.

"Farewell, little friend," he said. "I must find my way home somehow." His time underground had made certain things abundantly clear. He was eager to be surrounded by his people again, and to see Lucia.

The seal looked at him expectantly, and Bran smiled at her innocence as he returned to his small camp. After putting out the fire and collecting his things from the beach, he looked out to sea for her, but she had disappeared.

He had seen a herd of wild ponies in the distance up on the bluff, and with any luck, he had be able to use his skills to rope one and eventually ride it. He thought of his beloved Gethen and longed for his old companion. What a glorious time they would have had the day before, galloping along the ocean cliffs…

He started climbing up the cliff toward the bluff when suddenly heard a strange call. He turned around and to his shock saw a woman below him on the beach, naked and dripping wet, with long black hair and dark eyes, holding her wet clothes.

"Gods, woman!" he yelled, startled. She ran back into the surf, clothes and all, ready to dive back in the ocean.

"No! Wait! Don't go!" he called, bewildered as to where she could have come from, but she was already in the water, staring at him with fear in her eyes. He scrambled down the cliff, elated to have encountered another person.

"Are you hurt?" Bran spoke softly, wading slowly to where she was, but the closer he came the farther out she swam.

"No, please! Come back! Can you understand me? Is your village nearby?"

He made his hands visible, trying to make himself look less threatening.

"I won't hurt you," he said, but by now he was fairly sure she didn't understand him. Could she be from across the sea? One of the invaders women? If so, he would have trouble soon, as she would surely go and tell her husband (or master, if she were a slave) about him.

He waded further out, extending his hand. "Please," he said.

She was darker than the Saxon women, and smaller. Where could she have come from?

She would not come any closer, but at least she wasn't swimming away from him anymore. In a desperate act he saw a fish swimming by, and caught it with his bare hands.

"Are you hungry?" he asked, holding the fish up. She looked interested. "Come!" he said, encouraging her.

He slowly backed out of the sea, keeping his eyes on her. He had but recently left the fire, so quickly had it going again and sat upon the beach, roasting the fish and watching her, hoping to the gods his plan would work. It was the only thing left he could think of.

She watched him intently, eventually swimming a little closer. *Good*, he thought. *At least she's curious.*

He began eating the fish off the spear, and after a few moments she came out of the water, still holding her clothes, which appeared to be made from sealskin. She set them down carefully on a rock and slowly approached him. She took hold of his spear and he let her take it, holding his hands up in a gesture of surrender.

She pulled the fish carefully off the spear and then moved away to the rocks and began eating it.

"Do you have a name?"

Silence.

"Can you take me to your village?

Silence.

To his dismay she didn't understand a word he was saying, and beauty or no, he could not afford to waste any more time here. The morning would soon be gone.

"I must go now," he said softly, rising slowly to stand, so as not to startle her. He wondered again how she had come to be here. She was very young, and looked as if she might have been a shipwreck victim, living on this tiny beach alone. He couldn't bring himself to leave her here alone.

"Please, come with me." Again he held his hand out to her. She looked at him intently. Suddenly she slung her garment over her shoulders, took the spear, and came to him. She picked up his hand and examined it, looking back and forth between her own hands and his.

"Come!" he said, motioning toward the top of the cliff. He began walking up and to his delight, she followed him. Together they ascended to the top.

"Can you help me find the horses? Do you know where they run?" he asked her. He made a few horse sounds, hoping she would know what he meant, but she just smiled at him. *She must think I'm not right in the head,* he thought, imagining how he looked and sounded to her. He tried drawing a picture of a horse in the dirt with a stick, and still she looked at him blankly. Finally he gave up and headed off toward the open pasture, where he would likely find them himself. Again, she followed him.

As they walked inland, the landscape slowly undulated into rolling hills. Their path occasionally crossed over a brook where they stopped to drink. Bran noticed his companion slowly becoming more relaxed, even playful with him, as the day wore on. By late afternoon, Bran finally spied the herd of wild horses he had been looking for. He smiled and pointed them out to her. "Horses!"

She looked at him finally with understanding and followed him across the hills toward where the herd was grazing.

Bran looked at all of them, making his choice carefully. They looked strong, albeit a little small for his taste. Any of them would be perfect for her, although he wasn't sure if she could ride or not. If she couldn't, they would have a problem. Being the size and weight that he was, they most certainly would not be able to ride together.

Suddenly the girl ran to a mottled gray mare, shaggy with its winter coat. To Bran's shock, the horse didn't stop grazing. He slowly approached but the mare smelled him and looked up, ears pricked. The girl stroked the mare's muzzle and it relaxed. The horse was familiar with her.

"Do these horses belong to your people?" he asked, motioning all around them. "I must ask to borrow one, to return to my village." He hoped she could understand at least the urgency of his plea.

She got on the mare's back and then rode to where one of the larger mares was grazing. The woman reached over and touched her. Bran took this gesture as permission to approach. The horse shook its head and laid its ears back, but the woman again reached over and touched the beast soothingly and she calmed down.

He fashioned a bridle from his rope, thinking back to when his mother had first taught him to tie one so many years ago. He had been only a small boy at the time. He then walked up very slowly toward the side of the horse's head, speaking in low tones. He wooed the horse with all the skills of his tribe, and finally found himself upon her back, the bridle about her head.

"Let's go," he said to the woman, pointing the mare toward the East.

"I must get back to my village," he added.

Her blank look reminded him of how useless his words were, so he simply pointed again and started on his way. Again, she followed closely behind.

"You want to come along?" he asked her. *Well, she's welcome to,* he thought. She seemed able enough to care for herself, and her innocence was refreshing to him after so much darkness.

His plan was to ride inland, away from the sea. If all went well, he would begin recognizing the horizon within the next three days and then be able to navigate his way to his village. Hopefully he would find it still standing, or at least everyone he loved still alive. He prayed the warriors had been successful in keeping the cauldron-born at bay, and the men from the other clans had arrived as promised. He was suddenly filled with dread knowing he would have to tell Einon about what had happened to Gareth in the caves. *May the Guardians keep you well,* he prayed silently to his cousin, looking up into the sky.

After some time his thoughts returned to the present. He turned back to look at his new companion. She was wearing her seal skin barely slung about her, one breast and most of her skin exposed, but she seemed completely comfortable. He knew he had a strong resistance to the cold, thanks to his father, his mother had always told him, but hers obviously far surpassed his.

"I shall have to come up with a name for you if we are to travel together." he finally said. "I'm BRAN," he added loudly.

She looked at him strangely. He then smiled at his ridiculousness. The girl wasn't deaf.

"Bran," he said again more softly, looking over at her, placing his palm on his chest. *"Bran."*

He then pointed to her with an expectant look.

She simply patted her own chest.

He nodded, acknowledging the failure of his attempts at communication. He would simply *give* her a name. As they rode he ran through some names in his head, and finally settled on Ula; simple, pretty, and easy to say. If he remembered correctly, it was a name the people across the western sea gave their daughters which meant, "gem of the sea." It was perfect.

He stopped his horse and she stopped beside him. Again, he put his hand on his chest. "Bran."

Then he reached over and put his hand on her. "Ula," he said. He repeated this a few more times until she finally brought her own hand to her chest and barked out, "Ula!" then pointed to him and said, "Bran!"

He was beyond pleased with himself and laughed for joy. "Yes! That's it. I'm Bran, you're Ula!" They certainly would not be singing verses of mead hall songs around the fire anytime soon, but at least it was something.

They rode for the rest of the day, Bran picking up the pace, and Ula staying close behind him. Riding bareback was certainly not the most comfortable way to ride, but she seemed to be a natural at it. In fact, from the way she rode, he doubted she had ever been in a saddle. He watched her throughout the day. Escaped slave, perhaps? Fisherman's daughter? She looked unlike any of the clans he knew well.

When evening approached he resolved to talk to her more so that she could learn some of his words. "Ula, we must look for a place to sleep." He closed his eyes and tilted his head to one side against his hands. "Sleep," he said again.

She looked at him with understanding, but then galloped off toward a tree line perhaps a mile or so away. His horse soon followed with no signal from him. Once in the trees, she led the way, and soon the sound of water met Bran's ears. He followed her along a small stream. The last of the day's sunlight was coming down through the trees, and it was beginning to get colder. Eventually, the stream led them to a large waterfall feeding a pool, somewhat iced over, which the girl was obviously familiar with. To Bran's shock she jumped off her horse, ran to the water and dove in. Was she mad? That water was surely freezing!

"What are you doing!" he yelled. "It's nearly nightfall!" He jumped off his horse as well and led the animals to a tree at the water's edge and tied them up, waiting for her to emerge. He would need to get a large fire going.

"Ula!" he yelled after a minute, but she didn't come up.

"Ula!" he yelled again, more urgently.

Oh, gods…is she drowning? He pulled off his boots and sword and was just about to dive in when she emerged, smiling from ear to ear, with four fish in her hands.

"Bran!" she yelled back. She came out of the water, smacked the fish's heads on the flat rocks at the side of the pool and held them out to him proudly.

Shocked, he took them from her. How had she done it? Four fish in less than two minutes, with her *bare hands*?

"Thank you," he said, bewildered. He tried to give her his fur cape, both to warm her and so that he could keep his eyes off her naked body, but she refused it and motioned for him to follow her. She walked toward the wide waterfall feeding the pool. "Sleep!" she cried victoriously.

She was standing in a large stone cave behind the water, perfectly dry, with room enough for the horses as well. Bran had no desire to go anywhere near a cave, but he had to admit it was perfect. If the cauldron-born came roaming this far, he and his companion would be completely hidden, and the waterfall would likely keep the enemy from catching their scent. Not that he would not mind cutting off a few heads, but he didn't want to put Ula in any danger, and they certainly could not afford to lose the horses.

"Ula, good!" he cried. "Very good!"

"Good!" she said, proud of herself.

"Come, we need to get a fire started," Bran said.

He retrieved the horses and led them behind the waterfall, then set out to collect wood. She followed him and helped, smiling the entire time. She was indeed quite pleased with herself, and he was too, actually. Bringing her along had been a good decision.

There wasn't much dry wood lying about, so he cut a few dead limbs off nearby trees and hauled them back behind the waterfall where he chopped them into smaller pieces. When the work was done, he brought in some dry river rock from outside to make a circle for the fire and lit the kindling. Ula watched the flames in complete amazement. She reached out to touch them, but Bran caught her hand and stopped her. *How could she not know fire burned?* Perhaps she wasn't well in the head, he suddenly thought. It would explain how childlike she was…and why she couldn't speak…but she seemed entirely too clever in other ways for that to be the case.

"No, Ula. The fire will burn you," he explained. He didn't know if she understood him, but in any case she didn't try to touch the flames anymore.

"Wait here," he said, holding his hands out to indicate she should stay where she was. He went out to check and see if the fire or smoke were visible from the outside, and to his relief, they weren't. When he came back he found she had laid out her sealskin on the stones and was sitting upon it in front of the fire, completely naked again, eating her fish. He became aroused, but gratefully she was face-deep in a raw fish, guts and all, which did wonders to temper his desire.

She looked at him holding the fish she had caught for him and suddenly jumped up. She grabbed his spear and brought it to him, obviously remembering he preferred his cooked.

He smiled at her strangeness. "Thank you, Ula."

He took the fish over to the edge of the waterfall, cleaned and gutted them, and then brought them back on the end of his spear. He sat down across from her and roasted them, watching her. She finished her dinner and then laid her head down on her sealskin and looked up at him.

"Sleep," she said.

"Yes. Sleep," Bran said kindly. "Good night, Ula."

CHAPTER TWENTY

Islwyn

The night passed without incident, and at sunrise the next day, Bran and his mysterious companion set out again. It amazed him how she simply followed him without question or apparent concern for where they were going, but so be it. She obviously trusted him and perhaps didn't have a people of her own anymore, as he had assumed. He resolved to find her a husband in his clan if she wished it. She would have to get used to wearing a bit more clothing and learn their language, but that would not be hard for a woman as clever as she was.

The landscape rolled out before them as they traveled, growing wider and less rocky. As they made their way across the moorlands, a mountain range came into view, but sadly, Bran didn't recognize it. *Why did nothing look familiar?*

They rode hard for the rest of the day, reaching the foothills of the mountains by late afternoon, but still, he did not recognize the terrain. Suddenly, Ula began to assert herself and take the lead. It appeared at least *she* knew this land. At her insistence to travel in certain directions they finally came upon a river, which flowed south. Bran knew it would certainly lead them to a town or village, and eventually closer to his own.

"Good job, woman!" he praised, genuinely pleased with her.

"Sleep," she said proudly. She apparently now equated water with a safe place to sleep, and Bran smiled at her innocence.

As usual, she was quick to get in the water and soon had dinner sorted out. Bran knew he was outranked in that respect, so he focused his efforts on making camp instead. She soon tossed an impressive catch at his feet, smiling, her dark hair wet and glossy down her back and skin shiny from the water.

Suddenly, she sniffed the air and terror leapt into her eyes. She bolted into action, untying the horses and slapping them on the rump, speaking to them in a strange language Bran did not understand.

"What is it?" Bran asked her. He was smart enough to know by now that she could smell and hear things he could not.

She motioned toward the fire frantically, and as soon as he put it out she grabbed his arm and dragged him urgently toward the river. He looked around, surveying everything with a concentrated eye, and finally by the moon's light, he saw what it was that had stricken his companion with such fear. Far off in the distance, the movement of tiny pale figures rolled like an eerie mist across the moor toward the river: *Cauldron-born.*

She pulled at his arm with a crazed look in her eyes as she stepped into the river, and he followed, because her plan of taking to the water was actually a good one; swimming with the river's current would continue to take them south and would also hide their scent, hopefully throwing the cauldron-born off their trail.

He braced himself for the shock of the water and soon they were being carried away in the current, which was fortunately not very swift and deep enough that finding injury upon the rocks was unlikely.

Ula swam with incredible fluidity under the surface, nearly never coming up for air. He tried to keep up with her the best he could.

308

He finally raised his head out of the water to breathe, but she yanked it back down again. Soon he felt his lungs would burst. He slowly let his breath out and yanked his arm free to rise to the surface, but Ula stopped him and put her mouth over his instead, blowing air into his lungs and pulling him along as she swam. His knew his clothes, sword, rope…everything on his body was slowing them down, but they could not afford to leave anything behind.

After some time, taking breaths very sparingly, Bran knew he had to get out of the water. The cold was too much, and he could feel his body beginning to shut down. He brought his eyes out of the water, scanning the banks for any sign of the cauldron-born as they drifted. Ula came up too, her black hair making her near invisible in the water. She smelled the air and barely moved as they floated along quietly with the current, listening intently. He took her face in his hands and turned it toward him.

"I must get out," he whispered, pointing to the riverbank and swimming toward it. She looked at him in panic, but would not be left behind. She followed him, moving without a sound, constantly smelling the wind. He wanted to leave the riverbank, but she pulled at his arm again.

"Sleep," she said quietly. "Come." She ran silently along the bank and he followed, thanking the Great Mother she knew the land, and that heat was slowly returning to his body. They ran for a very long time before she stopped and pointed to the water.

"Come," she said, slipping in as silent as an otter and pointing downriver.

He followed her back with dread into the icy river, noticing the moon was high overhead. She allowed him to come up for air now, so apparently they had managed to leave behind their pursuers for the moment. The next time he came up he caught a whiff of wood smoke, and his heart leapt at their good fortune. Ula obviously smelled it as well and started swimming across the river toward the opposite bank where they crawled out of the water. Bran was struggling for breath and his muscles were cramped, but she didn't even seem to be out of breath.

What are you? he thought.

They finally got out of the river and she took his hand, pulling him toward the trees. There was no trail, but thankfully the night was clear and well-lit by the full moon. He walked alongside her, hacking away the brush to clear a path for them, and soon he could see a small bit of firelight in the distance. Ula walked faster, happy to see it, and urged him to hurry. The brush thinned out and soon they could pick out a pathway. Ula ran toward the light and he ran after her, worried, in case danger might be waiting. They soon came upon a simple round hut built within the trees with smoke rising through its center up into the night sky. Fishing nets hung from the trees, and much wood had been cut and stacked for the winter on either side of its small door peeking out from beneath a thatched roof. Symbols and signs were carved all around the door frame, and Bran recognized as Druid. Ula ducked and entered, and seconds later Bran heard an elderly man's voice call out.

"My child! My child, you've returned!"

Moments later, Ula came back out smiling and pulled on Bran's arm, leading him toward the door. Before he entered, the owner of the hut emerged into the moonlight; an old man, a bit frail-looking, with a full grey beard.

"Greetings. I am Bran. My clan lives south of here." he said, looking the old man over. "It seems you know my companion. Can you understand her? Do you know what clan she's from? She doesn't speak the common tongue."

"Oh, she speaks," the old man chuckled. "You just don't understand the language of the *selkie*."

"*Selkie*?" he said, searching his memory and finding only faint ideas. "From what land do they hail?"

"Not from any land," the old man said, smiling. "You've never heard of them?"

"No," Bran replied, a bit irritated by the elder's smugness.

"Just as well," he said, looking Bran over as well. "I can see you've been for a swim. I imagine you'd like to come in and sit by the fire?" he asked, knowing the obvious answer. "Please!" he urged, motioning for them to enter. "If you can fit through the doorway, that is." he winked. "I'll be back presently, I have something I must do."

Ula went in first and Bran followed. He had to stoop down and nearly crawl in, but once inside, the roof rose to a height that he could sit under comfortably. The heat surrounding them was like a mother's womb and he gladly shed his wet clothes and got as near to the fire as he could stand, almost as naked as Ula, who, as usual, sat down happily on her sealskin across from him. She pulled her fingers through her hair and stared at his body shamelessly, her eyes wide and round, as if it were the first time she had ever seen a man. Again, he fought his instincts, avoiding her gaze and looking into the flames instead.

Suddenly the skins covering the door of the small hut were thrown back.

"Bran!" he heard a boy cry.

Bran turned around, shocked to hear the sound of his name after so many days and nights alone.

"Gwion?" he exclaimed, recognizing the boy. "Gods, boy! How is it you're here?"

The old man came in after him. "He's been here a few days searching for you. I told him he had best stay here through the nights while the dark ones are roaming, and search for you by day."

Bran couldn't believe what he was hearing. A twelve-year old boy out here, alone, searching for him?

"Gwion, how is it that we are meeting here?" he asked. "How far are we from your home?"

"The Great Mother's handiwork, to be sure," the old man interrupted before Gwion could answer. "She protects those who trust her and weaves them together."

They joined Bran and Ula near the fire and the old man finally allowed Gwion to tell his story.

"Unfortunately we are nowhere near your village," Gwion told Bran. "We are far to the North, two weeks travel by foot from your village."

"Tell me first, is your mother well?" Bran asked.

"Yes," Gwion said, smiling at the mention of her. "She is safe. We fled to the island before the villa was attacked."

"Thank the gods," he sighed with relief. "I am sure you know Lucia came to my village in the company of the Sisters some weeks back. When I left she was delirious with fever, and speaking words of prophecy. I hope she's recovered since I've been gone."

"Lucia and I....Did you know we are cousins?" Gwion asked.

"No," Bran said, confused. "Why did you and your mother live as her servants?"

"Lucia didn't know who we were until recently. Her mother never spoke of her past, nor of us, to her. Women who leave the Sisterhood are sworn to secrecy about it."

"How did she find out, then?" Bran asked. He thought of Lucia and how she must have felt learning her servants were in truth her aunt and cousin.

"My mother told her when the three of us left the villa," Gwion answered. "Everything has changed, now."

"It has," Bran agreed, thinking of his own people. "The Sisterhood is good at keeping secrets, that is certain. I know nothing of them except the few things my mother told me. She visited the Priestess Rowan on occasion over the years."

"A wondrous woman," the old man interjected. "A true handmaiden to the Great Mother."

Bran turned to the old man, slightly irritated. "Might I ask your name, Druid?"

"I've been called by many. Druid is one of the more respectful ones," he said with a smile, "but you may call me Islwyn."

"Islwyn, do you know of Talhaiarn? He is also Druid, and counsel to my clan." Bran asked.

"Yes, of course," Islwyn replied. "Guardian of the Sacred Grove. No easy task in times like these."

Islwyn got up gingerly and walked to a small bed near the back of the hut and brought back wool blankets. He covered Ula tenderly with one of them and gave Bran the other, which he gratefully wrapped around his shoulders, regretting his impatience with the old man.

"He could use your help, I would imagine." Bran suggested.

"One does not need to be near another in body to help," replied Islwyn, putting various herbs from different clay pots into a wooden bowl. "Prayers and blessings know no boundaries, and those are what I contribute to the fight. I am no warrior, my friend. I am an old man, surprised each time I see the sun peek over the horizon and find all my teeth still lodged in my jaw.

There is much I am doing right here, and I will continue to do it as long as I draw breath."

He poured the contents of the wooden bowl into a cauldron of boiling water hanging over the fire. "Now, I am going to make you something to poultice that wound."

"That would be most welcome." Bran said. The blood was beginning to return to his limbs, and with it, the pain in his shoulder. He let go of his misgivings and thanked him.

"Bran," Gwion suddenly said, "there is more to tell, and I fear you will not welcome hearing it. You told me Lucia was among your people when you left, but she has since returned to the island in distress."

"What?" he exclaimed, suddenly remembering Aelhaearn's disdain for her. "Did Aelhaearn send her back?" he demanded angrily.

"No," Gwion said, shaking his head. "Her husband came for her."

"Her *husband*?" he exclaimed in surprise. "I thought he was dead!"

"It seems not. He came looking for her at your village on *Nos Galan Gaeaf*. She went with him, but he beat her and so she fled for the island."

A hot anger rose in Bran's breast. "Roman bastard!" he spat, furious.

"Truthfully, it surprised me to hear this," Gwion said. "Camulos was always kind to all of us, especially Lucia. We suspect something happened to him."

Bran didn't care how Camulos used to be. *And the Romans call us heathens!*

"Before she made it to the lake she was attacked by a wolf running with the cauldron-born. Luckily she was astride Gethen. Your sister gave him to her as a parting gift, as she was the only one he would suffer to ride him after you left. Surely if she had been upon the back of a lesser horse she would have perished. The beast wounded both of them very badly, but they are recovering."

Another wolf? Bran thought, his mind racing. *How many could there be? Or was the beast he had killed one and the same?*

"And now?" he asked anxiously. "How do they fare?"

"They were both healing well when I left," Gwion said.

"Good," Bran sighed. "I would have them both in my company as soon as possible."

"Soon, you will, but there is still more you need to know," Gwion added. "Your clan believed you died in the caves, and your sister has named Lord Aelhaearn Protector of the South."

A feeling of betrayal overcame Bran, even though he knew this had likely happened. He had thought on it much while trapped in the caves.

"My sister has forsaken me," he finally said, saddened.

"It has been two moons, my lord," Gwion added softly. "They had lost hope you would return."

At this, Islwyn spoke. "Lord Bran, in dark times, a clan needs a leader more than ever. Your sister merely did her duty and provided your people with one. Surely a man like you can understand this! And, from what news young Gwion brings, he has led your clan well. I would counsel you to rid your mind of thoughts of betrayal, for they will poison it, and instead be thankful your people have managed to keep the enemy at bay."

Islwyn looked him in the eye. "You are blessed to have escaped the Underworld! Think instead on that."

"Do you mean the caves?"

"Well, yes, but they were more than caves, I'm sure you realize. How else can you explain how you have come to be so far north? No, my friend. You were caught in one of the realms of the Underworld, and blessed to have made it out again."

Bran thought on the old man's words and realized he was right. There was no other way to explain it.

"Escaped, yes, but it seems the Underworld has followed me, its minions ever near; like a terrible dream I cannot wake from."

"This dream will end, like all dreams do," Islwyn said simply, ladling out the steaming herbs from the cauldron back into the wooden bowl. "And there is no need to fear them here. The dark ones will not cross running water."

"Is that so?" Bran asked, thinking on it. It was true he had never seen them in the pools within the caves.

317

"Yes. That is why I moved my home here." He walked over and sat down next to him, washed his shoulder, packed the hot moist herbs into the wound and then bound it tightly.

"My thanks," Bran said. The pain had begun to dull already.

Islwyn simply nodded. "Are you aware that we sit upon a small island within the river?"

"No," he answered.

"Over the past few moons I've managed to build myself this small home, and here I continue my worship and study in peace without worry of attack."

"You have no king or clan to serve?" Bran asked.

Islwyn let out a raspy laugh. "No, no, no…I chose long ago to live alone. I have always preferred the company of trees and animals to the company of people. I hope you take no offense to that confession. I am fond of occasional visitors, though, like your friend," he said, motioning to Ula.

"Yes," Bran said. He looked over at her fondly and saw she was sleeping soundly. "She is a mystery to me," he added. "Tell me what you know of her people."

"That is not for me to reveal," the old man replied. "If she desires to, she will find a way to tell you where she comes from."

Bran didn't press further. In a way, he enjoyed not knowing anything about her.

"She is a treasure," the old man added, gazing at her. "One not to take near any danger, my friend. You should leave her here. I'll see to it she gets back to where she belongs."

"She may do as she wishes," Bran answered, suddenly suspicious again. "I am not her master."

"Lord Bran, I know what evil you journey toward," Islwyn said, his face changing into one that instantly demanded respect. "If you care for her, then convince her to stay. I will make sure she gets home."

This time Bran didn't dismiss the old man's words. It was true he did not want anything to happen to her.

"Lord Bran, what will you do about Lord Aelhaearn?" Gwion asked, turning the conversation away from Ula.

Bran let out a long sigh of defeat. He could go back and challenge Aelhaearn, and likely win, but what good would that do?

"What's done is done," he finally responded. "I'll return home to give Aelhaearn my blessing, and return *Dyrnwyn* to my sister to present to him."

Dyrnwyn had been his salvation and only companion in the darkness of the caves, and he dreaded the idea of giving it up, yet he knew the sword did not truly belong to him. It belonged to his people, to be wielded by the one they called King and Protector. Aelhaearn now wore that mantle, and from the sound of it, had proven himself worthy. He would not attempt to wrench it from him. He would support Aelhaearn as King, and ask all those who would follow him do so as well. Divided, the clan would be weak, and he would suffer no blood to be spilled in his name. Instead, he accepted his fate and would seek to serve his clan in some other way.

"We will leave at first light," he said with finality, upset by everything he had heard and not wanting to talk about it anymore.

"Let us get some rest then," Islwyn said, reading his signal well, and going to lie down upon his small bed.

Bran lay back wearily upon the dirt floor, balling up the wool blanket and putting it beneath his head. Ula slept soundly near him. He didn't like the thought of leaving her behind, but knew his desires were selfish. She would be safe here, with Islwyn. He knew the old man spoke the truth; by his side was perhaps the most perilous place in the world for her to be.

As he lay there, watching the fire slowly die, he found his heart suddenly surprisingly content in spite of the news he had received. It was too full of gratitude for his freedom and the knowledge that his loved ones still lived to have any room for envy or greed.

Soon his thoughts faded away and he slept well.

CHAPTER TWENTY-ONE
The Legend of Arthfael

Bran awoke and saw that Gwion was not inside the hut. Islwyn was heating water over the fire, and Ula still slept soundly.

"I am preparing a fresh poultice for your wound," the old man said quietly, upon seeing him wake.

"Good," he answered groggily. Already his shoulder felt much better. "I would have the recipe for that poultice. I frequently find myself with such ailments."

"I can imagine," Islwyn said. "The young one knows how it is made. I have given him the herbs to prepare it for you. Change it at dusk and dawn until it has healed fully." Then he motioned toward Ula. "It would be best if you left without a word. I will tell her."

Perhaps the old man was right, but Bran found he couldn't bring himself to leave her without saying goodbye.

"I'm sorry, Islwyn, but I must bid her farewell," he said after a moment. "She would not understand."

The old man sighed as he ladled the herbs out of the cauldron with a shell into his wooden bowl. "Do as you wish, but she will not want to stay," he advised.

Bran dressed and collected his belongings, and then knelt down by Ula's side and gently woke her. She turned and looked up at him. Upon seeing him dressed she sat up with a start.

"No, no...Ula. Stay here with Islwyn. You cannot come with us," he said softly, putting his hands on her shoulders. "Please, stay."

She must have understood what he said because she latched onto him and did not let go, and Islwyn looked over at him with disappointment, raising his eyebrows and shaking his head. Just then Gwion came into the tent.

"I will speak to her," he announced, sitting down across from Ula and holding her hands. They looked into each other's eyes for some time, speaking in a tongue Bran did not understand, but he could tell by her manner that it wasn't going well. Finally Gwion stood up.

"She says she was told to stay with you, and she will not leave you until she is told to do otherwise."

"By whom?" Bran asked, bewildered, "and how is it you understand her?"

"I understand a great many strange things, my lord," Gwion answered. He said this without pride, simply as a statement of fact, and Bran wondered just how much he had underestimated him because of his physical years.

"I think you should allow her to come," Gwion advised. "We will be traveling down the river, and she is quite at home in the water."

"Down the river?" he asked suspiciously, wondering if Ula had suggested they swim all the way to his village.

"Yes, I have arranged for a boat that will carry the three of us most comfortably. We will be safe from the cauldron-born, and travel much faster than we would on foot."

"Well-done," he said to the boy. "She is welcome to do as she wishes, then."

Gwion relayed this to Ula, and her eyes lit up. Islwyn shook his head, begrudgingly accepting the group's decision.

Bran turned to him. "Your kindness shall not be forgotten, Islwyn. You have a home in the South should you ever wish it."

"I am honored, Lord Bran, but I am quite happy here," he replied.

Islwyn gave them blankets and food and said good-bye to Ula with tears in his wrinkled eyes, and Bran wondered how much of his desire to have Ula stay was borne of his own loneliness.

"May the Great Mother protect you all," he bid in farewell.

Soon the trio was on their way and walking along the river's edge.

"Where is the boat?" Bran asked Gwion.

"A few miles downriver," the boy answered, taking the lead, quickly finding a good path and charging ahead with no doubt in his direction.

"Gwion, how did you know where to find me?" Bran finally asked him. "Or that I even still lived?"

"I knew you were alive. I could feel it, and the animals speak to me. To know them is to have a thousand eyes and ears. Lucia knew you were alive as well. She feels such things."

"I count myself fortunate, then."

"Lord Bran, there is something you should know. Lucia told me many of your men gave their lives searching for you. Though they now call Aelhaearn their king, your people love you dearly, make no mistake. They will rejoice at your return."

Bran suddenly thought of Gareth's body, still down there in that dark place, and was overcome with regret that he had not been able to bring his friend's body out into the sunlight. Such a fate easily could have been his own.

"I hope so," he answered. "I am eager to be among them again."

The birds around them began to chatter incessantly as the sun emerged up over the horizon, illuminating the sky in soft pink. Ula suddenly moved up alongside Gwion and took his hand in hers, walking along happy and carefree, none of the fear of yesterday in her manner at all.

Looking before him, he suddenly felt as if he were traveling with two children. They were innocent and unarmed, yet ironically perhaps the most well-equipped to evade the darkness that hunted in the night.

"Gwion, I must reclaim Gethen from the isle. Could this be arranged?"

"I have a plan," Gwion said, "but in the end, I cannot speak for the High Priestess." After a moment he asked, "Bran, are you familiar with the legend of Arthfael and *Caledgwyn*?"

"Yes, of course," he answered. He had often heard the ballad sung. Arthfael was the only king to ever have ruled the island.

"He is the reason no boy-child is allowed to stay upon the island."

"Yes, but there is much more to the story than that," Gwion said. "I have heard it nigh a hundred times, and would tell it to you, if you wish it."

"Let us hear it, then," Bran encouraged. "A long story is a good way to pass the time, and we have much of it."

"Very well," Gwion said, and the three companions walked together along the river while Gwion told the tale of Arthfael.

"Once, long ago, there was a time when men lived alongside the women of the island. It began with Priestess Arwydd, who gave birth to a son whom she loved so much, she refused to send him from the isle to his father. She believed that if the Sisters were careful to raise their sons with respect toward the Great Mother, and shown nothing of war or hatred, they would not grow into the blood-thirsty, destructive men of the world outside."

"Her desire to keep her son and raise him on the island caused a rift within the Sisterhood. Some of the priestesses agreed with Arwydd, most especially those who had young sons of their own they did not wish to part with, and some insisted they should not question the Old Ways. In the end, somehow, Arwydd managed to get all the Sisters to agree to allow the sons to stay and be raised by their mothers."

"The first sons raised upon the island grew up to serve the Great Mother well. They were strong, yet compassionate and respectful. They served as noble ambassadors for their mothers and sisters, carrying messages to the other clans, and bringing back important news and goods that were needed. However, when they grew to be men and began taking lovers and becoming fathers, things naturally began to shift. Their children grew up very differently, being raised by both mothers and fathers, and many new longings competed with the Great Mother within their hearts."

"When Priestess Arwydd died, her only daughter, Gwyndolyn, became her successor as the Sisterhood's High Priestess. She also questioned some of the Old Ways, like her mother, and unlike any

High Priestess of the Isle who had come before her, she chose to take a Protector. Gwendolyn and her Protector ruled the island together, as was the custom of the other clans, equally sharing in the decision-making, and though life was not as simple or quiet as it had been the generation before, it was still fairly peaceful.

In her lifetime, the Priestess Gwyndolyn bore no daughters, only sons. Her eldest, Arthfael, was born with all the virility and ambition of the men of the outside world, and was said to be the most handsome man ever born to a mortal woman. He was restless and charming, and traveled off the island frequently. He felt the island should have a male chieftain, like the clans to the North, East and South, and one by one, through his stories of adventure and valor from the lands beyond, he converted many to his way of thinking."

"Without a daughter of her own to apprentice in the role as High Priestess, Gwyndolyn chose her sister's eldest daughter, Addfwyn, to teach and mentor as her successor. Unfortunately, Gwyndolyn died very young of a fever brought onto the island by the men, and Addfwyn came to her position far too soon. In her, Arthfael saw his opportunity. He easily seduced and charmed the young priestess, and Addfwyn fell deeply in love with him. It was not long before she named him her Protector."

"Slowly, Arthfael and his brothers brought the ways of the outside to the island more and more. He brought timber and limestone from across the lake to build a Great Hall like those he had seen in the lands beyond, with a tall tower so he could look out over the lake in all directions, and a courtyard around the Mother Oak for Addfwyn and her sister priestesses. In the Great Hall, banquets were held on the sabbats and the new sons and daughters of the island ate, drank, sang and fell in love like those of the other clans, and Arthfael and Addfwyn were content. However, the cost of this new life meant that many of the daughters who came of age under their rule chose to dedicate themselves to being mothers and wives rather than to the rigorous study and prayer involved in becoming initiated priestesses of the Great Mother."

"Those women who did choose to follow in the footsteps of their grandmothers separated themselves from the distractions of the court and clan by living in simple huts near the Sacred Pools and immersing themselves in the Old Ways. They were highly respected and consulted on holy days to give blessings and lead rituals, to heal and cure the sick or wounded, and to deliver babies. Soon it seemed an insult for Addfwyn to carry the title of High Priestess, as there were so many who were more knowledgeable and trained in the Old Ways and arts of the Great Mother than she was, and she knew this. She graciously stepped down, bidding the priestesses of the order choose a new High Priestess. They chose Seren (whom I believe your sister is named after, Bran), the eldest and most learned of them, to carry the prestigious title, and from that day forward, the people of the island simply addressed Addfwyn as their queen. Many believe her choice to abandon her vows to the Great Mother was the reason she and Arthfael were never blessed with a child, but that is something that cannot be proven."

"Over the years Arthfael grew restless. He did not consider himself a true king without a sword befitting his station, and was most envious of that wielded by King Meilyr, then chieftain of the South; the noble *Dyrnwyn* which now hangs at your side, Bran. The island had never known weapons, and had neither forge nor blacksmiths. Arthfael thus began his search for Eircheard, the legendary blacksmith who had forged *Dyrnwyn*, as no other would do. He journeyed to the South with gifts, asking King Meilyr if the blacksmith still lived, saying he wished to commission a sword from him, and that he would gladly pay Meilyr a handsome amount of gold for revealing his whereabouts.

King Meilyr agreed, but he did not want gold as payment; instead he desired a single flask filled with the water of the Sacred Pools, as it was said to cure any ailment."

"Arthfael knew it was blasphemy to barter with the sacred water, but he felt no harm could come from removing one flask to heal an old man. He delivered the flask to Meilyr, and, as agreed, Meilyr told him where to find Eircheard."

Bran was very familiar with the story of Meilyr and the water. Meilyr had used it to heal his wife, and eventually, his mother had descended from her line. As a boy he had been reminded of this every time he and his clan journeyed to the Crossroads for a sabbat celebration, for his mother would always take gifts for the Sisterhood, as well as offerings for the High Priestess to take back to the island and put beside the Sacred Well on her behalf. She knew she owed her life to the water that was granted to her maternal ancestor.

"Arthfael went to Eircheard and commissioned his sword, but insisted that he return to the island with him to make it, as he wished for the blade to be quenched and tempered with the water of the Sacred Pools. Eircheard agreed, eager to see the fabled island. Upon arriving and seeing the immense beauty of the woods in which Arthfael had built his forge, he chose to sleep under its roof and gather his own food rather than live among the clan. The king allowed him to do as he wished."

"Eircheard was a very wise and penitent man, and yielded himself to the will of the priestesses, promising he would never use the sacred water for any purpose they did not approve of, regardless of what King Arthfael commanded."

"The priestesses prayed about the arrival of the stranger to their island, and for guidance about what he had been tasked to do. To their surprise, the message they received was to allow Eircheard to forge the sword as he had been commissioned. Thus, with the blessing of the priestesses, Eircheard began his work, and when the time came to temper and quench the blade, the priestesses freely offered him water from the Sacred Pools."

"Eircheard forged the sword as an act of worship, inspired by the island and the purity which surrounded him in the grove. When it was finished, it gleamed silver-blue, illuminated from within as if liquid moonlight flowed within its blade. Before taking it to Arthfael, he presented it to the priestesses, bidding them bless and name it. They did as he asked, dedicating it to the Great Mother, and called it *Caledgwyn*."

"Eircheard proudly presented *Caledgwyn* to Arthfael, who cried tears of joy upon seeing it, for no sword forged before nor since was ever so beautiful in its perfection. Arthfael offered to pay him triple what was agreed upon, but Eircheard refused to take any payment at all, saying the privilege of living in such a sacred place was payment enough; that the sword was a symbol of his love and gratitude, and his only wish was for it to be ever-wielded in justice according to the Great Mother's will. Arthfael so promised, and Eircheard never forged another sword again, knowing none would ever be as perfect as *Caledgwyn*."

"For a time the island rested peacefully on the lake, and Arthfael was true to his word, but children grow to be men and women, and then have children of their own, and soon there were three generations living upon the isle. The priestesses were listened to less and less, as Arthfael and his clan grew tired of their constant warnings and prophecies. The water of the Sacred Pools was then used for the needs of the people, and all of the game on the island soon hunted down for food."

"With her holy places defiled and her name forgotten, the Great Mother sorrowfully removed her veil of protection from around the island. It wasn't long before invaders found it, and for the first time in history, blood was spilled upon its shores."

"Arthfael saw the invaders coming across the water from his great tower, and with zeal he hoisted *Caledgwyn,* eager to finally stain its blade in battle. He led an attack against the invaders, and when the first drop of innocent blood was shed, as always happens when men hoist swords, it is said the Great Mother looked down and wept. They say she wept from the new moon to the full, her tears falling incessantly day and night, flooding the lake until it covered the island, and under the waters of Lake Tegid it remained until every soul who had ever seen or lived upon it had died."

"Eventually the waters of the lake receded, revealing the island once again, but none who tried to reach it ever succeeded; it was protected again, more than ever. The Great Mother chose new priestesses to walk upon its soil again, and led them to her shores, and from that time, never again have any of her priestesses taken husbands nor raised their boys to the age of men upon its shores."

"Yes." Bran said after Gwion had finished. "I remember hearing some of these stories as a child, though never so completely. It is a tragedy what happened, but strong lessons are frequently learned in such a way."

"Yes, they are." Gwion nodded. "Bran, the reason I tell this tale is that it has long been believed the legendary *Caledgwyn* lies deep down in the heart of the deepest of the Sacred Pools, waiting to be raised by a worthy warrior in a time of great need. I believe now is such a time."

Bran inferred the boy's meaning and was shocked by Gwion's words. His first instinct was to chuckle and shake his head.

"Me?" he said. "I am no legendary hero, Gwion. Merely a warrior intent on surviving and protecting his clan."

"Heroes are not born, my lord." Gwion replied. "They are *made*--made when ordinary men choose to do extraordinary things."

Bran was yet again shocked by the child's wisdom, and put a reassuring arm around the boy's shoulders.

"You speak true, my young friend," Bran conceded. They walked in silence awhile before Gwion spoke up again.

"My lord, you are journeying to surrender your sword and position as king of your people. I know your warrior's heart must grieve over this, and I am offering you an opportunity to be chosen by the Great Mother herself, armed with a sword forged in dedication to her, and defend not only your own family, but the Sisterhood and Crossroads as well. Neither the Sisters nor Talhaiarn have a champion to protect them, and eventually, Cerridwen will overtake both of the holy places and dominate them. I have seen it, but fortunately the future is not a page written in ink. It is ever twisting in the mist, and we can adjust our sails to change it. It is the Great Mother who speaks through me, and she has bid me present you with a choice; the choice to embrace the highest expression of who you are, and serve her."

Bran was humbled by Gwion's words.

"I am honored she thinks me such a man, Gwion. You know my heart well. If the Great Mother considers me worthy, I can do nothing but submit myself to her and find out."

Gwion smiled. "This is good. I will send word to the isle that we are coming."

He didn't know how Gwion would do this, but he didn't doubt that he could.

"The boat is but a bit further downriver. We shall soon come to it."

Ula had been silent for miles, and Bran touched her shoulder to let her know he had not forgotten about her. She looked up and smiled at him, and then walked ahead with renewed energy. The boat was right where Gwion had said it would be, and soon they were pushing off from the dock.

"Who owns this boat?" Bran asked.

"A friend of the family, you could say," Gwion said. "He repaired it for us and made a few extra oars. A good man."

Bran took up the oars and Gwion took the rudder, directing them down into the center of the river. Ula nestled herself in the bow, obviously thrilled to be on the water. The current was flowing at a good pace, and Bran was pleased at the time this would allow them to make up.

"The river will take us to Llyn Tegid," Gwion announced. "We should be safe to travel downriver without stopping until we reach it. Once there I will get us to the island. There you will speak with my grandmother, and hopefully she will agree to my request on your behalf. Either way, I'll see to it that you are reunited with Gethen, if only it be on a skiff off the island."

And Lucia, Bran realized, gladdened. He suddenly remembered the day he had upset her by the lake and she had turned his dagger on him. He chuckled as he pictured her green eyes challenging him from beneath her wild red hair, whipped free by the strong wind that day. She had been so over-confident in her ability to protect herself that he had worried about her ever since, for he knew he could have taken that knife from her as easily as a toy from a child. She certainly did not lack a fighting spirit, but without the ability to match it, it would do nothing but stoke the fire in an attacker's loins. Taming a wild woman was akin to breaking a wild stallion, something that appealed to the conqueror in all men, and never did blood flow with more desire for conquest than in battle.

Suddenly a great splash broke him from his thoughts. He whirled around to see Ula had jumped into the river.

"What is it with that girl?" he exclaimed. "Ula!" he yelled.

"Bran, she *is* a *selkie!*" Gwion said, smiling. "She belongs in the water."

"Islwyn mentioned she was from that clan. Tell me of it."

Gwion laughed heartily. "They aren't a clan. Not as we think of one, anyway. She is a seal that can take the form of a woman."

"What?" Bran asked, looking at the boy blankly.

Gwion restated what he had just said a bit more slowly, picking up the sealskin which lay in the bottom of the boat for emphasis. "She is a seal, but can shed her skin and take the form of a human. You've never heard tales of such creatures?"

Suddenly Bran remembered the seal he had fed by the seashore a few days ago and how Ula had appeared shortly thereafter.

"By the gods, you're serious, aren't you?" he said to the boy in shock.

"Yes," Gwion said. "There are many creatures in the world like Ula, but they reveal themselves very seldom, for obvious reasons."

Bran nodded in vague understanding, watching Ula swim alongside the boat, feeling quite strange.

"Why does she not put her skin back on? Surely she would be warmer in that water." Bran asked.

"I don't know. She will when she wants to, I suppose." Gwion said.

Suddenly a fish flew out of the river and landed squarely in the boat, followed quickly by two more.

"Seems she's taken care of lunch," Gwion said, smiling widely.

Soon Ula's hands appeared alongside the boat and she swung herself blithely back into it. He stared at her in wonder while she tore into her meal. That was one of her habits he wasn't sure he would ever get used to, but at least he understood it now. She pulled her skin around herself after finishing her meal and rested her head in Bran's lap to sleep.

"She trusts you, Bran. Consider it an honor. I know of no men but you, me, and Islwyn who have been so blessed. There are many men who would steal her skin and keep her for themselves."

"What do you mean, steal her skin?" Bran asked, confused.

"She cannot return to her true form without her skin. Men have been known to capture *selkie* by stealing their skins. They are enchanting and make wonderful wives and mothers, but are never truly happy out of the ocean."

"Well, she seems happy now," Bran noted. "She can stay as long as she likes." He pulled some bread from his pocket and sunk his teeth happily into it.

"Oh!" he mumbled with a full mouth, "The joy of bread! I cannot tell you how much I have missed it!"

"I can imagine," Gwion said, smiling.

"Tell me more about this man claiming to be Lucia's husband," he asked, wanting to be sure he was out of the picture. "You said something happened to him."

"I suspect Cerridwen has something to do with it," Gwion said.

"Why him? What does a priestess of the isle want with a Roman?"

"What, indeed," Gwion said. "I suspect she knows of his marriage to Lucia, and that she has discovered Lucia has the Sight. It is the most coveted blessing among the women of the isle. She may mean to reach out to her and offer to train her. Knowing Lord Camulos was her husband, she likely turned him to her purpose first, and then sent him to your village to fetch her. With Lucia as her ally, and a centurion like Camulos to help lead an army and provide military counsel, she would strengthen her position immensely."

Knowing Cerridwen was purposefully seeking Lucia out made Bran want to have her at his side more than ever, where he could keep an eye on her.

"Perhaps this is dense of me, but it seems the island is not necessarily a safe place for her," Bran said. "If Cerridwen wants to return to it, can she be kept from its shores?"

"I don't believe that Cerridwen would go so far as to defile the island with bloodshed, nor bring men to its shores. If she were to return, she would so do alone and in peace. The island is the holiest of places to the Sisterhood, and home to the Great Mother. Not even she is arrogant enough to risk insulting her."

"That is good to hear, for I know where the Cauldron is, and want to return it there."

Gwion's eyes widened. "You found it?"

"Yes," Bran continued. "I spent days upon days exploring all of the wretched tunnels within those damn caves, and never could I find a way out, until finally I swam through an underwater chamber into another cavern. There, I emerged within a cave made of crystal, and within it sat the Cauldron. Unfortunately, it was too heavy to move, and there was no way to wrest it from the cave. There, within that same place, I was set upon by a great black wolf, like the one you described as attacking Lucia."

"Yes, a great black wolf…Such a creature was also the death of the great Belenus in the East."

No! Bran thought. *Not Belenus!* He stopped rowing, put his oars up and dropped his forehead in his hands, sitting in silence with the dark news. "Gods!" he cursed. *Would the darkness never cease taking his loved ones?* "Belenus has fallen?" he said in disbelief, bracing himself to hear the words again.

"I am sorry, my lord. Lucia told us he died a hero's death."

"I have no doubt," Bran said. "A more noble and brave king there has never been." With a heavy heart, he said a silent warrior's prayer for him and then took up the oars again. Soon thereafter he had a thought.

"Gwion?"

"Yes."

"After I killed it, its body twisted before me into the shape of a man. A deformed, black-haired man, with one eye that would not open."

Gwion was silent, his hand limp on the rudder.

"You killed him? Are you certain?" he finally asked.

"Yes. I severed his head and dumped him in the pool so there would be no way to resurrect him. There were creatures within that water that don't see very much meat. I am confident there is nothing left of him but bones."

Gwion shook his head in concern.

"What's wrong?" Bran asked.

"I fear you've killed Cerridwen's son, Morvran," Gwion replied. "If so, you will need protection from her. She will be inconsolable and full of wrath; whatever curses she is able to conjure, and they are many, she will place upon you. She loved her son more than anything."

Bran thought on Gwion's words. "Well, it was either him or me, and I chose me."

"Of course. I'm glad you did. Don't worry, the Great Mother has a plan. We must put ourselves in her hands."

"Easier said than done," Bran replied, pondering Cerridwen's wrath and weary of hearing such things.

'Yes. That is true as well," Gwion agreed.

For the rest of the day Bran rowed and Gwion guided the rudder. Ula lay in the bow of the boat, her hand and arm trailing in the water, occasionally jumping in to swim alongside them. The river's current was gentle, the air off the water fresh, and Bran found it all deeply soothing.

At dusk that feeling faded, however, and he began to watch the banks more intently, his eyes adjusting quickly to the dark he had come to know so well. Through the night, he and Gwion took turns at the rudder, luckily spotting no cauldron-born, and by morning they had traveled quite a distance downriver.

"At this rate we'll reach the lake by sundown tomorrow," Gwion announced happily. "Let me take the oars awhile. You can sleep. I'll wake you in a few hours."

"Be my guest," Bran said, grateful for the opportunity. He stretched out in the boat next to Ula. She came in close to him and rested her head on his chest, and Bran sighed in contentment, looking up at the stars overhead. If she didn't smell like raw fish he would kiss her on the lips, he thought to himself and smiled. He kissed the top of her head instead and welcomed the rest he needed.

As planned, they reached the immense lake late the next day. The distant island beckoned from behind the shifting mist, silhouetted against the pale setting sun.

Ula swam around the boat as Bran rowed powerfully toward it, sometimes emerging far off, then returning. She seemed excited to have deeper waters to explore.

It wasn't long before they were completely enveloped in mist, unable to see anything around them. Occasionally, Bran heard Ula splashing and laughing in the distance, but the sound never seemed to come from the same direction. Within the mist figures began to form, shifting and floating around the tiny boat, eerily hovering around Gwion, who sat completely still. Bran chose to look at the water instead, as the figures put him ill at ease. He watched the wakes the oars made as he pushed the water away, but then began seeing faces forming within the water as well.

"There are spirits about," he said warily to Gwion.

"There are *always* spirits about," Gwion responded. "You can simply see them here."

Suddenly, as if slipping into a dream, the bow slid upon the shore where so few men had set foot, and Bran felt more apprehensive than he had before entering the caves.

CHAPTER TWENTY-TWO
The Mist

"Someone is coming," Lucia said.

As if from very far away, she faintly heard her grandmother ask, "Can you see who it is?"

Lucia focused intently on the small figure in her vision. As she drew closer, she saw it was a small boat with two figures in it, but a thick mist swirled about them and obscured their faces from her. Then she noticed the mist was filled with spirits. There were so many of them! They clustered around the tiny boat as if they were feeding upon it, like ants swarming all over a piece of cake, and Lucia recoiled. She could see them under the water as well, their hands and faces upon the bottom of the boat. Then, all the faces turned toward her, and for the first time Lucia knew she could be *seen.*

She panicked and lurched out of her trance, her heart pounding out of her chest. She found herself sitting on the dirt floor of her small hut, peering into a dish of water. The sun had gone down and her limbs were stiff.

"Lucia?" A hand lightly touched her shoulder. "What did you see?"

She turned and looked into her grandmother's face. "Spirits," she answered, "swarming around a boat in the mist."

Rowan saw her fear. "They won't harm you," she said compassionately.

"That is not the way it felt."

"Lucia, you will become better at traveling within the Shadowlands, and dealing with whatever or whomever you meet there, but you *must* practice daily. As time passes, you will see that you'll be able to stay longer, move more quickly, and remember more after you return."

"I will," Lucia promised. She was shaken, yet still determined to become a Shadowmistress.

"What can you remember about the figures in the boat?" her grandmother prompted.

"I think it might have been Gwion and Bran...I couldn't see them, but I could feel them."

***

Lucia's vision of Gwion and Bran had come to her a week ago, yet they had not arrived. She had spent time with the scrying dish each day since, but she hadn't been able to muster the vision again.

"What am I doing wrong?" she finally asked Aveta in exasperation.

"Your fear may be keeping you from seeing," Aveta suggested.

"Yes, that could be true," she replied. She had been nervous about looking into the water since her last vision, and had shared her fears with Aveta. "--but I've often been fearful of my visions and they've come to me regardless."

"I suppose the difference could be that you are the one seeking the vision, rather than the vision seeking you. A part of you is coming to the altar, asking to be shown, yet another is fearful and does not want to see. You must deal with your fear if you want clarity."

Aveta's words rang true, but how did one go about stopping fear?

"How do I stop it?"

"Start by asking yourself what you are afraid of."

"I fear that I will be overtaken, somehow...helpless in a realm where I have no physical body to fight with."

"Anything else?"

"I have seen spirits before, many times. In fact, I will often see them when not in trance or asleep, and never have I felt as I did this time. These seemed especially tormented and intent on doing harm...I felt as if they were trying to turn the boat over."

"Many things live within the waters of the lake, both of this world and the Otherworld. Cerridwen insists the father of her children is a spirit of the lake."

Lucia was shocked by the idea. "That isn't possible, is it?" she asked nervously.

Aveta said nothing.

"That *isn't* possible, is it?" she asked again.

"Nothing is impossible, Lucia," Aveta said. "It has been known to happen among us. We sisters have no cause to lie to one another, for there is no shame nor pride in who fathers our children. In fact, it serves us ill when this happens and we bear sons, for we have no father to send them to when they came of age. That is

343

what happened with Cerridwen and her son, Morvran. Creirwy could stay upon the island of course and be trained, but Morvran would have to be sent away when he came of age. I suppose that is why she coddled him so much, trying to make up for this unfairness somehow--an unfairness that went beyond that of their sex, for though they were twins, the two babes were born complete opposites, Creirwy beautiful and fair, with a life full of the Great Mother's blessings, and Morvran dark and deformed, destined to be sent from here into a world that would surely revile him."

"But I don't understand how a spirit can father children. I've never understood it. The Christians believe this as well, that the father of their Lord was not a man, but a spirit who came to a virgin and put a child in her womb."

Aveta nodded and continued, "Cerridwen said a giant of a man appeared to her while she was walking alone along the shore one night. She attempted to shoot him with an arrow, but he kept walking toward her, even though she knew she had hit her target. He introduced himself as the Lord Tegid Voel, saying he had watched her grow from a girl to a woman, and that he would never rest until she was his. Cerridwen found herself overwhelmed with curiosity. She could not help but return to the shore each night following, where he would appear again and again, and eventually she was overcome with desire for him. She finally took him as a lover, but made him promise never to set foot upon the island again, for men were forbidden, and she knew well what had happened to her sister."

"He told her she would be blessed with twins; a boy and a girl, and that he would always watch over them. He then walked out upon the water and disappeared back into the mist."

"It all came to pass as he had said, and the babes were born the following June. This proves they were not Beltane babes, for they were conceived in September."

Hearing this story did nothing to assuage Lucia's fear, even though she didn't really believe it.

"So was he a god?"

"More of a lonely water guardian. Many water guardians and spirits envy the world of men, and take human lovers. The water can be a very cold and lonely place."

"This disturbs me, Aveta, for if spirits can love mortals, and get them with child, can they not also curse them?"

"Yes, of course," Aveta replied. "This is why you ask for protection, Lucia. You must always put yourself in the hands of the Guardians before venturing into the Otherworld, in the name of the Great Mother. She protects her daughters, so that they may go forth fearlessly into the mist and do her work."

Rowan suddenly entered the hut, interrupting their conversation.

"A boat has landed upon the shore," she announced.

"It's them," Lucia said, rising quickly to her feet.

She felt a spell of dizziness, no doubt from sitting so long in the same position on the floor, but steadied herself and followed Rowan and Aveta outside. Cold air met her skin through the holes in her shawl and snaked up under her dress as they walked. She would need to weave herself something warmer, for each day winter squeezed them more firmly in its grasp, and would continue to take them deeper into the darkness for the next few moons.

She stayed close behind Aveta, for a thick mist from the lake was moving in and around the trees, as it sometimes did, mingling with the smoke from the fires rising up through the center of their huts. The upper limbs of the giant oak disappeared and reappeared as they passed underneath it.

"The mist is strangely thick," she observed. "I don't think it's ever been this thick in the time I've been here."

"It happens sometimes. It can mean many things. Some good, some….*challenging*," her grandmother replied.

"How so?"

"When the mist is thick, it means the Great Mother is protecting us from something. Her protection is good, of course, but the fact that there is something we need protecting *from*, well…You can look at it however you like."

"I see," Lucia commented. Her uneasiness was apparently not unfounded.

"There are indeed many spirits about. Something has them restless," Rowan added.

Lucia grew uneasy.

They picked their way through the trees and down the narrow path that led to the small shore where, somehow, anyone who ever made it to the island seemed to appear. Why no one came upon it elsewhere was yet another mystery that she reminded herself to ask about.

Suddenly they heard footsteps approaching and branches crackling underfoot from the opposite direction.

"Gwion! Is that you?" Aveta called out.

"It is," Gwion's voice answered some feet away.

"Oh, thank the gods!" Aveta cried.

Soon Lucia saw Gwion's face over Aveta's shoulder as the two embraced, and Gwion smiled at her.

"Lucia!" he said happily.

"Gwion!" she replied, waiting for her chance to hug and kiss him as well.

"And you are Lord Bran," Lucia heard her grandmother say some feet ahead of them.

"Yes, I am he."

Lucia's heart began to pound uncontrollably at the sound of his voice.

"Come, we have much to talk about."

Lucia had no choice but to turn around and lead the way back through the mist the way they came, as the path was too narrow for anyone else to take the lead. When it opened up a bit, Gwion came alongside her and reached for her hand. At first, she thought he took it as a child would take a parent's hand, but she quickly realized he meant to lead her.

"Allow me, cousin. I know the way well," he said quietly to her. He had gotten taller in the past month, the first hints of manhood starting to show in his face. She squeezed his hand and he squeezed hers back in reassurance.

Behind them walked Aveta, then Rowan, and finally, somewhere back there, walked Bran.

"You found him, Gwion. Just as you said you would," Lucia said, proud of the boy.

"Yes. It took some time, but I did."

"I am so very glad."

"As am I," Gwion said, pulling her along by the hand.

Soon they were near their small group of huts and Rowan lead them all into the ruins of the castle whose courtyard the great oak sat within.

"We will meet in the old courtyard."

Then, suddenly, Lucia felt a large hand upon her shoulder.

"Lucia," Bran's voice said softly. She turned around to face him.

"Bran," she smiled. "I feared I would never see you again."

"Much has happened since we parted," he replied.

"Yes. More than in the entirety of my life before it." she said.

He smiled and nodded. "Sometimes the change we long for comes, and we find we regret it."

She shook her head. "I regret nothing. I am happier than I have ever been."

He gazed at her a moment, and she noticed her hands were shaking. Embarrassed, she hid them.

"Let us talk when this is done," he suggested.

"As you wish," she agreed, dizzy from the blood rushing through her body.

They walked together into the ruins of the old castle and followed Rowan into the once majestic throne room where a fire burned in the giant hearth. A lattice of tree branches now served as their ceiling, arching over their heads.

"Please, everyone, sit," Rowan said, looking small and frail next to Bran, and they gathered around the fire.

"Lord Bran," Rowan said, looking over at Gwion, "I'm sure you realize the rare privilege that my grandson has procured for you."

"I do, my lady," Bran said humbly.

"No man but Lord Talhaiarn has been permitted on our shores since the last High Priest of the Crossroads before him."

"Yes, my lady."

"It is only because of my grandson's gifts, and our desperate circumstances that you are here."

"Yes, my lady."

"That said, I will hear your request."

Bran had fought dozens of bloody battles and petitioned many a dangerous truce with clan and Saxon war lords alike, but never had he felt the particular uneasiness which he felt now, addressing the High Priestess of the Isle.

"My lady, as I was believed to be dead, my people have named Aelhaearn Chieftain and Protector of the South. My sister Seren has performed the rites, which I never received before becoming trapped in the caves of the enemy. Therefore, I am journeying to my village to present him with *Drynwyn*, as by rights it now belongs to him."

Bran paused a moment and took a deep breath, and Lucia wondered how much it bothered him. Surely quite a bit.

"I now find myself a warrior without a sword, nor a charge," he continued.

"It seems to me there are a great many things worth fighting for right now, Lord Bran," Rowan said impatiently.

"Indeed," Bran agreed. "This brings me to my request, Lady Rowan. Gwion has told me he believes the legendary blade of *Caledgwyn* rests somewhere within the Sacred Pools here on the island. I have come to ask you to allow me to submit myself to the Great Mother and attempt to retrieve it, and with it, return as many stolen souls to Arawn as I can. Should I succeed in resurrecting the sword, I pledge to prove myself worthy of it by protecting your holy Sisterhood against any who would seek to attack or defile it."

Rowan chuckled at this. "We have no need of a mortal protector, Lord Bran. The Great Mother protects us."

They all sat in silence at this statement until Gwion spoke up.

"Grandmother, she does indeed, but have you not noticed how many dark spirits now inhabit the waters about the island? How thick the mist has become? The threat from Cerridwen grows ever stronger, and you know nothing can keep her from returning. This is her home. She is a sworn priestess of the Great Mother, and she cannot be denied. The Sisterhood is in danger, Grandmother, and I believe you will need a Champion if Cerridwen brings her warriors with her. Let Bran submit himself to the Great Mother. If she does not approve, she will drown him."

Lucia was shocked to hear this, but said nothing. She looked at Aveta who nodded a "yes" to her silent question.

Rowan suddenly looked very tired. "I had hoped it would not come to this. The idea of war coming to our shores again sickens me, but I still do not believe we need a Protector."

"There is more, Grandmother," Gwion said. "Tell her, Bran."

Rowan turned toward Bran expectantly. "Tell me what?"

"My lady, I know where the Cauldron is. I have seen it," Bran replied.

The Cauldron! Lucia thought excitedly.

"Great Mother!" Rowan sighed, visibly pleased. "We are saved! Where does it lie?"

"Deep within a cave of crystal, far to the North…I found my freedom through a narrow crevice in the ceiling of that cavern."

"It must be rescued and brought back here, at all costs!" Rowan said emphatically. "Do you believe you can find this place again?"

Lucia had never seen Rowan show so much emotion.

"Yes," Bran assured her. "There is also a Druid by the name of Islwyn who lives not far from where it lies. I am sure we can count on his help, but the price for my service is opportunity. The opportunity to seek *Caledgwyn.*"

Bold, Lucia thought. Bolder than she had have been comfortable with.

Rowan looked at Bran as if he were a child. "How foolish do you think I am? What if you should perish? How would we find the Cauldron then?"

"I shall not perish, my lady," Bran said with complete conviction in his voice.

"Your over-confidence may very likely be the death of you, Warrior," Rowan warned.

Bran said nothing, and they all sat in awkward silence until finally Rowan spoke again.

"Lord Bran, if you will give me your solemn vow that you will do everything in your power to find and return the Cauldron to us, I shall grant you the opportunity you have requested."

"I will," Bran vowed. "You have my word."

"Very well," Rowan replied. "You have my blessing."

"Thank you, Lady Rowan," Bran said, bowing his head in respect.

"You must sleep here, however," she added quickly. "There should be more than enough wood to burn through the night, and I will send food, drink and blankets."

"I would be happy to see to it, Grandmother," Lucia offered.

Just then someone approached from the darkness and Bran bolted upright, his hand on the hilt of his sword.

Gwion smiled and laughed. "My lord! You forget where you are! At ease! It's but an old friend, come to visit!"

The sound of hooves on flagstone then greeted their ears, and out of the thick mist Gethen emerged like a dark apparition, walking regally into the throne room as if he were Arthfael himself. Bran let out a cry of joy and rushed to the horse, throwing his arms around the beast's neck.

"Oh, gods, how I've missed you, my friend!" he exclaimed, stroking him. Gethen nuzzled Bran's face and chest, and the sweetness of it brought tears to Lucia's eyes.

"Perfect. Now you also have a companion for the night," Rowan said. She rose to leave, and Aveta and Gwion followed.

Lucia leaned in close to Bran in passing. "I will return."

"I look forward to it," he replied.

The four of them made their way back to the huts, this time with Gwion out in front holding the torch.

"Lucia, you will soon have to make a difficult choice," Rowan said suddenly.

"What choice is that?" she asked, curious as to what she was referring.

"You will have to choose between being that man's wife or being the priestess you were born to be."

She laughed weakly in response, embarrassed by her transparency.

"Lord Bran has not asked me to marry him!"

"No, but I've been alive long enough to know how things will unfold. You don't need the gift of the Sight to see the potential of things around you if you simply take the time to notice."

"Ah," she said, not knowing how to respond.

Could this be true? Her excitement at the idea of it disturbed her.

Rowan turned around and put her hands on Lucia's shoulders, stopping her on the path.

"Lucia, you have been blessed with one of the greatest gifts that can ever be bestowed on a daughter of our clan. My hope, of course, is that you will choose the sacred path of a priestess and stay here with us, but you must make your own decision. I can only tell you that a man's love fades with time, as does his ardor, but a life in communion with the Great Mother is eternal and ever-satisfying. Think on that."

Lucia felt embarrassed and wished the subject had not been brought up.

"Grandmother, I don't know if I'm ready to speak of such things. I have always wanted a family…"

"You may still have children! It is encouraged!" Rowan argued. "Motherhood is the most sacred expression of the Goddess!"

"Yes, but what if I were to have a boy?" she asked, looking over at Aveta and Gwion. "I would have to send him away…"

"Yes, that is one of the sacrifices a Daughter of the Island must make," Rowan answered. "There is no meaningful path in life that will require none of you."

"Lucia, daughter," she continued, "I raise the question because I know you are happy here, and you are blessed with a natural understanding of things that others struggle their entire lives to grasp. You are *just beginning* to scratch the surface of the tremendous power you possess….It would be a great tragedy for you to leave this all behind and never fully bloom."

The joy Lucia had felt at seeing Bran now curdled in her stomach like sour milk. *Why must she choose?* Could she not study the ways of a priestess and also enjoy the love of a man? Understandably she would not achieve the status of Priestess if she chose not to stay upon the island, nor probably learn as much, but she had to believe there was a way to have both.

"Why do the priestesses of the other tribes have husbands and Protectors, then?" she finally asked.

"They do not know nor study the ways of the Great Mother as we do," Rowan answered impatiently. "We are as learned as the High Druids, and blessed in a special way by the Great Mother. The priestesses of the other tribes perform important rituals and rites for their clan, and provide strong leadership, but a priestess of the isle is *special*, Lucia. Why do you think the priestesses of the other clans journey here for advice? Why do you think they send their most gifted daughters here to be trained? This is a blessed place set aside for women who have been profoundly touched by the Great Mother. *And you are one of us.*"

"I am honored to have been so blessed," Lucia replied, feeling ungrateful, because for the first time in her life, she truly had felt honored. Up until the past few moons, she had ever scorned her gift. Now, she embraced it, and longed to learn as much as she could about it.

Aveta put her arm around her. "Mother, please…let Lucia enjoy seeing Bran again."

"That is how it starts," Rowan said with exasperation. "…with excitement and passion. Then, a hasty decision is made, and moons or years later, a woman once bursting with life and potential becomes a husk of the blossom she used to be, with nothing to show for her life but children hanging off her breasts and a husband grown fat off her cooking, secretly going off to the barn to lie with the milkmaid!"

"Mother, *please!*" Aveta protested.

Aveta turned to Lucia and spoke softly so that her mother could hear them, slowing down to put some distance between them.

"She speaks harshly, but it is out of love," she said.

"I know," Lucia replied.

"Bran is a good man," Aveta continued. "If he weren't, Gwion would not have risked his life to find him."

"I know that, too."

"She simply fears losing you, Lucia. I believe she hopes to train you to take her place when she passes on."

"What?" Lucia whispered, stopping in her tracks. "That cannot be true. You are a far better choice than I, Aveta!"

"You may think that now," Aveta replied. "That may even be true, now. But she sees things not only as they are, but as they could be, in their most perfect form."

They continued walking, and thankfully soon reached the huts.

"I am going to bed," Aveta said. "We can talk more tomorrow."

Everyone disappeared into the mist, and Lucia was grateful to be away from the conversation on the pathway. She went to collect blankets, food and ale for Bran and started her way back through the trees with a torch to light the way. Soon Bran appeared in her firelight and she nearly jumped out of her skin.

"I saw you coming," he said apologetically, relieving her of her load.

"Thank you," she said, calming herself.

"You've brought ale!" he cried with glee as he peered into the basket.

"Yes," she replied, "and the bread was baked this morning."

"Praise the gods!" he exclaimed, smiling widely. "Come! Drink with me!"

They made their way back to the throne room. He had fashioned a few benches from loose flagstones and had laid a blanket across them.

"Please, sit," he offered, setting the basket down in front of them.

Bran reached first for the goatskin and took a long drink.

"Ahhh...Gods! Like mother's milk!" he exclaimed, and then passed it to her. She drank in the hopes it would relax her and passed it back.

Bran then fixed his eyes on her.

"Lucia, what happened to you? Gwion said your husband came for you at the camp."

"Yes," she said, wishing it had never happened. "He found me somehow. I thought something seemed out of sorts with him, and he managed to anger Aelhaearn and some of the other men within moments of arriving, which was not something my husband would have done. It soon became clear he was not the man I once knew."

She had no desire to share the rest of what had happened with him. She would take that to the grave with her. She pulled a blanket around her legs tightly against the cold, still acutely aware of Bran's eyes on her. He threw more wood on the fire and wrapped his cloak around her shoulders.

"Go on," he encouraged.

"I don't know if he still lives or not. There were many cauldron-born about. And the black wolf, of course."

She looked over at Gethen who was munching on the apples she had brought for him.

"I thank the Great Mother every night that your sister gave me Gethen, or surely the next time you and I would have spoken it would have been in the Otherworld."

"Gwion told me some of the story," Bran said, reaching over and touching her hair. "I'm sorry I wasn't there. Husband or not, I'd never have let him take you. You would have been mine."

She did her best not to look away.

"Gwion said you and Gethen were badly injured by the wolf," he added.

"Yes," she said, her mind spinning at how to respond to his last comment. "Gethen has recovered more quickly than I have."

Bran looked at her leg with concern. "May I?" he asked.

She nodded and gingerly raised her tunic.

"I have just the thing for that," he said, kneeling at her feet.

The wound was still nasty to behold, but Bran's expression didn't change at all upon seeing it. He had surely seen far worse. He carefully removed the old bandages from around her thigh, and her heart started to race again at his touch. He took the herbs and gently packed them around the wound, looking up at her often, and then wrapped her thigh with bandages soaked in the warm water. The warmth radiated into her thigh, and almost instantly she felt the heat easing the ever-present ache and felt it begin to fade.

"It works well," she said, relieved, wishing his hands were still on her.

"Yes, it does," he said, smiling. "Could I get you to return the favor? My shoulder could do with a change of bandages as well."

He removed his tunic and sat down close to her; close enough for her to smell his skin and hair. Though much thinner, he was still twice her size, and she was overwhelmed with a desire to run her hands across his broad chest and wrap her arms around him. Fingers shaking, she removed the old bandages from his shoulder and did everything exactly as he had done for her. Her nervousness subsided as she concentrated on the task, and by the time she was done it was gone.

"There," she whispered as she tied a final knot, proud of her work. "How does it feel?"

He turned his head to look at her. "Much better."

His eyes lingered on her again and she felt her boldness return. She invited him in with an unwavering look, and finally he reached behind her neck and gave her the kiss she had imagined since their last parting. It began softly, hesitantly, until she put her hands up around his neck. Encouraged, he wrapped his arms around her and pulled her into him.

She had a vague sense of time passing, but how long that mythic kiss endured between them she would never know. All she knew for certain was that the stars seemed to race across the sky over their heads, stealing the night away from them like thieves.

Finally, Bran pulled away and looked into her face.

"I have to take you back," he said softly.

She stood up in response and nodded. He took her torch from the sconce on the wall and offered his hand to her, and they walked slowly back toward the huts where her sisters slept. Once they reached the edge of the circle he stopped.

"I cannot go any further," he said. "Good night, Lucia."

He kissed her one more time, and Lucia couldn't help but taste regret on his lips.

She left him and made her way to the hut she shared with some of the Sisters. Before going in she turned and raised her hand toward the single torch she saw burning in the woods, knowing that even though she could not see him, he was watching.

She prayed to the Great Mother to spare him.

CHAPTER TWENTY-THREE
Caledgwyn

Bran woke to the sight of Gethen's head hovering over his, and it made him laugh. He sat up and patted his horse and then went to rebuild the fire in the hearth from the leftover coals. He wondered where Ula was. She hadn't come back to the boat. Gwion had said not to worry about her, but he couldn't help but worry; he had made a promise to watch over her. He thought of the specters he had seen beneath the waters of the lake and shuddered to think of her swimming in those cold depths among them.

After awhile he was pulled from his thoughts by hunger pains. As if reading his mind, Gwion appeared under the stone archway that marked the former entrance of the courtyard with a basket of food.

"Good morning," the boy said.

"Good morning, friend!" Bran replied, happy for the food, but a bit disappointed it was not Lucia that had brought it.

"I've brought you some breakfast. Cooked eggs in the shell, some dried meat, and bread with butter and honey."

"A meal fit for the gods!" he said happily, thinking of how good they would taste. Gwion joined him by the fire and they ate together.

"I am worried about Ula," Bran confessed to him. "Where do you think she is?"

"In the lake, I'm sure," Gwion replied.

"I don't like it," Bran said. "If anything were to happen to her…"

"She will be fine," Gwion said assuredly. "She is far more resourceful than you believe."

"You should concern yourself instead with how you will find the blessed blade, *Caledgwyn*," a voice behind them suggested.

Startled, Bran turned around to see Lady Rowan had arrived.

"Does it not lie within the Sacred Pools?" he asked.

"Yes, and no. It lies within the realm of the Sacred Pools, but the pools hold many mysteries, and only a fool would believe he could simply dive in and retrieve it."

Bran had secretly been hoping it might only be a matter of holding his breath, for he had become quite good at it, but he also knew deep down that was wishful thinking.

"No one knows how deep the pool truly is. It appears differently to everyone. Some say it looks to be about ten feet deep, others say it is quite shallow, and still others claim it is so deep they cannot see the bottom. Whatever you see will be unique to you," she continued.

"Well, I'll dive in and swim until I find the bottom, then."

"As good a plan as any, my lord," Gwion interjected.

There is no way it could possibly be any worse than the pools in the caves. Or could it?

"If you're ready, then, I will take you," Rowan said, moving toward the pathway out of the courtyard on the far side.

Bran was quite sure he wasn't. He felt awkward and uneasy. He knew well how to prepare for a battle, but for this? What made a man ready or not?

"May the Great Mother find you worthy, Lord Bran," Gwion said.

He found the words encouraging and put his hand on the boy's slim shoulder in farewell before following the small, mysterious old woman into the forest.

They walked alongside a brook for an hour, the water rushing ever more swiftly as they grew closer to the source. She didn't speak to him, and he dared not speak to her. He felt like a great beast in that delicate place as he followed her, trying his best to keep from breaking branches or disturbing anything around him as they hiked up toward their destination.

Finally, to his relief, she announced, "We are here."

He followed her into a lush glade, its stones covered with deep velvet-green moss, a series of waterfalls and smaller pools all flowing from somewhere above down into a large, deep pool at their feet.

Rowan turned and looked intently at him.

"It is an honor and a sacrilege for you to be here, son of Agarah. No man has set foot in this sacred place since Arthfael. Not even Gwion. You would not be here, were it not for desperate times. Do not make me regret bringing you here."

"Yes, Lady. I am most honored. Truly," he replied humbly, and he meant it. "I will not shame you. If the Great Mother is displeased, I am prepared for her to do with me as she wills."

Rowan nodded, but he couldn't tell if she was satisfied with his answer or not. She turned away from him and continued upwards along a tiny path that led up to the source of the water.

Around the source of the spring were many garlands of flowers and fruit, some small clay figurines, and other offerings. He had heard many a tale about the healing waters of the isle, the Sisters most treasured and guarded resource.

"This spring has bubbled with fresh water for as long as anyone of the Sisters can remember," she told him. "Its waters can cure any ailment."

"Why is there mist rising off the surface of the pools?" he asked, wondering if there were also specters in these waters.

"Not mist," Rowan corrected. "Steam. The pools above flow with water as hot as that heated over a fire, and by the time it flows to the pools below, it cools to the warmth of mother's milk. The priestesses come not only to pray here, but also to bathe. Bathing in these waters is what saved Lucia."

Inwardly Bran rejoiced at his good fortune. He thought he would be searching for *Caledgwyn* in ice cold water in the middle of winter – it seemed he had been granted a warm bath instead!

"The water may indeed be comfortable, but what you encounter here may not be," Rowan cautioned.

At this he stiffened, worried she could read his thoughts. The idea disturbed him, but if she could, he might as well ask her what had been on his mind all morning.

"Lady Rowan," he ventured, "I know Gwion believes *Caledgwyn* lies somewhere within these pools, but do you?"

She looked at him a moment before answering.

"I've told you, the answer is not that simple. Generations of priestesses have bathed in these pools since the time of Arthfael. *Caledgwyn* has never been seen, but that does not mean it cannot be found here. We simply do not desire such things. Even if it were encountered by one of the Sisters, I doubt it would be touched. Arthfael was the reason the Great Mother was forced to abandon the Isle to the lake for so long. From that time, the Sisterhood has done all it can to forget him, sword and all."

He nodded in understanding. "Very well, then. Is there any advice you would grant me?"

"Undress and sit in one of the upper pools. Choose whichever one beckons to you, and listen to what the Great Mother has to say to you. That is my advice," she offered. "The rest is up to you."

She looked at him skeptically, Bran thought, which did nothing to reassure him.

"I must leave you now, Son of Agarah. May the Great Mother find you worthy of what you seek."

"May she, indeed," Bran said. "Thank you."

She began walking back down the path, but suddenly stopped and turned around to face him again.

"One more thing...I will give you only this one opportunity to obtain *Caledgwyn*. If you return from the glade without it, you will have failed and must leave the island immediately."

"I understand," he said.

Rowan disappeared into the misty trees, and he was left alone. He climbed up to the upper pools until he found one to his liking, took off all his clothes and lowered himself into it. He noticed the Sisters had put flat rocks into the pool to serve as benches. He tried clearing his mind to listen for a message as Rowan had suggested, but found his mind merely wandering.

Though he respected the gods, he had never prayed much. Not in earnest, anyway. He was a warrior, not a Druid, and sitting quietly was not something he had ever been able to do.

After an hour or so he gave up on hearing from the gods or guardians or Great Mother, or whatever spirits he was supposed to be communing with, and decided to get out and simply take his chances searching the pool below. He reached forward to get out, and to his surprise he noticed the pain in his shoulder was nearly gone. He eased himself back into the water, and his mind latched on thankfully to this, for it was a reason to justify sitting there. With his injuries fully healed, succeeding at finding the sword would be easier.

The longer he soaked, the less pain he felt in his shoulder. Soon he felt completely weightless, unable to tell where his body ended and the water began. He sat motionless, focusing on his reflection in the water. The water flowing into the pool caused it to shift and change, distorting his features. He saw the branches above overhead behind him. The water continued to soothe his body, and soon he felt no pain at all, and a euphoria began to flow through him.

Then suddenly he was bothered. It wasn't right, sitting there, relaxing like a queen in a hot bath while his people were being attacked by cauldron-born? *If the Great Mother has something she wishes to say to me, she will doubtless make it known!* he reasoned and stood up, irritated with himself. The cold air hit his skin like a whip, and he welcomed it.

He made his way toward the ledge where water poured into the deep pool below. He bent over, intending to dive in, when something caught his eye from behind the waterfall. A sword hilt, unmistakably! He stopped himself and nearly slipped over the edge. He moved across the strong current that flowed over the lip of the ledge, placing his steps carefully along the slick and mossy surface. There was nothing to hold on to – no branches, no rocks...

Suddenly he remembered he had brought a rope, and slowly made his way back across the treacherous rocks to go and find it.

He returned to where he had left his clothing and supplies, but to his shock, nothing was where he had left it. Not his clothes, his pack, spear, or, most disturbing of all, *Dyrnwyn*.

"Gods!" he cried out, secretly cursing Rowan. *She must have taken it all!*

He went back to the hot pool to think, for it was far too cold to stand there naked to the elements. He closed his eyes and his mind wound round and round the dilemma. *There was something there, behind the waterfall.* He had to get to it.

He would have to reroute the water flow and create a place where he could lie down and lean over the edge to take a closer look. He had built many rock walls in his life. He would simply build another. He got out and began moving heavy rocks into the water, stacking them up in a crescent shape with the arc against the current and the two points right up to the edge of the ledge just before the place in the falls where he had seen the sword hilt. It was slow work and he had to take breaks regularly to warm his body in one of the pools. Eventually his curved wall was high enough that the water began to flow around it. He flattened himself on the ledge and noticed something strange about it. It was far too uniform to be natural. He hung the top half of his body over it and saw why. It seemed the ruins of some kind of structure lay behind the sheet of water from above. He saw symbols for the cauldron and the Great Mother carved into certain stones peeking out from behind moss and plants, and an opening in the rock that surely led into some kind of temple. Then he remembered what he was really looking for; he looked suddenly to his left, expecting to see the sword hilt, but to his utter dismay there was nothing there. Nothing at all.

Suddenly he felt like a fool. Gwion had clearly said the sword lay *within the pool*, yet he had wasted the entire day building a rock wall to get to a place that didn't even hold what he was looking for. The days had grown short, and he knew there would not be much daylight left, but he could not leave the glade without *Caledgwyn*.

Frustrated with himself, he dove into the pool below. The water was a strange mix of temperatures ranging from warm to ice cold, which told him there had to be another water source besides the hot springs that fed into it. He opened his eyes and explored along the many crevices of its rocky bottom. He saw many small figurines and bits of jewelry or beads that had surely been offerings to the Great Mother from the priestesses. There were a few daggers as well, but no swords. Over and over he dove down, searching each section of the pool in turn, but finding nothing but small offerings. Out of curiosity, he followed a current of cold water, wondering where it was flowing from, and found it coming forth from behind some rocks that had clearly been stacked by human hands. Were they the remains of an old temple wall, put there to lessen the flow of cold water into the pool? He didn't know, but realized it wasn't beyond the realm of possibilities that the sword might be buried beneath them. He worked as long as he could removing the stones, and then swam up to the surface to breathe. He dove down again, and removed several more stones. Then, he saw what could be a pommel made from amber! He reached in to touch it, but he would have to remove a few more stones before he could free it. He swam up to the surface for another breath. It was late afternoon. He had to hurry.

He dove a third time and removed a few more rocks, revealing the unmistakable hilt of a sword, inlaid with amber and gold. His heart leapt at the sight. *Almost his!* He swam up to the surface once again to catch his breath, but when he returned to the place, yet as before, the sword he had surely seen was no longer there. He frantically moved the rocks around the place he had seen it, thinking it may have become dislodged by the current or moved while he was at the surface, but found nothing.

Night was falling. He wondered if perhaps in the grotto there might be torches or other things left behind that he could use to get through the night. He swam toward the dark opening beneath the waterfall and discovered rock stairs when he put his feet down. He climbed out of the pool and entered the grotto, reaching out on either side of him, his arms outstretched and his fingers trailing along the wet corridor. Warm water seeped down the rock over his hands, and the air became warmer and wetter the farther in he went. His senses were still very much attuned to the dark from his long stay in the caves, and soon he noticed the sounds around him changed. He knew he stood in a larger chamber, and thankfully it was warm enough for him to stay here and sleep. He found deer skins on the floor and imagined the priestesses used them to sit upon during prayer or rituals. He had not dared hope for such luck. He gratefully laid down in the darkness, covering his naked body with the skins, and relaxed in the warmth, his body becoming heavy and his breathing smooth and even. Suddenly from somewhere deep and quiet, a prayer rose unbidden in his mind.

"Blessed is your womb, Great Mother, from which all life is born. I have come to you naked and humble, as a child, to submit myself to your will. I am your servant. Use me as you wish."

He found himself drifting off to sleep, the prayer repeating itself to the rhythm of his breath.

Some things cannot be taken, my child. They must be asked for.

Shame overcame him. He was in a holy and sacred place dedicated to the Great Mother. He had been all day. Yet he had not offered her one prayer nor had he treated this place with the reverence it deserved. No, he had done nothing but throw rocks around, force her water to flow in new places, sat impatiently in her pools, and stomped around greedily plotting how he would take something he wanted. Not until now had he allowed himself to be guided by its peacefulness.

"I am ashamed, Great Mother. I ask for your forgiveness."

I forgive you.

"How may I serve you?"

Bring no death here. Shed no blood in my name.

"Great Mother, I seek Caledgwyn not to shed the blood of the living, nor to subject others to my will, but rather to return the dead to their peaceful rest; to return them to Arawn. Such work is the work of men; we are the reapers who plow the fields under so that new life may be brought forth. I ask for your blessing and the means to do this work. The name under whom blood will be shed shall be his, my lady, not yours."

Then it is not my blessing you need, child. It is his. Gain it, and you shall have what you seek.

This he had not expected, and he shivered at the prospect. No creature that roamed the earth, living or undead, struck fear into the heart of Bran, but the idea of meeting Arawn made all wise men anxious, be they slave, warrior, or king. The songs say that as your life drains out of you, you will hear his white hounds baying in the distance when they have caught your scent; the scent of a dying man who will soon bow down before him and be judged.

He could not sleep, consumed with the knowledge that he would have to call upon the one god wise men never dared to call upon, for to behold his face meant your heart no longer beat among the living.

CHAPTER TWENTY-FOUR
Annwn

Bran lay in the warm darkness for a long time, considering his words carefully. He dreaded saying them, but knew it was the only way. He stood and spoke.

"Great Arawn, Lord of the Otherworld, I humbly offer myself to you in service, and pledge my skills as an earthly Warrior to return the bodies of the cauldron-born to their graves, and thereby deliver unto you the souls that have been stolen from you by the sorceress Cerridwen. I ask for your blessing to pursue them."

He waited for an answer or a sign, and for what seemed a very long time none came forth, but gradually he noticed the air around him growing colder, as if a winter wind had somehow found its way into the cave. The sound of his breath and movements around him sounded smaller, and the space around him felt as if it were expanding. He reached down for the skins at his feet, but to his dismay found they were no longer there. He had no idea what awaited him outside the cave, and certainly didn't want to venture out into it naked, but it seemed he had no choice. So be it.

He followed the cold air outside and noticed that as he moved out of the cave his body felt lighter and lighter, the ground pulling at his feet less and less. His movements grew smoother, and soon he could not feel the hardness of the earth beneath his feet nor the coldness of the air against his skin. He eventually emerged into a pale landscape cast in a strange silvery light.

He felt quite vulnerable, and looked around for something to cover himself with. *If only I had my cloak!* He didn't know what to do next. He couldn't make out anything of interest on the horizon, for the land looked the same in all directions. He thought back on the stories of Arawn and the "in-between" that his mother had told him as a boy. He had always loved grisly tales, the more fearsome and bloody the better, and she told them with more skill than anyone, save his uncle, Einon.

He looked up and to his surprise found the horizon had shifted a bit. Things didn't look the same as they had a moment before. The change was disorienting and he found himself hesitant to leave the cave behind, wondering if he would be able to find it again.

Well, there is nothing to be done for it. Staying here won't accomplish anything. He moved forward in the hope that he would eventually find Arawn, or more likely, Arawn would find him.

As he walked, the landscape continued to drift and shift around him. He noticed that what he expected to see began to appear before him, which was disturbing, for what lay in the Otherworld he had imagined many, many times over as a boy.

Slowly a forest came into view, as if a fog that had previously hidden it was being lifted. *The dark forests of Glyn Cuch.* They were as he had always imagined them as a child, whenever his mother would tell him the tales of the legendary Pwyll, Lord of Dyved, who had met the Lord Arawn while hunting.

"What strangeness is this?"

Rough, grey-black branches of trees wove together, twisting all about him, as if conspiring to ensnare him. They soon surrounded him completely, but to his surprise he found if he moved forward, they dissipated, as if they were formed of nothing but ashes and shadows.

He moved faster through the bracken, tired of it obscuring his view, sailing through it impatiently. Suddenly through the branches he saw a light blinking in and out of view, small and faint in the distance, but discernible out of the corner of his eye. He moved toward it, curious and grateful to have something to move toward. *Could it be Arawn?*

He had no idea what the God of the Otherworld might really look like. He cautiously moved closer, and to his relief saw it was the form of a woman, her hair and skin luminous, beckoning to him like a candle lit by a lover in a window. Fearful she might disappear, he called out to her.

"Please! Hear me! I must speak with you…"

The trees faded away and he found himself suddenly in front of her, looking down into a deep valley with mountains on the other side.

Once she was near he was overwhelmed by a familiarity.

"Mother?" he asked tentatively, his soul feeding him the answer.

"Yes," the luminous being answered. "You've been thinking of me."

It was true. He had wondered if he would find her here.

"I always draw near when you think of me, only here the soil that thoughts are planted in is much richer. You will find they bloom into being very quickly, so I would caution you to take care what you plant, my son."

"I don't understand."

"Why do you think the forest appeared? Was it not what you expected the world of Arawn to look like? Do you think this is truly where he lives, or that he even hunts as men do in such forests?"

"I don't know. Until now, for me, the Otherworld of Annwn was nothing but the speculations of men and the songs of the Druids."

She laughed. "And now? Now do you think this world consists of anything more than that?"

He became confused. The sky around him darkened, clouds forming ominously in the distance.

"It seems a storm is brewing," she said. "One that I'm sure will clear up when you come to understand what I mean. When you do, you will know how to find Arawn."

His mother's words continued to perplex him.

"One more bit of advice," she offered. "The more you explore this world, the easier it is to forget the world of the living. You must strive to remember why you have come."

"I am struggling already, Mother," he admitted. He knew he didn't belong there, and that he had come to find Arawn, but he could not remember why.

"Did I come for you?" he asked.

"No, son. Not for me. You came to offer yourself to Arawn, and do his bidding in the world of men."

She took his hand and traced the symbol of the cauldron into it. The mark stayed upon his palm and she pressed her thumbs into it.

"You must remember," she insisted.

"Yes," he answered, looking down at the symbol.

"I will be with you always," she said in farewell, and her spirit began floating away, vanishing into the mist.

He anguished at her departure, as if he were yet again a small boy. He cried out to her, but she was already gone, and yet again he was left standing alone in the pale landscape.

The clouds had lengthened into smooth grey fingers that reached across the vast sky, and though many of the features of the countryside still shifted, there were now certain things that did not; the most noticeable a distant dark fortress set within the mountains on the horizon, and a dry and rocky road stretching out for miles in front of him.

He moved his weightless, ghostly feet swiftly along the road, noticing he was now somehow dressed, his cloak billowing behind him on a breeze he could not feel. The mountains looked to be days away, and he thought of Gethen. He would be glad of both the horse's speed and company right now.

Suddenly he sensed something gaining on him from behind, coming toward him at an alarming speed. He turned around in fear, and to his surprise the road he traveled upon did not appear behind him, only in front of him. He couldn't hear anything, but he knew something was coming for him. He suspected it might be Arawn's hounds and didn't want to risk an encounter with them. He looked off the road for a place to hide, and a large boulder appeared. Gratefully he got behind it to watch the road, but to his dismay, the road was no longer visible at all. He looked back toward where he had been for any sign of the animal, but saw nothing. He rose to his feet, and to his shock found the road rolled out from beneath where he now stood toward the structure in the distance.

It wasn't long before he sensed he was being pursued again. This time he would not run. He turned and readied himself, and suddenly felt the weight of a spear solidify within his right hand. His confidence soared as he waited, weapon poised, until suddenly a dark figure burst out of nothingness onto the road, nearly knocking him over, and after a moment of astonishment he smiled in relief. His pursuer was a dark and regal form he knew well, with eyes pearlescent and luminous in the pale light, and a violet hue dancing on the curves of his body as he moved.

"Always faithful, you are!" he grinned, recognizing Gethen's spirit. "Even in the Otherworld!"

He and Gethen were soon soaring as one being at astonishing speed through the rugged landscape, at times seeming to fly over the land, everything shifting slightly around them except for the road unfurling in front of them toward the dark fortress in the distance.

The road began descending into an ever-darkening valley, becoming narrower as forest crowded in upon it from both sides.

Unlike the shadowy forest he had first encountered, its thorns and branches scratched and tore at flesh and hair, as real as any he had ever encountered among the living. It swallowed them into its web, arching completely over the road they traveled upon and obscuring the silver light from the sky. Soon they had to slow to a walk until the road eventually widened again, the trees thinning out, and they emerged along the shore of an immense dark lake. The mountains looked down upon the water ominously, like hags lamenting the loss of their youth in a mirror, clutching the now huge and foreboding fortress within their craggy knuckles.

They traveled along the road around the edge of the lake. Its waters were clear and still, its bed filled with smooth, white stones. He found the scene beautifully peaceful until he realized they were not stones at all, but countless human skulls resting deep within the clear water, stretching as far as the eye could see.

They rode along the shore until they reached an immense archway, some forty feet high, perhaps, made entirely of bones and antlers. Perched high upon it were hundreds of ravens, Arawn's sacred messengers. He wondered if they indeed served as escorts for the souls of the dead, as it was believed among his people, and if so, where their charges wandered.

They rode cautiously beneath the arch, all of the birds' heads turning in unison to watch them pass beneath it. Not one black eye was trained on anything else, and his uneasiness increased as they passed through, for now he knew the birds' eyes were on his back. The road began climbing steeply up the mountainside, taking them ever closer to the fortress.

Suddenly the sky filled with black wings and an ear-splitting cacophony of shrill cries, and a cloud of darkness moved overhead.

"I believe we have just been announced," he said nervously to Gethen as they continued up the steep mountain trail, but soon a much more disturbing sound filled the air.

The hounds of Arawn.

Bran panicked, knowing he could not slay them for fear of angering Arawn, but he would not let them tear him or Gethen apart, either. *Think!* he chided himself, but there was no time to think. The huge white hounds soon surrounded them, baying and bellowing up into the sky, red ears and eyes menacing in the night.

Neither horse nor rider moved. Bran attempted to protect them by thinking of armor for their bodies, food to subdue the hounds, or even the two of them taking flight above the jaws which snapped at them, but nothing changed, no matter how desperately he willed it. It was as if he now stood within another's dream, not his own, where his will had no dominion.

Then, to his relief, a beautiful apparition appeared on the road and quieted the hounds. They went to her in perfect obedience and sat at her feet.

"Name yourself and why you've come," she said abruptly to him.

He dismounted and knelt respectfully, bowing his head, looking into the palm of his hand. The cauldron his mother had drawn for him was still there, reminding him of his purpose.

"I am Bran, son of Agarah, and I seek audience with the great Lord Arawn. I wish to offer myself in service to him."

"To what purpose?" she asked.

"As slayer of the cauldron-born," he answered, his eyes still on the ground in front of him, not daring to look up without her bidding. He felt her eyes upon him, considering his words.

"Rise and follow me."

He stood and did as she commanded, Gethen walking closely behind him. She was obviously no slave, so he surmised she must be Arawn's queen.

They floated silently along the lonely road, winding up toward the massive fortress until they reached a vast chasm of darkness. Nothing could be seen within its depths, but strange and disturbing sounds drifted up from far below, hinting at what lay beneath.

A great bridge appeared as Arawn's queen stepped to the edge of the chasm, and he followed her out upon it, but Gethen refused.

"That's fine, friend," he said kindly. "Wait here for me."

She was already half way across the chasm, the hounds ever at her thighs. He feared that when she reached the other side the bridge might disappear again, so he ran to close the gap between them.

With her back turned he could look at her more closely without fear of reproach. Her dark hair was twisted and piled on the top of her head, revealing a long, slender neck and graceful shoulders. He noticed a mark on the back of her neck, but he couldn't make it out. She was nearly as tall as he was, her long legs striding swiftly across the bridge. The wind blowing up from the chasm beneath floated the light fabric of her gossamer dress all around her, revealing different parts of her body as she walked, mesmerizing him.

Finally, to his relief, they reached the other side, where they passed under yet another archway. The tell-tale ravens were perched upon it, and he wondered if they were the same birds he had encountered before.

He followed her into the gaping dark maw of the fortress and down a long, high corridor carved out of rock. The skeletons of a thousand men held torches down both sides, lighting their way. The hounds now left her side, rushing toward the end of the corridor, no doubt eager to return to their master.

Bran's heart pounded in anticipation of meeting the powerful being who lay beyond the corridor stretching in front of him, and he fought back a feeling of panic. Everything he had come to say seeming like folly and insolence to him, but it was too late now. His fate was sealed.

The corridor led to a huge chamber with a massive fire burning in the center of its floor within a brazier the size of his clan's motherhouse. It burned without wood, and without smoke, but sent heat and light in all directions. Above the flames he saw a giant figure seated upon a raised dais upon a throne built of bones. The hounds lay at his feet, looking as docile as such frightening creatures possibly could.

Bran walked apprehensively around the fire to the other side, unsure of whether he should look up, but he could not help his curiosity.

The god Arawn was three times the size of an ordinary man, massive and broad-chested with a mane of dark hair, and frighteningly translucent skin through which his skull could be seen. His clothing was dark and fine, a great fur cloak fastened about his neck. He sat widely, feet planted firmly on the ground, and elbows resting upon his giant throne. He had terrible eyes, the milky color of the blue ice that lay at the heart of the glaciers in the North, and they peered down on Bran. As the god wore no discernible expression, Bran had no indication of what his disposition might be toward him.

Bran knelt in submission, summoning all of his courage to find his voice.

"Lord Arawn, I am Bran, son of Agarah. I've come to submit myself to you."

"Submission to me is not a choice," the Dark Lord spoke, shaking the entire chamber and setting Bran's heart to pound.

"Know I have heard well your oath to serve me, son of Agarah, and you shall fulfill it, either among the living, or here among the dead, as I see fit to command."

"Yes, my lord," Bran replied, trembling at the second possibility. "There is a sorceress among the living known as Cerridwen who steals the dead from their graves and grants them life through the Sacred Cauldron. Her cauldron-born roam among us, feeding upon the young and weak…"

"All predators feed upon the weak. This is the way of things."

"My lord," Bran began again carefully, knowing if he could not convince Arawn to send him back, he would spend eternity here.

"You surely know then that Cerridwen seeks to rule the Crossroads and the doorway to the Summerlands, setting herself above you, usurping your right to end life, and the Great Mother's to grant it. Could you not use a faithful servant among the living?"

There was a long silence, and finally Bran dared to glance up and saw Arawn stroking the head of one of his hounds. He prayed he had finally managed to say something the god found of interest.

"Cerridwen is indeed blessed beyond her sisters."

Arawn looked toward his queen, who gazed back at him with a strange knowing.

"She is a favored child among the Gods. She breaks the rules, but we cannot help but smile at her cleverness."

Bran grew anxious again over the tolerance Arawn bore Cerridwen.

"However, she shall not be indulged. She will be made to answer for her misdeeds. As for the souls she has stolen from me, it is true that I need the assistance of a mortal. They are beyond my reach, trapped in the in-between."

Finally, a flicker of hope!

"Behold me, son of Agarah," the terrible voice then commanded.

Bran looked up to see Arawn had leaned forward, his horrible form arching over him like a great mountain, his red cape flowing from his shoulders over the gruesome dais of bones like a sheet of blood.

"Though all men dread my coming, if they knew what lurked in the in-between, they would welcome me with open arms," the ghastly skull said. "For the souls who suffer there unfairly, you shall serve me among the living and reap them in my name."

A wave of immense relief washed over Bran, and he almost laughed with joy knowing he would again see the blessed light of day.

"However, I will require a few things of you, to ensure your loyalty."

Relief was quickly replaced by dread as he pondered what Arawn would require of him.

"Those who have my blessing wear my mark," the god began. "I will know you in the world of the living by it. Serve me well, and you may live among your people for as long as you desire. This is my gift to you in return for your service."

"Yes, my lord," Bran replied.

Arawn's queen descended the dais and went to the fire, a long delicate wand in her hand with a circular amulet forged upon its end. She placed it into the fire until it glowed white-hot.

"Bow your head," she said to Bran.

He did as she bid, and she smiled, a bit cruelly. She walked behind him and pressed the brand upon the back of his neck, right where he had seen her own mark, searing the symbol of Arawn into his flesh. The pain was unbearable, and he could not help crying out in agony. When the deed was done, she leaned down and kissed the mark, and miraculously the pain disappeared as quickly as it had come upon him.

She whispered in his ear, "That is my parting gift to you, Warrior."

With that she returned to her lord's side.

"Go, son of Agarah." Arawn said dismissively.

Bran lowered his head to the ground in respect and then left the throne room, stealing one last glance at Arawn's queen on his way out.

He found he moved with much more speed and power as he left Arawn's fortress, and when he reached the chasm the bridge expanded out in front of him as it had for Arawn's queen. He ran across it in long strides and called out to Gethen, who was soon at his side.

Soon upon his back, they galloped off down the road, underneath the first archway, along the lake and through the valley and forests, never stopping until they arrived at the cave through which he had entered this world.

"Farewell, good friend," he said to Gethen. "I'll see you again on the other side."

Bran dismounted and went back through the doorway he had entered this world through, and there he waited.

***

Daylight crept into the grotto, illuminating the green moss and paintings in the temple around him.

I have returned.

He rose and walked outside where the light of dawn greeted him, reflecting upon the surface of the pool. He gazed thankfully into it, and noticed the figure of a woman emerging just below the surface, her hair floating around her face and dancing about her breasts in the water. She offered him the blade of a sword, lifted delicately upon her fingertips, just below the surface of the water. He reached in and took it, wondering if his hands would actually touch metal or if the vision would disappear, but it was cold and solid. He gripped the hilt in his hand, squeezing it in reverence, and then the apparition slowly faded away, disappearing into the watery depths.

He held the magnificent sword up to examine it, tilting it back and forth in the light, and then with a final prayer of thanks to the Great Mother, left the glade with what he had come for.

CHAPTER TWENTY-FIVE
Lost Daughters

Lucia was weaving when Gwion came to her.

"He has done it!" the boy said, smiling. "Bran wields *Caledgwyn*."

"What?" she cried. It had been a week since Bran had gone to the glade. Gethen had returned to the village without him, and Lucia had feared the worst.

"Where is he?"

"In the courtyard," Gwion said. "He asked for you."

Lucia quickly set her work down and wrapped a shawl around her shoulders, eager to see him.

"How long has he been there? Has he eaten?"

"No," Gwion said. "He looked weak."

"Does Lady Rowan know?"

"Yes, I told her first. After speaking with him she left for the glade, saying she did not wish to be disturbed, and sent me back to bring him food and water."

Lucia grabbed a basket to that end, and took the blanket from her bed.

"Let's go," she said.

"Why don't you go ahead?" Gwion suggested. "I'll be there shortly."

Lucia smiled inside, knowing he had given her a gift. After filling the basket with food and drink, she set out toward the old courtyard, thinking of what Bran's accomplishment meant to the war they were fighting.

Soon she entered the courtyard and saw him, his back turned to her, stoking a fire in the ancient hearth. He heard her approach and turned around, a smile on his face. He did indeed look pale, but happy. She went to him and bent down to rest the basket at his feet in front of the hearth, feeling no trace of the awkwardness that she had felt before. When she stood up he wrapped his great arms around her, pulling her into his chest, and time ceased moving for her. She didn't want to speak, nor be spoken to, nor move. She wanted nothing but to be there, suspended in the perfection of that moment with him, forever. He must have known somehow, for he remained silent and didn't pull away. He waited until she finally did.

"You're hungry, I'm sure," she said.

"I am," he admitted.

She sat and reached into the basket she had brought, offering him a round loaf of bread and a flask of ale.

"You've done it," she said excitedly, eyeing the jeweled hilt at his side in wonder. "I knew you would succeed. It was your destiny, Bran."

"I'm glad you believed so," he replied. "I was not as confident as you."

With that he reverently held up his prize for her to examine. The sword was indeed the most beautiful Lucia had ever seen. Its hilt was inlaid with intricate patterns made from ivory, amber, and gold, but its real beauty lay within its blade, which gleamed as if reflecting the moonlight even though it was the sun which shone in the sky above them.

"Where did you find it?" she asked.

"It was not to be found, but rather to be given," he answered.

She smiled and nodded in understanding, and then noticed dried blood on the back of his shirt.

"Are you injured?" she asked, concerned.

"No," he replied. "There is more to the story. I needed Lord Arawn's blessing before the Great Mother would grant me the sword. To obtain it, I made an oath with him. I wear his mark now."

"What?" she cried.

Shocked, she jumped up to look at his back. She pulled his shirt down gently and saw a brand between his shoulders that shone like silver in the light, the skin around it raw and red.

She gasped at its intricacy, amazed by how it shimmered like metal, though it rested on skin.

"I have given my oath to Arawn that I will not rest until I've hunted down all of the cauldron-born, releasing them from the in-between and into his hands. My work will not be done until the dead walk the earth no more, and the Cauldron is returned here where it belongs."

Just then Gwion entered the courtyard.

"I knew you could do it, my lord," he said, smiling.

Bran smiled back, holding up the sword for him as well.

"Take it!" Bran urged.

Gwion did, and he, too, was mesmerized by the blade's beauty.

"It is perfect," he whispered, moving it from one hand to the other.

"Tomorrow I ride south," Bran announced after a moment, "and after presenting Aelhaearn with *Dyrnwyn*, I'll raise a company to ride north with me to find the Cauldron. Returning it here is the first step. Without it, Cerridwen cannot resurrect her warriors nor create new ones. It is a helpless battle as long as she possesses it."

"I am coming with you," Gwion announced.

Bran smiled. "I expected so."

At that Gwion left to go and spend the rest of the day with his mother, and Lucia was glad. Aveta had missed him so terribly.

"I wish to come as well," Lucia said boldly.

Bran shook his head. "No, Lucia. You will stay here with Aveta and your grandmother."

How dare he dismiss her like a child! "But I can be of great service!" she cried indignantly. How could he not see the value in her coming along? She argued with him until he finally grabbed her by the arms.

"Gods, woman!" he exclaimed in frustration. "Why are you so eager to put yourself in harm's way again!"

Lucia's anger melted away as she realized the truth of why he had wanted her to stay behind.

"Let me travel with you as far as your village, then," she said with a softer tone. "Let me help your people as I did before."

Bran was silent for a moment and Lucia took heart in seeing that he was considering her request.

"So be it," he finally said. "You can come south with us if you give me your oath not to leave the safety of the camp again, nor try to follow me north."

She smiled at her victory. "I swear it," she promised.

"Gods, but you're stubborn!" he said, and though Lucia noted genuine frustration she also noticed the hint of a smile.

"Lucia, there's something I want you to know," he said after a moment, his smile fading.

"What?" she replied nervously, wondering whether it would be good or bad. Before he could tell her, Gwion called out from the trees.

"Lord Bran! Ula has returned!"

Gwion entered the courtyard accompanied by a naked woman with wet hair. The moment the girl saw Bran she ran to him and threw her arms around his neck.

Who is she? Lucia wondered, staring at her nakedness in shock.

"Ula!" Bran cried happily, a grin on his face, as if a puppy had ran to him rather than a naked woman.

Lucia felt eclipsed, her heart sinking at how overjoyed Bran was by this strange woman's arrival. *Gods. Was she what Bran had wanted to tell her about?* Her stomach began churning with emotions, none of them good.

Bran found a blanket and wrapped it around the woman and then turned to Lucia.

"This is Ula. She led me to Gwion and Islwyn, who healed my wounds. I owe my life to her."

Ula turned to look at Lucia, her face full of smiling innocence, but Lucia could manage nothing more than a nod in her direction.

"Within the lake are creatures that travel the rivers that flow through it, and even out to sea and back. There is nothing that happens in or around the waters of this land that they do not know," Gwion said. "I bid her speak to them, and they have told her the Cauldron no longer rests within the grotto."

"What?" Bran said, dismayed.

"I believe she's taking it to the Crossroads," Gwion said with concern, "and she would not chance taking the Cauldron to the Crossroads if she weren't sure she could overtake it."

Bran seemed undaunted. "With Talhaiarn's knowledge of sorcery, Aelhaearn wielding *Dyrnwyn*, *Caledgwyn* in my own hand, and the strongest warriors of the four tribes, I cannot see how she could possibly defeat us. She is one woman with a host of puppets, and though they are far more gruesome and strong than the average warrior, they can be killed as ordinary men. My only worry is time. We don't know if she's already there, or on her way."

"Indeed," a voice behind them said, and everyone turned abruptly to see Rowan descending from the opposite side of the courtyard from the trail that led to the pools. The old woman's ability to approach without being seen or heard was deeply unnerving, for one never knew how long she had been there watching or listening before making her presence known.

"My daughter is not a fool. She rarely fails in judgment. If what the *selkie* says is true, she surely has the upper hand, and we must find out why," she cautioned.

"I poured all my knowledge into my daughter in the hopes she would one day be honored as High Priestess after me. She has instead chosen to wield that power in her own name, rather than the Great Mother's. You must not underestimate her. She is extremely shrewd, and Morvran is said to be a terror unlike any other in battle."

Bran shook his head. "I believe Morvran is dead," he said simply, and Rowan looked over at him in shock.

"What?" she asked in confusion. "Why?"

"A black wolf nearly twice my size attacked me in the grotto where I discovered the Cauldron. After I managed to kill the beast, its body transformed from wolf to that of a deformed man that Gwion assured me was Morvran when I described him."

Rowan suddenly looked frail and leaned against the oak in the courtyard, clutching at its bark with her thin hand as if it would hold her up.

"Her rage will know no bounds," she finally said. "Though Morvran was her greatest burden, he was also her greatest love."

She turned and looked Bran in the eye. "You will never be free of her wrath. Or his father's."

"His father?" Bran asked with surprise.

"His spirit dwells within this lake," Rowan said. "This explains the mist," she added. "He is angry."

Lucia saw Bran struggle for a moment, as if trying to choose his next words carefully.

"Lady Rowan, I know Morvran was of your blood, and for this I ask your pardon."

"You did what you had to," Rowan replied, again her competent self. "My greatest sorrow now, I fear, is that the same fate awaits my daughter. She will never compromise, nor come under anyone else's authority. Not now. She has gone too far to return to us."

Rowan suddenly looked very old to Lucia.

"I have work to do," she finally said in farewell, leaving the small party alone in the courtyard.

398

There they sat--a young boy, a young girl, a single warrior and herself, Lucia thought. She looked toward the sky above the moss-covered stones of the last great tragedy that had come of defying the Great Mother's ways, and wondered anxiously what the gods had planned for them.

CHAPTER TWENTY-SIX
The Journey Home

Bran rose and packed the boat early the next morning, but interrupting all of his tasks and worries were thoughts of Lucia. Something about her had called to him since their first meeting, but thankfully it had remained relatively silent. Now it surfaced with a vengeance, demanding his attention, which he found immensely frustrating. Gods willing, there would be time for such matters later, provided any of them survived this damn war, but such distractions were a luxury he could not afford right now. Then, complicating matters further, was Ula. He was not blind to how she looked at him, and was fairly sure it would only be a matter of time before she offered herself to him. He would have to refuse her, and then what? What were the *selkie* like when spurned? He did not know, and he did not want to find out.

As if she had heard his thoughts, Lucia suddenly appeared on the shore with her arms full of supplies. Her damn green eyes pulled him in and the smell of her punctuated the conversation he had just had with himself.

"Will you fetch Gwion and Ula?" he asked flatly, taking the supplies from her. "We should have left already."

Her expression changed. "Is something wrong?"

"No," he snapped.

"Are you certain?" she asked again.

"I am anxious to leave, that's all," he said, half-smiling and hopeful she would take that as an explanation. She did not seem convinced, but did not pry further. Instead, she made it worse.

"Last night, you said there was something you wanted to tell me," she asked.

She seemed as irritated as he was now, her tone defensive.

He had hoped she would not remember. Emboldened by ale, he had foolishly almost confessed his feelings to her, but sober it no longer seemed prudent. What could he do about it now, anyway?

"I'm sorry," he replied sheepishly. "I don't remember."

"I see," she said.

He was unable to tell if she was relieved or disappointed. Thankfully, Gwion showed up with Ula before she asked any further questions.

"How do you propose we get Gethen back across the lake?" he turned and asked Gwion.

"On the large skiff the Sisters use. My mother and a few of the other Sisters will cross the lake with us and then row the skiff and boat back once we're across. We should tie them both together so we don't get separated in the mist."

"Good," Bran said. "Let's get started."

After a bit of a struggle they were finally on their way, the women in the boat ahead of them navigating, barely visible through the mist which was now nearly solid. Ula swam happily alongside them, and Bran and Gwion rowed the large skiff as evenly as they could, so as not to spook Gethen who stood upon it like a great statue carved of black marble.

Once they were on their way, Bran let out an audible sigh of exasperation.

"What troubles you, my lord?" Gwion asked.

"Many things, Gwion, but this morning it is women," he confessed.

"Ah, I see," Gwion said. "Lady Lucia, or Ula?"

"Both," he answered.

Gwion smiled. "I imagine many men would be pleased with such a dilemma."

"I suppose they might," Bran admitted, "but I require a clear head at the moment."

"Understood," Gwion replied, but then his smile suddenly disappeared.

"What is it?"

"There is something in the water," Gwion said nervously, looking down into the lake. "Something *big*."

Bran looked down into the lake as well, and sure enough, he saw a shadowy form moving beneath the skiff. Very large, indeed. Gethen became restless, pawing at the skiff and causing it to teeter, and Gwion reached up to calm him.

"Gods! Where is Ula?" Bran cried, suddenly remembering she had been in the water.

"She is fine," Gwion said. "It is you it wants, Bran."

"Me?" Bran asks, surprised. "Why?"

Suddenly the skiff was hit from beneath with tremendous force. Gethen struggled to regain his balance, and all three are nearly thrown into the water.

"Gods!" Bran yelled. "What is it?""

"The *afanc*," Gwion replied with dread.

"What the bloody hell is that?" Bran asked, standing and taking up his spear.

"I have never seen it before, but the songs say it has swum the waters of this lake for at least a hundred years."

"Well, I won't risk your life or my horse's, so if it's me it wants, I will take the fight to it!" Bran said.

Before Gwion could protest, Bran put his dagger between his teeth and dove into the water to search for the creature, but the water was too murky.

He heard Gwion yelling a warning from up above, and then suddenly something clamped down upon his leg and dragged him rapidly toward the bottom of the lake.

He was grateful he had trained to hold his breath for so long, but even so, he knew he would drown if he could not free himself quickly. He stabbed at the creature as hard as he could, but his hide was like armor. Finally, he managed to find an eye, and knew he was saved. He jabbed his dagger deep into its eye socket and twisted its eyeball out, and finally it released its hold on him. He swam as quickly as he could toward the surface and burst forth to fill his lungs.

Once he regained his breath he looked around anxiously for some sign of his companions, but the mist surrounding him was so thick he couldn't see a thing. He called out as loudly as he could, over and over, but no one returned his call. He was disoriented and had no idea which way to swim, so simply continued to tread water and yell. He gave up after ten minutes, finally realizing he was on his own and out of earshot of his companions.

He decided he had better start swimming in *some* direction, and hoped desperately for two things – that he was swimming in the direction of the shore, and that the *afanc* would not be back.

***

"What is happening?" Lucia cried in terror.

"Bran has disappeared," Gwion's voice called anxiously out of the mist. "He dove in after the *afanc*."

"Oh, Great Mother," Aveta said, distressed.

"The what?" Lucia asked, growing more upset by the second.

"The *afanc* is a lake-dwelling demon," Aveta explained, "much like a dragon, but with fins."

"*What?*" Lucia cried.

"I'm afraid this might have something to do with Tegid Voel," Aveta said. "He must know of Morvran's death, and that Bran is responsible. The *afanc* serves him."

"What are you saying, Aveta?" Lucia asked urgently. "Bran!" she called out frantically. "BRAN!"

She could hear Gwion rowing the skiff closer and soon Gethen's massive black form appeared through the mist.

"We need to get Gethen off the lake," Gwion said. "We cannot search for Bran like this. We must go back to the island."

"Yes," Aveta agreed.

"Will he be alright?" Lucia asked, but no one answered her. She began rowing, and Gwion stayed close behind. After some time, the island shore reappeared. Gethen was eager to dig his hooves into land and leapt off the skiff as soon as it slid upon the sand.

"All we can do is appeal to Tegid Voel and ask that Bran be spared, but he is sure to ask a price," Aveta warned.

"What kind of price?" Lucia asked nervously.

"I don't know," Aveta replied. "Hurry, we must speak with Rowan. The others can finish up here."

Lucia followed Aveta and Gwion through the trees back toward the huts, her mind racing. "How do we find this Tegid Voel to make him an offer?" she asked impatiently.

"He is not of our realm," Aveta explained. "We cannot go to where he dwells."

"What are you saying?" Lucia snapped angrily. "That Bran is lost to us?"

"I would never say that, child," Aveta corrected, putting her arm around her shoulders in reassurance, but Lucia wanted none of it and strode on ahead, eager for solid answers. She reached the motherhouse first, and found her grandmother was waiting. She did not seem surprised at all to see her.

"You could not cross, could you?" she said.

"No," Lucia replied.

"I feared this might happen," Rowan sighed. "He knows already."

"Who is this Tegid Voel?" Lucia asked. "He sent some horrible beast called an *afanc* to attack us."

"A spirit of the lake. He lives between the mists," she answered simply, as if that were a sufficient explanation. "Is the *selkie* with you?"

"No," Lucia answered. "She didn't return to the boats after it happened."

"With any luck she has gone to your warrior's aid," Rowan said. "She is likely his only hope. Being of the water, Tegid Voel may listen to her. Pray that she can convince him to spare Bran, or I doubt you shall see him again."

**

Bran was beginning to lose strength when suddenly he sensed something swimming near him, and before he knew it, it had latched on to his hand. In a panic he yanked it away and raised his

407

dagger in defense, but suddenly Ula's face appeared in front of him, her big black eyes looking fearfully at his weapon.

"Thank the gods, Ula!" he cried breathlessly, lowering his dagger and overwhelmed with joy at seeing her. "I thought I would surely drown here!"

She again reached for his arm and he let her take it, scarcely able to keep his head above water anymore. She pulled him along when he slowed down, swimming powerfully with him in tow.

Some time later the mist thinned out, and finally he saw her stand up and walk out of the lake. He put his feet under him and did the same, following her up on the shore.

Bran couldn't help but notice she seemed especially somber, no trace of the regular childishness or fun in her manner. Perhaps she was worn out from searching for him? He hated the idea of having been a burden. He had not even managed to kill the *afanc*, and now a *woman* had come and rescued him? *Gods.*

Ula sat down on the bank to rest, and Bran collapsed on the ground next to her, so thankful to feel the solid earth beneath his bones. After catching his breath, he turned to her, and to his surprise she suddenly threw her arms around his neck and wrapped her legs around his waist, holding him tightly with all her limbs, clinging to him like a child who didn't want her father to leave. However, fatherly feelings were not the sort he was experiencing, and he tried his best to ignore them.

*No, can't do this…*his mind asserted, bringing his body under control, but then she began to kiss his neck and face.

"Ula, *anwylyd*..." he said tenderly, stopping her. "We cannot."

She pulled away and looked at him, confused, obviously not understanding. Bran very much doubted she had ever been refused before, and no wonder. He simply held her, and she finally accepted this, resting against him. He looked around and wondered where they were. Had she taken them back to the island? Which shore of the lake had they come upon? He had no idea.

Eventually Ula unwrapped herself from around him, and he went to collect wood for a fire. She was quick to jump up and follow him. They returned to the shore with wood, and Bran lit a fire for them while she dove into the lake for fish.

They soon shared a quiet meal together, Ula occasionally looking up at Bran, that same sad demeanor upon her. Bran had thought she would be happier now, but no. She seemed even more troubled than before, and it worried him deeply.

After they finished their meal, she leaned over and wrapped her arms around him again, more tightly and desperately than ever. Then, without a word, she walked to the water and slipped back into the lake.

Hours later she had still not returned.

***

"My lord!" a voice cried, shaking him.

Bran woke to see Gwion's face hovering above him with the morning sky behind it.

"Gwion! Thank the gods! Is Ula with you?"

"No," Gwion replied in a soft tone. "She isn't."

Bran stood up and saw Lucia and Gethen approaching from the lakeshore.

"Bran!" Lucia cried out when she saw him, quickening her pace. Soon she was in front of him. "You're alive!" she exclaimed, throwing her arms around him.

"Not to my own credit, I'm afraid," he answered, holding her tightly in return. He had not been embraced as much in his entire life as he had been in the last day.

"I'm sure I would have drowned in that lake, or frozen to death, if Ula hadn't found me and led me to shore. We must find her."

Gwion nodded somberly. "She loved you, Bran."

Now even Lucia looked sad.

"What is going on?" Bran asked, looking suspiciously back and forth between the two of them. "Why do you both look as if you've just been to a burial?"

Lucia looked at Gwion. "Tell him, Gwion."

"Tell me what?" Bran asked, growing impatient.

"Ula offered herself to Tegid Voel, in exchange for your life."

"*What?*" Bran exclaimed in shock.

"She agreed to stay and be his companion, if he would let you go," Gwion explained.

"Oh, no, no, no…." Bran moaned, suddenly feeling sick to his stomach, remembering Ula's sad, dark eyes, and how desperately she had clung to him the night before. It all made sense.

"What does this mean for her?" he asked anxiously. "What sort of spirit is this Tegid Voel?"

"A lonely one, as most lake-dwelling spirits are," Gwion said. "He is something of a giant, but he is certainly not cruel."

"On the contrary," Lucia said, obviously trying to muster some cheer, "he is said to have romanced and seduced Cerridwen most utterly. Perhaps Ula may come to love him."

They both meant well, but Bran was feeling worse by the moment.

"*Gods*, I didn't ask for her to do this!" he cried out in frustration.

"Of course not," Gwion said, "but you must understand it was the only way. Had she not done this for you, you would surely have been taken by the lake. Make no mistake about that. No amount of strength or will could have saved you. Besides, he is not a tyrant. Much worse situations have befallen the *selkie* than becoming the wife of as powerful a water guardian as Tegid Voel."

Bran considered this but it did not comfort him. "Well," he resolved, "I'll not disgrace her by sitting here idly, when she's made such a sacrifice for me," he finally said somberly, masking his shame and walking over to Gethen.

"We need another horse. Gethen cannot carry three of us," he said. "Lucia, could you call upon one of the farmers who worked your land, perhaps?"

"Yes," she replied. "There is one I know who will surely help me. He lives not far from here."

Within an hour Lucia had led them to an old farmhouse, but insisted on going alone to speak with its owner. Some time later she returned with a dappled mare.

Bran was pleased. "Well done. We'll make much better time now."

"We will," Lucia agreed. "This is Braith," she said, stroking the mare.

Then, to Bran's surprise, she suddenly looked as if she might cry. She looked over at Gwion, her eyes welling with tears.

"Colwyn thought we had all died in the fire, or had been taken by the 'blood-drinkers', as he called them. He saw the villa burning, and he and his boys ran to help fight the fire. His wife insisted on going as well..."

At this, her voice broke down and Bran surmised the rest. She struggled not to sob, and suddenly he realized that these people were the first friends or family she had lost to the cauldron-born. He put his arms around her rather than saying anything, and after a moment or two she managed to compose herself and pulled away.

"He asked about you and your mother, Gwion. I told him we'd been living with family and that I'd come back to check on the villa and found it burned. He asked me if I had plans to rebuild it in the spring, so I know it still sits in ruins. Camulos lied to me about having it rebuilt. He had no plans to bring me back here."

412

"He would have taken you to her," Gwion said with certainty.

Bran cursed the man's name at the thought, and hoped he had some day have the opportunity to crush him for it.

The narrow trail they followed eventually led to the main road south, and Lucia brought her horse up alongside her companions. The road meandered along through the trees for awhile until it began to climb upward toward the crest of a long ridge. As they came to the top, Bran looked over to see Lucia smiling into the wind as she gazed down onto the vast rolling moor that unfurled in front of them.

"Let's see how fast you are, shall we?" she said to her mare, kicking her in the flanks. The mare took off like a lightning bolt and Lucia shrieked with joy.

Always eager to run, Gethen gave chase immediately and the two horses thundered across the moor. Lucia's hood flew back in a gust of wind, releasing her copper curls, and Bran smiled as he watched them explode and dance wildly behind her like flames.

Even carrying Gwion's added weight Gethen could not be outrun, and he was quickly alongside the mare. The two horses ran head to head until they reached the river.

"I don't recognize any of this," Lucia announced breathlessly when they finally stopped. Her cheeks were red from the cold wind, and Bran was stunned by how green her eyes looked above them.

"We are not traveling the same way you came before. This way is faster," he explained. "She is a good horse," he added, nodding toward Lucia's mare.

"Colwyn said to keep her," Lucia replied. "He can't afford to feed her anymore." She shook her head sadly. "Poor man. He is alone now, trying to take care of that farm without his sons and his wife. I don't see how he can possibly manage."

Bran could see how worried she was, and it was obvious she felt responsible for what happened to him.

"Lucia, I will make certain he has help, or a place in our village if he wishes it," he offered. He knew well how guilt ate away the soul.

"You will?" she said gratefully.

"Yes. I know where to find him."

She smiled at him in such a way that he knew she would have run to kiss him if she had not been in a saddle, and that was thanks enough.

The rest of their journey was thankfully uneventful, and by mid-morning on the third day they had neared Bran's village.

"We're almost there," he announced happily, filled with gratitude.

"These times are bringing all manner of men back from the dead," Lucia said to him. "You will be one of them today."

"That I will," Bran replied, almost to himself.

They crossed the open meadow where he knew they could be seen approaching, and soon a young man rode out to meet them.

The look on the boy's face at recognizing him was a mix of shock and joy.

"Lord Bran!" he cried. "You're alive! Lady Seren will be so pleased!"

"Yes, boy. Ride back and tell her."

"Right away, my lord!"

The boy turned his horse around and rode hard back across the meadow, and Bran smiled.

CHAPTER TWENTY-SEVEN
Bran's Return

"My Lord *Pennaeth*!" Gawain yelled, galloping into the battle camp and quickly dismounting.

Aelhaearn tossed his ax aside and strode quickly over to the youth. "What is it?"

Gawain lowered his voice so that none but Aelhaearn heard his message. "Lord Bran has returned."

"*What?*" Aelhaearn asked in shock. "Are you certain? You have seen the man with your own eyes?"

"Yes, I spoke with him near the meadow ridge. He travels with Lady Lucia and a boy," Gawain answered breathlessly. "I have told no one else, as you requested."

"Keep it that way," Aelhaearn commanded. "I must go immediately, for they've surely reached the village by now. I'll return before sundown."

"Yes, my lord."

Before Aelhaearn left, however, he went to seek counsel with Einon. He found him in the makeshift forge he had set up, mending horseshoes and weapons.

"How do you fare this morning, *Pennaeth*?" the old man asked, looking up from his work.

"I may not hold that title long," Aelhaearn replied skeptically. "Bran has returned."

"What?" Einon exclaimed. "Gods be praised!" He looked up toward the unseen deities, gratitude on his face.

"Do you think his return will divide the clan?" Aelhaearn asked anxiously.

"Gods! Must we talk of such things so soon? The man has survived the caves!" Einon cried in protest, but the look Aelhaearn gave him quickly made him realize the answer was yes, they did need to speak of it.

"Perhaps, is the answer," he conceded respectfully. "You cannot deny he may wish to reclaim his position. Whether it will divide the clan will depend much upon Seren and what stand she takes. The Council looks to her in matters they cannot decide upon themselves."

This did nothing to reassure Aelhaearn. Seren bore her brother a love and respect that he had never been able to compete with, and he had always resented it.

Einon continued. "I would have you remember, though, that Bran was never actually sworn in as *Pennaeth* of the clan - *you* were - and you have carried the title with honor. You've kept the cauldron-born from our doors, and I know of no man who does not bear you respect for it."

Aelhaearn was encouraged by his words. "Let us go and greet him, then."

Aelhaearn barked some orders to the warriors in the camp as they made their way out, and soon he and Einon were galloping toward the village. When they arrived, they found Bran and his companions surrounded by a happy crowd that had gathered to greet them.

Einon quickly dismounted and impatiently pushed his way through to where Bran stood. "Thank the gods, Bran! Embrace me!" he bellowed, throwing his huge arms around him.

"Einon," Bran beamed, returning the warm greeting. "I am so glad to be home. This is Gwion," he said, reaching back and putting his hand on his small companion's shoulder, leading him forward. "He is grandson to the High Priestess Rowan and a friend of Lady Lucia, who has also returned with me."

"Your grandmother is well-respected among our people," Einon said to the boy. "Welcome back, Lady Lucia," he added, nodding respectfully in her direction.

Aelhaearn made his way over much more slowly, preferring to watch from a distance. *Gods, Bran had wasted away. And why had Lucia returned?*

Bran seemed to feel him watching, for he looked his direction and made his way over with Lucia, Seren and Gwion close at his heels.

He made his way over to him.

"Like three little lap dogs," Aelhaearn thought in disgust.

"Bran, it's good to see you alive! We'd thought you'd surely met your end in the caves."

"I thought surely I'd never see the light of day again," Bran replied. "Seems the gods have spared me." He looked Aelhaearn up and down and glanced around the village. "Much has changed," he noted.

"Much indeed," Aelhaearn replied, his tone a bit cautionary. "You'll have to tell us the tale of how you escaped the caves tonight. I'm sure it is a tale that'll keep everyone close to the fire."

"It will, indeed," Bran agreed.

Aelhaearn then turned toward Lucia. "Where is your husband?" he asked her, glancing quickly at Bran for a reaction and hoping this would stir the hornet's nest.

"They ran into cauldron-born on the road and became separated," Bran answered for her. "Lucia and Gethen were badly wounded, but made it to the isle. Her husband's whereabouts are unknown."

"I see," Aelhaearn said, disappointed. He approached Lucia.

"Let it be said, my lady, that if your husband comes here in search of you again, I will not hesitate to part his head from his shoulders."

"Understood, my lord." she said, casting her eyes down.

"*Pennaeth*," he corrected.

"Understood, *Pennaeth*," she repeated.

She seemed much more compliant than before, he noted with surprise; most likely ashamed or embarrassed by what had happened, and rightly so.

Seren then spoke. "Brother....I'm sorry...."

"For what, sister?" Bran turned and asked her.

"We sent many men into the caves to search for you, but most did not return." She paused a moment and put her hand on Bran's arm, and then added, "Gareth went in searching for you, and is still missing as well."

Bran sighed heavily. "He is not missing, I am afraid. I found his body in the caves," he said. "I am grateful you did not send any others."

Seren fought back tears, but did not break down in front of her people. Within moments she was herself again. "I am sorry to hear this. Seeing you alive, I had hoped he might yet live as well," she said with disappointment.

Bran simply shook his head.

"There is more," she said, looking at Aelhaearn and then back to her brother. "We needed a chieftain in your absence, more desperately than ever, as the cauldron-born suddenly began attacking nightly."

The clanspeople gathered in the village suddenly quieted down, waiting to see how Bran would react to the words that followed.

"We had given up hope that you still lived, and the Council and I made the decision to swear in Aelhaearn as Chieftain."

Aelhaearn readied himself for a confrontation, but was surprised to see that Bran seemed unphased by the news.

"I understand," Bran said. "I am glad there was such a man here to do what I could not."

Aelhaearn was shocked. He had been prepared for any reaction but acceptance.

Bran looked him in the eye. "Lord Aelhaearn, I have come home to present you with the sword of our people. Let it be done tonight, amongst the warriors," he said, offering his arm.

Seren looked concerned, but Aelhaearn ignored her and stepped forward to clasp Bran's forearm in return.

"I must admit, I did not expect this," he confessed.

"Gwion brought me news of all that had happened here in my absence, and at first, I will admit, it was my intention to return and reclaim my place. Now, I see it is yours. You have proven yourself more than worthy. My destiny lies elsewhere."

Aelhaearn was more than pleased by his good fortune, but was also wise enough to be wary of it. It seemed too good to be true, and he knew such things almost always proved to be just that.

***

"Seren, how can you be sure he has not been bewitched?" Aelhaearn asked. He had been arguing with her for an hour but she would not see reason.

"Speak no more!" she cried. "I've mourned my brother every night since he disappeared, and now that the Great Mother has returned him to us, you would have me believe he is bewitched? No! This rottenness comes from your jealousy! You should count yourself fortunate that he brings no challenge to your title!"

Seren's eyes were flashing with rage, and Aelhaearn knew he had to choose his next words carefully. He waited for a moment, and lowered his voice.

"All I am saying is that he spent two moons in the caves, and we must be wary of this possibility. That is all," he said calmly. "Think also on the boy. Tell me, how is it that the finest trackers in the Eastern tribe could not find Bran, yet a boy of no more than twelve years or so was able to, supposedly in the Northern wilderness? Not even Taranis' people venture that far to the North! You know this!"

She was quiet, and he hoped she was considering his words.

"I admit, what the boy has accomplished is....*impressive*," she finally conceded.

"Yes," he said, encouraged. "Seren, I know you love your brother more than anyone upon this earth...and I would be a cruel man to try and rob you of believing he has wholly returned to you. I ask only that we watch him and his companions closely over the next few days. That is all. Would you fault me for this? It is my sworn oath to protect this clan, and I do not take my oaths lightly. I make no accusations; I merely ask for caution."

Seren stood and faced him. "Be cautious, then, but know this: if you should plot against my brother behind my back, or attempt to bring him any harm, I will see to it that you suffer well for your efforts. Do not make the mistake of thinking you are more powerful than I am."

Aelhaearn was taken aback by the vehement force exuding from Seren, and his blood boiled at her threats. He lost his temper and grasped her by her arms, pulling her face close to him so she could not help but look into his eyes. He could crush her if he wanted to, and he wanted to be certain she knew it.

"Priestess or not, do not speak to me like that," he warned through clenched teeth. "You would do well to remember that I am *Pennaeth* of this clan, whether you regret it or not, and our people respect me and do *my bidding*. You will as well!"

She stared back at him defiantly, but she couldn't fool him. He saw the proper amount of fear filling her eyes, and it satisfied him. He released his grip on her and left her alone to think on it.

Earlier that morning he had sent for the warriors to come to the village to welcome Bran home and witness the handing over of *Drynwyn*, as well as collect supplies for the camp and spend a night with their women. They had arrived that afternoon, and when the work was done they had gone to spend time with their women or families.

That had been hours ago. Now, dusk was falling and Aelhaearn could hear the warriors had already gathered in the motherhouse and were well into their cups. It was obvious everyone was eager for a bit of warmth and comfort, and he knew the feast would be good for morale; even the most hardened of warriors tires of blood. He stopped for a moment and tilted his head back to look up at the stars. He took a deep, long breath and said a prayer of gratitude. *Dyrnwyn* would finally be his, and the threat that had been prickling him for moons was finally gone.

When he entered the hall he noticed Seren sitting next to Bran, speaking with Lucia and the boy, and suddenly his good mood turned a bit sour as he pondered what lies they might be telling her.

He went to his place across from the entrance of the motherhouse and sat upon the furs laid out for him. A servant came quickly to fill his drinking horn. He kept an eye on the four, growing ever more anxious.

Suddenly Bran stood and all eyes looked toward him.

"Brethren, I am so grateful to be back among you again."

Cheers erupted through the motherhouse, the clan crying Bran's name, wishing him a long life and children, and other such things.

"I stand here tonight to acknowledge the great Aelhaearn as Chieftain and Protector of the South, and am honored to present him with the sword of our people." Then Bran approached him, knelt down in respect, and held out *Dyrnwyn*.

Aelhaearn was filled with immense joy at the sight. *The great warrior, Bran, kneeling at his feet, offering him the thing he had wanted more than anything in his life.*

He looked down proudly at the scabbard holding the beautiful hilt of *Dyrnwyn*, took it from Bran, and drew the beautiful sword, holding it up, watching in amazement as the light danced like blue flames along its blade from hilt to tip, flowing mysteriously upwards. What a glorious, glorious sight! *His.* The dream he had held since his boyhood had actually come to pass--*Chieftain of the Clan, with Dyrnwyn at his side.* He turned it round, staring at it in awe and respect. He still could not believe Bran had parted with it. The clan cheered, and his dream was complete.

"A weapon fit for a king," Einon said to him proudly.

"Yes," he answered. "Yes, it is."

"With your skills in the forge, *Pennaeth,* you can appreciate it more than most," Einon added. "I know I do."

Aelhaearn smiled. "I can scarcely believe it will now hang by my side...after thinking we had lost it forever..."

"It is a blessing to have it back where it belongs," Einon said.

Suddenly, Aelhaearn found his fear of Bran and the situation ridiculous and chided himself for it. Let them make any move they wish--for even with the help of a sorceress, what match is an emaciated warrior, a woman and a boy against a Firebrand wielding *Dyrnwyn* with a tribe of southern warriors at his command? *None at all.* In a sudden burst of overwhelming gratitude and good will, he stood and raised his drinking horn high.

 "Let us drink to our beloved brother, the Lord Bran, who has cheated the Lord of Death and escaped the bowels of hell to drink among us once again!"

Everyone cried out and raised their horns in tribute, the men clapping Bran on the back and the women crawling over the skins and floor mats to kiss him.

Only Seren did not cheer. Instead, her eyes stayed fixed upon Aelhaearn like stone, no smile upon her lips, obviously still angry with him. Aelhaearn found it strange that not so very long ago he had been unable to think of any woman but her. Now, he found himself wishing she would disappear.

The next day Aelhaearn went to the forge and gratefully found much work to be done. He often took refuge in metalwork when he needed to think. For hours he settled into the comforting rhythm and force of his hammer blows as he mused over the past few days.

Bran came seeking him later in the day. "Aelhaearn, we did not have time to speak last night before you retired."

Aelhaearn glanced up from his work. "There was plenty of time. You chose instead to waste the evening speaking to women." he replied, not ceasing his hammering.

Bran ignored his comment. "I will come straight to the heart of the matter," he said, pulling a sword slowly from the scabbard at his side.

Aelhaearn was robbed of his breath. "How did you come by such a sword?" he asked in wonder.

"This is the legendary *Caledgwyn*," Bran announced.

Aelhaearn was shocked at the mention of the ancient weapon and shook his head in disbelief. "That's not possible," he said, but the sword before him gleamed as if it were forged from moonlight by the Fae, and whether or not it was truly the legendary *Caledgwyn*, he was wise enough to know whatever he beheld was something far beyond what the hands of ordinary men were capable of.

"Now I understand why it was so easy for you to give up *Dyrnwyn*," he said slowly, his disdain for Bran returning. "You now wield a weapon for the ages."

427

"Make no mistake," Bran replied, "it still pains me to have parted with the sword of our people. That blade was my only companion in the caves, and my salvation time and time again. Without it, I surely would have died in there. I will always think of *Dyrnwyn* as a close friend. I have no such bond with this weapon yet."

"Then trade it," Aelhaearn challenged.

"That I cannot do," Bran answered. "The Lady Rowan allowed me to petition the Great Mother for it. It was my good fortune that she saw fit to grant it to me. In return, I gave my oath to serve her, and this is the weapon I've been blessed with. It is not mine to trade, any more than *Dyrnwyn* may be traded by the Chieftain of the South. I am now Protector to the Sisterhood."

"The *Sisterhood*?" Aelhaearn scoffed. "They have lived safely on that island for generations without the help of a Protector. No one can approach their shores without them knowing of it. They have no need of a Protector!"

"They do now," Bran answered.

"If you say so," Aelhaearn replied sarcastically. "I don't understand why you would want to serve them, but as the men's tribes already have chieftains, I suppose the women were the only choice you had left, weren't they?"

The look in Bran's eyes confirmed to Aelhaearn that his comment had hit its mark, and it pleased him.

"I did not come to argue with you," Bran retorted angrily. "I have reason to believe Cerridwen may try and take the Crossroads soon, and I have come to ask if you and the clan warriors will ride with me to defend it. Maur and his men have already pledged to do so."

"I see," Aelhaearn said. "Who has told you she means to do this?"

"We've heard she's taking the Cauldron there. I plan to return it to where it belongs."

"Heard from whom?" Aelhaearn repeated. He noted Bran's hesitation, and came to the conclusion that his news was nothing but rumor. "I'm sorry, Bran, but hearsay is not reason enough for me to lead my warriors away from the fight we know is here. Cauldron-born still roam the countryside, and I'll not leave our village undefended." He looked back down to the metal on his anvil and continued hammering, finally looking up again when he had noticed Bran had not left.

"I wish you a safe journey," Aelhaearn said, looking forward to Bran's departure. "If the rumors prove true, send word and we will follow."

Bran nodded, obviously irritated. "Farewell, then. We leave at dawn."

Aelhaearn didn't believe for a moment that the Great Mother had anything to do with Bran obtaining *Caledgwyn*; such a weapon could only have been summoned by the most powerful sorcery, and a warrior the likes of Bran could not possibly be content without a clan, living alone and doing the bidding of women. He thought on it a bit more, searching for the explanation that would satisfy all of his unanswered questions.

What if Cerridwen had approached Bran in the caves, and offered him a title greater than Chieftain of the South in return for helping her? What if she had obtained the sword for him? The more he thought on it, the more he was convinced it was what had to have happened. He had no way of proving his suspicions, and knew he could not discuss them with Seren, but there were others who could help him discover the truth.

Aelhaearn sent a servant to look for Gawain, who had proven himself quite trustworthy. Among other things, he had kept his word to deliver news of Bran's return to him alone. Gawain was an Eastern tracker whom Aelhaearn had granted permission to stay and live among their clan. He had had fallen in love with one of their young women, and as she no longer had a father, needed Aelhaearn's approval to marry her. It happened often, in fact. The men of the East loved the women of the South. No doubt they longed for some heat in the bedroom with all the difficult women they had at home. Likewise, managing to seduce an Eastern woman and melt her icy exterior was a challenge many a Southern man aspired to.

Gawain soon arrived at the forge.

"Gawain, I want you to accompany Bran and his party," Aelhaearn commanded. "They ride at dawn. Pay close attention to all you see and hear, and then you'll report back to me. I have reason to believe he may betray us."

"Yes, *Pennaeth*," Gawain replied dutifully.

***

Seren was tending the fire and Lucia was sitting with Llygoden and the twins around it in the motherhouse, working bread dough upon stones. Lucia had spent the day with the women at the task, hearing of all that had happened in her absence, and likewise sharing news of their sisters on the island.

Suddenly Bran entered and announced to his sister that he had chosen his men and they planned to leave at first light the next morning.

"What? You've just arrived!" Seren protested.

"I came only to deliver *Dyrnwyn* safely into Aelhaearn's hands and ask for his support at the battle that I suspect will soon arrive at the Crossroads. Now, I must go to Talhaiarn. Maur and his men are coming with me, but Aelhaearn will not leave the village undefended for anything less than certain proof that she plans to attack. I do not hold this against him. He is right to put the safety of the clan first. I will send word once I learn the truth of it."

"We can certainly spare some of our warriors. If nothing else, we should send a few of our fastest riders with you. They could bring word back should it be true."

"See if you can convince him of it, then. My words have fallen on deaf ears. My return has not pleased him. Less so your disdain of him over it."

"Yes, we have quarreled," Seren admitted.

Lucia had indeed noticed Aelhaearn glaring over at Bran from his place at the banquet the night before. He left long before the songs had ended.

"Then go to him and mend things," she heard him say to his sister. "Lives are at stake, Seren."

"I will go to him and make it right. You shall have the riders, if nothing else."

Bran then looked over at Lucia. "Lucia, come with me," he said, walking outside.

She stopped her work, dusted off her hands and followed him. A cold rain had fallen all day, and the late afternoon sky was grey and cloudy. She pulled her shawl closer to her against its chill.

"Walk with me," he said.

She was pleased to finally have him all to herself. The past week had been spent constantly in the company of others; Gwion, the Sisters, his people. Occasionally, he would look over at her and pull her to him with his eyes, and she would long for everyone to disappear.

He offered her his arm, and they walked a long time, rarely disturbing the silence of the forest, listening to the rhythm of the slow raindrops on the leaves of the trees.

"Lucia, Gwion is coming with me."

"What?" she cried in surprise. "You won't take me, but you'll take him? He is just a boy! Less trained in a fight than I am!"

Bran shook his head at her comments. "You know that isn't true, Lucia. He has a vision that reaches beyond even what Talhaiarn can see, and that vision is a weapon far more powerful than *Caledgwyn*, or a thousand warriors. He is the reason she will fail."

"But he is just a boy…" she whispered, terrified for him, and for Aveta.

Bran reached down and took her hand. "I'll protect him," he promised.

She looked up at him and he bent down to kiss her, and she reached up and pulled him closer. *Don't stop…*she thought, desperate for his touch. But he did stop, for twilight had begun reaching its long, dark fingers across the sky and in between the trees.

"Come, it's getting dark," he said, and they slowly made their way back. Fires could be seen in the distance like friendly beacons as they approached the village, and although Lucia was near frozen through, she didn't care. She dreaded their time alone coming to an end. They were too soon back in the village, but to her surprise, instead of leading her back to the motherhouse, he took her across the village to his hut. He held back the skins that covered the door.

"Stay with me," he said.

She walked in and sat upon the large pile of furs on the ground, watching him as he started a fire. Soon the hut was almost too warm, and he came and sat down next to her, looking at her the way he had before, only now were no others, and no darkness to stop them. Now, *finally.* He leaned in and kissed her, and she melted into him, wrapping her arms around his broad shoulders. He undressed her, and then himself, and soon all she felt was his skin on hers…his lips on her neck and face, his arms around her, his hands behind her neck and fingers clutching her hair.

His body crushed her into the furs beneath them, as if he were made of stone or oak, at once making her feel both dominated and protected by the same forceful power he had turned on so many enemies.

Finally she was overcome. He followed her into that place soon after, and then wrapped her around him like a cloak, caressing her skin and holding her close to him. She watched the shadows from the flames dance around them, listening to his heart pounding in her ear, and breathed in the smell of him, hoping desperately that there would be a next time.

CHAPTER TWENTY-EIGHT
The Alliance

Aelhaearn moved and struck, getting the better of his opponent yet again. He and his warriors had been training all morning, and he had yet to be bested.

"Gods, you were near impossible to best before, but with *Dyrnwyn* in your hand I'm not sure it can be done!" gasped Beynon from the snowy ground beneath him.

Aelhaearn swelled with satisfaction. It was true, he felt nearly invincible with the weapon in his hand.

"Next!" he yelled lustily. Another of his men attacked, and so it went, all through the morning, until all his warriors were all spent.

Finally, hungry, he sheathed his beloved prize. "We will train again tomorrow morning," he said. "See to your other duties."

The men dispersed, and Aelhaearn walked about the camp seeing to various tasks. Thankfully Bran was gone. He had left with that queer blonde boy and the Northerners two mornings ago, and returning to his normal daily routine had improved his mood considerably.

He wondered how long it would be before Gawain returned with any news. With proof of betrayal, he could see to it that Bran and all his companions were executed, and Seren would be able to do nothing about it. Bran's sword would then belong to him by right.

He went into the forest to hunt, but there wasn't much daylight left. The days had grown extremely short as they were deep in the heart of winter, and twilight was soon upon him. On his way back, he noticed the silhouette of a lone woman on the path in front of him.

"Woman!" he yelled at her. "Are you mad? What are you doing out here? Get back to the camp! There may be cauldron-born about!"

As she came into view his heart nearly stopped.

"Are you not pleased to see me, Firebrand?" she asked.

He had nearly given up on ever seeing her again, and approached her as he would a skittish horse, afraid she would disappear. Then he noticed she was with child.

"The Great Mother has told me it will be a boy-child, blessed with the Firebrand, like you," she said, putting her hands gently on her belly.

"*What?*" he gasped. The idea of a son filled him with immense pride, and he was overcome with the desire to possess this woman.

"Where have you been?" he asked, pulling her to him. "Why have you not come to me again until now?"

"Let that not concern you. I have been where I was needed. Now, I am here, with you," she offered. "*You*, Firebrand, the strongest chieftain of them all."

He wanted to pull her into his cloak, and never let her out of it. He wanted her for his queen. The clan admired power in their women, and her beauty and power would completely eclipse Seren's.

"Stay and be my queen," he demanded, reaching down to touch her face, excited by the thought. "Raise the boy here, among his people."

"We have much to talk about," she said, pulling away.

Aelhaearn feared she meant to leave. "Stop!" he cried, quickly casting a ring of fire around the both of them.

She looked around her in delight and laughed. "Wondrous!" she exclaimed. "You are wondrous!"

She turned toward him. "Firebrand, there is much I have to say that you will perhaps not enjoy hearing."

"There is nothing you could say that will anger me," Aelhaearn said.

"I fear there is much," she replied.

"Not if the answer to one question is yes," he said.

"What question is that?" she asked.

"If you will swear to all the gods and guardians that my blood beats within the body of the babe you carry in your womb."

"I swear that this is so," she answered, "and I have come to make you an offer, Firebrand, for you are the strongest of all the chieftains of the Great Circle; stronger than Neirin, who was easily seduced and wagered the Helm of the East in prideful folly, and stronger than Taranis, who promised my unborn babe the Shield of the North in exchange for ale and my legs wrapped around him for a night."

Aelhaearn stared at the woman in front of him now in caution and wonder, dazzled by her brilliance and in awe of her cunning, as he finally realized who she was.

"*Cerridwen,* he whispered.

"Yes, I am she."

"You have all the relics but one, now."

"Yes," she answered. "All but the one you carry."

"You swear you carry my child, and yet you just admitted to having lain with two others? Do you take me for a fool?"

"Don't take me for a common woman, Firebrand," she warned. "The father of this child is three-fold."

Aelhaearn backed away from her. "What do you mean, 'three-fold'? What sorcery is this?"

"I have also bedded the chieftains of the North and East, but to one grand purpose--to take the best of their seed and yours, and with it knit together within my womb the future High King of the Four Tribes. He will be blessed with the Firebrand of the South, the bardic singing voice and earthy passion of the North, and the cunning vision and mind of the East, and of course the gifts that come with having a mother of the Isle. With these gifts, along with the relics, he shall have no rival. He shall be my most beloved and wondrous creation, and all will bow to him." After a moment, she added, "I have never lied to you, Firebrand."

Indeed, she hadn't. She had not revealed her true purpose, to be sure, but she had never lied.

"Your kinsman, the Lord Bran, murdered my son, and I intend to make him pay for it with his life," she said. "I understand the two of you have had your differences, and now I am in need of a Protector who is more god than man; a man like you, Firebrand. You've been blessed by the Guardians with a gift that lifts you far above your brothers."

It was true. He had always believed he was meant for something better, something beyond ruling his own tribe. Why else would he have been given such power, if not to wield it?

"Should you choose to protect me, Firebrand, I promise I will share power with you that goes beyond this world and stretches into the next...Power that no man who has walked the earth has ever known."

Aelhaearn believed her. Against all logic, he believed her, and the idea of raising this momentous child as *his* son, with the feared and powerful Cerridwen of the Isle as *his* queen, filled him with unquenchable ambition.

"My love," Cerridwen said softly, "you and I will rule the four tribes from the Crossroads. There we will raise the boy as your son, and he shall rule after you. Bards will sing for generations to come of you both." She came closer and looked up into his eyes. "...and Bran, and his sister who foolishly spurned you? They will kneel at your feet, and at the feet of the one who will come after you."

Aelhaearn was completely won over, picturing that sweet victorious moment. He looked at her intently.

"I shall be your Protector," he agreed, "if you agree to bring me the Helm and the Shield, and swear to the Great Mother and all the Guardians you will *never again* lay with any man but me, for as long as your heart continues to beat."

"That I can promise you easily, Firebrand," she said, "for I want no man but you."

CHAPTER TWENTY-NINE
Talhaiarn

"Father."

Talhaiarn turned and beheld his eldest daughter for the first time in years. She looked so like her mother it shocked him. Were it not for his own eyes staring back at him, he would have sworn Rowan stood before him, grown young again.

She came and sat down next to him under the Oak where he had been praying, and there they stayed for a long time, saying nothing, simply watching the winter sky slowly fade over their heads. Perhaps they both knew that once she said the words she had come to say, they would likely never be able to sit together again.

"Father," she finally began, "I cannot stop what is going to happen here. It has grown far beyond my power to control. I am merely a vessel for the Great Mother. It is what she wants for our people."

"No, Cerridwen," Talhaiarn said sadly. "That isn't true, child. She wants nothing of the sort, and you *can* stop this. You need but return the Cauldron to the island, where it belongs. I can help you, if you'll let me."

"You're wrong, Father. Although you are the High Priest of the Grove, you are still a man, and only a woman can truly understand what the Great Mother wants," Cerridwen insisted. "Ask yourself, why have I been blessed with the ability to bring back life, if not to use it?"

"Daughter, you're wiser than this," Talhaiarn said in frustration. "Healers *preserve* life, and to do so is noble, but when a soul has been called by Arawn, you have no right to call it back! Your cauldron-born suffer! Their souls cry out from the in-between, begging for peace! What you are doing is wrong!"

"This is why what I've started *must* be finished, Father. All the relics of the Great Circle have been pledged to me, and I now have the power to open the door to the in-between and end their suffering. I can call the souls of the cauldron-born back to their bodies, bodies now made stronger and more powerful by the Cauldron. They will not have suffered in vain, for they will be honored as the fathers of a new race of wiser men with no fear of death, for they will have overcome it!"

Talhaiarn shook his head, thinking it was never those with simple minds who truly suffered, but rather those who were gifted with an understanding far beyond that of common men and women.

"Father, there is more," she said. "When harvest time is upon us again, I will bear a son blessed with all the most sacred gifts of our four clans. I wish to raise him here, at the Crossroads, with you as his teacher and the Firebrand as my Protector. Together we shall raise him into the High King of our legends. When he is grown to manhood he will wear the Helm of the East, bear the Shield of the North, and wield *Drynwyn*, for the relics were never meant to be kept apart. They were meant to be wielded together by a man worthy of being High King of the Great Circle. Imagine, Father…your grandson, High King of a clan of men and women with the power to refuse death, growing in knowledge of both the seen and unseen, until they tire of this world and *choose* to leave it. Through the Cauldron and the Crossroads, we possess the power

442

to cleave the chains of death from our ankles! *I know how*, Father. We can free ourselves, and any whom we choose, forever. Our clan will prevail over its encroaching enemies, and the Great Mother shall never be profaned nor forgotten. *We have within our grasp the power to refuse Arawn's call*, we need only close our fist around it!"

Talhaiarn looked at the passion in his daughter's eyes, and wanted to weep.

"It cannot be so, my daughter," he said. "You overreach, and offend the gods. We are not meant to live forever, nor any one of us to rule from so high a throne. Here you may stay, and raise your child, but the relics must be returned to their clans, and the cauldron-born slain, their souls released to Arawn. You must pay your debts."

Cerridwen stood up, angry tears welling in her eyes.

"And what of the debts owed to my son, my Morvran? The gift of light and wisdom I brewed for him, stolen! His apprenticeship, stolen! And now, his very life! He was sent long before his time to Arawn at the hands of Agarah's Saxon bastard! What of these debts? Shall they go unpaid?"

"Daughter, he was my grandson. I grieve for what has happened to him, but you must find acceptance, or your rage will be your Keeper. We cannot change the past."

"No, we cannot, but as perhaps I will be made to pay my debts, I shall find the coin to pay them by demanding what is owed my son. Gwion will use his gifts to serve me and the unborn son in my womb, and Bran will pay for Morvran's death with his own!"

Tahaiarn despaired as he searched for words that would penetrate his daughter's angry heart, but he had begun to lose hope that any of them would take root.

Then, suddenly a man appeared at the edge of the grove. At first, Talhaiarn thought it was Bran, for he was quite tall.

"Don't hurt him," Cerridwen turned and said to the man, who came and stood beside her.

"As you wish," the man replied.

Suddenly a ring of fire sprung up around Talhaiarn, trapping him where he sat, and he realized quickly who his captor was.

"Aelhaearn," he said sadly.

Cerridwen walked away, leaving her father with the Firebrand, and Talhaiarn did the only thing he could do.

He prayed.

Grant, Goddess, Thy protection;
And in protection, reason;
And in reason, light;
And in light, truth;
And in truth, justice;
And in justice, love;
And in love, the love of the Goddess;
And in the love of the Goddess, gwynfyd.

Goddess and all goodness.

444

CHAPTER THIRTY

The Trees Speak

Bran rode with Gwion beside him, the Northerners following with their dogs. Aelhaearn had conceded to send an Eastern messenger along with them named Gawain, whose hawk could fly a message back to the village quickly should the rumors about Cerridwen attacking the Crossroads prove true.

Over the last hour the laughter and stories of the Northerners had slowly faded away from behind them. The horses seem agitated and the dogs clearly smelled something. Bran stopped, watching and listening for anything out of the ordinary, his spear at the ready.

Then Gethen suddenly refused to move forward. Bran gave a comforting stroke to the side of his neck and surveyed the area, but saw nothing.

"Cauldron-born," Gwion whispered to Bran. "We must be near one of their lairs. The dogs smell death."

Bran turned and yelled to the others, "Cauldron-born! We must get to the keep before dark!"

"Let them come, the worms!" Maur cried out from the back. "My ass itches from sittin' in this damn saddle! I'd welcome an excuse to get out of it!"

Bran shook his head and said, "Be careful what you wish for, brother."

They doubled their pace, reaching the river at twilight, and stopped briefly to let the dogs and horses drink. Bran stooped his giant frame down to the water to fill his goatskin, becoming more and more vexed by the anxiety gnawing at his stomach.

"Not much further," he said to Gwion, standing up and shaking it off. "Let's go."

The party was soon riding up the side of the mountain toward Talhaiarn's keep. As they approached the entrance, Gwion said with concern, "There is no one here."

Bran suspected the worst. Talhaiarn was an old man, and though his knowledge was vast, he was certainly no longer a warrior. They entered to find Gwion was right. No horse, no torches, and worst of all, no Talhaiarn.

"We will search for him at first light tomorrow," Bran announced. "Bring the horses into the main hall. Maur, bar the door behind you."

"But what if Talhaiarn returns in the night?" Maur replied in concern. "We will have locked him out of the only safe keep for miles around."

"I will know if he comes," Gwion said.

"How will you know that?" Maur asked, looking at him strangely.

"He will know," Bran confirmed, reassuring Maur. As they settled in, each man attending to his personal tasks, Bran took Maur aside and said in a low voice, "The boy will soon outshine Talhaiarn in his abilities. In fact, I believe he may have already."

"Is that so?" Maur queried doubtfully.

"Yes," Bran said, glancing over at Gwion. "Have you noticed how animals are drawn to him? Wild or tame, it matters not." He motioned toward the boy, and sure enough, all three of the Northerners dogs, normally ever at their masters' heels, were sitting as close to him as possible upon the floor, tame as puppies.

Bran chuckled. "They want nothing to do with you."

"Come on!" Maur cried in disbelief. He walked over to Gwion and, with some effort, managed to sit down on the floor next to him.

"Can you speak with them, boy?" Bran heard him ask Gwion earnestly.

"Not with words, no…but I can sense what they feel," Gwion replied.

"Tell me about Madoc," Maur asked. At the mention of his name the dog looked up expectantly.

"There is not much I can tell you that you don't already know," Gwion said, reaching over and stroking the dog's coat. Suddenly Gwion giggled. "Well, maybe a few things."

"What?" Maur asked nervously.

"He doesn't like it when you snore," Gwion replied. "He can't sleep."

At that, Eurig and Heilyn burst into peals of laughter from across the hall.

"I don't snore!" Maur protested.

"Oh, please," Eurig said. "It's bad enough we have to suffer through it, but even your dog can't stand it!"

It seemed Maur realized protesting was pointless, so he didn't.

"Very well," he said instead, "Let's talk to your dog. See what secrets she has to tell."

Gwion looked to the great grey hound sitting at Eurig's feet.

"She likes living in the South away from your clan, because she can have you all to herself."

Heilyn jumped at the opportunity to tease his brother. "Whoa! Yes, that's true. The Southern women haven't much taken to you, have they?"

Eurig smiled smugly. "Oh, come now, brother! I think we both know who takes more women to his bed!"

"Well, of course you do! But only because I'm a married man," Heilyn protested. "Besides, you may take more women to your bed, but at least mine comes back every night."

At this everyone burst into laughter, and Bran found he couldn't help but chuckle as well.

"Go ahead, have yourselves a laugh, you've earned it!" Eurig said smiling. "I don't care!" He reached down and wrapped his arms around the huge dog's neck. "Yes, I believe you, my sweet darling," he cooed to her like a baby as she licked his face. "Yes, that's right. You're my favorite girl!"

Suddenly, their merriment died as all three of the dogs turned and growled in the direction of the fissure in the rock wall that had been chipped away at to serve as a window. Bran was at the opening in a flash and quickly spied the reason for the dog's alarm; a great white owl was perched just outside.

"Let her in!" Gawain cried urgently. "She has a message."

Gawain hadn't said a word since they had set out, and Bran had almost forgotten he was with them until that moment.

Gwion turned and spoke to the dogs, and they calmed down. Gawain then beckoned to the owl. It sailed swiftly through the narrow opening and landed gracefully on his outstretched arm.

"It's Blodewydd," Gawain said in surprise, "our queen's owl." He untied the leather pouch from her talon, and inside was a message written on a piece of birch paper, written in a delicate hand.

He read the message and let out a weak cry. "Gods, no!"

"What is it?" Bran demanded, taking the tiny parchment.

"Enemy has the Helm," he read with a heavy voice.

"Damn!" Maur cried, shaking his head as if trying to rid his ears of the words. "No, no, no! Damn the bloody gods! I knew that boy of his was not ready to rule."

"We don't know what happened," Bran quickly said in Neirin's defense, "nor how bad things might be in the East. Do not forget the enemy bested Belenus, and that was no easy feat."

"True," Maur conceded, backing down a bit, "but I cannot help but feel Ambisagrus would have made a better chieftain."

449

"Ambisagrus is not of our clan!" Gawain suddenly yelled in anger, surprising everyone with his display of emotion. "Don't speak of things you know nothing of, Northerner!"

"What I know is that Neirin has failed to protect the Helm, after only two moons of having it in his possession. That's what I know!" Maur shot back angrily.

Bran quickly stood between them and bellowed, "We shall not fight amongst ourselves!"

Maur and Gawain backed down, and Bran added with a tired sigh, "Let's put our efforts into finding Talhaiarn instead. With him missing and the news we've just received, I'm sure the rumors are true. Gawain, send your hawk to Aelhaearn and tell him the battle lies here now. I think it is safe to say we can count on that, at least."

"And what of Blodewydd?" Gawain asked.

"Send her back to your queen with a message for Neirin to come with as many men as he can spare, and that Talhaiarn is missing."

"Perhaps he can redeem himself," Maur said under his breath to Bran, but Bran did not respond.

***

As soon as light began to creep in through the small windows, Bran and his party set out to search for Talhaiarn. The sun was still hidden behind the hills, and the air was bitter cold. Gwion shivered in his thin tunic, his lips blue. *The poor boy has no more meat on him than a sparrow*, Bran thought. He would have given the boy his cloak, but it would surely trail behind him on the ground.

450

Instead he gave him his wool tunic, which though shorter, still hung down to the middle of his little stick-like legs.

"There are six of us," Bran said. "Let's pair up and search different areas, then meet back here before nightfall. Hopefully we'll have found him by then."

"We'll find him," Maur said optimistically. "If we can just get our dogs to come to us, we'll give them the scent and be off."

The dogs were still clustered around Gwion, tails wagging, licking his cold little hands. "Go!" encouraged the boy, shooing the dogs back to their masters.

"Well, then!" Maur said, glaring down at Madoc as he returned, looking sheepishly up at his master. "Come back now, have you? Ha! Boy, the beasts love you, to be sure!" The dog saw Maur's smile return and his tail set to wagging again, happy his master was not cross with him.

"Gawain," Maur said gruffly.

"Yes?"

"Apologies for last night. Come with me."

"As you wish," Gawain said after a moment, seemingly satisfied. The Easterners were by nature a very calm and reasonable folk, quick to forgive. "I wish I had my hawk. She would be helpful."

"We can depend on Madoc. He won't let us down," Maur assured him. "Come on!"

With that, the pair headed up the steep mountain path.

"We'll search along the river, then," Heilyn said. He bent down to offer one of Talhaiarn's robes to their dogs to smell.

"That leaves us with the path leading down to the Grove," Bran announced to Gwion. They turned and set off down a steep and narrow trail leading into the trees, Gwion in the lead, who knew the way. He had lived there not so very long ago, studying under Talhaiarn, and had traveled the path frequently with him. Bran followed the boy with some difficulty, his feet crushing into the earth where Gwion's barely left a mark, and his large frame breaking branches where Gwion slipped through like a young fawn, but he managed to keep up, never letting the boy out of sight.

The early morning light slowly began to descend between the branches of trees, casting a frosty veil of pale light on everything below. Talhaiarn had taken much care to hide and protect the Grove, and the markings leading the way to it were imperceptible to Bran, but not to the boy. The forest around them spoke to him in a language only he understood.

They walked very slowly and carefully, looking at the ground frequently for footprints or freshly broken twigs.

Bran's thoughts wove round and round the fortress and how nothing had been disturbed within it. There had been no sign of a struggle, so that meant there were two possibilities--either Talhaiarn left the fortress alone, or he had left with someone he trusted.

"His horse was there, so we know he was on foot," Bran said, thinking aloud, "and there was a drinking horn when we arrived still wet with ale, which means he had not been gone for long before we arrived."

Gwion picked out the path easily, stopping occasionally to lean into a tree and press his cheek against it, as if the tree were whispering to him, telling him which way to go. Then, suddenly Gwion stopped dead in his tracks.

"What?" Bran asked.

"It's as if the trees suddenly stopped breathing," Gwion said, listening. After a moment he said, "It's a warning. We need to turn back."

Such was the tone in Gwion's voice that Bran did not argue.

***

Bran and Gwion made it back to the keep before the others, but before long they had all returned and gathered in the hall.

"Something's happening in the Grove," Bran announced, "and my guess is that's where Talhaiarn is, but we're too small in number to attack without knowing what awaits us. Hopefully Gawain's hawk has already reached the South and the warriors are on their way. Tomorrow we must gather as much food, wood and water as we can before nightfall, and hope the men arrive soon. We've no idea how large her army might be."

The others gave their accounts of what they had found, and it was not encouraging. Tracks and kills had been found everywhere. There was certainly no shortage of cauldron-born roaming the area.

The next morning they rose before dawn. Maur and his men went hunting and managed to bring back a deer which put everyone in better spirits. After dressing their kill, they chopped wood for the rest of the afternoon. Gwion took care of the horses and weapons, and Gawain and Bran hauled water into the fortress, filling every barrel and basin they could find.

"Bran, I could try to get closer to the Grove and see what is happening there," Gawain offered as they worked.

Bran considered it. They needed to know what kind of numbers they were dealing with, and truly, the Easterners were unrivaled in their ability to track an animal or enemy undetected. As Bran's clan was referred to by outsiders as "the Firefolk", the Easterners were often referred to as "the invisible ones", and had earned the name well.

"Do you think you could find the Grove without assistance?" Bran said. "The markings are near impossible to see. Gwion knows the way, but I can't let him go with you. There are at least four women who would boil me in oil if I let anything happen to him."

"I'll speak to him," Gawain said. "He can tell me what to look for, and I'll find it. I am not as good a tracker as Neirin, but I'm certainly one of the best in our clan."

"If you think you can manage it, it would certainly give us an advantage. Set out tomorrow and find out what you can."

"I'll leave when the sun rises," Gawain agreed. Bran nodded and turned to go, but Gawain stopped him.

"My lord," he said apprehensively, "there's something I need to tell you about Lord Aelhaearn."

"What?" Bran said, his gut tightening.

"He sent me with you, not as a gesture of good will, but rather with orders to watch you and the boy," Gawain admitted. "He believed you might have been plotting with the enemy. I am telling you this because I fear he may not send the men you've asked for."

"*Bastard!*" Bran seethed.

"My lord, I am ashamed for agreeing to do it. It is quite obvious where your loyalty lies. Please forgive me."

Bran was angry, but not at Gawain. The next time he saw Aelhaearn, he had be sure to break more than a few of his bones.

"We can depend on Lady Eirwen and Lord Neirin," Gawain said encouragingly. "I am sure they will send all of our warriors to fight, especially now that the Helm has been taken. As you know, if captured in battle, the relic belongs to the victor. I am certain none of our warriors would refuse the opportunity to win it back."

"Well, send for them and pray to your Guardians they make it here in time," Bran agreed. "It sounds like they've been under attack, but perhaps as she has what she wants from your clan, now, she'll let them be."

"Yes, let's hope that's true. Either way, they'll travel in small groups and avoid the well-traveled roads," Gawain replied. "I'll suggest they approach from the North, down through the mountain pass and avoid the valley. There are many cauldron-born about for them to come that way. But they *will* come, my lord. I'm sure of it."

Bran nodded. "Even so, if what you say about Aelhaearn is true and he doesn't send the men we've asked for, we'll need more. I'm going to send one of the Northerners to petition Taranis for the rest of his warriors."

"Wise," Gawain said. "I do not know Aelhaearn's heart, but it is obvious he does not trust you."

"Nor I him," Bran said in disgust, hoisting two huge buckets of water onto his shoulders.

CHAPTER THIRTY-ONE
A Call to Arms

The night passed without incident, which was unnerving to Bran. *Why did the enemy have no interest in the fortress?* It was near impregnable, and the most valuable battle asset in the area, yet they had neither heard nor seen any sign of the enemy since they had arrived.

Heilyn and Eurig had ridden North at first light to tell Taranis that Talhaiarn had been captured, and Gawain had left as agreed to find out as much as he could about what was happening in the valley.

Now, it was simply Maur, Gwion, and himself at the fortress, and Bran's anger toward Aelhaearn grew by the hour. He used it as fuel for his work, and accomplished much.

By late afternoon Bran began to worry about Gawain, watching all paths up to the fortress in turn as he worked, hoping he had succeeded in doing what he had so confidently said he could, but when the last of the sun disappeared Gawain had still not returned.

"Shall we go after him?" Maur suggested.

"No," Bran answered. "Not by night. They would likely capture the rest of us."

"Is that what you think? That he's been captured?" Maur asked.

"I fear it is likely."

"We should go in," Gwion suddenly said. "They're hunting, and not far from here."

"Gwion, what of Gawain?" Bran asked him as they moved into the keep. "Can you sense if he's in danger? Does the forest speak of such things?"

"I sense he is somewhere safe, for now, at least," Gwion answered.

"They're as slippery as fish, those Easterners," Maur interjected optimistically. "My guess is he's roosting up a tree, looking right down on the enemy, counting them out for us."

"For all our sakes, I hope you're right," Bran said as he bolted the door behind them. He knew if Gawain should fail, they would be no closer to knowing what they were up against and down one very valuable asset.

The three of them worked madly over the next few days preparing the fortress to receive as many warriors as possible. Then, on the afternoon of the third day, as Gawain had promised, the Easterners arrived. Neirin met with Bran, explaining they had indeed gone north around the valley as Gawain had suggested and come down through the mountain pass. Some of the camps had been attacked in the night, but thankfully they had managed to fight the enemy off without losing too many men.

Small groups of Easterners steadily streamed in and went to work, and within days the fortress was fortified and a well-organized battle camp had been built around it. Bran took comfort in seeing the Easterners hawks perched about the camp, knowing they had gained hundreds of eyes to watch the valley down below through the night.

Then, to everyone's relief, Gawain returned.

"Thank the gods!" Bran exclaimed upon seeing him. "What news do you have?"

"Much to tell, my lord," Gawain replied breathlessly. "I am ashamed to say the reason I am late is that I became lost, but finally I succeeded in making it to the Grove without being seen."

Bran knew the way to the Grove was well-hidden, but he had never heard an Easterner utter the word, 'lost', and it took him by surprise.

"A new sort of cauldron-born roam the night," Gawain continued.

"What do you mean, *new sort*?" Bran asked.

"There are some who hunt together. They walk upright, and carry weapons."

"And you're sure they're cauldron-born?"

"Yes, they have the same milky-eyes, and they never speak."

Bran suspected Gawain spoke of the older ones.

"How many were there?" he asked.

"I think it would be best to assume there are many."

Bran knew this would certainly change the fight. The older ones were nearly impossible to kill one-on-one.

"What of Talhaiarn?" he asked.

"He is in the Grove, trapped within a ring of fire which seems to burn without a source, for there is no wood beneath it upon the ground."

"But he lives?" Bran asked.

"Yes, he lives," Gawain said, then proceeded with a bit of hesitation, "but I regret to say it is Aelhaearn who is keeping him within the fire."

"What?" Bran cried incredulously. He and Aelhaearn had always had their differences, but the one thing that had made the man tolerable was that he loved his clan. Bran never would have suspected him of such a betrayal.

"But why would he serve the enemy now?" Bran wondered aloud. "After leading the clan against the cauldron-born for moons? He hates them as much as the rest of us do."

"It would seem he loves power more," Neirin answered for Gawain. He had been silent up until then, listening to Gawain's tale intently. "I am sure he believes he has the upper hand, but I can tell you from first-hand experience, unfortunately, that he does not."

Bran slowly began to realize all of the implications of Aelhaearn's betrayal. He had surely received the message for help that they had sent with Gawain's hawk, but if he had already turned against them, he would have kept it from the clan and instead gone to aid the enemy. Suddenly he began to fear for his sister as well.

"Has my hawk returned?" Gawain suddenly asked, as if he could read Bran's mind, his face full of concern.

Bran knew what he was thinking. "I don't know," he replied apologetically. "There are so many of them here now that your clansmen have arrived," he said, looking over at Gwion. "If she is here, Gwion can find help you find her."

This seemed to put Gawain at ease, and so he continued.

"I decided to watch the Grove through the night to see what numbers she commands. I could hear when the creatures awoke in the forest around me, and saw many as they went out to hunt. From what I could tell, I would guess they number in the hundreds."

"Then we need all the warriors we can get," Bran said disheartened. "Thank you, Gawain. You've been very helpful. Go with Gwion and find your hawk."

They left, and Neirin approached Bran.

"I'll head south," he volunteered. "You and I both know the bird is dead. We can't risk sending another one that might also be shot down. Let me go, and I swear on my father's honor, I'll bring your men back with me."

Bran nodded, knowing Neirin was likely right about the bird.

"Bring Seren as well," he added. "We need another Firebrand, and she can fight better than some of the men. Tell her to bring the women who can fight and aren't nursing children. They can defend themselves if necessary. We need them to cook and take care of the wounded."

"I will," Neirin said confidently. "I'll be back in three days."

"May the Guardians speed you there," Bran said in farewell.

***

Taranis arrived the following morning, blood-thirsty Northerners in his wake.

As usual, their arrival raised spirits, and soon the fortress and all of its surrounding areas were full of men, campfires, and tents made out of skins and furs.

"What are we dealing with?" Taranis asked Bran in the heart of the fortress.

"Things are much worse than I expected, and I didn't expect them to be good," Bran said with disappointment, ashamed of what he had to say next. "Aelhaearn has betrayed us. He fights for the enemy, and holds Talhaiarn captive in the Grove. We also have the damn cauldron-born to deal with. Apparently they've become more cunning. At least some of them."

"What do you mean, Aelhaearn holds Talhaiarn captive?" Taranis cried, spewing profanities at length. "I'll gut the traitor!"

"Rightly so," Bran agreed, but inwardly hoped the honor of doing so would be his own.

"And what of Talhaiarn? Is he injured? We must free him!"

"I've sent for my sister," Bran said. "If anyone can get through to Aelhaearn, or free Talhaiarn from his trap, it's her."

"How long before she arrives?" Taranis asked anxiously.

"Neirin left this morning to get her, he's promised to return in three days."

"Three days?" Taranis cried in alarm. "Talhaiarn could be dead by then! We can't sit here for three days, knowing he's in danger."

"What would you have me do, then?" Bran asked, exhausted.

"If the Grove is guarded by cauldron-born, we'd have the advantage during the day. Could we not simply attack the Grove all at once, from all sides, and free him?" Taranis suggested. "We could send the trackers in first to choose the best approaches, and then close in on them with all the warriors we have!"

"And once we're all in the valley, then what?" Bran asked. "You forget, friend, Aelhaearn is a Firebrand. All he needs to do is set the forest on fire around us. We'd be choked out, or burned alive!"

This seemed to stump Taranis, and he sat and thought awhile. "I can't believe the bastard betrayed us," he finally said, shaking his head. "Where's Einon? Can he not talk sense into him? He loves Aelhaearn like a son."

"He's in the South as well," Bran replied. "I suspect he knows nothing of this, but he will, soon enough."

"And it will tear him apart," Taranis said.

"I think I should go in myself and take Aelhaearn out," Bran suggested.

"The hell you will!" Taranis said in a way that did not invite discussion. "I'm coming with you."

"And then what?" Bran said. "What if both of us perish? That leaves Neirin alone to command all of the warriors, and he has the least experience of us all."

"He has Ambisagrus. That man knows more about war than anyone but you," Taranis countered.

Bran considered the two of them going in further, but glanced down anxiously at the Shield of the North on Taranis' arm.

"We can't risk taking the Shield to the Grove. It's the only relic the enemy doesn't have. If it's captured, she'll have the power to open the Crossroads. You should leave it behind."

Taranis looked at Bran as if he had three heads. "Are you mad? Have you forgotten the power the Shield gives it's bearer? It's the only way we'll even *make it* to the Grove. We're warriors--not fox-footed, nearly invisible Eastern trackers. Our footprints sink deeply and we do not move quietly, but with the Shield held before us, we'll be protected by the Guardians of my clan and none will see nor hear us approach. You'll be able to deliver your beautiful *Caledgwyn* right into the heart of the Grove, where it can destroy the enemy from the inside out!"

Taranis' plan was a good one, but he couldn't help thinking this was all part of Cerridwen's plan. She had managed to gain three of the relics, but needed the fourth to open the Crossroads. If Taranis took the Shield anywhere near the Grove, Bran feared she would surely find a way to capture it.

"You're right, the Shield would give us the advantage, yet you cannot deny taking it so close to the enemy is a huge risk," Bran said. "I will agree as long as you promise that as soon as we make it to the Grove you'll turn around and bring it back here. I'll stay and see the job done, or die trying."

Taranis wanted to protest, but upon seeing Bran's face thought the better of it. "Done. You have my word," he promised instead. "The Shield's been passed from father to son within our clan for generations, and I'll be damned if I don't see it passed on to my own." He paused a moment and then added, "I've finally found my queen, Bran."

"Is that so?" Bran said in surprise. Taranis had an insatiable appetite for women, and Bran had seen him devour many a maiden over the years. To think of him married was nearly impossible. "You, my friend? Forgive me, but I won't believe it unless I witness the hand-fasting myself!"

Taranis laughed. "I'd not have believed it either, not if a thousand Druids would have foretold it, but this one's a goddess, she is. She's playing cat and mouse with me right now, but she carries my son, and once we've won this battle I'll find her and take her for my queen."

"Not of your clan, then?" Bran asked.

"No, not from any clan within the Great Circle. I don't know where she's from, but she's the greatest beauty you've ever seen. On top of that, she can brew an ale that near enslaves a man, and you should see her dance! The most bewitching of the faerie could not entice you more."

"Well, whether I see a hand-fasting come this spring or not, any woman capable of taming a heart as wild as yours, even for a season, I must meet," Bran said with a smile.

"That you shall," Taranis promised. "Come this May there'll be a wedding for the ages!"

"I'm sure it'll be quite the celebration," Bran said, happy his friend was in love.

"Aye, that it will--a week's worth of feasting and dancing all night, just like we used to!" Taranis said, slapping Bran on the back. "And what of you, brother? Anyone special been warming your bed?"

Bran thought of Lucia, suddenly wishing he had her to look forward to that night, but instead it would be the cold ground again.

"There's a woman I favor," he answered simply.

"One of your own?" Taranis asked.

"No, from outside the Circle as well."

"Nothing better than the taste of something new, eh?" Taranis said with a chuckle.

"True," Bran replied, almost to himself. He thought of Lucia's body wrapped around his and how her curls had spilled over his chest while she slept on his shoulder.

"Let us discuss our plans with Ambisagrus," he said, changing the subject.

"Saw him earlier," Taranis replied. "He's up the mountain a bit."

Bran knew Ambisagrus would have good battle counsel, and he looked forward to planning the attack with him. Taranis led the way and they soon came upon him sitting on a boulder, sharpening a well-cared for blade. The fur of a great black wolf lay across his shoulders, no doubt his own kill. Bran thought the warrior likely killed any wolf he encountered now, after the recent tragedy that had befallen Belenus. Bran thought of how nobly he had defended his adopted king, and it wasn't hard to understand why Maur had thought him a better choice for chieftain, Southerner or not.

"Ambisagrus!" Bran called in greeting.

The hero looked up, relieved to see him, and replied, "Seems we've got plenty of men and weapons, but what have we for a plan?"

"That's what we've come to discuss," Bran said. He told Ambisagrus everything that Gawain had reported, as well as what he and Taranis had spoken of.

"I'm with Taranis," Ambisagrus said after hearing it all. "We need to rescue Talhaiarn and get him back here where he can guide us in these matters of sorcery. We've no idea what we're up against, and I'll not walk my men into a trap or an inferno."

"Nor I," agreed Bran.

Suddenly, Gwion appeared on the path, and all three men turned to look at him.

"I am going with you," he announced simply. "I understand her, and I know the way."

To Bran's surprise, neither Taranis nor Ambisagrus disagreed.

CHAPTER THIRTY-TWO

Lost and Found

It was unanimously decided that Bran, Taranis, and Gwion would go to the Grove and attempt to rescue Talhaiarn with the protection of the Shield. They left as soon as the sun came up, Gwion leading the way, Taranis' hounds at his heels and Taranis close behind, his Shield providing protection for them as they made their way through the dense forest.

Half the day had passed by the time they reached the outskirts of the Grove, but Gwion stopped short of entering.

"What is it?" Bran asked quietly.

"No one is here," Gwion replied.

"No one?" Bran asked. "Are you sure?"

Gwion nodded.

"What of Talhaiarn?" Taranis asked.

"I sense him," Gwion said, "but from far away."

"He's escaped, then!" Taranis concluded happily.

Gwion said nothing and proceeded carefully. Bran regularly looked overhead and in all directions, but he neither saw nor heard anything unusual.

They moved slowly to the edge of the large circular grove. An immense oak reigned at its center, her dark branches heavy with acorns and her gnarled roots twisting deep into the earth, clutching it for surely dozens of feet in all directions. Alder, birch, rowan, hazel and ash trees encircled her like graceful dancers around a bride, reaching toward the sky with fingers intertwined and feet rooted in the silver stream that curved around their ankles like a delicate crescent moon.

"Where is he?" Bran said, expecting the worst.

"I tell you, he's escaped!" Taranis said optimistically.

They entered the Grove and suddenly Taranis exclaimed, "Great Mother, the bloody Cauldron!"

Bran looked and there it was, a strange, unearthly light dancing around it. The dogs would go nowhere near it, giving it a wide berth and quickly crossing to the other side of the Grove.

"Do not touch it," Gwion warned the others. "It serves only her now." He then walked solemnly to the Oak and leaned against her trunk like a child against his mother's thigh. He stayed there a long time, as if she had a heartbeat that he was listening to.

Suddenly the dogs began to bark incessantly, and Gwion left the tree to investigate. Moments later they heard him beckon.

"I've found Talhaiarn," he announced somberly from across the stream.

Bran and Taranis rushed over to where Gwion stood and looked down to behold Talhaiarn's body lying beneath a yew tree, his hands crossed peacefully across his chest and face pale with death.

"No!" Taranis cried, kneeling down and kissing the old man's worn hands. "Gods, no!"

Bran swam inwardly in rage and failure at the sight.

Gwion knelt down and touched Talhaiarn's body, and after a moment announced, "Hemlock."

"The cowards *poisoned* him?" Bran cried in disbelief.

"No," Gwion said, pausing. "He took it himself."

"What?" Bran cried in desperation. "Why?"

Gwion took Talhaiarn's hands and was silent for awhile.

"He is in the Underworld," he finally said. "He has gone to speak to Arawn. The hemlock was the only way. There wasn't time for anything else."

"What do you mean, there wasn't time for anything else?" Bran cried. "I entered the Underworld and returned, and have none of Talhaiarn's knowledge."

"You entered by way of the Sacred Grotto, where the veil is thinner than anywhere we know of, sent with Rowan and the Great Mother's protective blessings. From anywhere else, it is not so easy. It takes much time and preparation," Gwion explained.

Suddenly all of the branches began to crack and fall from the two alder trees flanking the Oak.

"Collect the branches," Gwion instructed. "Each of your best warriors are to take one and make a spear of it, whittled by his own hands, and carry it into battle."

One had fallen not far from where Bran stood, and he knelt down to pick it up.

471

"He says don't mourn him," Gwion continued. "He can do more good from where he is. Once things are set right, he will continue on to the Summerlands." At this, Gwion smiled, but then his smile withered.

"What?" Bran asked.

"He says you must cut his head from his body so that Cerridwen cannot bring him back from the dead."

"I cannot," Bran flatly refused. Desecrating the body of a High Priest was something he simply could not do.

"She'll come back, and unless we can stop her, she'll put his body in the Cauldron," Gwion said. "A man as powerful as Talhaiarn would be a terror resurrected, my lord!"

"No, that won't happen, because we're going to carry him home," Bran said emphatically. "Tonight he shall have a proper burial among his kinsmen."

Gwion and Taranis agreed, and as Talhaiarn had instructed, they collected all of the alder branches that had fallen. Bran lashed them together with rope and laid Talhaiarn's body upon the bier, and the three began the slow journey back.

**

That night, the men of the Circle burned their High Priest's body by the light of the moon, their heavy hearts set more than ever against the enemy. As the body burned, Bran presented each of his warriors with an alder branch and bid them whittle a spear from it, as Talhaiarn had commanded.

Their eyes were watchful and full of sorrow and anger as they worked, ready to slaughter any who dared to disturb their ceremony, but strangely, none came.

None, save one.

Only Taranis saw her, watching from the cover of the trees.

Was he seeing things? He blinked, blaming his confusion on lack of sleep, but he was sure he had seen a woman in the trees and went to investigate.

"By the gods!" he cried suddenly upon seeing the woman's face more clearly.

She startled and ran into the trees, and Taranis regretted his outcry.

"Wait!" he yelled, but she didn't stop, so Taranis gave chase.

"Enyd! It's me! Stop!" he called, but still she ran.

As he chased her he wondered if he had been mistaken. Maybe he was chasing after a woman traveler who had gotten separated from her people and been drawn to their fire. Either way, he had to know. He put more effort into the chase, wishing he had his dogs with him. They would not let her get away. After a time she burst into a clearing where a man stood waiting and ran behind him.

Thieves! Taranis suddenly thought, chiding himself for his foolishness.

"Your weakness for women will be the death of you," the man said in disgust, drawing his sword.

473

"And your *weakness* alone will be the death of you," Taranis replied confidently. He paid the man little mind, knowing a thief was no match for him in a fight. He drew nearer, determined to get a good look at the woman's face. *He had been so sure it was her.*

He moved slowly toward the pair, hand on the hilt of his sword, and looked round the man's shoulder to the woman standing behind him.

"Enyd!" Taranis cried out, utterly confused. There was no mistake. It was her, but why did she not answer him?

"Why do you pretend not to know me, woman?" he asked, truly crestfallen.

"Oh, she knows you, better than you know yourself," the man said, drawing a sword Taranis knew all too well. "It is *you* who do not know *her.*"

For the first time, Taranis looked closely at the face of the man who threatened him.

"Aelhaearn," he said with disgust, recognizing him. The brute must have kidnapped Enyd in order to lure him away from the camp.

"Don't worry, my love," Taranis said reassuringly. "I'll slay this traitor and take you home!"

Taranis lunged at his enemy, striking a mighty blow that knocked him back, but Aelhaearn merely laughed. He returned the attack, delivering blow after blow, but Taranis deflected them all, sparks flying in all directions each time *Dyrnwyn* struck the Shield of the North.

Both men had bodies and wills forged from hard work and an unyielding stubbornness that demanded everything of their enemies. They matched each other, time and time again.

"You have no idea who that woman is, do you?" Aelhaearn asked through labored breath.

"She is my future queen, and the mother of my unborn son, and tonight you will die for bringing her here!"

Taranis looked over at Enyd, and by the light of the moon saw tears in her eyes, which encouraged him, kindling his fury to new heights. He soon had the better of the Firebrand, knocking him to the ground violently.

"She has played you for a fool," Aelhaearn gasped up at him in desperation. "You call her Enyd, but she is known far better by her true name: *Cerridwen*, Daughter of the Isle."

Shock washed over Taranis, stunning him, and he made the mistake of turning to look over at his queen, but she had disappeared.

No, it couldn't be, Taranis thought at first, but slowly the truth sunk in like a bitter poison. She had played him for a fool, indeed.

Aelhaearn took advantage of his opponent's confusion and rose up again, sword in hand, and cast a ring of fire around them that Taranis knew only the victor would step out of.

His blows began to lose their focus as the passion of his fight drained out of him, realizing Enyd had used him. He didn't deserve to hold the Shield of the North any more than Aelhaearn deserved to wield *Dyrnwyn*.

475

Aelhaearn could smell his doubt and attacked with renewed force, driving him into the fire over and over again, until, inevitably, Taranis made the fatal mistake of putting his Shield between himself and the flames.

Aelhaearn quickly drove *Dyrnwyn* through his unprotected breast, and Taranis of the North fell to his knees and died of a wounded heart.

***

Dawn broke, but neither Bran nor the men had slept. It was late into the night before they had realized Taranis had disappeared. Gwion had found Madoc roaming the fortress looking for his master, and told Bran, who began to search for him. When it became clear Taranis was nowhere to be found, Bran went to Ambisagrus who immediately had the Eastern trackers light torches and search the surrounding areas. The Northerners joined the search, eager to find their king, weapons at the ready should they encounter cauldron-born.

It wasn't long before the trackers found a clearing with scorched earth and burned trees where a fight had clearly taken place, but there were no bodies to be found, and only two pair of tracks leading away from it.

Things were bleak. The enemy surely had the Shield, for if it had been Taranis who had been the victor in that fight, he would have returned.

Now that the enemy had managed to capture all four relics, they were out of time. Neirin would not be back with the men of the South until the following day, at the earliest, and by then it would likely be too late. The best they could hope for was that the South would arrive in time to help finish the battle.

Bran sought out Ambisagrus and found him in the fortress stable with his horse.

"We have to take the Grove and hold it until the others arrive," he said.

"That we do," Ambisagrus answered somberly, stroking his horse.

They discussed various options, but in all of them they both knew they would be attacking blindly. They had no idea what awaited them.

"It's a bloody hell of a place for a battle. Those damned things crawl through the trees like spiders. I prefer a good, honest fight on a battlefield where I can see my enemy coming," Ambisagrus grumbled.

Bran did too, but that was decidedly not what was in store for them. Instead, they had be fighting in the dark of night, made even darker by a thick canopy of treetops, without horses or much room to swing a sword, against an enemy that would likely attack from overhead or the ground below.

"We should leave now while we have the advantage of daylight," Ambisagrus suggested. "Leave a few men here with some of the dogs for protection. When the South arrives they can send them down into the valley, where hopefully some of us will still be alive with some fight left in us."

"Agreed," Bran said. "I'll rally the men."

Bran circulated throughout the tents of the Northerners, giving orders to prepare for battle that were well-received in spite of the odds. Talhaiarn's death and the disappearance of Taranis had fueled the rage and blood-lust of the warriors, and they were eager to take skulls in honor of their leaders.

Within the hour the men set out for the Grove, Gwion leading the way, and Bran found it unsettling that those with the most experience fighting the cauldron-born were not among them now for the most important battle of all.

CHAPTER THIRTY-THREE
The Grove

They reached the Grove and it was decided the Eastern archers would watch along the outer edges as well as from the trees with as many arrows as could be hoisted into the canopy, and armed with their daggers for close combat. The Northerners would surround the Grove ready to meet the cauldron-born with their spears, and hopefully, gods willing, Southern steel would arrive by nightfall.

It was late afternoon when Gwion came to Bran, a worried look upon his face.

"She is coming," he told him.

"Ambisagrus!" Bran yelled, "Ready the archers!"

Bran watched their surroundings intently, Gwion close by his side. After some time he spied a lone woman approaching. She stepped lightly into the Grove, features fine and kind, with dark hair flowing down her back.

How could such beauty be responsible for such darkness? he thought, but what disturbed him most was the feeling that he knew her, somehow, as if they had perhaps played together as children long ago.

"The thief who stole my son's birthright, and the murderer who took his life, here together," she said softly, bringing him out of his thoughts. "It would seem the serpent has swallowed its own tail."

Even her voice was familiar, he thought.

Suddenly Bran heard Gwion cry out and he turned to see Aelhaearn holding his dagger to the boy's throat with one hand, the Shield of the North in the other. He was covered in blood; blood that Bran knew belonged to Taranis.

"Treacherous dog," Bran seethed, drawing *Caledgwyn*. "Before the gods, you shall die today!"

"Sheath your sword, Chieftain of Women," Aelhaearn spat. "Or I'll gut this servant boy and you can watch him die at your feet."

"Better a defender of women than a coward who threatens innocent children," Bran challenged.

"This boy is a thief," Aelhaearn shot back, "and today, he will pay for what he stole."

"How dare *you* speak of crimes?" Bran yelled at him in disgust. "You who betrayed your clan, and stand covered in the blood of a fellow chieftain who trusted you."

Bran moved a bit closer, taunting him. "How many others have you betrayed?" he demanded. "I'd bet my life you were the coward who murdered Cadoc in his sleep, out of lust for his title!"

At this, Aelhaearn attacked him, as Bran hoped he would.

"Run!" Bran commanded Gwion, and the boy did as he was told, leaping like a rabbit out of Aelhaearn's grasp and disappearing into the trees.

"No fire in the Grove!" Cerridwen warned Aelhaearn as she ran in pursuit.

Bran soon learned Aelhaearn had no need of fire, however. He now wore the Helmet and wielded both *Dyrnwyn* and the Shield, attacking with a focus and intensity Bran had never seen in any adversary. He could barely keep him at bay, and he knew without *Caledgwyn*, he would have no hope of beating him.

Then to make matters worse, out of the corner of his eye Bran noticed silhouettes closing in from the trees around them.

"Bloody hell! Cauldron-born by day?" he thought in panic.

It seemed they had underestimated the enemy yet again, and he wondered how much blood it would cost them.

He heard the Northerners engaging the enemy as cauldron-born converged on the Grove from all sides, some upright wielding weapons, as Gawain had described, and some more animal-like, moving eerily on all fours, like deformed dogs at the heels of their grotesque brothers, their pale skin blending into the white birch bark, occasionally visible against the darker trunks of the other trees. The figures approached with an ease that seemed to defy gravity, twisting along in ways Bran did not think a human skeleton capable of. They slid around objects in their path, at times moving across the ground like snakes. He became more alarmed as their features came into view, their cloudy eyes most disturbing of all. He had never seen them clearly before, having encountered them only in the darkness of the caves.

Bran heard arrows rain down on the cauldron-born from the trees, followed by the fierce voice of Ambisagrus leading men into the fight, but the cauldron-born were stunned for only a moment. They struck back with inhuman strength and agility, the older

ones overcoming the Northerners quickly, the younger
scrambling up the many trees to yank or knock the archers down
to the forest floor below where they were swarmed and fed upon
one by one. Screams of agony filled the Grove, and Bran's hatred
for Aelhaearn boiled over.

"How could you betray your people?" he cried, exhaustion and
despair setting in. "Cerridwen is using you! *You mean nothing to
her.*"

"Yes, she is," Aelhaearn agreed, "and I am using her."

With that, Aelhaearn struck a blow so forceful that Bran lost his
balance and toppled backward over one of the Oak's huge roots.
Aelhaearn was on top of him in seconds, and pinned Bran
helplessly against the ground with the Shield and pointed
Dyrnwyn at his throat.

Bran knew he was beaten. He thought fast, and from beneath the
cover of the Shield, managed to push *Caledgwyn* deep between the
roots of the Oak, where it disappeared. He would not suffer it to
be taken by this man.

"What did she offer you?" he asked Aelhaearn, truly wondering
at the answer.

"Something I'd wager you'd do just about anything for right
now," he answered, looking down at him. "The power to refuse
death."

With that he forced Bran's throat down against the root he had
tripped over.

Bran fought with all of his strength, panic lending him power, but it was no use. He could not move.

Aelhaearn raised *Dyrnwyn* high and brought it down swiftly on the back of his neck.

A moment later, Bran was as shocked as Aelhaearn to find his head still attached to his body. Bewildered, Aelhaearn raised his sword again.

"Wait!" Bran heard a woman's voice call.

Cerridwen had returned, and Bran prayed she had not succeeded in finding Gwion. He felt her hands move his hair away, and touch the brand on the back of his neck.

"What in bloody hell is that?" Aelhaearn said.

"None of your concern," she said. "Tie his hands and hang him from a tree so he can no longer interfere."

She then leaned down and whispered directly into Bran's ear.

"I know to whom your Death belongs, Warrior. Consider yourself twice blessed, for you shall see today something no mortal has ever seen before."

Aelhaearn did as he was bidden, and tied Bran's hands behind his back. He dragged him beneath one of the Oak's strongest limbs, and to Bran's horror looped a rope around his neck and hoisted him ten feet in the air. The pain was excruciating, but Bran's heart continued to pump, demanding he stay and bear it. He had no choice but to watch helplessly what was happening below.

Cerridwen called in the Guardians, inviting them in, and then walked the perimeter of the Grove, casting a ritual circle, whispering something that Bran did not understand. From where he hung, he could see hundreds of cauldron-born pressing in, pacing restlessly along the edge of the circle, their cloudy eyes glowing eerily in the trees, the blood of his slaughtered brothers dripping from their lips and hands. Where were his men? Had they so easily been defeated? He saw none of them below.

Seren! Bran prayed desperately, hoping somehow his sister could hear him.

Just as the last of the sun's light disappeared, Cerridwen walked to the center of the grove directly underneath the Oak and raised her arms. The cauldron-born then swarmed into the Grove like insects and began climbing the Oak, pressing their bodies into her, guttural sounds emerging from their throats. They seemed ravenous, as if longing to feed upon her, moving up along her trunk and into her limbs, their long fingernails digging into her bark.

Then, Bran thought he felt the Oak *herself* began to move, the limb he hung upon changing its position. He squinted in the faint light, wondering if perhaps the movement he felt could have come from the parasites that leeched upon her, but soon there was no doubt.

Oh, Great Mother... he thought in horror, not believing what he saw.

The Oak shuddered in labor pains, pushing her roots up and spreading them apart, straining out of the forest floor that held

484

her. The cauldron-born became frenzied in anticipation of what was about to happen, and Bran was overcome with dread.

Some of them fell from her limbs down between her roots and were crushed as her enormous trunk began to split, cracking in the center, but the rest rushed toward the opening, their fingers invading it, squealing fervently trying to pull her apart. Again she twisted, her roots moving outward, her branches shaking, and the crack opened wider. They writhed and screamed in delight, as the gap was now nearly large enough for a body to fit through…

Then the Oak suddenly split wide open with a crack as loud as a thunderclap. The cauldron-born trampled over each other, scrambling and falling over the hundreds of acorns that blanketed the ground in their desperation to get near the opening.

With the cauldron-born preoccupied, Bran tried to use the opportunity to call for help, but he could not speak. The rope was too tight around his throat. He held on as long as he could, but eventually the blackness claimed his consciousness.

***

Bran suddenly felt the rope from which he hung being sawed upon from above. He tried to see who labored to cut him down, but he could neither lift nor turn his head. Suddenly the rope snapped and he fell from the tree limb down into the chaos below. He struggled to his knees and got himself to the cover of the bracken as fast as he could.

"My lord," he heard someone whisper urgently to him in the dark. He looked up to see Gwion kneeling at his side.

"The South has arrived. Even your sister has come to fight," the boy told him, cutting the rope from his hands.

Hope returned to Bran's heart as he worked blood back into his wrists and sat up and drank the water Gwion had brought him. Once he could feel his hands again he rose up, encouraged by the familiar sound of his clan's battle cries. He quickly retrieved his sword, pulling it out from where he had hidden it.

"Go and hide while we finish this!" he commanded Gwion, and then ran into where the battle was thickest.

"Surround the tree!" he called to his clansmen, his voice finally returned. "They cannot be allowed to cross over--slay them all!"

The warriors were encouraged by Bran's appearance, and belted forth mighty battle cries.

Not far from where he fought, Bran suddenly noticed fire bursts. *Aelhaearn*, he thought. Finally he would have his revenge. He ran swiftly toward his enemy but upon reaching him was shocked to discover the fire came not from the hands of Aelhaearn, but from the hands of a boy, engulfing cauldron-born in flames.

How could this be? **Another** *male Firebrand?*

He ran to the boy's side and began decapitating the burned victims when a familiar voice greeted him.

"Brother!"

Stunned, Bran took a closer look and realized it was his sister who fought at his side. Cadoc had indeed taught her to fight well, far better than Bran had assumed. She had shaved off her hair like the ancient Firebrand warrioresses of old used to do, and had bound her clothing tightly to her body, leaving nothing for her flames to ignite but their enemies.

As the battle waged on, Bran watched intently for any sign of Aelhaearn or Cerridwen, until finally they appeared within the opening of the oak which now had gotten much wider.

"Slay the witch!" Bran heard Ambisagrus cry from across the Grove, and he looked over to see the old warrior surging toward Cerridwen.

"Stay here," Bran said to his sister.

"Like hell I will!" she cried, moving ahead and burning a trail for them through the cauldron-born. Bran delivered repeated executions as he moved toward where Cerridwen stood, Aelhaearn defending her as she worked to open the doorway to the Otherworld for her dark children.

Ambisagrus attacked Aelhaearn, but like Bran, was driven back easily.

Seeing the traitor blaspheming the relics of their clans while he slaughtered his own brothers drove Bran to a fury beyond that which he had ever felt before, and he launched himself like a terrible warship across the sea of writhing flesh which separated them, *Caledgwyn* culling waves of cauldron-born like wheat as he hacked his way toward Aelhaearn, heads rolling into the rifts in the earth opened up by the Oak's shifting roots. Tragically though, before Bran could reach him, Aelhaearn dealt Ambisagrus a death blow, sending the great warrior deep beneath the sea of clamoring bodies.

Enraged, Seren burned a path toward Aelhaearn and attacked him, but he easily tossed her aside into the swarm of cauldron-born. Bran was quick to run to her rescue, pulling her out from being trampled or ripped apart.

"Seren! Leave this fight!" he demanded, grabbing her by the shoulders, but before he could see her to safety, Aelhaearn attacked him, and their swords met again with a deafening clash.

"She's never been obedient," Aelhaearn said, "but she will be. As will everyone when this is done."

Bran fought with all the strength and skill he had, but could gain no ground, all the while watching as cauldron-born took down dozens of his fellow clansmen.

"We must retreat," he heard Neirin call out to him from across the Grove, but Bran knew this was their only chance to defeat their enemies. It was now, or never.

"No, we cannot give up!" Bran cried back, even though he had been in enough battles to know a loss when he saw one.

Suddenly, the cauldron-born stopped attacking and turned toward the opening in the tree which was now big enough for a man to walk through, and swarmed toward it more desperately than ever.

We have lost, Bran thought despondently. The cauldron-born outnumbered the warriors three to one, and the doorway would soon be wide enough for them to pass through.

She had done it.

Cerridwen had opened the door to the Otherworld.

Bran didn't know what to do. He hadn't allowed himself to entertain the possibility of failure, and so was momentarily stunned, unable to think.

Suddenly, *Caledgwyn* was struck from his hand, and Bran instinctively reached for his spear and drove it through his attacker. To his shock, its body turned to ash.

"Take up your spears!" he bellowed to the warriors around him. He finished three or four more cauldron-born, turning them to ashes, and soon his warriors realized what was happening. They quickly traded steel for their wooden spears, and slowly gained a slight advantage in the fight. Bran thought they might recover the ground they had lost, but as the sun began to dip beneath the horizon, the cauldron-born gained strength and fought more fiercely. One by one, the warriors of the Great Circle disappeared beneath the enemy swarm, and Bran finally choked out the command he knew he must give.

"Retreat!" he yelled.

What few warriors remained attempted to fight their way out of the Grove, but it was no use. They were now completely surrounded, and Bran knew none of them would make it out alive. He said a silent prayer to Arawn on their behalf, asking that they all be swiftly guided to the Summerlands for their bravery.

Then, something happened that no one but the gods took notice of, until a lone child's screams of agony rose above every sound in the Grove.

"Bran!" Seren yelled. "The boy jumped into the Cauldron!"

Bran ran toward the heart-wrenching sound in a panic, but just before he could peer over its dark lip, the Cauldron split in two with a thunderous clap that seemed to shatter the sky, its dark halves falling apart to reveal Gwion's broken body.

The cauldron-born who had not managed to cross over collapsed to the ground like empty sacks, and a deathly quiet descended upon the Grove. Even the river seemed to be holding its breath.

Bran ran to where the Cauldron lay split open and knelt down to pick up Gwion's crushed body. He cradled him like a baby, and soon sobs burst forth from his chest as violent as if he had lost his own son.

Then, out of the corner of his eye, Bran spied something huge and dark emerging from the doorway of the Oak into the Grove. He looked up and recognized a terrible sight he had seen once before.

The ominous figure of Arawn moved into the Grove, towering above them all some fifteen feet high, clutching cauldron-born in his huge skeletal hands as easily as if he had pulled up a patch of weeds. He dashed them to the ground where his white hounds soon had them ripped to pieces.

Bran saw Aelhaearn leap to stand protectively in front of Cerridwen, foolishly challenging the God of Death, but neither fire nor the weapons of men could harm the Lord of Annwn. The black giant struck him but once, easily throwing him off his feet, knocking both Shield and Sword from his hands and the Helmet from his head.

"Firebrand no more, you shall henceforth wander the earth in exile stripped of your gift, unable to speak or make love to a woman. Life will yield no pleasure to you, and though you will beg me to come for you, like a disemboweled warrior begs for me upon the battlefield, I will not come."

Aelhaearn quivered, bleeding at the feet of the great god, eyes cast down in fear.

"I warn you, should you take your own life, you will enter a hell far worse than the one you suffer here, for you will never find the Summerlands until you have redeemed your injustice here. *Be gone.*"

Aelhaearn dared not turn his back upon Arawn, and so backed himself away, crawling into the trees.

Then Arawn turned toward Bran. Terrified, Bran kept his eyes on the ground in front of him and Gwion close to his chest, making his submission clear.

The great god came and extended his massive hand over the boy that lay in Bran's lap, his fingers spread over him like the limbs of a tree.

Golden light slowly began to emanate forth from Gwion's body toward the center of Arawn's great palm, until it formed a point so small and brilliant that Bran could not bear to look at it. Suddenly, Bran no longer felt the weight of Gwion in his arms, and looked down to see his body was gone.

Then with the golden seed of Gwion's soul within his hand, Arawn turned to the woman Cerridwen. Her face and hands were on the ground, and to Bran's shock he realized why he had found her so familiar to him. There, upon the back of her neck, lay the same unmistakable silver mark he himself bore. *The one she herself had given him; the Mark of Arawn.*

The Lord Arawn stood over her, as solid and silent as a great black statue except for his red cloak, which floated eerily around him on the invisible breeze of the Underworld. He looked down upon her for a long time, and she did not lift her head nor speak, her upturned hands shaking with supplication and surrender.

Bran could not hear the words he spoke to her, but Cerridwen shook her head against them in refusal, crying, "No, I won't!"

Arawn picked her up from the ground as if she were a small child, and placed his golden palm that held the soul of Gwion upon her belly.

"No!" she protested.

But she would. Arawn set her back down in the Grove and then disappeared back through the Oak he had come through, carrying in each hand a broken half of the Cauldron. His hounds took the other relics up in their massive jaws and followed their master through the doorway. After they disappeared into the blackness, the tree twisted and turned, her trunk closing behind them and her roots reaching forth and grasping all of the dead, pulling them into their final resting place deep down in the earth beneath her.

When all was as it had been before, Bran heard the deep and terrible voice of Arawn thundering within him.

Consider your oath fulfilled, Son of Agarah.

What few warriors remained built a mass pyre for their dead in the Grove, and there Seren burned them in a fire so hot, it seemed summer had returned. They sang songs of the Summerlands to their fallen brothers through the night until the dawn broke, and then left Bran and Seren behind, eager to return to their families.

As they made their way back to the Fortress, Bran pondered the bittersweet victory they had won; a victory that had finally set them free from the terrors of the night, but had been bought with the steep price of many, many lives.

"Our people wait for you at the Fortress," Seren said after some time.

"All of them?" Bran asked in surprise.

"Yes, all that are now left," Seren replied sadly. "Lucia dreamt of a hawk with wings of fire, bearing a message from you insisting we journey to the Crossroads and leave none behind. She has never been wrong before, so I heeded her warning. We met Neirin along the way, who said he had come seeking the warriors. We sent the women to the Fortress and bid them barricade themselves inside. Lucia is there with them. I came along with the men to fight."

Bran's heart leapt at the mention of Lucia, but then was as quickly overcome with shame as he realized how many warriors would not be returning to lie in the arms of their lovers tonight.

"Our people," Bran murmured softly. "Our people are now mostly women and children robbed of husbands and fathers."

"Yes. It seems you are a Chieftain of Women twice-over," she replied sadly.

"So it would seem," Bran answered. He thought deeply about the Crossroads and how it now stood without a guardian, and the loss of life all the clans had suffered.

"I fear returning home and finding it in ruins," Seren said anxiously.

"We won't be returning home," Bran said suddenly, the words surprising him as they came out, as if some unseen force had uttered them. "The North sits without a chieftain, and Neirin is still very young without Ambisagrus to advise him any longer. Both clans have lost most of their warriors, and amount to little more than small villages now. I plan to unite us as one tribe, here at the Crossroads."

Seren said nothing for awhile, considering her brother's words.

"You mean to lead us all, then?" she finally said.

"Uniting our clans is what we must do to survive." Bran answered. "I believe I can do that."

"That you will, Bran of Agarah, because it is what you were born to do," said a familiar elderly voice moving toward them from the path ahead, "and I'm here to help you do it."

Bran smiled as its owner came into view. "Islwyn!" he exclaimed, moving to embrace the old man. He was comforted by his presence, as if some part of Talhaiarn might yet live among them again through the old Druid. It seemed he had come to stay, but

Bran did not ask, for fear of a disappointing answer. Surely they had had enough of those today.

Bran yearned to see Lucia, but dreaded the blow he would have to inflict upon her with the news of Gwion's death. A blow which she, in turn, would have the horrible burden of delivering to the child's mother.

No, although they had vanquished their enemies, there would be no victory songs tonight, nor for many nights hence.

CHAPTER THIRTY-FOUR
Farewell

Aveta longed desperately for some news, for it had been almost a month since Lucia and Gwion had left the island with Bran. She had sent word to the Sisters in the South but had not received a reply and her patience had run out. After much consideration, she decided to brew the Seeing Tea.

Brewing the Seeing Tea was something every Daughter of the Isle knew how to do, but the process was long and demanded much of the body and mind. The older you were, the more painful and difficult the effects of the tea could be on your body, as well. It had been years since Aveta had last drank the tea but she was certain it would be worth it to gain the knowledge she craved.

Aveta rose at dawn the following day. She enjoyed the quiet solitude of the morning as she scanned the forest floor and under the roots of trees for the mushrooms and herbs she needed. Most of them she found very quickly. Trees and plants were something she understood the way others understood animals or people. She admired their silent vigil and quiet knowledge, and the way they adapted to survive whatever obstacles were put in their way. She had always loved growing and nurturing them, and there was nothing more satisfying to her than pushing her hands into good, dark soil.

After gathering everything she needed from the forest, she made her way to the meadow. She walked along the stream bed that led through the birch grove, stopping a moment to admire the sky through its cathedral of white tree trunks. The small yellow leaves that had managed to survive through autumn into winter winked and fluttered at her, and she smiled at their tenacity.

The path wound through some brush, and then opened up into the meadow she remembered playing in as a child. As she wandered through the meadow looking for her herbs, she slowly began to notice the sun growing warmer and warmer, and wildflowers beginning to dot the outer edges of her vision. She looked up, and to her surprise found they were blooming all around her. Their bright faces peeked out from between new green rushes, and butterflies courted them, teetering on a fresh springtime breeze. Winter had somehow turned to spring in the meadow, and Aveta smiled in recognition of the handiwork of the Guardians of the East.

Their voices came to her upon the wind, calling, *"Run and play, Avie!"*

Hearing the name of her youth, Aveta suddenly felt like a child again....

Her body felt younger, and so it was.
Her heart, lighter, and so it was.
Her mind, clearer, and so it was.

She surrendered to it, taking her shoes off and running through the meadow. She no longer felt any aches or pains in her joints or limbs as she ran, feeling her hair bouncing everywhere. When she could finally run no more, she tumbled down in the grass and lay on her back, staring up at the beautiful early morning light.

She watched the clouds move across the sky and the sun rise higher, until suddenly she remembered she was there to find something. She sat up with a start, as if waking from a dream, and found herself once more in a winter meadow. There in the snow next to her hand, like a small parting gift, was the final ingredient for her tea.

***

The sun was directly overhead. Aveta gathered the wood of several different trees, set it aflame and began to chant, walking clockwise around the fire.

Slowly she felt the innocent joy of her morning turning into passion and strength, quickening and coursing through her body. She began to hear drums...Her heart beat to the same rhythm, and her blood rose. Soon the rhythm took over, and when she was no longer able to contain the energy building up within her, she burst forth into a dance. With each revolution, she gave herself over to the rhythm more and more, surrendering herself...

Her dance spun on and on, until slowly the landscape began to change around her. The trees faded in and out, at times becoming almost completely transparent. She caught glimpses through the smoke of spirits dancing across from her, the ever-growing heat distorting their images. The earth beneath her bare feet felt drier and drier with every step, and soon she no longer felt cool grass beneath them, but warm dust.

Sweat ran down her body, and soon she felt suffocated by her robe and pulled it off so she could move freely. Naked she danced, luxuriating in the heat of the fire on her skin.

Through the smoke she glimpsed a red arid land under a blazing sun. With each turn, the image strengthened and grew, taking up more and more of the space around her, until finally it surrounded her. She danced around her fire which was now set upon a mesa, strange cliffs vaulting above her into a vast blue sky arching majestically overhead and spanning out in all directions. Atop the cliffs were luminous beings. *Guardians.*

Her thoughts and feelings became different colored vines of light, emanating out from her in all directions. Those which rang true in her heart went forth as flames of light, but those which were fearful or doubtful looked dull, their path crippled and without direction. She willed the flames of the fire to rise and burn the weak ones before they could escape, and focused on a chant of powerful Truth.

"Dance with me!" she cried, welcoming the Guardians into her circle. The Guardians accepted her invitation, and descended on trails of light which spiraled upwards into the sky in an ever-expanding arc. They began to move with her, weaving patterns of light around and between each other. Aveta was overwhelmed with gratitude, humbled beyond measure that they would choose to grace her so.

Eventually the fire burned down to a few logs, and the Guardians returned to their place atop the cliffs, and the tapestry of energy they had woven together settled upon Aveta as a mantle of radiance and protection.

She glowed with the color of late summer apricots, looking to be once more in the prime of her child-bearing years. Her hair had become shiny, skin creamy and smooth, her breasts round and full. Aveta felt sexual and fertile again, her bones strong and muscles supple; she was beautiful again. She thought back to the many lovers of her youth, the passion of those memories surging within her as she remembered what it felt like to be worshipped and held and dominated, the thrill of being fully ravished and fulfilled by a man's desire, and then basking together with him in ecstasy. She gave thanks for all of the men who had taken her to such bliss, and most of all, for the spark of passion planted within her womb that had become the miracle of her only child.

As the sun began to set, she slowed her dance to a simple walk. She looked up toward the cliffs, and saw they were fading. The trees began to return around her, and slowly with each step she felt more and more grass beneath her feet. The fire had burned down to a huge bed of glowing coals. She stood in silence for awhile, breathing deeply, until the last flame died and just the coals remained.

***

Aveta stepped lightly on the path to the pool, as sure-footed and silent as a fox, disturbing nothing as she moved. She walked alongside the stream, carefully pushing aside tree branches and stepping over river rocks, the late afternoon light dancing on the water as she hiked ever-upward through the thickening brush. Dusk was approaching. Her surroundings become greener and the sound of the water louder as she climbed. Moss clung to every tree and rock, and a fine mist began to fill the air around her, letting her know she was almost there. Finally she glimpsed the pool through the trees. She went to the water's edge near a clear eddy where she could look into the water's depths through her own reflection.

She chose a place she had sat many times before, her heart beating a bit faster. For being a Daughter of the Isle, looking into the water had always been surprisingly frightening for her. As peaceful and beautiful as the Sacred Pools were, their waters often revealed frightening or disturbing things from within. As a girl, she often felt as if she were drowning, and would wrench herself from trance in a panic. She had often wondered why she had not been born to the Northerners, with their deep love of the earth and talent for growing things. She felt much more at home with them. Her mother had explained to her that despite her natural talents, she had been born as a daughter of the West for a reason, and that reason was why her heart beat so fast; the water had lessons for her, and she would need to face her fears with courage if she wanted to learn them.

It helped her to have the clear joy of the morning and the strong energy built up by dancing around the fire as she faced the water. She felt prepared, and found a place to greet her reflection.

The woman staring back at her from her reflection was serene, she thought. The past few years had been hard, but they had not broken her or taken those things away from her. After awhile, she dared to look past herself into the depths of the water, and waited for what would emerge.

She was unaware of time passing, and didn't fight her thoughts. She simply stepped away from them, watching them from above, like looking down upon a stream she no longer swam in. Once she felt ready, she asked the spirit world for a guide. Often loved ones from the other side answered the call and came to guide seekers through the water, as it was notoriously disorienting.

The first person who came up from the water to greet her was Gwion's father, and her heart melted with melancholic joy. Images of the nights they spent together floated toward her; his kind and handsome face, the moon overhead, waking up next to him….She felt his love washing over her, holding her, and relaxed into his protection, finally allowing the water to take over, simply breathing, surrendering to the steady sound of the currents swirling all around her, so entranced she was barely conscious of twilight falling upon the glade.

Images and emotions began to assail her with greater force. She was suddenly holding little Gwion the night they fled her sister's wrath and left the island, terrified inside, but pretending not to be so he would not be afraid. She was rocking him, holding his head, singing to him. *"Everything will be alright"*, she heard herself say to him…Next, she was kneeling in front of him, holding his shoulders, looking into his face before she left him with Talhaiarn, again, hiding her fear and anguish, and then, an image of her son came to her that she could not bear to see.

No!

Frantically she tried to pull away from it, but couldn't. The more she resisted, the deeper the water pulled her beneath its surface. She looked up and could see her own face high above the water peering down, but she couldn't move. *Panic.* She began to thrash, unable to breathe, desperately reaching toward the surface but unable to reach it in time…

And then, blackness.

***

Aveta awoke, shivering and cold upon the ground, her feet still in the water. The sun had set and the stars were out. She sat up, wondering how long she had been unconscious, and wept at what she had been forced to see.

Time passed, and again she looked past her face into the water, resigned to it, willing to surrender. This time, Gwion came to the surface, and upon seeing his face a sickening feeling of loss engulfed her...the loss of love and the searing pain of being left behind, but this time she didn't fight. She let the images come to her, and offered herself up to the message they brought.

Instead of pain, however, she suddenly found herself a young mother again. She was nursing her infant son beneath a tree, his green eyes looking up at her in complete trust and love, the moment as vivid as if she were truly there. She felt the grass against her ankles, the bark of the tree against her back, and the summer breeze on her breasts. She was warm and content, *so happy*. She bent down to kiss Gwion's golden head, and the smell of his hair made her weep.

You can come here whenever you wish, Aveta, the water whispered to her tenderly.

Aveta held her baby close to her, rocking him, letting the water's message in.

This moment is eternal, as all moments are, Aveta. They belong to you forever. There is no such thing as loss.

***

When she was ready, Aveta allowed the sound of the water call her back to the grove, and opened her eyes. She reached into the pool and filled her small cauldron, drank from it, and then filled it a second time.

She returned to the embers of the fire she had danced around that day, and set her cauldron upon it. When the water began to boil, she added the herbs she had collected that morning, and then lay down to sleep. Mother Earth cradled her in her arms and would perhaps speak to her in her dreams as her tea brewed through the night. Aveta felt comfortable there, her cheek against the solid earth that she knew would always be there. She pressed her palms into it and stared up into the night sky, listening to the sound of her breath until she fell asleep.

***

The next morning the tea was ready, and the fire had died. Aveta drank it all, then lay down with her cauldron at her side should she need to vomit.

She folded her hands across her belly and focused on the pale sunlight coming down through the branches of the trees overhead, and soon felt the tea traveling through her blood and quickening her heartbeat, changing her thoughts. It had been a long time since she had drank the tea, but slowly she recognized where she was going. Her mind cleared, and her body felt as light as autumn leaves or butterfly wings; so light, in fact, that she sat up and came right out of it and began to float up, occasionally looking down at the silver thread that tethered her spirit to her body trailing behind her as she rose into the heavens.

She flew far above the island, rising higher above the clouds until they were all she could see for miles around. They glowed a golden pink, like the roses she planted alongside Lucia's villa wall. Below her as she flew, the clouds become a sea which eventually broke upon a shore that stretched on forever. Towering above the shoreline were rugged cliffs, and over the cliffs tumbled waterfalls created by rivers that wound like melted silver through miles of rolling green hills dotted with groves of trees. Beyond the hills lay golden meadows filled with wildflowers, and beyond those, foothills undulated into rugged mountains that cleaved majestically into the air.

These were the Summerlands as her soul knew them, a place for her to come and pray and ask for guidance. Sometimes the Great Mother would speak to her upon the seashore, while she listened to the waves crash upon the beach, and sometimes when she sat beside a river, toes in the water, leaning against a tree. She had even sat perched on the edge of the cliffs a few times, watching the gulls sail out over the ocean and smelling the salty air, but today, Aveta longed for something far more mundane.

Aveta longed for the home she once shared with Lucia and Gwion by the lake, and her garden, and the hearth she had cooked so many meals upon. She imagined it, and it appeared around her, shimmering into view in the middle of her meadow; the lake, the villa, the garden....All of it. The path along the lake unwound before her, and she followed it through the barley field and the apple orchard.

She looked across the lake and saw the island, awash in golden light, glittering like an emerald in the mist. She walked up the path to her garden. The sun was shining down upon its fat cabbages, string beans, peas, onions and carrots, all ready to be picked. Her basket was right where she expected it to be, and she knelt down and harvested all of them, one by one. She shoved her hands joyfully into the soil, the smell of the earth filling her nostrils, and breathed in deeply.

"I've come to speak to you, Great Mother," she said, pulling carrots from the ground.

"I am here, child."

"Tell me of my sister. Can anything be done for her?"

"Her pain has driven her to desire power she does not understand, and cannot wield, but this is her path."

"Must she die?"

There is no death.

"Must her body die?"

All bodies must die.

Aveta knew she was not asking correctly. "Must she be *killed*?" she finally asked, fearing the answer.

"No, but balance must be restored. Sacrifices must be made."

"What kind of sacrifices?" Aveta asked fearfully.

There was no answer from the Great Mother.

"What *kind* of sacrifices?" she repeated, looking up into the sky.

Just then, the stable door swung open, and a beautiful white-winged horse trotted out.

"Hello, Mother," she heard.

She smiled, recognizing her son's chosen form in this realm.

"Hello, my son."

The horse came close and nuzzled her shoulder. She stood and put her arms around his great white head, and her face into his mane.

"It is I who must make the sacrifice the Great Mother speaks of."

"What?" she whispered. "No!"

Tears welled up in Aveta's eyes as she suddenly realized she had known this truth from the day Gwion was born. It all became clear; the deep fear she carried in her heart, the pang of anxiousness whenever they were separated for more than a few hours; why she had wanted to spend every waking moment with him from the time she held him as a newborn in her arms. Women became so vulnerable after giving birth! From the moment a woman holds her infant in her arms, her heart splits in two and no longer belongs to her alone...Her child carries a half of it about, bouncing along through life, sometimes dangling it carelessly, oblivious to how much pain he can cause.

"I took something that was not mine to take, Mother."

"You were a child! *A child*, Gwion! It was not your fault! It was an accident!" she cried.

"It was no accident. What power has been taken must be paid for. The Great Mother helped me see this."

"This isn't fair! How can this be?" she felt herself falling as she had before, falling toward the blackness....

"Aveta, this was Gwion's choice before he was born to you. He knew the path his life was to take, as you knew yours."

"Mother, I need to show you something. Come with me," Gwion said.

He spread his wings, unfolding them high above her head, and kneeled down for her. She climbed on his back, and soon he was galloping through the barley field, faster and faster. She wrapped her hands around his mane as he stretched out his wings and took off from the ground, vaulting higher and higher into the sky.

Suddenly they were surrounded by blackness. Below them Aveta could hear wailing. The sound was agonizing. She felt dizzy, her heart pounding in fear. She couldn't keep her hands closed and struggled to hold on.

"Don't give in to the blackness, Mother. Don't let go," she heard, and felt herself being pulled back into the light...his golden light.

"Stay with me," rang huge and booming in her mind, and Aveta took a deep breath, steeling herself against the blackness, gripping his mane.

"What is this horrible place you have brought me to?" she asked.

"Around us are the souls that once lived inside the bodies Cerridwen stole from their graves and forced to awaken again.

Now they are trapped here, unable to find the Summerlands, for Arawn cannot reach them."

"This is what Cerridwen has done?"

"Yes, and it must be made right."

Aveta felt their breath on her skin, and their voices in her ears. She felt their desire, their misery, and their desperation. As her eyes adjusted to the dark, she began to see them. More and more swarmed in, closer and closer to them. They were attracted to Gwion's light, like fish to a lure. Again she started to feel dizzy.

"It is not safe for you here. I am taking you back," Gwion said.

She felt his great wings surge again, away from the grasping hands, and the cries of agony increased to a pitch far worse than when they arrived. She clutched his mane and lay her body down, resisting the power of the blackness until fresh night air greeted her nostrils, and she gratefully filled her lungs with it. She opened her eyes, and though the sky was still black, she found it gloriously dotted with stars. Below them a herd of wild stallions ran in a vast open field.

Gwion flew down to the herd, and soon they were running with it, smoothly thundering through the landscape with the other horses, Gwion in the lead, his wings folded tightly against his sides, securing her on his back. The wind blew away her fear, and she let out a joyful cry.

There is no loss. There is no death.

He showed her his world, flying over fantastic vistas until eventually they came to land in a stone circle built on the edge of a cliff, overlooking a vast sea.

"I first came here as a small boy," Gwion told her. "I was terrified; terrified of Cerridwen's anger, terrified of leaving the island, but most of all, terrified of how huge the world had become. After the potion touched my lips and swam in my blood, I gradually became aware of every pulse of life around me – every cricket's song, every stroke of a butterfly's wing, every rise and fall of the waves on the lake. I could hear the wayward chatter of a million unseen creatures, see light flowing between them, and feel the turn of the heavens above. I felt like an infant again, clinging to you, afraid to eat or leave your side. Do you remember?"

"Yes, of course," Aveta answered, remembering those horrible times. She had felt so helpless. "I would take you to a quiet place in the forest and hold your head, and rock you until you calmed down. When that wasn't enough, I would bind a cool wet cloth around your ears and eyes."

"Yes. Eventually I learned I could create my own places; places like this one. So I did, and in these places the Great Mother came and spoke to me. She told me I could come here whenever I needed her, and I have, many times. Sometimes when I come, others are here. Sometimes it's an old man who teaches me about my gifts, and sometimes a child who just wants to play. Now that I've shown you the way, you can come here too, to visit me when you miss me. I'll know when you're here, and I will come," he promised.

They stood in the stone temple looking out over the sea for a long time. Aveta then looked around, memorizing every detail, so that she could find her way back again.

"Are you ready to return?" Gwion finally asked her.

"Yes, I am ready," she replied sadly.

Aveta climbed on Gwion's back again and he returned her to the place where her sleeping body lay on the ground. She slid off his back and put her arms around his great white neck.

"May I say goodbye to you as I know you?" she asked. "I want to embrace my son. More than anything, I want to hold him once more."

The body of the horse then transformed into the familiar body of her son as a small boy. She scooped him up in her arms and held him close a long time before setting him down. He then changed into a boy of five, all skinny legs and golden hair, and he wrapped his little arms around her legs like he used to when they would encounter a stranger. She tousled his hair, and as she did, he grew taller, his face changing, until he became the young man she knew.

"I love you, Mother," he finally said. "I will miss you."

Tears welled up in Aveta's eyes. "I love you, too, my son. I have been so blessed to be your mother. Do what you are meant to do."

With that, Aveta returned to her sleeping body, fearful of the grief that awaited her on the other side, but resigned to face it courageously.

EPILOGUE

Cerridwen speaks:

The Lord Arawn bid me bear the golden child as my penance; to give back to the world the life I had unjustly taken, and serve him in the Underworld as Guardian of the Cauldron, which was never again to return to the world of the living.

I fled to a solitary place and waited as the babe grew heavy in my womb. I cursed him for the pain I suffered, the sleep I could not find, and the food I could not eat. In my anger toward Arawn, I vowed to smother the child before he drew his first breath - but when the babe came into the world, he shone forth with such glorious perfection I could not bear to do it.

Instead, I set him adrift upon the sea; if the Guardians willed it, the babe would live. My time in his life was over.

The moment the child left my arms, the ground opened up beneath my feet, and Arawn burst forth to claim me.

Once again at his side, I suddenly knew I had always been so, from the beginning and for eternity; my time upon the earth as the mortal woman, Cerridwen, had been but a fleeting moment...

I am, and have always been, Queen of the Underworld, consort to Arawn.

ABOUT THE AUTHOR

J.M. Hofer lives in Salt Lake City, Utah where she works in the travel industry. In her spare time she studies dance, history, mythology, Celtic studies and foreign language.

Islands in the Mist is her first novel, and was one of five semi-finalists out of 2,000 in the Sci-Fi/Fantasy/Horror genre in the 2013 Amazon Breakthrough Novel Award Contest.

She is currently working on the sequel to *Islands in the Mist*.

Made in the USA
Charleston, SC
31 July 2014